continued ...

Highlander in Her Bed

"[A] randy paranormal romance.... The premise is charming and innovative.... This novel definitely delivers a blast of Scottish steam."
—*Publishers Weekly*

"A yummy paranormal romp."
—*USA Today* bestselling author Angela Knight

"A delightful paranormal romance. The writing is poetic, compelling, and fun, and the story features an imaginative premise, crisp dialogue, and sexy characters whose narrative voices are both believable and memorable. HOT."
—*Romantic Times*

"A superb paranormal romance." —*Midwest Book Review*

"A sexy, humor-filled romance with delightfully amusing characters. Artfully blending past and present, *Highlander in Her Bed* is an entertaining read. Well written. Readers will enjoy this one!" —*Fresh Fiction*

"Appealing and amusing. Sizzles with passion."
—*Romance Reviews Today*

"A whimsical read that will have you panting from start to finish! Mackay knows what a Scottish romance novel needs and socks it to you! Red-hot sizzling chemistry ignites from the moment Sir Alex materializes in front of feisty Mara ... a sure-bet bestseller." —*A Romance Review*

Must Love Kilts

Allie Mackay

A SIGNET ECLIPSE BOOK

SIGNET ECLIPSE
Published by New American Library, a division of
Penguin Group (USA) Inc., 375 Hudson Street,
New York, New York 10014, USA
Penguin Group (Canada), 90 Eglinton Avenue East, Suite 700, Toronto,
Ontario M4P 2Y3, Canada (a division of Pearson Penguin Canada Inc.)
Penguin Books Ltd., 80 Strand, London WC2R 0RL, England
Penguin Ireland, 25 St. Stephen's Green, Dublin 2,
Ireland (a division of Penguin Books Ltd.)
Penguin Group (Australia), 250 Camberwell Road, Camberwell, Victoria 3124,
Australia (a division of Pearson Australia Group Pty. Ltd.)
Penguin Books India Pvt. Ltd., 11 Community Centre, Panchsheel Park,
New Delhi - 110 017, India
Penguin Group (NZ), 67 Apollo Drive, Rosedale, North Shore 0632,
New Zealand (a division of Pearson New Zealand Ltd.)
Penguin Books (South Africa) (Pty.) Ltd., 24 Sturdee Avenue,
Rosebank, Johannesburg 2196, South Africa

Penguin Books Ltd., Registered Offices:
80 Strand, London WC2R 0RL, England

First published by Signet Eclipse, an imprint of New American Library,
a division of Penguin Group (USA) Inc.

First Printing, January 2011
10 9 8 7 6 5 4 3 2 1

Copyright © Sue-Ellen Welfonder, 2011
All rights reserved

SIGNET ECLIPSE and logo are trademarks of Penguin Group (USA) Inc.

Printed in the United States of America

This one is for Horatio, Hercules, and the gang, for everything they are and do. Only their intrepid leader knows how much their extraordinary support means to me. Hopefully she also knows how much I love and appreciate her.

ACKNOWLEDGMENTS

This book's heroine loves Scotland passionately. I share that love and have done so all my life. My family hails from the Hebrides, so loving Scotland comes naturally to me. So does yearning to be there, to return again and again to the special places that beckon so strongly. Scotland is extraordinary, a magical place held in awe by so many. The mere mention of words like "glen," "heather," or "mist" can make someone's face light up. Eyes then glisten, and pulses race, the longing for the Highlands touching hearts. Toss in a kilted man with a sexy Scottish accent, let the pipes skirl and the drums roll, and women everywhere swoon.

In my previous career as a flight attendant, I was fortunate to travel the world for decades, visiting many fascinating lands. Beauty can be found everywhere. Yet I cannot name one place that stirs souls like Scotland. Even those who have never set foot there, like Margo Menlove at this book's beginning, are fierce in their love of the Highlands.

Margo is my nod to dedicated Scotophiles everywhere. I hope that, like her, you'll someday visit the land of your dreams. And if, like me, you're already a frequent Scotland visitor, I know you'll agree that the magic never fades. Each trip proves anew that Scotland is so much more than a destination. It's a passion that burns forever.

Margo's journey will take you to some of my favorite West Highland places. Gairloch, Badcall, Badachro, and Redpoint, as well as other locations, all exist. I've changed hotel names, and Badcall Castle is pure fiction. But even these fictitious places are based on a blending of real hotels and castles I know and love in this area. If you visit, you'll be as enchanted as Margo. I just hope that you don't land on one of Wee Hughie's whirlwind tours. Scotland is meant to be savored, enjoyed with leisure and lots of *ooh* and *ahh* moments.

For the curious, Magnus MacBride could've existed. The Norse ruled the Hebrides for several hundred years and their fierce assaults on Scotland's isles and mainland coasts lasted even longer. Somerled, the great warrior chief of Clan Donald in the twelfth century, fought the Vikings tirelessly and eventually chased them from the Hebrides. He comes closest to how I envisioned Magnus. The book's setting is an area that was a frequent and favored target of Viking raiders. Their legacy lives on in a wealth of culture and tradition, place-names, archaeological finds, and even character traits and physical features. The melding of Celtic and Norse gives us the Highlander so beloved today.

Three special women helped me take Margo to Scotland. Roberta Brown, agent extraordinaire, who is also my dearest friend. She is an angel on earth. Kerry Donovan, my supertalented editor, for her excellent input and direction. Thanks, too, to my copy editor, Michele Alpern, for her sharp eye and skill. Ladies, I'm grateful.

Much love and appreciation to my very handsome husband, Manfred. He might not slay Vikings, but he keeps all trouble from my door and guards my turret, always. I couldn't do this without him. As ever, my little Jack Russell, Em. My four-legged soul mate, he holds my heart in his paws. I hope he knows how much I love him.

"Loving Scotland isn't just my greatest passion.
It's who I am."
   —Margo Menlove, founder of the Bucks County
                        Kilt Appreciation Society

Prologue

Badcall Bay in the Northwest Highlands
A fine summer's eve, 1250

"Spawn of Satan!"

Magnus MacBride, proud Highland chieftain, drew rein on the heathery ridge just above the sheltered cove of Badcall Bay and stared through smoke-tinged clouds of choking haze at the six many-oared Viking longships, beating swiftly away from the coast and toward the open sea. His men thundered up beside him, each one jerking his steed to a sudden, jarring halt. They were fierce fighters, well armed and battle-proven. But just now they could do no more than rattle their swords and shout their outrage.

Not that Magnus heard them above the roar of his own hot blood pounding in his ears. Or the terrible hammering of his heart that raced in time with the flashing oars of the longships as they sped across the waves, almost flying and leaving great plumes of spray in their wake. Magnus glared after them, shock and dread slamming into him like a hundred hard-hitting fists. White-hot fury scalded him, squeezing his chest and making it impossible to breathe.

The hot, ash-filled air also made inhaling difficult, but that unpleasantness was the least of his concern. Now, this moment, his entire world had contracted to hold only those six fleeing longships.

Nothing else existed.

Even at this distance, he recognized the garishly colored sea dragon painted on the square sail of the largest Norse vessel.

The coiled, fire-spewing monster was the emblem of Sigurd Sword Breaker, the worst of the heathen Norsemen who terrorized this coast. His hasty departure and bloodthirsty reputation left no doubt that he was responsible for the thick columns of smoke rising from the fishermen's cottages lining the foreshore beneath the ridge.

The most times peaceful hamlet was a raging inferno.

Black, acrid smoke that stank of more than burning roof thatch came to Magnus and his men on the wind, stinging their eyes and scalding their lungs.

The smoke also obliterated their reason for being there.

Knowing it as well, the horn blowers and drumbeaters at the rear of Magnus's party fell silent. Even his piper quit his strutting and stood stunned, the rousing skirls of his blowpipes dying away to a pitiful moan. Brought along to herald Magnus's arrival at Badcall village—a journey made to collect Liana Beaton, his soon-to-be bride—these men, too, swiped at streaming eyes and gaped at the hellish scene.

And it *was* hell.

Badcall Bay was now a place of the dead.

No screams or cries rose above the wicked crackle and roar of the flames.

Whoever might remain in the little fishing community at the foot of the steep and rocky cliffs lived no more. And if anyone did yet draw breath, God's mercy on them, for they'd met a terrible and undeserved fate.

Bile rose in Magnus's throat and he welcomed its bitterness, wishing he could take on the agonies suffered by the hapless fisherfolk of Badcall Bay. He couldn't, regrettably. But he was sure that giant, unseen hands had clamped tight iron bands around his chest. His pain was that great, especially when Liana's innocent face flashed before him.

A maid still, for they'd shared only chaste kisses. Her wonder that he'd defied station and tradition in desiring her for his wife had driven him to prove to her that he loved her above all else. He'd vowed to protect her always, keeping her safe from all ills and ensuring that her family and village would prosper. And—the memory speared him—he'd sworn to fill her days with happiness and her nights with boundless passion. Together, they'd raise strong sons and beautiful daughters, showing the naesayers that no other bride would have better suited him.

How she'd smiled when he'd made those promises.

Now, as he remembered, instead of seeing her eyes alight with pleasure, he saw them wide with horror.

Unspeakable terror that—he was certain—would never have visited this quiet place if not for him.

Viking sea raiders cared little for heaps of fish nets and strings of dried herring.

But they would have known—and rightly—that any Highland chieftain worth the title would shower his bride-to-be and her family with riches.

Those coffers of silver and coin would have been the spoils that attracted the Norsemen.

"Calum!" Magnus swung down from his saddle and signaled to one of the horn blowers, an older man who had once been a renowned Viking-fighter but now handled horses better than he wielded a sword. "Take young Ewan"—Magnus jerked a glance at Calum's grandson—"and see the garrons away from this smoke. The rest of us will go down to the village and put out the fires. We'll find you when we're done."

He didn't add that they'd be burying the burned and the slain.

It wasn't necessary to put words to such a ghastly task.

Calum nodded, grimly.

He knew better than most what awaited them along the shoreline.

"Ewan and I can tether the horses and come back." The older man's gaze flicked to the cliff edge, where a steep track began its zigzagging descent to the little bay. When he looked back at Magnus, he straightened his broad-set shoulders and spat on the ground. "You'll be needing all hands when you get down there."

"Aye." Magnus gripped Calum's arm, firmly. He hoped his old friend—a man who was much like a father to him—would leave it at that.

He was also thinking fast.

The cliff path was too treacherous for a man of Calum's years. Especially one with a knee that was wont to give out on him, however much the doughty warrior chose to make light of his occasional stumbles. And Ewan had yet to bloody his sword. Magnus didn't want the devastation below to be the lad's first taste of carnage.

"I'd rather you and Ewan guard the horses." Magnus seized the first excuse that came to mind. "Sword Breaker and his men likely slaughtered the village cattle and took the meat onto their longships." That was true enough. "They may have left someone behind to search for other beasts and then hasten them away to a hidden landing beach to be fetched later."

Magnus doubted it. But he was grateful to see Calum bobbing his bearded head. "If such men should appear, you and Ewan can dispatch them."

"Aye, right you are." The old man's chest swelled. "We'd make short work of the ravaging bastards." He patted his sword, looking fierce. "They'd ne'er see the blow that felled them. We'd be on them that quickly."

"Good, then. See you to it." Magnus stepped around him, making for the cliff edge, where the others were already pounding down the track.

Calum maneuvered in front of him, blocking the way. "She may no' be down there, laddie," he warned, voicing Magnus's worst dread.

Liana in the hands of Sigurd Sword Breaker would be a fate worse than death. The Viking sea raider was known for committing atrocities on those he sought to ransom. And if any attempts at rescue were made . . .

Magnus blotted the thought from his mind, unable to bear connecting the woman he loved with the Norseman's blackest villainies.

But if Sword Breaker had her, he'd upend the world to free her.

Calum leaned close then, his gaze direct. "You'll do well to brace yourself. I fought Sword Breaker's father, Thorkel Raven-Feeder. I know what they do—"

"I'll find Liana, where'er she is." Magnus clapped the old man's shoulder, silencing him. Then he turned and raced after his men, tearing down the steep, dizzying path as quickly as his hurrying feet would carry him.

The scene at the bottom was worse than he'd imagined.

He glanced wildly about, staring at the chaos. Beneath his feet, the ground tilted dangerously, almost bringing him to his knees.

"Liana!" He shouted her name, knowing she wouldn't answer him.

Fire-blackened—or butchered—bodies were everywhere, littering the crescent-shaped strand in glaring testimony to how savagely they'd died. No mercy had been shown. Each slashing wound displayed how ferociously the Norsemen had wielded their spears and axes.

They'd also been free with their torches. Every cothouse, byre, and fishing shed stood ablaze. The smoke was denser here, great billowing clouds that filled the cove with an ominous, suffocating stench. Magnus's men ran about, shouting and battling the flames. Many had stripped naked and were using their plaids to beat at the fires.

Magnus ran, too, ripping off his own plaid and swatting at the leaping flames as he dashed from one sprawled and broken body to the next, searching for his bride.

He was almost to her father's cottage—now a soaring wall of fire—when one of his men pounded up to him, red-faced and panting.

"Magnus!" The man clutched at him, breathing hard. "We've found one still alive! It's Liana's grandmother and—"

"Liana?" Magnus's hope flared. He stared at his kinsman, willing the answer he wanted to hear. "What of her? Has anyone seen—"

"She's with the old woman." The man's tone made the world go black. "They're there"—he pointed to a rocky outcrop at the edge of the cove—"together, both of them. The grandmother doesn't have much longer. She's been grievously set upon. Liana . . . your bride . . . I'm sorry, Magnus. She is—"

"Dead." Magnus's heart stopped on the word. He couldn't breathe or move. He went rigid, his entire length freezing to icy-hard stone even as agony hollowed him, leaving him emptied of all but searing denial.

He saw Liana now, her lifeless body there on the sand, beside the rocks. Several of his men knelt around her, their heads respectfully bent. One of them cradled the old woman, leaning down to catch whatever last words came from her blood-drained lips.

A great cry burned in Magnus's throat, but he couldn't tell if he was yelling or if the terrible, earsplitting sound was the thunder of his blood.

Then, somehow, he was at Liana's side. He flung himself to his knees, pulling her into his arms, holding her limp form against him. She looked only asleep, for her body wasn't broken and mangled like the others. Her fair hair was unsullied and shone bright as always, spilling around her shoulders. But her eyes were closed, her lashes still against the whiteness of her cheeks.

"No-o-o!" He tightened his arms around her, burying his face in her hair, still so cool and silken. Just as her skin was yet smooth and warm, almost alive.

He heard footsteps then and looked up to see one of his men approaching, pity in his eyes. The man set a hand on Magnus's shoulder, gripping hard. Magnus glared up him, grief and rage turning him feral.

"She isn't dead, see you?" He raised a fist, shaking it at the heavens. "She's only stunned, I say you. She'll waken soon and—"

He broke off, staring at the blood on his hand. Bright red and fresh, it colored his fingers and the whole of his palm, hideous rivulets trickling down his arm.

Liana's blood.

"Nae!" He held her from him, his heart splitting when her head lolled to the side. He stared at her, looking closely, seeing what he'd missed before.

There was a large crimson stain at her middle, dark, glistening wet, and deadly.

It was then that the madness seized him.

He threw back his head and roared, allowing the pain to rush in. Blackness filled him and his vision blurred to a burning, red haze. But he kept his hands steady as he lowered her onto the plaid that someone had spread out for her beside the old woman, who—he saw at once—had also taken her last agonizing breath.

Soon, he would see them buried. He'd put them, and all the others, to peace as best as possible in such a fouled and heinous place.

But for now, he gave in to his rage and leapt to his feet, a beast unchained. He ran to the water's edge, where he whipped out his sword and plunged it deep into the wet sand beneath the cold and swirling surf.

He clenched his hands, glaring through the smoke to the now-empty horizon. "Sword Breaker, hear me!" he bellowed, yelling with all his lung power. "There is no rock large enough to hide you! No shadows black enough to keep you and yours safe from me, Magnus MacBride!"

He strode into the water, shouting the same words again and again as he glared out to sea. He shook his fists at the rolling waves, ranting until several of his men came for him. They took him by the arms, dragging him back to shore.

Back to a life that was forever changed.

The Magnus MacBride who stood on the strand—his heart turned to stone and his blood boiling with rage—was a different man from the one who'd wakened that morn, eager and joyful to ride out and fetch his bride.

From this day on, he would live only for vengeance.

Chapter 1

Ye Olde Pagan Times
New Hope, Pennsylvania
The present

Margo Menlove was born loving Scotland.

She lived, breathed, and dreamed in plaid. At the ripe age of sixteen, she'd single-handedly convinced nearly all the girls in her high school—and even a few of the female teachers—that there was no man sexier than a Highlander. In those heady days, she'd even founded the now-defunct Bucks County Kilt Appreciation Society.

Now, more than ten years later, locals in her hometown of New Hope, Pennsylvania, considered her an authority on all things Scottish.

And although she was officially employed as a Luna Harmonist at the town's premier New Age shop, Ye Olde Pagan Times, advising clients according to the natural cycle and rhythm of the moon, many customers sought her assistance when they wished to plan a trip to Scotland.

Sometimes when one of those Glasgow-bound travelers consulted her, she'd surprise herself with how well she knew the land of her dreams.

She really was an expert.

She knew each clan's history and could recognize their tartan at a hundred paces. She prided herself on being able to recite all the must-see hot spots in the Highlands in a single breath. Her heart squeezed each time she heard bagpipes. Instead of ballet, she'd taken Scottish country dance classes as a child and could dance a mean Highland fling before she'd entered kindergarten. Unlike most non-Scots, she even loved haggis.

And although she didn't wish to test her theory, she was pretty sure that if someone cut her, she'd bleed tartan.

She loved Scotland that much.

Her only problem was that she'd never set foot on Scottish soil.

And just now—she tried not to glare—a problem of a very different sort was breezing through the door of Ye Olde Pagan Times.

Dina Greed.

Margo's greatest rival in all things Scottish. So petite that Margo secretly thought of her as Minnie Mouse, she was dressed—as nearly always—in a mini tartan skirt and incredibly high-heeled black boots that added a few inches to her diminutive but shapely form. The deeply cut V neckline of her clinging blue cashmere top drew attention to her annoyingly full breasts. And her cloud of dark, curling hair shone bright in the late-autumn sunlight slanting in through the shop windows. She was also wearing a very smug smile and that could only mean trouble.

Sure of it, Margo shifted on her stool behind her Luna Harmony station and reached to rearrange the little blue and silver jars and bottles of organic beauty products that shop owner, Patience Peasgood, urged her to sell to those seeking celestial answers. With names like Foaming Sea bath crystals or Sea of Serenity night cream, all inspired by lunar seas, the cosmetics made people smile.

Even if most Ye Olde Pagan Times regulars found the prices too steep.

Margo secretly agreed.

No one loved a bargain more than her.

But just now she was grateful so many of the Lunarian Organic products cluttered her counter. If she appeared busy, fussing with their display, Dina Greed might not sail over to needle her.

At the moment, the pint-sized brunette—who never failed to make Margo feel like a clunky blond amazon—was browsing around the aisles, her chin tilted as she peered at sparkling glass bowls filled with pink and clear quartz crystals. She also examined the scented oils and reed diffusers, and then drifted away to study the large selection of herbal teas and cures. Willing her to leave the shop, Margo eyed her progress from beneath her lashes.

Instead, she stopped before a display of white pillar candles arranged in trays of small, river-polished pebbles, then moved on to the bookshelves set against the shop's back wall, where she stood watching Patience Peasgood carefully unpack a box of newly delivered books on medieval magic and Celtic and Norse mythology.

Neither woman looked in Margo's direction.

Yet—the fine hairs lifted on her nape—she was certain someone was watching her.

Margo shivered. She wondered if it was her—Dina Greed did ride her last nerve—or if a shadow had passed over the sun. Either way, the whole atmosphere in the shop suddenly felt a shade darker.

It was a creepy, unsettling kind of dark.

Margo knew that Patience, a self-taught white witch, had been experimenting with new spells in recent days.

Watching the shopkeeper now, Margo hoped her employer hadn't unwittingly unleashed something sinister. It wouldn't be the first time Patience's well-meant magic backfired and caused more trouble than good.

"She's going to Scotland, you know."

"Gah!" Margo knocked over a bottle of Sea of Nectar body lotion. Whipping around on her stool, she came face-to-face with Marta Lopez, the Puerto Rican fortune-teller who became Ye Olde Pagan Times' Madame Zelda of Bulgaria each morning when she stepped through the shop door.

"Geesh." Margo pressed a hand to her breast as she stared at her friend. "Didn't anyone ever tell you it's not nice to sneak up on people?"

Instead of backing away, Marta stepped closer, lowering her voice. "I thought you'd want to know before she ruins your day. That's why she's here." She flashed a narrow-eyed glance at Dina Greed's back. "She wants to make you jealous."

She is! The two words screamed through Margo's Scotland-loving soul, turning her heart pea green and making her pulse race with annoyance.

"How do you know?" Margo tucked her chin-length blond hair behind an ear, hoping Marta wouldn't notice the flush she could feel flaming up her neck. "Are you sure? Or"—she could only hope—"is it just gossip?"

Dina Greed had been making noise about going to Scotland forever.

So far she'd never gotten any closer than *Braveheart.*

But the way Marta was shaking her head told Margo that this time her rival's plans were real.

"You should know I only ever speak the truth." Marta smoothed the shimmering purple and gold folds of her caftan. "One of my cousins"—she straightened, assuming an air of importance—"works at First Class Luggage and Travel Shoppe. She told me Dina was in there two days ago, buying up a storm and bragging that she was about to leave on a three-week trip to the Highlands.

"She even has a passport." Marta imparted this bit of info with authority. "My cousin saw it when Dina insisted on making sure it fit easily into the tartan-covered passport holder she bought."

Margo's heart sank. "She bought a tartan-covered passport holder?"

"Not just that." Marta's eyes snapped. "She walked out with an entire set of matching tartan luggage. It's a new line First Class just started carrying. I think my cousin said it's called Highland Mist."

Highland mist.

The two words, usually the stuff of Margo's sweetest dreams, now just made her feel sick inside. As long as she could remember, Dina Greed had deliberately targeted and snatched every one of Margo's boyfriends.

Three years ago, she'd also somehow sweet-talked the manager of a really lovely apartment complex Margo wanted to move to into giving her the last available apartment, even though Margo had already made a deposit.

Now she was also going to Scotland.

It was beyond bearing.

"So it is true." Margo looked at her friend, feeling bleak. She also felt the beginnings of a throbbing headache. "Minnie Mouse wins again."

Marta shot Dina a malice-laden glance. "Maybe she'll fall off a cliff or disappear into a peat bog."

"With her luck"—Margo knew this to be true—"some hunky Highlander would rescue her."

"Leave it to me." Marta winked. "I have lots of cousins and one of them practices voodoo. I'll just put a bug in her ear and have her—"

"Margo!" Dina Greed was coming up to the Luna Harmony station, her dark eyes sparkling. "I was hoping you'd be here today. I need your advice about—"

"Scotland?" Margo could've bitten her tongue, but the word just slipped out.

"You've heard?" Dina's brows winged upward in her pretty, heart-shaped face. "It's true. I'm really going. In fact, I'm leaving"—she smiled sweetly—"in three days. But that's not why I'm here."

She set her tasseled sporran-cum-handbag on the counter and unsnapped the clasp, withdrawing several typed sheets of paper. "This is my itinerary, if you'd like to see it. I'm doing a self-drive tour and will be concentrating on all the places connected to Robert the Bruce." She twinkled at Margo, well aware that the medieval hero king was one of Margo's greatest heroes.

"I've been planning this trip for years, as you know." She clutched the itinerary as if it were made of gold and diamonds. "I don't need your help with Scotland."

Margo forced a tight smile. "I didn't think so."

Out of the corner of her eye, she saw Marta swishing away, making for the back room where she did her tarot readings. Margo hoped she'd also use the privacy to call her voodoo-expert cousin.

She looked back at her rival, wishing she had the nerve to throttle her.

"So what can I do for you?" She hated having to be nice. "Are you looking for some good cosmetics for your trip?" She tapped the Ocean of Storms shower gel. "All the Lunarian products come in travel sizes."

"No, thanks, but that's close." Dina held out a hand, wriggling her fingers. "I'm on my way to have these nails removed"—she glanced down at the diva-length red talons, clearly fake—"and someone mentioned you might have a tip for keeping my real nails from breaking.

"They aren't very strong and"—she gave Margo another sugar-infused smile—"I'll be exploring so many
castle ruins and whatnot, you know? I'd hate to damage
them when I'm off in the wilds of nowhere."

"Oh, that's easy." Margo felt a spurt of triumph. "Just
be sure you always file them on a Saturday," she lied,
knowing that was the worst possible day for nail care. "If
you do that, they'll stay hard, resistant to breakage, and
never give you any problems."

Margo smiled.

Friday after sunset was when the moon's magic
worked on nails.

"My fingernails thank you." Dina tucked her itinerary into her furry sporran purse. "I really must go. It's
been lovely seeing you. But"—she was already halfway
across the shop—"I need to pack. I'll stop by when I'm
back and tell you about my trip."

"I'm sure you will," Margo muttered when the shop
bell jangled as Dina swept out the door.

Free at last, she released a long breath. It was good
that her nemesis left when she did, as she might have
exploded otherwise. She could maintain her always-be-
gracious-to-customers demeanor only so long. Dina had
pushed her close to her limits. A white-hot volcano of
anger, envy, and frustration was seething inside her.

On the trail of Robert the Bruce.

Highland Mist luggage.

Margo frowned. She wouldn't be surprised if the
other woman wore plaid underwear. She *had* left her
mean-spirited residue in the most times tranquil shop.
Sensitive to such things, Margo shivered and rubbed her
arms. They were covered with gooseflesh. And the odd
dimness she'd noticed earlier had returned. Only now,
the little shop wasn't just full of shadows; it'd turned icy
cold.

Of course—she saw now—rain was beginning to beat against the windows and the afternoon sky had gone ominously dark. Autumn in Bucks County was known for the night drawing in rather early.

Still . . .

This wasn't that kind of chill.

Margo sat frozen on her stool. She wanted to call out to Patience or even Marta, sequestered in her back room, but her tongue felt glued to the roof of her mouth. She glanced over to the bookshelves, seeking the reassurance of Patience's familiar presence.

Instead, she found her palms and her brow dampening.

Her ill ease only increased when the door jangled again and she caught the backs of Patience and Marta as they dashed out into the rain. The door swung shut behind them, leaving her alone.

She'd forgotten it was Marta's half day.

And Patience had told her that morning that she'd be leaving early to join friends for high tea at the Cabbage Rose Gift Emporium and Tea Room out near Valley Forge. Margo had agreed to close the shop on her own.

It was an unavoidable situation.

But she regretted it all the same.

Especially when—oh, no!—she saw the shadow by the bookshelves.

Tall, blacker than black, and definitely sinister, the darkness hovered near where Patience had stood earlier, sorting the new books. And—Margo stared, her stomach clenching—whatever it was, it oozed an ancient malevolence.

It wasn't a ghost.

She knew that unquestionably.

This was more a portent of doom.

Then there was a loud rumbling noise outside and—as a quick glance at the windows revealed—a large cement mixer that had been stopped in front of the shop lumbered noisily down the road, allowing the gray afternoon light to pour back into the shop.

The *shadow* vanished at once.

And Margo had never felt more foolish.

She wiped the back of her hand across her brow and took a few deep, calming breaths. She shouldn't have allowed Dina Greed and her upcoming Scotland trip get to her so much that she mistook a shadow cast by a construction truck for a gloom-bearing hell demon.

She didn't even believe in demons.

Ghosts, you bet. She'd even seen a few of them and had no doubts whatsoever.

She was a believer.

But demons . . .

They belonged in the same pot as vampires and werewolves. They just weren't her cuppa. And she was very happy to keep it that way.

She was also in dire need of tea.

Knowing a good steaming cup of Earl Grey Cream would soothe her nerves, she pushed to her feet and started for Marta's tarot-reading room, a corner of which served as Ye Olde Pagan Times' makeshift kitchen.

She was almost there when she heard a *thump* near the bookshelves.

"Oh, God!" She jerked to a halt, her hand still reaching for the back room door. The floor tilted crazily and she was sure she could feel a thousand hidden eyes glaring at her from behind the bundles of dried herbs and glass witch balls that hung from the ceiling.

Every spell gone bad that Patience had ever done flashed through her mind. Once, Patience tried to cast protection over migrating frogs she'd heard about on the news. She didn't like thinking of the amphibians crossing busy roads. Within minutes, Ye Olde Pagan

Times had been overrun with hopping, green-skinned frogs.

Another time, she'd tried to spell the air conditioner into working better and frost suddenly appeared on every surface in the shop. Icicles even grew from the ceiling and hung like frozen swords in the windows.

Lately, she'd been trying to gain the power to see true history by murmuring spell words over the white spaces between lines in books. Patience wanted to examine a few specialized books on early witchcraft to learn the truth behind medieval witch hunts and trials.

Margo shuddered to think her employer might have summoned a foul-tempered warlock.

Or something worse.

Very slowly, Margo turned. She half expected to see the shadow again.

There was nothing.

No ghosts, demons, or other beasties crept along the bookshelf aisles.

She certainly didn't see a warlock.

But a book had fallen, lying open and facedown on the polished hardwood floor. Margo went to retrieve it, glad to know the source of the noise and intending to return the book to the shelf. It was from Patience's new shipment and the title jumped at her.

Myths and Legends of the Viking Age.

For some inexplicable reason just seeing the words, red and gold lettering on a brownish background, sent a jolt through her. It was so strong, and forbidding, that she almost walked away, leaving the book where it was on the floor.

Stubbornness made her snatch it up, the painful shock that sped through her fingers and up her arm as soon as she touched the book underscoring why she really needed to heed her instincts.

Could Patience's spell-casting pursuits have thrown magic on the books, rather than on Patience herself?

Had her employer enchanted the merchandise?

Margo was sure she didn't want to know.

But she'd had enough—enough of everything—and she wasn't going to let a book get the better of her. So she ignored the burning tingles racing along her skin and peered down. She immediately wished she hadn't, for the book had opened to a two-page color illustration of a Viking warship off the coast of Scotland.

Margo could have groaned.

She didn't care about the fierce-looking Norse dragon ship.

But the oh-so-romantic landscape was a kick to the shins.

Beautiful as a master painting, the illustration showed a rocky shoreline with steep, jagged cliffs soaring up around a crescent-shaped cove. The sky above boiled with dark clouds and looked as wild and turbulent as the churning sea. Margo's heart responded, beating hard and slow. It was such places that called to her soul. In fact, she often dreamed of just such a Highland coast.

She brought the book nearer to her face and strained her eyes to see because the light in the shop seemed to be fading again.

Now, looking more closely, she saw a man on the golden-sanded strand. He stood at the water's edge, his long dark hair tossed by the wind. Clearly a Highland warrior, he could've been ripped from her hottest fantasies. Big, strapping, and magnificent, he'd been painted raising a sword high over his head and yelling. He was staring out to sea, glaring at the departing Vikings, and his outrage was so well drawn and palpable she could almost hear his shouts.

Margo shivered, feeling chilled again.

She glanced at the windows, but this time there weren't any big trucks blocking the afternoon light.

Everything was at it should be.

Except when she looked back at the illustration, the man had moved and was now actually in the water, with the foamy surf splashing about his legs.

"What?" Her eyes rounded. Waves of disbelief shot through her entire body. Worse, she could hear the rush of the wind and the crash of the sea. She also felt the scorching heat of flames all around her, the air even smelling of burnt ash and terrible things.

Somehow—in the space of an eye blink—the illustration had come alive. Margo suspected Patience's magic had gone awry again. Not that it mattered *why* she was seeing what she was. At the moment, it seemed real. Leaping flames were everywhere, raging up behind the enraged Highlander and even consuming the pages, the heat scalding her fingers.

"That's it!" Margo flung the book aside.

She pressed both hands to her cheeks and stood, breathing hard. She would not accept the crazy spiral of madness whirling inside her.

She didn't care how many demon-shadows lurked in the aisles between the bookshelves or how often a painted Highlander chose to stride into the surf in his own illustration. She especially didn't want to consider how drawn she'd felt to the hot-eyed chieftain. She'd not just felt the fires burning around him; she'd also experienced a flare of pure molten heat all through her body.

And she was having none of such nonsense.

Patience's skills weren't that formidable. And her mistakes brought on visitations from frogs, frost, and suchlike. Sexy, hot-eyed Highlanders with swords were not in Patience's range of talent.

Margo knew what ailed her.

She simply had a vivid imagination. And, today, she'd also had a lethal dose of Dina Greed–itis.

But she was okay now.

The rain was lessening and already she could hear the muffled voices of people passing along the sidewalk, and the swish of car wheels on the road's wet pavement. It was a perfectly ordinary October afternoon and even the shop seemed warm and welcoming again.

Feeling better, she gave herself a shake and went to fetch the Viking book. It'd landed near a tiered display of tinkling tabletop fountains. And when she picked it up this time, nothing happened.

No tingly thunderbolts burst into her fingers.

The light didn't dim and the floor stayed steady beneath her feet.

Even so, before she returned the book to the shelf, she thumbed through its pages. It wouldn't hurt to take one last peek at the illustration. She wasn't surprised when she didn't find it. In fact, there wasn't anything even similar to what she'd seen.

Margo let her fingers slide down the book's spine. Its glossy-smooth cover felt so normal. Cool and smooth to the touch.

She really had imagined everything.

Too bad she was sure that the fearsome Highland warrior and the wild and rugged seaward coast where he'd stood would haunt her forever.

And wasn't that the story of her life?

She might know Scotland better than anyone else. And her heart was certainly in the Highlands. But she only ever went there in her dreams.

Now they'd never be enough again.

She wanted that Highlander on the shore.

A man the illustration's caption had called Magnus MacBride, Viking Slayer.

Chapter 2

"Did you know, Greer, that Norsemen say fate is inescapable?"

Magnus MacBride, famed as the Viking Slayer, glanced at the big man standing near him at the water's edge. Built like an ox and with a huge red beard, Godred Greer couldn't know the fury coursing through Magnus's veins. Though if the traitor had looked close, he might've seen a muscle twitch in Magnus's jaw. Or the murder in Magnus's eyes when he turned his gaze back to the dark blue line that marked the edge of the sea.

As it was, Godred merely spat onto the sand. "I make my own path."

Magnus nodded. "So men say."

He stepped closer to the surf, pretending to watch the waves rolling in. In truth, the bloodlust was on him. Soon he'd do what he did so well, take vengeance and right terrible wrongs. Eager to begin, he opened and closed his fists and let his lips curve in a smile that would've shriveled Godred's gizzard if the bastard could have seen his face.

But he kept his back turned, his eyes on the sea, for this scene of carnage held the power to scald his innards, even after five long years.

No ribbons of flame or thick plumes of smoke fouled the air, black, ominous, and reeking. And no dragon ships could be seen beating for the open sea. But the crescent-shaped strand was a place of graves, and the wind whistling past its craggy cliffs still echoed with the cries of innocents. Many of the rocks along the shore remained blackened, and within the charred and rotting ruins of cothouses, the dark-stained hearthstones lay cold.

It was a meet place for purging evil.

And now that he was here, Godred the betrayer only a sword swipe away, Magnus reached to pull the leather tie from his hair, letting it swing loose about his shoulders. That, too, he'd learned from the Vikings.

They killed with unbound hair.

Beside him, Godred seemed unaware of his approaching demise. "You chose an ill site to counsel, Mac-Bride." He joined Magnus at the surf's edge. "This place is no better than a corpse hall."

His words made Magnus's anger surge.

Taking a tight breath, he glanced down the shore to where Godred's sister, Donata, walked near the remnants of a burned fisherman's hovel. A small but shapely woman, she had bold eyes and a mass of dark curling hair that glistened like a raven's wing. Her cloak was also black and she wore jangling bands of silver and jet around her neck, wrists, and ankles. Her exotic scent drifted on the sea wind and her presence only riled Magnus the more.

Not because she tempted him.

No woman had done that since Liana, God rest her soul.

But no female—even the sister of a foe—should witness what he meant to do to Greer. Though he knew why the man had brought her.

Donata Greer was rumored a witch.

Just now, Magnus would swear she was weaving some dark magic over him. Her lips moved in a chant he couldn't hear and each glance she flashed his way held poison. Whatever she was about, it boded ill.

Magnus steeled his spine.

He feared nothing. But he wouldn't sleep well with such a female beneath his roof.

Godred Greer didn't go anywhere without her. She advised his every move. Or so the prattle-mongers claimed. A shame, for Greer, that she hadn't warned him to ignore Magnus's summons to Badcall Bay.

A pity, too, that the gutted fisherman's cottage where Donata now stood was so close to where Liana had been found, dead on the sand.

The memory sent white-hot pain spearing through Magnus's chest. A wave of anger crashed over him, but he fought the red haze. He needed his wits, even if he could hardly wait to fill the air with the stench of Godred's blood. That glory would come soon enough.

For now . . .

"You speak true." He turned back to the miscreant. "This strand is a burying ground. It's tainted, blood drenched, and unholy. But where else could we be sure no Norsemen might observe our tryst?"

He swept out an arm, indicating the devastation. "There's nothing here to attract them." He could scarce keep the outrage from his voice. "They ply waters where they're assured of rich plunder. And they seek places where they'll meet little resistance."

"We all know that." Godred looked to the cliff path and then back to Magnus. "I didnae come here to waste breath o'er pagan raiders. Your man said you wished the strength of my swords." He frowned, glancing again at the cliffs, where several of Magnus's guards were making their way down to the strand. "I was told you're offering land and wealth for a score of good fighting men?"

Magnus smiled openly now. The men on the cliff were a signal, letting him know they'd dispatched Godred's own guards who'd been waiting above.

"I will make you a rich man, that's true." Magnus just didn't say he'd do so by sending the craven to Valhalla, where he could enjoy the splendors of Odin's feasting hall. "But first I'd hear why the pagan raiders haven't ravaged your stretch of this coast."

"They know better." Godred swelled his chest. "My men's prowess is known, even to those thieving bastards. What I'd hear"—his eyes glinted suspiciously—"is why you'd dare to ask."

"Sigurd Sword Breaker has returned." Magnus's tone hardened. "Word is he seeks to settle here. He craves a good haven and boat strand for his dragon ships and sweet grazing for cattle." Magnus watched Godred carefully. "He wouldn't leave such ripe lands as yours untouched, no matter the fierceness of your men."

Godred spat again, this time into the surf. "Who am I to know that devil's mind?"

Magnus shook his head, letting the wind toss his hair. "Do you know much of Norse gods? Perhaps that Odin gave up one of his eyes for the gift of a golden tongue? Could it be that you've allied yourself with a deep-pursed, land-hungry Norse warlord? That you've surrendered your loyalty to this land for the promise of Viking silver?"

"You snake!" Godred's eyes bulged. His face turned purple. "I've ne'er heard such lies!"

"You're the liar." Magnus stepped forward and threw

back Godred's cloak to reveal the bastard's rows of silver and gold arm rings. "Vikings use such baubles to reward men who serve them well. Including fools who believe empty promises made to them. Such men have arms bright with the rings that bought their loyalty. They—"

"Cur!" Godred jerked his cloak from Magnus's grasp. "You wear no less. All men speak of your arm rings. See them now, glittering on your—"

"My arm rings mind me of each sword Viking I've slain." Magnus flexed his muscles, proud of the rings. "I wear different ones each day and have taken them all myself, one silver or gold ring from each dead Norseman. They aren't gifts from a Norse warlord. I bear them openly and ne'er hidden beneath a dark mantle.

"Nor"—he yanked the silver chain from Godred's neck—"do I wear one of these!"

Magnus clenched his fist around the Thor's hammer charm and then flung the necklace into the sea.

"You dinnae need such an amulet to feel close to Viking gods." He slapped his sword hilt. "I mean to speed you into their presence."

"Odin's arse, you will," Godred snarled, reaching for his own brand. But before he could unsheathe it, Donata ran between them, flinging herself at Magnus.

"Touch him and you're damned!" She beat his chest with her fists, her dark eyes wild. "You and yours will burn in your god's hell. Your children and theirs and all the offspring to come after them will be cursed on this earth and in every world beyond."

"Hah!" Magnus hardly felt her blows. "Your words are wasted. I dinnae have children. And I'll no' be making any, either."

"You'll soon wish you could." She lifted a hand to slash her cheek, flicking the blood from her talonlike fingernails into Magnus's face. "I curse you to want a woman so badly that you won't be able to breathe, eat, or even take a step without burning for her."

Magnus swiped the blood off his face. "I desire no woman."

"You will." Donata's eyes narrowed, glittering madly. "She'll be a woman you can never have. She'll haunt your dreams and you'll see her everywhere, but she'll remain as distant as the stars."

"The woman I loved is far away." Magnus wiped his fingers on his plaid, unmoved. "She's dead."

"Another woman lives. And you'll want her with a fever that will scorch your veins. You'll chase after her, never catching more than air." Donata tossed her head, her voice rising. "You'll lose your reason, wishing yourself dead. That is my curse on you!"

Magnus laughed and seized her arms, lifting her off the ground. "I live in hell. You cannae curse a man already damned."

"Nae, but I can kill you." Godred drew his sword, flashing it from side to side.

"You'll have your chance." Magnus smiled, relishing the fight.

"No chance, your death." Godred glared at him. "Release my sister."

"Och, I shall." Magnus broadened his smile. The cold smile men came to fear these last bloodred years.

Knowing Godred wouldn't strike so long as he held Donata, he threw a glance to where his guardsmen stood near the bottom of the cliff path. They were six, all clad in mail and well armed. Two clutched bulging leather sacks.

"Ewan! Come take her back up the cliff. And"—he ignored Donata's flailing legs and clawing fingers—"dinnae let the lady scratch you."

"I willnae." Ewan, a strapping lad and Magnus's youngest warrior, came sprinting up to them. Without glancing at Godred, he scooped Donata into his arms and carried her away, across the strand.

She fought Ewan's grasp, still hurling curses at Magnus, her voice shrill.

Just before Ewan reached the cliff path, he looked back over his shoulder. "I like 'em with spirit! She's no bother whatever."

"No foolery, lad." Magnus whipped out his sword as he spoke, his eye on Godred's glinting blade. "We dinnae make war on women. She's to go to a nunnery, along with Greer's other ladies."

"My women are no' your concern." Godred swept his steel in an arc that would've slit Magnus's gut if he hadn't leapt aside fast enough.

"You no longer have any women." Magnus scythed his own blade, cutting the air, taunting. "My men are seeing them to a new home, a place where they'll enjoy the benevolence of Holy Church."

"You lie." Godred made another vicious swipe, clipping Magnus's arm. "They're at Castle Greer."

Magnus tossed back his hair, ignoring the sting at his elbow. "Castle Greer is no more." He whirled his blade in another hissing arc, forcing Godred down the strand. "I have many men. Some used my ship, *Sea-Raven*, to make a swift visit to your hall after you left this morn. They burned your keep while others saw your women away. All that remains is a blackened hillside and"—he lunged, slicing Godred's cloak—"that which was mine.

"Alan, Donnie, bring the sacks!" Magnus raised his voice above the clash of swords. "Show this dung beetle what you found when you dug beneath his hearth."

Two large men with broad chests and thick arms crossed the strand and hurled the heavy pouches at

Godred's feet. The bags clinked as they landed. Magnus slashed down with his sword to split open the largest sack, and a river of silver and gold spilled onto the sand. Coins, rings and necklaces, jewel-rimmed drinking horns, silver cups and candleholders, several large Celtic brooches, and even a fine warrior's helmet inlaid with gold.

"You did fire my hall." Godred paled, staring at the plunder.

"I retook what was mine." Magnus raised his sword, pointing the tip at Godred's belly. "Thon treasure was part of my Liana's bride gift. Sigurd Sword Breaker kept most of it, I'll vow. But he paid you a good share for letting him know where he could find such bounty."

"You'll have no joy in it." Rage burned in Godred's eyes. Snarling, he swept his blade in a furious arc, aiming for Magnus's side. He roared when he missed by less than a hairbreadth.

Magnus spun away, whirling with lightning speed and bringing his brand against Godred's in a blur of sparking, ringing blows that sent his foe staggering backward into the surf. Magnus fought like a fiend, sweeping his blade from left to right, cutting and slashing until a bright tide of crimson spilled down Godred's mail-clad ribs.

"Whoreson!" Godred slipped in the waves washing the sand, but kept lunging, clumsily now. His swings grew wilder, each one missing by inches, slicing air. "Killing me changes naught." He grunted, stumbling again. "Sigurd will sleep in your bed, hump your woman—"

"I have no woman!" Magnus roared, rage almost blinding him. "And you are dead!" He charged, his sword clashing furiously against Godred's blade, the force of the blows knocking Godred to his knees.

"Stand and die!" Magnus snarled, glaring. "I'll no' kill a kneeling man." He whipped his blade, flashing it within a breath of Godred's neck. " 'Tis time for your blood to color the sea and feed the gulls." The wheeling birds were already gathering. "They will grow fat on your flesh."

"Nae, yours!" Godred surged to his feet, howling as he swung his sword. He cut air again and this time the blade flew from his bloodied fingers and disappeared beneath the breakers, sinking into the sea.

"Greet Odin!" Magnus lunged, his sword taking Godred's throat in a single vicious swipe. Godred crashed into the water, blood fountaining in a hot, red arc, splashing onto the sand and staining the waves' frothy spume.

He toppled, writhing and jerking, clutching his opened gullet, as the surf washed over him. His face said he knew he'd not be greeting Odin or any other Norse god, dying without a weapon in his hand. Then, at last, he gave a pitiful, gurgling cry, and a final twitch, his hate-filled eyes glazing.

It was done.

Panting, Magnus glared down at his foe and then slammed his sword, *Vengeance*, into the wet, bloodred sand. The blade quivered, singing death's song, her steel humming with the force of Magnus's fury.

Alan and Donnie came forward then, both men spitting on Godred's corpse.

"Shall we bury him?" It was Donnie who spoke, his tone revealing that he'd sooner slice his own throat than give Godred even that courtesy.

"Nae. We leave him." Magnus gazed out over the empty, rolling sea. He didn't look at his men, or what was left of the bastard he'd once thought of as a friend. "The gulls will have done with him. The tide and wind will take whatever they leave behind."

It was a kinder fate than Magnus's own.

He closed his eyes then and shoved both hands

through his hair, not caring that his fingers were sticky with Godred's blood.

Vengeance had been served.

Nothing else mattered.

He did draw a tight breath, the echo of Godred's slur squeezing his chest, pummeling his heart. " . . . *Sigurd will hump your woman.*" Liana had been spared from suffering that horror. And he, Magnus MacBride, Viking Slayer, wouldn't sully her memory by taking another bride.

He didn't even lay with whores.

Donata's curse couldn't touch him. Any lust that burned in him was killing fever.

And looking down at Godred's hacked and mangled body only fueled the flames of his anger.

So he knelt and—as he always did—slid a twisted gold ring from Godred's limp arm. When he stood, his blood finally cooling, he turned to Alan and Donnie. "Gather the coins and whate'er else spilled from thon bags"—he jerked his head at the bride goods fanned across the sand—"and take them with Godred's sister and his other women to the first nunnery that will have them. The coin alone will buy the ladies a good life behind cloistered walls.

"I'll no' have any of the treasure at Badcall Castle." A wash of distaste rolled over him. "No' after the grief it's wrought."

Donnie and Alan exchanged looks. Glances that made Magnus's anger start to ignite anew. He arched a brow, waiting.

Alan spoke first. "Those bags hold a fortune, lord."

"They cost me more." Magnus yanked his sword from the sand, wiping its blade on his plaid. "Something far more precious and that all the world's gold cannae replace."

Alan looked down, shamed. "I dinnae mean—"

"Godred's bitches willnae thank you." Donnie glanced across the strand to the cliff path. From above, Donata Greer's angry voice could be heard shrieking at Magnus's men. "One o' them bit me when we carried them from Godred's hall. See here"—he rolled back his sleeve, showing the bite mark—"the kind of hellcats—"

"That's all the more reason to gift them with a new life of prayers and penance." Magnus sheathed Vengeance. "Begone now. Take the treasure and Greer's sister. If you ride swiftly, you'll catch the others before dark."

And before the sight of the tainted bride goods could stab more fiercely into Magnus's heart.

The pain was already beyond bearing.

As was his surety that, in the midst of cutting Godred to ribbons, he'd glimpsed a beautiful naked woman standing in the surf, looking on in wide-eyed horror as he'd given Greer the final blow.

Dripping wet and with water streaming down her body, the spume glittering in her shining, sun-bright hair and on her shoulders, the droplets sparkling like jewels on the lush swells of her breasts. She'd looked straight at him, crying out as he'd swung his blade.

Her scream was silent.

He'd blinked and she was gone.

Her image had stunned him. And even in that bloodthirsty moment, he'd wanted her. Desire, hot, swift, and powerful, had swept him, making him burn with a need such as he'd never felt before.

Not even for Liana.

It was a blaze of passion that could only have been conjured by dark magic. And that slew him more roundly than if he'd felt the cold steel of Godred's sword slicing into him.

He no longer had any use for women.

And he certainly didn't want to lust after a will-o'-wisp summoned by Donata to plague him. Doing so could only give credence to what his men had been harping on for so long. His determination to follow the sword path, his fierce quest for vengeance, was finally getting the best of him.

He was losing his wits.

Hours later, once again at Badcall Castle, Magnus stood on the raised dais of his great hall and looked out at the men enjoying their supper. Blessedly, he didn't catch the merest glimpse of an unclad siren, her shimmering, soaking length slipping through the shadows to taunt him. There was nothing to stir his vitals. Whoever—*or whatever*—he'd seen had vanished with the tide.

He could've laughed out loud with relief.

Instead, he drew a tight breath and put the naked beauty from his mind.

Donata's screeches and his own joy in savaging Godred had clearly left him befuddled. There could be no other explanation. Wet, bare-bottomed vixens didn't appear out of nowhere and then disappear before a man's eyes.

More like, she hadn't been there at all.

Willing it so, he stood straighter. Then he sent one more probing glance about the hall, just to be sure that all was well, the evening progressing as it should.

And it was.

Thick candles on the long tables illuminated his men's bearded faces as they applied themselves to a meal of ale, bread, and cheese. And enough roasted meat to satisfy an army. Braziers burned in corners, spending warmth, as did the fire on the large central hearth. But it was a dark night and cold wind lashed at the shutters, the icy air seeping in to chill the poor souls unlucky enough to have claimed seats beneath the hall's small, high windows.

Magnus glanced down when his dog, Frodi, shuffled over and leaned into him. He reached to rub the beast's bony shoulders. Magnus's friend and companion of many years, Frodi knew him better than any man and no doubt sensed his restlessness.

The seething anger that coiled inside him always, twisting his gut even now.

Triumph should be surging through him.

Godred Greer was a he-ass and had deserved to die. Seeing his blood stain the sand and hearing his last groans fill the air had satisfied him. Magnus's only regret was that his death hadn't been slower. A more torturous end for the black-hearted fiend who'd brought such horror to the innocent fisherfolk of Badcall village.

He'd sold Liana's and her people's lifeblood for the glint of silver and gold.

Now he'd paid the price of his greed.

But Sigurd Sword Breaker yet lived.

And until Magnus warmed his hands on the Viking warlord's death pyre, he'd know no peace.

He'd never know happiness.

Fortunately, he also knew that if he kept standing at the dais edge, staring out into the smoky hall, more than one of his well-meaning men would take it upon themselves to try to foist jollity on him.

They did so more and more often of late.

And to his increasing annoyance, their idea of merriment frequently took the form of some poor big-bosomed, lusty-natured kitchen wench whose well-tested charms they believed would make him smile again.

The problem with their logic was that Magnus liked not smiling.

He also enjoyed his peace, so he returned to his place at the high table, a magnificently carved oaken monstrosity crafted centuries ago as a gift for the wife of a long-dead MacBride chieftain. Determined to be left alone, he pretended interest in the beef ribs he piled onto his trencher. If he was careful, no one would notice that he intended to slip most of his supper to Frodi.

The old dog needed meat on his bones.

And Magnus's prickling dread that he'd glance up to see a naked, spume-covered Valkyrie jiggling her breasts at him ruined his own appetite. Since Liana, other women left him cold as winter's frost. The large-eyed, flaxen-haired vision from the strand had burned him like the sun.

He could still see her blue gaze piercing him. Her stare had locked with his as if she'd been real.

Donata's curse echoed in his ears, damning him.

Furious, he looked down at his beef ribs.

His anger at the sorceress knew no bounds. His body's reaction to the woman who hadn't been there might have him passing on his supper for a fortnight.

Perhaps even longer.

Something told him that a mere fourteen days wouldn't be enough to banish her memory.

Gods pity him.

"You're no' fooling anyone, lad." Calum, the aged warrior Magnus loved like a father, gripped his wrist just as he tried to give Frodi a choice bit of beef. "Truth is"—Calum leaned close, lowering his voice—"men are starting to worry about you."

"Humph." Magnus jerked free of Calum's grasp and gave Frodi the tidbit.

He also scowled.

His men couldn't dream the worries crashing through his head just now. Unless the louts were too fearful to admit it, not a one of them had seen the tempting sea witch.

Valkyrie, goddess, water nymph, or whatever she'd been.

"My men have no cause to fret." Magnus spoke in his hardest tone.

Then he reached for his ale and took a long swig, setting down the cup with a *clack.* "They saw me blood-drenched and grinning at Badcall Bay a few scant hours ago. They looked on as I opened Godred's gullet and sent the bastard to Odin's corpse hall.

"An unfit man couldn't have done the like." Magnus poured himself more ale. Then he gave Calum a narrow-eyed glance. "My men, and you, are fashing yourselves o'er naught."

"No one will argue your fighting skills." Calum returned his stare with irritating reason. "You could cut down any one of us before we had our swords half-drawn. Every man in this hall knows that. But"—he spoke in a tone that made Magnus feel like a lad of twelve—"look in the shadows of thon window embrasure and tell me what you see."

Magnus bit back a curse and followed the older man's gaze. "I see Maili, the smithy's daughter."

"Is that all?" Calum pressed him. "You see nothing more? What's the maid doing?"

"Maili is no maid, you old goat!"

"Aye, well, she has other talents to commend her, eh? And old I am, 'tis true. My eyes aren't what they were...." Calum shook his head, feigning a troubled look. "So make an auld man happy and tell me what she's doing, there in the shadows."

"By Thor, Odin, and Loki!" Magnus snarled his favorite Norse oath. Then—knowing Calum would pester him all night if he didn't do as bidden—he twisted around to peer deeper into the alcove's shadows.

He saw at once why Calum was needling him.

Maili, a plump wench with an unruly mass of flame-bright hair and saucy eyes, sat on one of the alcove benches. She'd opened her bodice to air her full, round breasts and her nipples were taut and thrusting. And—Magnus scowled—the little minx had a hand beneath her skirts. When she caught his stare, she smiled and quickly flipped her hem, giving him a glimpse of the fiery red curls betwixt her slightly parted thighs.

"Damnation!" Magnus whipped back around. "You lecherous old goat"—he shot a furious look at Calum—"you knew fine what she was doing."

Calum had the gall to jut his bristly chin. "Could be I asked her to help me show you why men are talking. Other men wouldn't be wearing a glare about now. They'd be halfway across the hall, their itch for a bonnie lass setting wings to their ankles.

"See there." Calum paused as one of Magnus's guards joined Maili in the embrasure. The man pulled her close, lowering his head to her breasts. "It isn't healthy for a man to live for war glory alone."

"I live for many things." The words sounded hollow even to Magnus. Calum spoke true and knowing it only made him the more furious. "My warring keeps Maili and others safe of a night."

That was something his old friend couldn't argue.

Unfortunately, his words put an even more belligerent glint in Calum's eyes. "That may be. But Maili didn't tempt you just now, did she?"

"So?" Magnus scowled, his night now fully ruined.

Calum didn't blink. "Your men fear you've gone monk."

"And if I have?" Magnus's voice was dangerously low.

"Then you're treading on perilous ground." Calum speared a chunk of cheese with his eating knife. "MacBrides are a superstitious lot. There be some"—he broke off a corner of the cheese, chewing with annoying deliberation—"what think built-up seed can poison a man, even work its way into his head and clog his brain. If you don't soon spill—"

"I spill blood, you nosy arse!" Magnus half rose from his laird's chair.

Lightning quick, Calum's fingers closed around his arm again. And this time when the older man narrowed his eyes at Magnus, the fierce look on his face prickled Magnus's nape.

He dropped back into his chair, a strange dread making his chest tighten. For a moment, the firelit hall seemed to darken and he imagined he heard the tinkle of Donata's silver bangles. *"See, you are damned even here, in the heart of your home."* Her taunt hushed across his mind, then whispered away, leaving him doubting his senses.

Calum was watching him sharply.

Magnus frowned. "What is it?"

"'Tis odd you'd speak of spilling blood." Calum's blue eyes glittered in the torchlight. "Orosius thinks you'll die soon. He—"

"Hah!" Magnus shot to his feet, the sorceress forgotten. He searched the hall for the burly, big-bellied seer. The only man able to strike terror in Magnus's heart, Orosius saw truths, heard the voices of the dead, and cast runesticks with unparalleled skill.

Orosius claimed the gods walked beside him, but he also suspected they'd caused him to lose part of his left ear in a long-ago sword fight. Retribution, he believed, for trying to use his talents as a seer and rune master to hear more than he should.

The gods didn't like when such blessed mortals believed themselves grand.

Now Orosius was cautious and respectful of his gift. He never used his abilities for gain and refused coin for his wisdom, accepting only ale and viands in payment. And, as need required, peat for his fire.

Calum glanced over his shoulder then, as if he didn't wish anyone else to hear him. "Orosius—"

"What did he see?" Magnus's pulse raced. If Orosius saw him fall, he would.

The seer never erred.

And even if Magnus didn't fear death, he wasn't ready. He couldn't leave this earth until Sigurd Sword Breaker breathed his last.

"Well?" Magnus flashed a glance out over the hall. "Is Orosius saying someone will lop off my head? Slit my belly and wade in my blood?"

"He saw nothing the like." Calum took a bite of cheese. "And you needn't keep bending your neck looking for him. He's in his cottage, sleeping off the strain of his vision. I can tell you what he saw."

Calum peered at him. "It was you lying with a dead woman."

Magnus's eyes rounded. *"Lying with—"*

"He saw you naked, the both of you, and you taking the woman in passion." Calum was blunt. "Orosius believes she was Liana."

"I ne'er touched Liana." Magnus felt his blood chilling.

"Not in life." Calum made light of his protest. "That's why Orosius is certain you're about to leave us. Liana dwells in the realm of the dead."

"How does he know the woman was Liana?" Magnus's heart began knocking, a terrible suspicion squeezing his innards. "Did he see her clearly?"

"Nae." Calum confirmed his dread. "He only saw her back and the fairness of her hair. The woman's face was turned away from him."

"She could have been anyone."

"You haven't touched a woman in o'er five years." Calum voiced what they both knew. "Who save Liana could tempt you into her bed?"

"No one." Magnus's denial came harsh.

And it wasn't the truth.

The naked Valkyrie could have seduced him.

If she'd been real, he wouldn't have been able to resist her. Just imagining lying with her fired the blood in his veins. Such a woman in the flesh could have scorched him with flames that burned from his loins clear to his heart.

Not that he need worry.

She didn't exist.

Chapter 3

Magnus MacBride, Viking Slayer.

The name stole Margo's breath and made her pulse quicken. Even now, hours after returning home from Ye Olde Pagan Times. Real or imagined, he'd awakened her passion like no flesh and blood twenty-first-century man had ever done. She suspected Patience's broken magic lingered on the book, opening a channel her employer hadn't realized existed, allowing the long-ago Scottish hottie to seem so real. Whatever the cause, she could easily imagine him. Clearly, in bold, vibrant color as if she were right there with him in his time and on that distant shore.

Discovering him only reminded her of the great tragedy of her life.

She'd been born in the wrong century.

She'd definitely been plunked down on the wrong side of the Atlantic.

Men like Magnus MacBride didn't walk around modern-day America. They didn't even frequent New Hope, cozy and quaint as it was. Her most recent dating disaster had been a computer programmer who'd been a lousy kisser. He'd attracted her because he was a history buff. But he was a Civil War reenactor and not a medieval-Scotland enthusiast. Since ditching him, she'd lost interest in romance.

Unless . . .

There really was such a thing as Highland magic. True, ancient power, steeped in the old ways, and so much stronger than Patience's dabbling. The kind of magic that would let Magnus manifest in front of her.

Her sensible side knew it would never happen. That part of her urged her to save her swoons for certain Scottish movie stars, so popular in recent years. Real flesh and blood men who actually existed, even if their Hollywood status made winning their hearts equally impossible.

If she could get to Scotland, she'd surely meet a real live Highlander who'd knock her socks off.

But he won't be the one you want.

The whisper swirled through Margo's mind, making her start. It was a woman's voice, lilting, intimate, and entirely unreal. A shiver ran through her and she rubbed her arms, edgy. Surely Patience's spelling wasn't adept enough to make her hear voices that weren't there?

Magnus hungers for you.

The voice came again, laced with a trace of malice this time. Margo tensed, the fine hairs on her nape lifting as the lights in her apartment flickered and—for a moment—darkness pulsed around her. She knew she was alone, yet she couldn't shake the odd sensation that someone else was with her, watching her.

Someone who didn't like her.

But she gave herself a shake and pushed the ridiculous notion from her mind. A quick glance around her apartment, ensuring that she was alone, helped restore a sense of normalcy. What she couldn't do was wrest her thoughts away from Magnus MacBride.

Not that fantasizing about him bothered her.

A girl was entitled to dream. Doing just that, she rolled her shoulders, pressed a hand to the small of her back. She stretched, fighting off the strain of a long day as her mind conjured a whirl of delicious scenarios featuring herself and Magnus MacBride.

He *was* dream worthy.

Big, strapping, and hot-eyed, his long, dark hair tossing in the wind, and his powerful biceps thick with silver and gold arm rings. He was more perfect than any man she'd ever seen. Her total fantasy brought to life by a few vivid brushstrokes. She'd give anything to have seen him when he was rock hard and solid. Even as paper and ink, every magnificent inch of him made her hot and tingly.

If she could have her very own Highlander, she'd choose him.

She had splurged on his book, *Myths and Legends of the Viking Age*. She'd dipped into her emergency gas and grocery money to buy it. The tome now held pride of place on her glass-topped coffee table. Scenic Highland postcards and pictures she'd cut from glossy Scottish travel magazines winked from beneath the table glass, providing a fitting background for such a braw Highland warrior.

It didn't matter that his two-page color illustration had mysteriously disappeared from the book.

He'd been there.

And that was enough.

Now the book was hers.

Too bad Magnus MacBride wasn't.

Like it or not, he belonged to a long-vanished time. These days, there wasn't much need of Viking slayers. Not even in Scotland. But that didn't mean she couldn't indulge in a bit of wistful imagining. After all, her apartment—a small one-bedroom arrangement on the second floor of an 1840 stone house—was filled with everything a dedicated Scotophile needed to pretend herself into the Highlands.

Margo excelled at such romanticizing.

Now, three years after moving into the old house, she was glad that Dina Greed—damn her eyeballs—had finagled her way into the modern, more spacious apartment Margo had thought she'd wanted so badly. That all-the-bells-and-whistles complex might boast a clubhouse, a swimming pool, and tennis courts, but it didn't have atmosphere.

Nor would the buildings creak and groan when wind whistled round the eaves.

Margo liked creaking and groaning.

Windy weather reminded her of the cold air and gray skies of Scotland. As did her treasures like the mock-medieval strongbox she'd once found sitting alone and forlorn beside a Dumpster. A bit battered, but with a fine humped lid and banded with only lightly rusted iron straps, the chest held her collection of Scottish guidebooks and maps. Another prize was her plaid-covered wing chair, a marvel she'd picked up for next to nothing at Aging Gracefully, a vintage-clothing shop not far from Ye Olde Pagan Times.

The chair had been part of the shop fittings, not merchandise for sale. But Margo was such a good customer at Aging Gracefully that the owner, Ardelle Goodnight, allowed her to make the coveted purchase.

Margo reciprocated by interesting her Luna Harmony clients in Ardelle's heirloom wares.

Just now she glanced at her watch, pushed up from her beloved tartan chair. She'd had a strange, tiring day and the evening dark was closing in. The afternoon's rain had returned with a vengeance and thick, gray mist blew past the windows. Wind rattled the panes—the

Fieldstone House *was* old, the windows made of ancient, wobbly glass—and the sound was making her sleepy.

What she needed was a hot shower, a cup of Earl Grey Cream tea, and then bed.

If she was lucky, she'd dream of Magnus MacBride, Viking Slayer.

As long as she wasn't plagued by images of Dina Greed winging her way across the Atlantic, heading for the Highlands, she'd be satisfied.

That would be a nightmare.

But the gods who loved Scotophiles were good to her.

The instant she went through to her bathroom, a heather-scented haven filled with fluffy, lace-edged towels and Lunarian Organic soaps and bath foams—Patience gave her a generous discount—all thoughts of her rival vanished. She pulled back the curtain of her ancient claw-foot bathtub and turned on the shower.

Steam quickly filled the room, looking almost like Highland mist against the backdrop of Margo's heather-vista wallpaper. Thick, silent, and enveloping, the make-believe mist gave her a cozy feeling of connection to the wild northernmost part of Britain she loved so much.

Her beloved Scotland.

That faraway land of hills and moorland, foaming waterfalls and deep blue lochs, where she should have been born. Kilties, bagpipes, and castles set her heart to pounding, not hot dogs, baseball, and apple pie.

But all wasn't lost.

Someday she'd walk the waterfront of some remote Highland village, stand on a spectacular cliff edge, and watch the sea crash against jagged, black rocks. She'd lose herself in the hills and breathe the scent of pine and wild thyme. Or, better yet, stroll past a thick-walled croft house in a quiet glen and catch a whiff of peat smoke on chill autumn air.

As soon as her ship came in, she'd be on her way.

It was so nice to dream....

Somewhere a dog barked.

Margo frowned as she stripped out of her clothes. There weren't any dogs at the Fieldstone House, regrettably. She really loved them and hoped to have one of her own someday. But she didn't yet, though if she learned that someone had locked a dog out in the rain, she'd try and persuade the owners to let her adopt the poor thing.

Dogs were meant to be loved.

Not left to shiver in the cold, wet dark.

Fortunately, the dog stopped barking—Margo hoped that meant he was now safe and warm, curled before a fire or on someone's comfy couch—and that was good because the night was turning fierce. Rain drummed on the roof and dense, gray fog pressed against the bathroom's tiny window, turning the light of a nearby old-styled lamppost into a smear of glowing yellow haze.

Margo blinked.

For a moment, she would've sworn the edges of the luminous blur flared red. But when she looked again, the eerie light was gone.

Even so, she turned to the broad windowsill and lit three white pillar candles. Set in trays of small, river-polished pebbles, the arrangement was a gift from Patience, who always murmured warding spells over every candle to leave Ye Olde Pagan Times.

Patience believed in doing her part for the community by sending each customer home with a blessing. She claimed the spell would protect the patrons whether or not they realized they'd left with a charmed candle. Or scented oil and reed diffusers guaranteed to not only spend fragrance but keep negativity at bay. Himalayan salt-crystal lamps did more than lend cheer and ambience to a room with their soft, orange glow. They also soothed hectic lives, bringing balance and healing to body, mind, and spirit. All thanks to Patience's gentle murmurings.

No one ever guessed.

Margo knew.

And she hoped the white candles would chase the odd shivers racing down her nerves again. Watching Magnus MacBride quicken to life on a book page might've been beyond amazing, but something else had lurked in the shop's dimly lit rows of bookshelves.

Something evil, she was sure.

And she wanted none of its residue tainting her.

Imagining a strange woman's voice taunting her had been bad enough.

So she climbed into her heather-purple-painted claw-foot tub, reached for her favorite Ocean of Storms shower gel, and stepped beneath the hot, pounding water. A good vigorous scrubbing would revive her and—she hoped—cleanse and shield her aura.

Ocean of Storms did foam better than any other shower gel. Almost iridescent, the creamy bubbles reminded her of sea spume. The fragrance was a dream, filling the air with the mysteries of wild, windswept seas and just a touch of rich, musky amber. She closed her eyes and breathed deep, letting the scent soothe her, carrying her away. . . .

"Precious lass . . ."

Margo's heart thumped as she imagined how Magnus would greet her. His voice would be deep and richly burred. Every word would be buttery smooth, pure Highland seduction.

They'd be on the strand from the book illustration

and he'd stride up to her, taking her face in his hands and kissing her deeply.

She could picture the scene so well, even the sheer black cliffs rising behind him. Her breath caught at the vividness of her imagination, fantasy letting the tile and wallpaper vanish until she saw only jagged, basalt crags. Mist wreathed the cliff tops and the air filled with the cries of seabirds and the roar of the surf.

Magnus would break the kiss then and look deep into her eyes. *"I'm waiting for you, lass. Come to me, soon."*

Margo was sure that was what he'd say. And the thought sent a rush of feminine need racing through her.

"Kissing you is no' enough...."

Margo bit her lip and stopped soaping herself as she imagined his voice. It'd be darker and sexier now, full of the soft, musical undertones that made a Scottish accent so curl-a-girl's-toes irresistible.

Margo's heart beat faster and she took a shallow breath. Desire stirred, her body heating as she let her imagination lead her onward.

She went willingly.

It was too tempting to pretend he was kissing her. Too delicious, imagining his love words spilling through her like smooth, sun-warmed honey. Seductive, molten, and so deliciously Highland that if only they were real, her heart would split wide, and she knew she'd ache with the pleasure of hearing him.

God help her if he spoke Gaelic.

Sadly, her imagination had its limits.

Much as she loved Scotland, she'd never learned Gaelic.

She could paint his world vividly. With her mind's eye, she could even see screeching seabirds speeding past, swooping low over her head on their way to the rocky, many-ledged crags.

She could almost believe she *was* in a rock-lined, cliff-hemmed cove.

Everything seemed so real.

Nearby, a dog barked again—it sounded like the same one as earlier—and from the corner of her eye, she imagined that she caught a glimpse of a large, scruffy-coated beast running along a black line of seaweed near the water's edge.

Big waves crashed there, the endless *whoosh* and booms echoing along the headland.

Margo's heart began to thump, heavily. She inhaled deep, exhaled slowly.

It didn't help.

She blinked, and the dog disappeared into the mist. But glistening tidal rocks and steep cliffs met her eye no matter where she looked. Her bathroom had disappeared. And she still heard the sea.

The rhythmic pounding could be only her own blood rushing in her ears. It wasn't every day she imagined herself up close and personal with a dream-spun hunk of pure Scottish sexuality. But real as it all seemed, it wasn't. She hadn't been transported anywhere, much as she wished she had been. She was still in her heather-clad bathroom.

Rain hammered on the roof and splattered the window, same as a moment ago. And the shower still splashed around her and spilled down her naked body. But the water chilled her now, as did the cold bite of racing wind.

Wind like none she'd ever felt and that smelled of deep, clean waters, full of ice and strong, northern currents.

A peek past her shower curtain showed that Patience's candles still burned, though their flames now looked more like distant torchlight or even beacons.

And the red-rimmed light of the garden lamppost was now a fire-edged moon, casting its lurid path across a sea that shone like beaten silver.

But her sexy-voiced Highlander was nowhere to be seen.

He'd left her dream.

Or so she thought until she pushed her dripping bangs back from her face. The air seemed to shift then, and he reappeared in all his kilt-clad glory. She blinked, her jaw slipping.

Her heart went wild, thundering madly. Exhaustion and soap in her eyes were surely playing tricks on her, for he looked even more magnificent now. Afraid the dream would shatter if she even breathed, she stood still. But a bit of shampoo slipped into her eyes and she reached to dash at the suds. At once, two large hands clamped around her wrists, lowering her arms to her sides.

"Stay with me. I'll show you bliss as you've ne'er known." His voice was darker now, richer than ever, and his eyes smoldered with passion.

He gripped her possessively, crowding her with his wide shoulders and big, hard chest. He looked like a mythical Celtic god, full of power and passion. Glittering silver and gold rings banded the hard muscles of his upper arms. And his full, sensual mouth promised ecstasies beyond her wildest imaginings. Wind whipped his silky black hair, drawing her attention to his bold, chiseled features. He had a proud, handsome face, strengthened by fierce slashing brows. His eyes were dark as midnight and, just now, staring straight into her soul, bridging forever as if time and distance didn't exist.

Anything was possible in dreams.

Margo just wished this were reality.

She tried to say something, but the pure sexual magnetism of him fuzzed her mind. He stepped closer, the heat from his big muscle-packed body warming her, making her tremble. "You want this, aye?"

Not waiting for an answer, he cupped her chin and lowered his head, kissing her again.

"Yes . . ." Margo wasn't about to argue.

This was her fantasy, after all.

As if from a great distance, she could feel the pounding cascade of her shower. She also felt his big, strong hands glide down her sides, to her hips. He splayed his fingers across her bottom, kneading her flesh, pulling her close against him.

She melted, wishing fervently this were real.

At least six feet four, he towered over her, his great height making her neck ache because she had to tip back her head to peer up at him. Unlike in the book illustration, he now wore his sleek raven hair tied at his nape, but his dark eyes burned with the same heat that had so captivated her at Ye Olde Pagan Times.

Only now that fire was one of desire, not fury.

And just looking up at him, dream-spun or not, made her heart race and her sex clench. She went liquid with want, everything female in her melting. Urgent need pooled into a hot, throbbing ache that burned at the very center of her.

As if he knew, his fierce gaze turned even more heated. Pulling her closer, he gave her a slow half smile that could only be called provocatively wicked.

Dangerous.

"Tell me you want me." He touched her wet hair, smoothing a strand behind her ear. "I am made of rock and ice, as strong"—his fingers slid along the curve of her cheek, then skimmed her chin—"as the cold steel of Vengeance, my sword. But you, lass, have the power to bring me to my knees."

"I know. . . ." Margo couldn't breathe.

His touch, now an oh-so-light caress across the sensitive skin beneath her ear, sent jolts of pleasure shooting all through her. Her lower belly grew heavy, tingling with female desire. Her nipples tightened, making it impossible to hide her excitement.

He looked out at the empty sea and then back at her. Holding her gaze, he slid the edge of his thumb across her lower lip and back again, teasing her. "I know what you want, sweet one."

Then give it to me, she almost dared him. She wanted him. Every tall, strong, and handsome inch of him. She especially wanted the hard ridge of inches tenting his kilt. But as so often in dreams, her lips wouldn't form the words. She also knew that any attempt to alter the natural flow of a dream could have adverse effects. Such as waking up alone, wet, and shivering in a shower that had gone icy cold. With her luck, she might then slip and conk her head on the edge of the tub, winning a goose-egg-sized bump and days of throbbing pain.

His dark gaze flicked over her. "You tempt me greatly."

Margo swallowed, the hunger in his eyes stirring a storm of arousal inside her. His deep voice seduced her, its richness spilling through her, warming her, as if the smooth, honeyed tones held ancient magic. A spell that strengthened on each word he spoke and that left her hot, needy, and aching.

Everything else about him . . .

Just breathing in the same salt-kissed air electrified her and sent wicked-hot shivers spearing through her from head to toe.

Margo could see that he knew.

His smile was almost predatory.

She did want him to kiss her again. This was her fantasy and she might as well enjoy every moment. But instead of pulling her even tighter against him and granting her wishes, he paced away from her and then whirled back around. His scorching gaze made her very aware that she was naked.

Thank God she exercised.

For every baked potato slathered with butter, sour cream, cheddar, and chives that she devoured—she was such a potato zealot—she made good her indulgence with a minimum of one hundred sit-ups and crunches.

Her belly was tight, her waist trim.

Her hot-eyed Viking Slayer was pure male perfection. She'd already given him a thorough head-to-toe sweep and knew by the fall of his kilt that his broad, plaid-draped shoulders and brawny arms weren't the only well-muscled parts of him. He was more than amply endowed, and having once led the Bucks County Kilt Appreciation Society, she knew exactly what Highlanders wore under their kilts.

Better said, what they *didn't* wear.

The thought almost made her climax.

Especially when he dropped his gaze to her breasts, letting his focus settle on her taut and straining nipples, so eager for his attentions.

Margo bit her lip again. The ache inside her was unbearable now.

"O-o-oh, lass." He shook his head slowly, his gaze not leaving her nipples. "You would heat a thousand Highland nights." He took a step closer, and another, pausing about three feet away from her. He stood at the sea's edge and the surf broke white behind him, the foam swirling around his ankles as the water hissed across the sand.

He didn't move or blink. He only held her gaze, and Margo knew he felt the awareness crackling between them. The pull binding them felt almost alive, burning the air, and the power of it sent delicious shivers along her nerves. Her heart beat wildly. Her pulse quickened at how conscious he was of her naked breasts. Hearing him admit in his deep burr that he desired her made her breath catch. The seductive words reverberated through her body, touching her intimately.

"I need you, lass." He clenched his fists at his sides, so tightly that his knuckles gleamed in the moonlight. "In another place and time"—he spoke as if this were real, his gaze dipping to the juncture of her thighs—"I'd do more than kiss you. I'd drag my tongue o'er every inch of you, sating myself until your hot, womanly taste was branded on me forever."

"Oh, God . . ." Desire washed through Margo, a hard, fast torrent.

She'd been verging on a climax and his words— spoken in his husky Scottish accent—were speeding her close to that bright, looming edge of ecstasy.

She closed her eyes, almost there.

Then he suddenly slid his arms around her and pulled her close, slanting his mouth over hers in a hard, bruising kiss. He released her as quickly, stepping back as if she'd scalded him.

Margo frowned, not liking this turn of her dream.

"Now begone from here before I forget this isn't real." He dragged his sleeve over his lips, his gaze burning her. "If we meet again—where'er—I'll no' be responsible for what I might do."

Before she could argue—or even blink—he turned and strode down the strand, slowing his pace only when the large scruffy dog she'd seen earlier bounded up to him. Without breaking stride, he reached down to pat the dog's head. Together, they hastened along the water's edge until they both disappeared into the mist, leaving her alone.

Except she still heard a Scottish male voice, soft and lilting, but nothing at all like Magnus MacBride's deep, buttery-rich burr.

She was still cold.

Absolutely freezing . . .

And—somehow—she was no longer in the shower. She came awake slowly, not wanting to leave the cocooning darkness. She felt almost hungover, even though she'd had nothing stronger than Earl Grey Cream tea. Vaguely, she remembered coming into the living room, moving like a sleepwalker. Her grogginess told her she'd slept deeply. And that it was late. Rain still drummed on the roof, though the sound was only a light patter now. Somewhere, a Scottish voice did rise and fall, the musical tones filling her ears, pulling her from the hazy mists of her dream.

Crathes Castle's ghost is a Green Lady. The voice droned on, clearer now. *She's most often seen in the room given her name, the Green Lady's Room, where she paces back and forth, then pauses by the fireplace. . . .*

Margo started when she recognized the voice. "Oh, no!"

Her eyes popped open. Fully alert now, she found herself curled naked in her plaid wing chair. Well, wrapped-in-a-big-bath-towel naked. And judging by the cramp in her legs, she'd been wedged into the chair for hours.

Her feet had even gone to sleep.

She stared across her living room at the soft glow of her television. A well-known Scottish medium peered back at her from the screen. She couldn't recall his name, but he appeared weekly on a popular British ghost-hunting show.

Her heart plummeted as she stared back at him, watching him lead a small group of ghost enthusiasts through Crathes Castle in Scotland's Royal Deeside.

She loved the show and had never missed an episode. Apparently she hadn't skipped this night's investigation, either.

But she *had* taken a shower.

And then, in the confused half-awake, half-asleep state that haunts the weary, she'd stumbled in here to watch *Ghosting Britain*.

There could be no other explanation.

Her hair was still damp. She'd even tended her nightly ritual of slathering on moisturizer. Her skin felt sleek and silky smooth. She could smell the fragrant jasmine notes of Sea of Nectar body lotion. She'd just been so tired that she didn't remember flipping on the television.

What she remembered was dreaming of Magnus MacBride.

How his voice had deepened when he'd talked about *dragging his tongue over her* or *sating himself on her taste*. She could still feel his kisses, so hard, rough, and plundering. His mouth crushing down over hers, stealing her breath, surprising her as his tongue plunged between her lips to twirl and tangle with her own, making her burn . . .

She was still on fire.

She was also hungry.

So she scrambled out of her chair, ignoring the jabs of a gazillion needles shooting up her legs when she put weight on her feet. Quickly, she knotted her big purple towel more securely around her breasts.

Then she headed for the kitchen.

She was halfway there when she realized she could devour everything in her fridge—and even her cupboards—and she'd still be ravenous. She craved something a mere midnight snack would never satisfy. And it was a hunger that would only worsen as the night progressed and she soon found herself alone in her bed.

This time, she wouldn't sleep.

She'd spend what remained of the night reliving her dream and what it had felt like to be held and kissed by the Viking Slayer.

Chapter 4

Early the next day, across time and in a far-distant place, Magnus strode from Badcall Castle, making for a certain thick-walled cottage. Nestled atop a pine-clad knoll, Windhill Cottage required visitors to climb a rough track through dense bracken and to be wary of hidden bog slicks. But there were rewards for the effort. One of the finest was the welcoming curl of peat smoke that always rose from Windhill's thatched roof. A great, huge-bearded seer dwelt at the cottage, preferring seclusion to cast his runes, watch the roll of the sea, listen to the wind, or whatever else he did in his endeavors to unravel the mysteries of fate.

This man was Magnus's reason for leaving his hall on such a chill and drizzly morn. And why he carried a basket of smoked herring on his arm.

Orosius was an unlikely prophet, but skilled at reading signs in elemental forces. Or through other means he didn't care to divulge.

Most times, Magnus appreciated the seer's wisdom.

Just now he only wanted to put an end to Calum's blether about the realm of the dead and a naked, golden-haired siren he knew wasn't Liana.

He hoped she wasn't the temptress conjured by Donata.

The lushly curved vixen who'd appeared to him twice now. Once when he'd cut down Godred, and—he frowned—in the heated dream that robbed his sleep and left him so angry this morn. More than that, for ever since she'd visited him in the night, his tongue ached to tease and taste her. He'd wakened to find his entire body so tight that even breathing was an agony.

His loins . . .

Magnus's scowl deepened. He quickened his pace, glad for the damp air, the cold wind fretting his plaid. And for Frodi's loyal presence as the old dog trailed him up the steep rise. A journey that, thanks to the spume-flecked maid from the sea, had never struck him as so torturous.

Such intense, bone-aching lust hadn't seized him since the first time he'd thrust his head beneath a woman's skirts and breathed in the tangy musk of female desire. It galled him that he now felt an overwhelming urge to fill his lungs with the naked beauty's feminine dew. Shoving the desire from his mind, he avoided a jumble of loose, moss-covered rocks and then leapt over a narrow, rushing burn.

Without doubt, the sea siren had cast magic over him.

He'd have been fine if she hadn't taunted him by placing her hands on her hips, offering him such a grand view of her full, round breasts and her shapely, succulent thighs. The lush triangle of dark gold curls that set his blood to simmering.

Even then, he might have remained unaffected.

But his dream self had kissed her.

And she'd sighed her pleasure, parting her soft, ripe lips. Somehow, before he realized what was happening, his tongue was tangling with hers and they were sharing breath, the intimacy scalding him.

If the vixen hadn't wished to seduce him, why had

she kissed him back? Why deepen the kiss and let her tongue twirl so hotly with his, if not to drive him to madness?

Why burst into his life wearing naught but pearls of water and sea foam?

She'd even leaned into him when he'd seized her, melting against him so that he felt the delicious burn of her tightened nipples. The soft, beckoning heat of her woman's place and the silky-wet delights waiting beneath her tangle of golden female curls.

He might have been dreaming, trapped in the thrall of Donata's curse, but he could almost taste the naked beauty now. He knew she'd be honeyed nectar on his tongue. Sakes, he'd kill a man just to run a finger down the slick, molten center of her.

And that need fashed him greatly.

Especially as he was certain Sigurd Sword Breaker or Donata Greer had worked some kind of dark, carnal magic to send the seductress to plague him. Donata would laugh when he succumbed to the vixen's charms. Sigurd would wait until he mounted her and then plunge a blade through his back, piercing his heart.

Only his foes could hatch such a plan.

His own mind was too filled with his need to sharpen his sword on his enemies' bones for him to bother conjuring bare-bottomed, pert-nippled females to addle his wits and rob him of his nights' rest.

"Come, Frodi." Magnus frowned when his dog stopped to sniff heather. "The female is a proper pest. I want Orosius to banish her."

Frodi swiveled his furry head, seeming to grin at Magnus before trotting back to his side. The dog's swishing tail gave the impression he agreed that the seer could spin such magic.

If anyone could vanquish the sea witch, it was Orosius.

Magnus trusted in the seer's power.

But his hopes dimmed when Orosius opened the door as he neared the cottage. The seer was known for his moods, and the way he scratched his tattered ear at Magnus's approach didn't bode well.

Orosius had lost much of his ear to an enemy's sword years ago and believed the injury was the gods' retribution for using his gift unwisely. He tugged the damaged ear only when he wasn't of a mood to scry. The fierce look he pinned on Magnus was equally telling. His wildly mussed hair signaled that he'd only just risen.

It was clearly one of those mornings when Orosius desired his peace.

Magnus didn't care.

Letting his own brows snap together, he strode on toward the low, whitewashed cottage. "Orosius! I'll be having a word with you."

"Humph. I knew you'd be coming." Orosius continued to scratch his ear. "Felt it in my bones, I did." A huge man with piercing, silvery eyes, a bulbous red nose that had surely been broken more than once, and a great, bushy black beard, he filled the doorway.

He was also blocking it, deliberately.

His odd eyes narrowed. "Calum couldn't keep his tongue from flapping, eh?"

Magnus forgot his intention to treat the seer with respect. "I'd rather you put such tidings in my own ears before filling Calum's head with nonsense."

Orosius gave him a chiding look. "As it happens, I meant to tell you. That long-nosed Calum darkened my door before I had a chance."

"You could've come straight to Badcall."

"Harrumph." Orosius rocked back on his heels and glared at Magnus. "I need to sleep after seeing the like. And with everyone tromping a track to my door of late, I haven't had my rest."

"You can sleep after I've had my answers." Magnus glowered back at him. "What's this about seeing me dead?"

"Only what I saw, no more."

"You erred."

"Be the first time, if I did." Orosius bristled. "I'm not a storyteller, spinning tales to fill a long, cold evening." He swelled his chest, looking proud. "I speak true, whether or not my words are pleasing."

"Then I'll tell you what pleases me." Magnus drew himself up likewise. "Standing in Godred's blood was more than satisfying. And I'll no' be dying until I've danced in Sword Breaker's guts."

"Could be that's so." Orosius shifted and a waft of peat smoke drifted from the cottage's dim interior. "I didnae see your end happening. I only saw—"

"I know what you saw." Magnus's gaze met the seer's. "And it wasn't me with Liana."

Orosius's heavy black brows drew together. Instead of answering, he peered at the basket of smoked herring in Magnus's hand.

"Be that your tribute for me?" Orosius's sharp eyes narrowed on the fish. "I still have two strings o' herring hanging o'er my fire from your last visit. What I need is more peat to burn."

"You'll have your peat." Magnus turned a sour glance on a fresh curl of smoke whirling out into the cold morning. He knew if he peered around the corner of the cottage, he'd see a peat stack nearly as high as the one that supplied Badcall. "Truth is, you're better supplied than most."

Looking belligerent, Orosius folded his arms over his barrel-sized chest. "If my kettle isn't kept simmering, there's no steam to scry—"

"Is that where you saw me in the realm of the dead?" Magnus gave him an equally hard look. "Peering in the steam off your cauldron?"

"I could've seen what I did in the bottom o' my ale cup." Orosius didn't budge from the door. "Where and what I saw changes naught."

"It does if the woman you saw wasn't Liana." Magnus half turned to glance at the dark clouds racing in from the sea. Thunder sounded in the distance and cold wind thrashed the red-berried rowan tree next to Orosius's cottage. "I say"—he swung back around to fix the seer with a stare—"your scrying showed me in the thrall of a she-demon summoned by Donata Greer, the sorceress."

Orosius thrust his chin. "I dinnae mistake what's shown to me."

"Let me see what you saw and we'll know."

"Begad!" Orosius looked horrified. "Suchlike would flatten me for days. You dinnae ken the power needed to share even a glimmer of what I see."

"You showed me how Liana died." Magnus's voice hardened.

"That was long ago and she came to me in a dream, wanting to reach you." Orosius's eyes gleamed with defiance. "If she wished to be seen now, she would've shown me more than the back of her head."

"You didn't see Liana." Magnus was sure of it.

"Humph." Orosius snorted.

Magnus frowned. The seer was his last hope.

And the cantankerous lout's foul mood grated on his nerves.

Orosius was an ogre.

And Magnus was weary of him. He also pushed past him into the low-ceilinged cottage. A small fire burned in the central hearth, where Orosius's black kettle hung on a chain above the smoldering peats. It was there that Frodi chose to sprawl on the stone-flagged floor.

Orosius went to stand beside the dog. The red glow from the peat lit his hulking form, making him look even bigger, almost like an oversized troll with his large nose and wild hair. "Bad things happen when folk go poking into things they aren't meant to be a-seeing."

"I'll take my chances." Magnus folded his arms. "Say your scrying words."

"Mayhap I'm no' of a mind to see your nekkid arse again." Orosius balked. "Once was enough."

"Dinnae test me, Orosius. One glimpse is all I'm asking. Then I'll be on my way."

"And I'll have my peat?"

"Aye, and as much as Ewan and two lads can cut in a day."

The seer pulled on his beard, considering. "I'm descended from a long line of sages. . . ." He paused to glance at the steam rising above his cauldron. "They watch o'er me. I'm no' sure they'd approve. The lass was bare-bottomed and—"

"And you saw me having her, what?" Magnus stepped forward, going toe to toe with Orosius. "That's what Calum told me. Will you be denying it?"

"Nae." Orosius reddened.

"Then"—Magnus leaned close—"you'll no' be showing me aught that I haven't already seen."

Orosius spluttered.

Magnus grinned and held out his hands, palms downward. "Take my hands now. Put your feet o'er mine. That's how you did it last time."

"Botheration!" The seer snapped his bushy black

brows together in a fierce scowl. But he placed his hands on top of Magnus's and dutifully rested his toes over Magnus's own.

Then he closed his eyes as he muttered a string of nonsensical words. When he stopped chanting and opened his eyes again to peer into the steam, Magnus knew the seer was looking into another world.

Magnus saw nothing.

Until Orosius's hands began to tremble and a peat brick popped, sending up a shower of sparks to join the cauldron's whirling steam. In that moment, the heavy black kettle and even the cottage's peat-stained walls vanished, leaving only clouds of glittering blue-white smoke that swirled around Magnus and the seer.

Magnus's nape prickled.

Then the air shivered, the mist parted, and his breath caught, the world seeming to stand still, as he gazed upon a beautiful crystalline landscape that could've been the domain of the gods.

It was a lofty headland, luxuriantly wooded and stretching forever. Soft afternoon light slanted across trees dressed in autumnal scarlet and gold, while cloud shadows dappled a sea of endless moors. Rich, heather-clad hills rolled into the distance, finally melting into shimmering blue at the edge of sight.

And in the midst of the sunlit haze, Magnus saw himself lying on his plaid as a beautiful, lushly curved woman rode him to ecstasy. Her sleek thighs gripped his hips, and the way she held her head tilted to the sky showed how much she enjoyed being astride him. They were both naked, their clothes strewn about the heather as if they'd undressed hurriedly. And from where Magnus looked on, the woman had her back to him, just as Orosius had claimed.

Her body gleamed in the strange golden light, and her

full, sweetly curved bottom moved with a fluid rhythm that made Magnus's blood surge with urgent, almost feral need. Fair, shining hair swung about her shoulders. And even without seeing her face, he knew she'd have creamy, flawless skin and huge sapphire eyes.

He recognized her without question.

She wasn't Liana.

She was the Valkyrie.

And it wasn't her shorn hair that gave her away, though her lack of Liana's hip-length tresses should've alerted Orosius to his error. Nor was it her ripe shapeliness where Liana had been so slight.

It was her intensity.

Her passion singed the air, burning him.

It was torture to see her yet not feel the hot, silken glide of her naked skin against his. Tormented, he ached to know the slick wetness of her woman's flesh as she rode him. Magnus stared at her, his loins heavy with longing. When her body arched and he saw a shiver ripple through her, he didn't care if Sword Breaker had paid Donata to conjure her. Or even if the sorceress had summoned her on her own, to punish Magnus for her brother's death.

All he knew was that he wanted her.

She rose and fell above him, the sight making a ragged breath catch in his throat.

He needed to see her breasts. Cup their fullness and taste her nipples ...

"Damnation!" He jerked away from the seer and strode forward, straight into the fire.

The image shattered, spinning away in a burst of blue-white sparks.

Darkness swirled, blotting the world.

Magnus tripped, his foot colliding with one of the stones edging the fire. He couldn't see beyond the deep, whirling shadows.

"You great lackwit!" Orosius grabbed his arm, yanking him back just as he crashed into the heavy black cauldron on its chain.

Frodi leapt to his feet, bolting away as scalding broth sloshed over the kettle's rim. The liquid missed Magnus's legs, but spilled onto the hot peats with a loud *zish*-ing sound. Smeary ash covered Magnus's feet, and puffs of soot floated in the air, drifting down onto Orosius's stew, ruining his meal.

The seer glared at him. "I told you no good comes from peering at things no' meant to be seen again. You wasted a good morn and spoiled my supper, you did. Now you can take your pestering self and—"

"The runes." Magnus glanced at a lumpy leather pouch on the table. "Cast the runesticks for me. I need to know who the woman is."

Orosius planted his bulk between Magnus and the scarred wooden table. "You had your look and now I'll be having my sleep. Thon beauty was Liana." He folded his arms. "Herself, and you, in the realm o' souls."

Magnus knew better.

He wiped a hand over his brow. His head was beginning to ache worse than if he'd drunk a barrel of soured ale. "Liana was an innocent, you he-goat." He put back his shoulders, not liking the smirk on the seer's face. "She wouldn't—"

"Pah." Orosius waved off the objection. "Mayhap you teach her the like after you join her in the otherworld?"

"That was Badcall, no cloudland of the dead." Magnus brushed past the seer to scoop the rune bag off the table. He thrust the pouch into Orosius's hands. "I'll leave after you cast the runes."

"Ho!" Orosius's eyes narrowed, cagily. "Rune casting is heathen Norse magic. Pagan sorcery, you scolded, last time I shook out my sticks in your hall."

Magnus frowned, remembering. "You said they speak true."

"Aye, so I did."

"Then cast them."

The seer lifted a brow. "You may not like what they say."

"I don't care for any of this." Magnus could feel annoyance inching along his nerves. "I only want the truth."

"So be it." Turning to the table, Orosius opened the pouch and withdrew the runesticks. Gleaming white, they were bundled by a red silk thread. Orosius set his fingers to the string, but he glanced once more at Magnus before he released the slender sticks.

"Do it." Magnus nodded.

Orosius closed his eyes and held out the runesticks. Then he opened his hand, letting them clatter onto the table. Leaning forward, he peered at the jumbled sticks for a long time. At last, he straightened and turned to face Magnus.

"The runes have spoken." Orosius's tone made the cottage seem gray and cold.

"And what did the sticks say?"

"What I knew they would."

Magnus's stomach knotted. "And what was that?"

"That the maid—"

"You mean Donata's temptress." Magnus wanted clarity.

Orosius scowled. "The sticks didn't choose to show me who she is. Though"—he swelled his great chest—"I'm still for thinking she's Liana."

Magnus glanced at the fallen sticks, then back at the seer. "Just tell me what the runes said."

Looking annoyed, Orosius drew a long breath. "That the maid," he repeated, "is nowhere you can reach her.

You could search the whole world in its length and breadth and not find her.

"She is"—Orosius's silvery eyes met Magnus's—"beyond this realm."

Magnus looked back at him. "That's all?"

The seer nodded.

And it was then that the truth hit Magnus, settling on his shoulders like a weighted cloak.

He didn't care who, or what, the naked woman was.

But it did bother him that the runes said she was beyond his reach.

And that could only mean what he'd dreaded.

He was cursed.

In her own world, Margo lay as still as she could beneath her bedcovers. Night noises sifted through the curtains, but the scratch of tree branches against the wall and the rattle of rain on the window weren't what she wanted to hear. She especially resented the *tick-tick-tick*ing of her bedside clock and the distant wail of a siren.

She'd have preferred the sound of wind and waves. She'd rather be standing atop high black cliffs that dropped to a dark, foaming sea. She'd hoped to reclaim her earlier dream, slipping into a place where she could breathe in cold, streaming air that smelled of heather, peat, and salt spray. Her beloved Highlands, where Magnus MacBride would be waiting for her, eager to answer her passion with his own.

Instead . . .

She felt the weight of twenty-first-century America close in on her. The siren's whir faded, but—somewhere—the annoying rumble of a garbage truck replaced the noise. She frowned, wanting to forget the asphalt and concrete world outside her bedroom and return to the peace of the sea- and landscape of her fantasy. She'd read somewhere that a shattered dream could be retrieved if the dreamer didn't move before falling back asleep.

She hoped cracking her eyes didn't count as moving.

But something jarring had wakened her and she needed to be sure she was alone in the deep grayness filling her presunrise bedroom.

If—horrors!—five thirty a.m. could even be considered early morning.

As a dyed-in-the-wool night owl and with Patience allowing her to begin work at noon, Margo rarely wakened before nine. Anything earlier was the middle of the night to her. And weird noises that intruded into her sleeping hours were not looked on with kindness.

Such disturbances could also be dangerous.

New Hope wasn't a crime hub. And the Fieldstone House had never been burgled. The old house and its gardens felt safe, always. Margo believed the land possessed a sanctuary-like aura. As if no harm could touch anyone who lived within the property's rambling bounds.

Even so . . .

She clutched the edge of her comforter, digging her fingers into the soft, downy warmth of the splurged-on duvet she'd restyled with yards of Isle of Skye tartan, nabbed off the bargain table at Aging Gracefully.

Margo peered into the darkness, her body still.

Blessedly, nothing stirred anywhere.

She hadn't been awakened by an as yet unheard of Bucks County serial killer.

Satisfied, she snuggled back against her pillows and nestled deeper beneath her plaid comforter. She needed only to focus. So she concentrated on images she wanted to see. Mist rolling down steep, rocky hillsides, then flashes of autumn-red bracken, the deep purple of heather. Nothing happened, but anticipation made her heart beat fast and hard. Soon, she'd catch a whiff of heather, the mist would swirl, and she'd see her proud Highland warrior. She tried to imagine him standing with one foot on a boulder, his dark head tilted back as he stared up at the cloud-veiled sun. Steel would glint at his side and strength would pour off him as he gripped his sword hilt, all arrogance and challenge.

For the space of a dream, bliss would be hers. . . .

She closed her eyes, trying to get there.

But just when the Highland scene began to rise around her and she thought she might drift away to the distant place she loved so much, a shrill noise rang out in the silver-misted air.

It was her cell phone.

And the persistence of its tinny rendition of "Scotland the Brave" dashed her hopes, grounding her in the real world of her darkened bedroom.

Margo sat bolt upright and glared at the clock on her bedside table. The alarm's glowing green hands told her that it was just five forty-five a.m. Not even six o'clock. If she had any doubts, a glance at her window showed that it was still darkest night outside.

Not even the tiniest shimmer of light seeped through her drawn curtains.

Yet her cell phone's imitation bagpipes kept screaming.

And she was going to kill whoever had the nerve to call at such an ungodly hour.

Grabbing the phone, she flipped it open and slapped it to her ear. "Who is this?"

"Margo! *Finally.*" Marta Lopez's voice held a touch of hysteria. "I've been trying to reach you all night."

"Oh?" Margo's annoyance turned to apprehension.

"I've been calling nearly every hour, on the hour, since midnight." Marta sounded breathy, excited. "I know you're a sound sleeper, so I let it ring."

"I was sleeping deeply." Margo's irritation returned. Now she knew what had wakened her earlier. "What's so important that—" She broke off, a terrible thought rushing her. Marta didn't sound upset, but still . . .

Margo braced herself. "Has something happened to Patience?"

"No." Marta actually laughed. "It's nothing to do with her, though she was with me when—"

"When what?" Margo prodded, not wanting her friend to launch into one of her drawn-out spiels. Marta could be theatrical. And much too long-winded if not checked. "What's happened?"

Marta took a breath. "This afternoon, after Patience and I left the shop, we were having high tea at the Cabbage Rose Gift Emporium and Tea Room out near Valley Forge."

"I know." Margo pulled a pillow onto her lap.

"We ran into Ardelle Goodnight of Aging Gracefully as we were leaving. She invited us to her place to see some vintage caftans before she puts them on sale. She thinks they'll sell quickly and she thought Patience or I might want a few of them. So—"

"You woke me up in the middle of the night to talk about caftans?"

Marta laughed again. "Of course I didn't, you silly bean. I called about Scotland."

"Scotland?" Margo felt her eyes rounding.

"Yep." Marta's grin came down the line. "Your beloved Highlands and all that. Those heather hills may not be as far off as you think."

"What?" Margo was all ears now. "What does Scotland have to do with Ardelle Goodnight and her caftans?"

"Only that"—Marta managed to make her voice sound like a drumroll—"Ardelle mentioned she'd run into Donald McVittie and he—"

"Donald McVittie?" Margo scooted up higher against her bed's headboard.

Donald McVittie was a great kilted teddy bear of a balding, beer-bellied American Scottish male who owned and ran New Hope's premier Scottish shop, A Dash o' Plaid.

Margo liked him.

Especially as Donald saw it as his duty to the Auld Hameland to quicken shop visitors' interest in Highland culture, whether or not they made a purchase. He was also a sponsor of Bucks County's annual Scottish Festival. For people like Margo who couldn't afford a plane ticket to Glasgow, the event was the next-best thing to being there.

Donald's A Dash o' Plaid stall was always her favorite stop at the fair.

Margo adjusted the phone against her ear. "Is Donald looking for help at his booth?" The festival was soon, only a week or so away. Margo had pitched in a time or two in the past. A Dash o' Plaid was popular. "If so, and if Patience can spare me, then—"

"No, no—it's nothing like that." Marta was waving a hand in the air. Margo knew from the tone of her friend's voice. "Donald is doing a raffle at the Scottish Festival.

"He's giving away lots of neat things. But the grand prize is"—Marta's voice rose—"a trip to Scotland!"

"Oh, my God!" Margo's heart hit her ribs. "You're joking, right?"

"Not a word." Marta went all excited again. "Wait a minute. I wrote down the details. . . ." Margo heard rustling noises through the phone. Then Marta was back on the line, sounding triumphant. "One lucky soul will win a guided coach tour that'll hit all of Scotland's classic sites. Highlights are castles, Loch Ness, and"—there was a sound like a finger moving down a piece of paper—"Culloden

Battlefield. The outfit running the trip is Heritage Tours, one of most respected touring companies in Scotland."

"Oh, Marta!" Margo was going to swoon. "I've got to win."

"I know." Marta soothed now, her voice almost motherly. "And you will. Madame Zelda of Bulgaria feels it in her bones. And think about this." She laughed again. "If the timing is right, your plane to Scotland could pass Dina Greed's homeward-bound jet. Just imagine how much that would annoy her when she finds out.

"She'll head right for Ye Olde Pagan Times to needle you with an account of her trip through the Highlands. Then Patience and I will smile and tell her too bad, she can't see you that day.

"You're touring Scotland. And"—Marta's voice swelled with glee—"surely having a grand time."

"Oh, Marta . . ." Margo couldn't speak.

Blood roared in her ears and her mouth had gone horribly dry. She tried to thank her friend for calling— she felt so guilty for being annoyed when the phone rang—but no words would come. Her throat had closed, and although she hadn't cried in years, her eyes were watering. They stung badly and blurred her vision.

"Now you sleep, love." Marta's voice came as if from a distance. "I'll see you in the shop later and we'll think up a battle campaign. . . ."

Margo nodded mutely.

Then she flipped shut the phone. Her friend was right. She'd need a strategic plan for the raffle. And she hadn't been lying to Marta when she'd said she had to win the vacation to Scotland.

She did have to win.

Losing would be unbearable.

Chapter 5

Margo saw the envelope the instant she approached her Luna Harmony station at Ye Olde Pagan Times. It was almost noon, but it could've been any hour inside the little shop. The real world rarely crossed the shop's threshold. Margo knew instinctively that the note somehow transcended the ordinary. The air around the card almost shimmered. Margo's pulse quickened as she stepped closer. Thick, cream-colored, and tied with a purple-and-green tartan ribbon, the beautifully hand-cast card shone from its hiding place in a cluster of blue and silver jars and bottles of Lunarian Organic beauty products.

Patience took pride in making the richly textured stationery and cards herself, using only recycled cotton and other natural materials.

They sold well.

This card bore Margo's name in her employer's bold, slanting script.

Intrigued, she peered at the envelope, ignoring the tinkle of chimes as someone stepped through the shop door. She heard Patience's usual "How may I help you?" coming from where the older woman stood arranging bundles of sage-and-herb energy cleansers.

But Margo's attention stayed on the card.

All morning—she hadn't been able to fall back asleep after Marta's call—she'd experienced a sense of something shifting in her favor. It was a feeling she recognized as a foreshadowing. A strange, unshakable promise that, very soon, her luck would change, turning good.

The sensation had been so strong. And it remained powerful, strengthening as the day wore on. Now, when she saw the plaid-beribboned card, her heart filled with the ridiculous hope that the envelope held Donald McVittie's assurance that—somehow, someway—he'd make sure that she'd win his Scotland vacation raffle.

Donald liked her.

And he knew how much she loved Scotland.

He understood why she collected old maps and guidebooks of the Highlands. She'd once confessed to him how often she pored over the brittle pages, tracing special routes with her finger until the ink blurred and the place-names faded, becoming illegible.

Donald would nod sagely, his usually merry face turning solemn. He'd then tell her she felt *the pull*. The irresistible lure Scotland held for anyone who thrilled to misty, heather-covered hills, tartan, and the wild, heart-pumping skirl of pipes.

But unlike her, he knew those hills. He walked them at least twice a year, more often if he could justify getting away from A Dash o' Plaid long enough to make the journey he fondly called a homecoming.

He always told Margo she'd get there someday. Donald liked to make people happy.

He was also much too honest to cheat in the drawing.

Even for her.

Margo frowned, sliding her oversized handbag off her shoulder and stowing it behind her counter before she could tarnish her karma by wishing that Donald were a shady, unscrupulous character. A less-principled man who'd stoop to any means to see her leave the Scottish Festival as a grand-prize winner, the Glasgow air ticket and the tour itinerary clutched in her hand.

Just now, her palm itched as if such victory were already in her grasp. Her eyes scratched, too. But that was because she'd spent the morning scouring every Scottish research book in her personal library, searching for mentions of Magnus MacBride, Viking Slayer.

A half-mythical warlord, his name was legend and even struck dread into fearless Viking hearts. His sword, Vengeance, drenched the Highlands with the blood of his foes, the Norsemen. Down the centuries, bards made him such a hero that many believed his memory would live on until Scotland's last peat fire turned cold and time itself faded.

Such quotes were all she could find.

The Internet proved even more pointless. She kept stumbling across repetitions of the scant snippets from her books. There weren't facts anywhere. Just exaggerated, larger-than-life accounts that could only leave one to conclude that he hadn't really existed.

Margo wanted to believe he'd been real.

If only she could get to Scotland, she might be able to prove it. She just needed a bit of luck and then—

"So are you going to open our card or not?" Ardelle Goodnight strode up to Margo's Luna Harmony station, her strong voice carrying as she planted two heavily ringed hands on the counter's edge. About Patience's age—midfifties or somewhere thereabouts—Ardelle had a shock of thick gray hair and the kind of huge, shelf-like bosom that made her resemble the figurehead on an old-time sailing ship. She was a formidable woman, straight-spoken, with piercing blue eyes that didn't miss a trick.

In medieval times, and if she'd been a man, she'd have been the warrior you'd have wanted fighting at your side.

Or—Margo blinked at her now—holding your back against the enemy.

Ardelle couldn't stand Dina Greed.

That alone made her Margo's hero.

"I thought the card was from Patience." Margo reached for it now, not surprised when the shop seemed to recede, then snap back into place, the instant her fingers touched the textured envelope.

The card held powerful energy.

And that could mean only one thing.

"Patience spelled the card." Margo's fingers tingled just from holding it. "And she's the one who wrote my name on the envelope."

"The card holds the good wishes of us all." Ardelle looked triumphant as Patience and Marta stepped up to flank her. "Donald's well-wishes are in there, too." She reached across the counter to tap the envelope. "Open it and you'll see."

Margo glanced at her. "Donald's?"

The other three women nodded, smug as coconspirators.

"He might be too fair-minded to tuck your raffle ticket up his sleeve, but"—Patience echoed Margo's own sentiments—"he isn't above helping you tilt the odds in your favor." She smiled, her gaze flicking to the card. "Donald would love to see you win."

"Oh, God." Margo's throat began to thicken. She had an idea what her friends had done. "There's only one way I'd have a decent chance of winning and that's if I bought a slew of raffle tickets."

The three women's grins said they agreed.

"Don't tell me you did something I can't allow." Margo began to untie the envelope's tartan ribbon. Her fingers shook so badly, she couldn't undo the knot.

Her friends' smiles grew brighter. "We only did what you'd do for us. If"—Marta spoke for them all—"the tables were turned and our own dreams were about to go up for auction, as it were."

"We know what Scotland means to you." Patience plucked the card from Margo's hands and deftly removed the ribbon. She gave the card back to Margo. "It isn't much. Pin money, really."

"There's no such thing." Margo's vision was blurring. Pin money added up and paid monthly bills.

Margo knew the value of dimes and nickels. She even respected pennies, which she collected in jars.

And her friends knew that twenty dollars' worth of raffle tickets was all she could afford. Even that amount would pinch her. Ever cautious and frugal, she used tea bags twice. She boiled her tap water rather than buying bottled water from the grocery. She brought a packed lunch to Ye Olde Pagan Times and ate out only when a newspaper offered discount coupons for a restaurant. And rather than go to a gym, she walked and rode her bicycle whenever she could, saving gas money along with whittling her waistline.

She never splurged.

Her family called her discipline walking. Someday she planned to write a book on living thrifty.

Yet . . .

She ripped open the envelope. Dollar bills fluttered onto the counter, some dropping onto the floor. Tens, twenties, and singles, there seemed no end to the stream of money that spilled into her hands. Some notes whirled into the air, fluttering about like green-winged butterflies, the sight making her breath catch and her heart pound.

Each dollar told her how much she was loved. And made Scotland seem more a reality than ever before in her aching-to-get-there life.

She stepped back from her counter, one hand pressed to her chest.

Margo swallowed. The hand she'd clapped to her breast trembled as several of the airborne dollars settled on her shoulders. One landed on her shoe.

Her friends were grinning. Ardelle—who would've believed it?—blinked hard and then dashed a tear from her fearsome face.

She recovered quickly, lifting an iron gray brow. "We surprised you, h'mmm?"

"You—" Margo couldn't get words past the thickness in her throat.

"Good heavens, what have you done?" Margo found her voice. She looked from Ardelle to the other two women, and then back to Ardelle. They *had* stunned her. And she was torn between hugging and scolding them.

"I can't accept this." She started scooping up dollars, stuffing them back into the envelope. "It's too much and—"

"It's two hundred and fifty dollars." Marta snatched the envelope from Margo's hands and slapped it onto the counter. "Fifty each from us and a hundred from Donald, and we won't take back a dime."

"I'm not touching it." Margo held up her hands, palms outward. "And"—she braced herself to make a confession that still astounded her—"you couldn't have known, but I emptied my stash of mad money before leaving for work. I'll be using that cash for raffle tickets.

"It's enough." She lowered her hands and folded her

arms, hoping to deter objections. "I'll have a fair chance of winning the raffle."

She hoped.

Her emergency fund—kept in a long-emptied tin of Maisie's Hand-Baked Oatcakes, an import from Scotland—hadn't offered a tidy sum. She'd counted enough crumpled one-, five-, and ten-dollar notes to make ninety-six dollars. She'd then scrounged small change from the bottom of her purse to gain a round hundred.

That was a lot of money for a girl on a shoestring budget.

But she'd hoped for a bit more.

Three hundred and fifty might buy her a good chance at winning the trip to Scotland.

Still . . .

"Read the note." Marta slipped a card from inside the envelope and handed it to Margo. "Our wishes will bring you luck. Patience"—she flashed a glance at their employer—"spoke a blessing over them."

Margo took the card, opening it. She read the words aloud. "'All your life, you've loved a special place hewn of rock, wind, and the sea. Now the time has come for you to go there. You'll walk the hills with a spring in your step and thrill to the cold wind in your hair. The scent of heather and peat will delight your senses. Cloud shadows on the moors will rush to greet you and the whole of that wild landscape will embrace you as one of its own.'" Margo's resistance crumbled more on each word. She glanced up, meeting her friends' gazes before reading the last few lines. "'Be welcomed by loch, bog, and wood. Show wonder to each shimmer of mist. Watch, listen, and absorb, until your heart is filled and you know you're home. It is there you belong. So mote it be.'"

"We all pitched in to write it." Ardelle spoke briskly.

Marta dabbed a tissue to her nose while blinking eyes that swam with brightness. "We sat down last night and tried to remember all the things you most wanted to see and experience in Scotland."

"We left out the 'tang of cold brine' and haggis." Patience drew herself up, smoothing the pink and orange swirled folds of her caftan. "And you know"—she pinned Margo with a stare—"once such a blessing spell is cast, only a fool would rebuke it."

"I don't know what to say." Margo kept her hand tight against her breast.

Her friends' words said it all.

And she *was* tempted.

Never had she come so close to ignoring everything she believed in. She'd sooner burn in hell than be beholden to anyone. And—she couldn't deny it—her pride wouldn't let her accept charity. She believed in working for everything she had, and if she couldn't afford certain luxuries, she'd rather do without.

But such sharp longing pierced her that she could hardly breathe.

"It doesn't matter." She put down the card, her denial breaking her heart. "I know you mean well and I love you for it. But I still can't take the money. My own hundred dollars will have to do. That's a lot of raffle tickets and—"

"There will be thousands of visitors at the Scottish Festival." Ardelle frowned at her. "They'll all be buying tickets."

"Which"—Margo stood straighter—"is another reason I shouldn't snare more than a hundred chances to win. The other people will be just as keen to—"

Marta snorted. "Name one person who loves Scotland more than you do."

Margo couldn't.

Dina Greed came to mind. But her passion for the

Highlands came when *Braveheart* hit the movie theaters. Margo had been born loving Scotland.

"It still wouldn't be fair." Her principles made her argue.

"Hah!" Patience came around the counter and laid her arm across Margo's shoulders. "Have you forgotten everything I've taught you? There could be ten, even twenty thousand visitors to the festival and the winner would still be the person meant to win."

"Then snapping up two hundred and fifty additional chances won't make a difference." Margo wriggled free. "You'd be wasting good money."

"We'd be investing in your energy." Patience tutted. "You'd have confidence knowing you'd bought so many tickets. That boost would go out into the cosmos, increasing your chances of winning."

Margo bit her lip. She knew Patience was right.

So she used her strongest objection. "It's still a lot of money."

"Oh, sure." Patience waved a dismissive hand. Then she turned away, looking to Marta. "Madame Zelda"—she used Marta's tarot-reading name—"how much money have you brought the shop with your weekly readings from clients who live at the Fieldstone House?"

Marta smiled. "Thousands of dollars, I'm sure. Maybe more, as old Mrs. Beechwood comes twice a week, sometimes more. She doesn't lift a finger without first stopping in for a consultation."

"And I wonder where the Fieldstone House residents heard that you're so good at reading the tarot." Patience rubbed her chin, feigning ignorance.

Margo felt her face warming. She did praise Marta's skills to everyone she met, especially her neighbors at the Fieldstone House.

"I see you know where those clients come from." Patience surely saw Margo's flush. Not finished, she glanced at Ardelle. "And you, dear"—her voice boomed—"didn't you tell me a while back that you heard Margo suggest to an Aging Gracefully customer that we carry an excellent blend of moon-grass tea?"

"The woman had a bad cough." Margo recalled the day at Ardelle's vintage-clothing shop. Silverweed, called *moon grass* at Ye Olde Pagan Times, did soothe aching throats. "I couldn't help but offer a tip. The woman was popping industrial-strength lozenges that weren't helping her at all."

"And now that woman, Octavia Figg, orders our moon-grass tea by the case. She's been doing so for over six months, claiming the tea also calms her nerves. I could take a Caribbean cruise on the money she brings the shop." Patience smiled triumphantly, her point made.

Marta and Ardelle grinned like fools.

Margo knew she'd lost.

There wasn't any point in further argument.

She was going to purchase 350 of Donald McVittie's raffle tickets.

Centuries away, in a distant place even Donald McVittie had never been, Magnus came instantly awake and frowned into the shadows of his bedchamber. He thought about punching his pillow, rolling over, and returning to sleep. But his entire body tingled with a warrior's knowing and he was on his feet, reaching for his sword with the speed and agility his enemies knew to dread.

For weeks he'd been waiting, trying to guess where his foes would next strike. But no matter how well he'd come to understand the Northmen, or how often he stared out across the sea, his gaze on the horizon, he couldn't guess where or when the Vikings' long, lean dragon ships would glide out of the mist and then gain speed, their oars flashing like demon wings as they raced to the shore, eager to raid, plunder, and kill innocents.

Now he knew what to do.

He'd draw the Vikings ashore and slaughter them when they landed.

Even if only a handful of their loathsome, beast-headed ships fell for his ploy, the lesson he meant to give them would teach them fear.

At the least, it would warn them to stay away from his shores.

There were two things Vikings dreaded. One was losing men. Not because they feared death. As long as they died well, clutching a sword or battle-ax, Odin's feast hall awaited them and they went there gladly. But for the living, a reduced number of warriors meant a weakened fighting force. Replacing lost men was difficult when the raiders roamed so far from their own northern shores.

Magnus buckled on his sword, a slow smile curving his lips. He was good at whittling down the number of fighters in a Viking war band.

He took equal pleasure in diminishing the crew on a Norse longboat. After all, every oarsman could wield an ax or a sword as wickedly as his oars bit the waves. And—Magnus tied back his hair with a leather band— soon he'd treat his foes to their other great dread, a burned ship.

More than one, if the gods were kind.

Somewhere a cock crowed, and Magnus glanced at his shuttered window. The barest hint of gray was just beginning to edge the fading blackness. And—he snatched his plaid off a chair—a light drizzle was falling. He could also hear the sea foaming on the rocks beneath his castle walls.

Soon, he would lay his trap for an unsuspecting Viking fleet.

Bloodlust stirring, he threw open the lid of the strongbox at the foot of his bed and looked down at the glittering sea of silver and gold arm rings that filled the chest. He might have to secure a second coffer. He hoped so, fervently. But this morn, he simply grabbed a handful of the shining bands and slid them onto his arms.

He was ready.

With luck, he'd soon have reason to undo the leather string binding his hair. He'd smile then and shake his head, letting the strands swing free around his shoulders so that his foes would see his loose hair and know at once that he'd come to kill them.

And after he'd sated himself on vengeance, he'd make another visit to Orosius.

The sea vixen might not be of his world, but he was certain she was close.

So near he could taste her.

Chapter 6

Magnus MacBride, Viking Slayer.

Help me win. . . .

Margo repeated the silent words like a chant, letting them fill her mind and—she hoped—sending a heartfelt message into the cosmos.

It was the morning of the Bucks County Scottish Festival and, quite possibly, the most important day of her life. The only moment that could surpass today would be when her Atlantic-crossing plane landed at Glasgow International Airport, bringing her to the land of her dreams.

If she won Donald McVittie's raffle drawing.

Unfortunately, she couldn't shake the feeling that everyone crowding the parklike grounds of the Cabbage Rose Gift Emporium and Tea Room shared her sentiments. Celtic festivals did tend to draw people who claimed to love Scotland. Margo could spot such folk at a hundred paces. Their eyes shone with the same sense of wonder she always felt when she walked around the fairgrounds and immersed herself in so much Highland culture and atmosphere.

It was tartan triumph, alive and breathing.

What Scotophile could resist such a perfect blend of bagpipes, haggis, and plaid?

No one that Margo could see. Everyone milled about in awe, their hearts soaring and passions roused. A group of middle-aged couples near the duck pond behind the tea room even wore matching sweatshirts that read *The Home Glen Is Calling Us*. Margo had no doubt that each one of them wanted to win the seven-day guided coach tour of Scotland.

As, she was sure, did everyone else enjoying the brisk autumn day.

And that knowledge was killing her.

When a large, forceful-looking woman barged past her wearing a huge pin proclaiming in rhinestones that she loved the *Auld Hameland*, Margo didn't perish. But she did get a queasy feeling in her stomach. The woman had a determined air about her and she was heading straight for the Cabbage Rose's plaid-decorated auditorium, where Donald's drawing would soon take place.

The woman was competition.

Margo bit her lip as her rival for the trip marched across the grass. Tweedy and with her iron gray hair perfectly coiffed, she looked as if she could afford well over three hundred and fifty dollars' worth of raffle tickets. Though—one could hope—if that was true, she could probably also purchase her own air ticket to Scotland. Perhaps even a private kilt-wearing chauffeur once she arrived there. So maybe she hadn't dropped as many raffle tickets into Donald's tartan-wrapped drawing box as Margo had done.

Margo fervently wished the gorgon bought only one chance at the Heritage Tour.

Just then, pipes skirled and drums rolled from the far side of the duck pond. The stirring tones came from a meadow near the edge of woods that were appropriately draped in fine, drifting mist. The parade ground where, Margo knew, the local piping-band competition was gearing up. As so often, "Scotland the Brave" seemed to be the tune of choice. Margo's heart began thumping, her breath catching with all the fierce longing she felt for her beloved Highlands.

And they *were* hers.

No one loved Scotland more.

Who else would spend hours printing his or her name, address, and phone number on the backs of 350 raffle tickets?

Donald McVittie hadn't wanted to spoil the moment with everyone in the audience scrambling to check raffle numbers, so he'd insisted that people write their personal information on the tickets in block letters.

Margo's hand still ached.

She suspected her fingers might be permanently cramped.

But just now the screaming pipes were calling her, so she started forward before she could check herself. She never missed the piping drills. Only this year she'd vowed to stick close to Donald McVittie's A Dash o' Plaid booth. She hoped her hovering presence—and her silent prayers to Magnus MacBride, Highlander of her dreams—might somehow deter other Scotland zealots from purchasing raffle tickets.

So she quickly turned back to Donald's stall, hoping she looked suitably formidable.

A Dash o' Plaid appeared annoyingly inviting.

Donald had left earlier, claiming he was needed in the auditorium, where preparations were under way for the Scottish luncheon buffet and the festival highlight, the drawing of the grand-prize trip to Scotland. But Donald's son, Donald Junior, bustled about the tartan-hung booth, encouraging passersby to stop, blether, and—Margo could throttle him—pick up tickets for the raffle.

"Wee Hughie MacSporran, famous Highland author

and historian, will be guiding the tour." Donald Junior's voice boomed from the other side of the stall as he beamed at two twentysomething girls wearing too much makeup and plaid rayon fanny packs. "He's known as the Highland Storyweaver and is also the founder and owner of Heritage Tours. He's quite an authority on Scottish history and—"

"Does he wear a kilt?" One of the girls popped her gum.

Her friend giggled. "I'm more interested in what's under his kilt."

"Is that him?" The gum popper snatched a book off the display table. *"Royal Roots: A Highlander's Guide to Discovering Illustrious Forebears,"* she read the title aloud, peering at the large, rosy-cheeked Scotsman on the cover. He was kilted, but he looked more like a pudgy teddy bear than a wild and rugged Highlander.

"He isn't too sexy." The girl slapped down the book.

"Any man in a kilt is hot." The giggler picked up another MacSporran title, *Hearthside Tales: A Highlander's Look at Scottish Myth and Legend*. She eyed the author's photo critically. "He's at least six foot four." She glanced at her friend. "I like big men. I wouldn't mind tooling around the heather with him."

"Who says he's big where it counts?" Her friend popped another gum bubble.

Ever a diplomat, Donald Junior ignored the girls' comments and launched into a spiel about how Wee Hughie MacSporran was directly descended from Robert the Bruce and that the author was at the festival, come all the way from Scotland to draw the grand-prize winner.

The news drew a bored sigh from the gum popper. But the other girl nearly swooned. Squealing, she danced a little jig.

"You've sold me," she gushed, swelling her breasts. "I'll take twenty tickets."

Margo stiffened.

She'd die if one of those girls won the trip.

Death by Highland envy.

There were surely worse ways to go. But she'd rather go to Scotland.

Trying not to show her annoyance, she reached to examine a tartan sash. Lovely in rich shades of dark green and blue and just enough threads of black and pink to make it special, the sash had caught her eye the instant she'd arrived at the A Dash o' Plaid booth. But such sashes—each one imported from Scotland—were expensive, so she'd resisted temptation and busied herself looking over the assortment of kilt pins, Scottish-themed figurines, refrigerator magnets, and coffee mugs.

She frowned at a pile of *Real Men Eat Haggis* bumper stickers.

At a dollar each, even they were beyond her budget.

She'd put every dime she could spare into the drawing box.

Getting nervous, she drifted back to the rack of tartan sashes. They were exquisitely made and so quintessentially Highland.

Margo sighed.

Wistfully, she smoothed her fingers along the soft, pure wool. The lustrous weave seemed alive to the touch, warm and beckoning. Conjuring images of wild cliffs and castle ruins edged against dark, brooding skies. She could feel the cold, racing wind and smell the earthy richness of peat smoke in the chill, damp air.

This was why she loved A Dash o' Plaid.

The booth held magic, always.

But when she looked up from the pretty tartan sash, her dreams of heather, misty hills, and glens shattered.

The gum popper and the giggler were stuffing what appeared to be way more than twenty dollars' worth of raffle tickets into the drawing box.

Donald Junior looked on, a pleased smile on his ruddy face.

The raffle benefited a good cause.

The McVitties—who rescued border collies in addition to running A Dash o' Plaid—were donating every penny earned to a local no-kill animal shelter.

And they were personally matching the sum.

Needy animals would benefit.

Margo loved animals. She had the scars to prove it because she was known to veer her bicycle to avoid colliding with the occasional squirrel, raccoon, or other critter that sometimes dashed across her path. She never minded such scrapes or bruises. If the animal escaped unscathed, her little bit of pain was well worth it.

She applauded the McVitties' dedication.

Even so, she resented every raffle ticket the two girls had purchased.

And that made her feel like a terrible person.

But her annoyance didn't go away.

"If I win"—the giggler started kissing her tickets before pushing them into the slot—"I'll put a tilt in Wee Hughie's kilt before you can say *Braveheart*."

The gum popper rolled her eyes. "If he's called 'wee' because of the size of his *haggis*, you won't be able to tell."

Donald Junior's smile faded. He was fussing with an assortment of coffee mugs stamped with thistle designs or colorful pictures of a bagpiper in front of Edinburgh Castle.

The two girls nudged elbows, clearly enjoying his discomfiture.

Margo frowned at them, not caring if they noticed.

When they did, they both opened their eyes exaggeratedly wide, treating her to a scathing look that showed they thought she was an obsolete dinosaur.

And maybe she was.

Because—she lifted her chin and gave them a glare that could've frozen much of Iceland—their attitude only made her think of older, distant times when men like Magnus MacBride, Viking Slayer, would've dealt swiftly with such crude and rude manners.

Men like Magnus had honor, she knew.

In his day, insults weren't taken lightly.

But this was the here and now, another age and a different world. As if they sensed how much that unalterable fact irritated Margo, both girls uttered two words that Margo would never allow to pass her lips. Then they sashayed off toward the Cabbage Rose, their hips swinging.

Margo shuddered.

It was almost more palatable to think of Dina Greed in Scotland than those two twits.

"They'll no' be winning," a sprightly, old-ladyish, and definitely Scottish voice trilled behind Margo.

"Gah!" Margo whirled around, almost colliding with a bright-eyed Scotswoman.

"You needn't fash yourself, lassie." The tiny woman winked at her. "All things happen as they should and"—her blue eyes twinkled—"*when* they should."

"Ahhh . . ." Margo didn't know what to say.

"Fie on them." The woman shot a glance at the girls' retreating backs. "There be words for their kind, but"—she set her hands on her hips—"I'm a lady."

Any other time Margo would've smiled.

But she'd been caught out.

The old woman had clearly seen her watching the girls. And somehow she knew Margo burned to win the raffle and that—how embarrassing—she wished everyone else buying a ticket would lose.

Margo's head pounded slightly and she felt a teeny bit dizzy. Almost as if she'd stepped into another dimension, silly as the thought was. Donald Junior was still standing a comfortable arm's length away, but somehow the distance felt like miles. Behind him were racks of ready-made kilts, tartan skirts, and—for the less discerning—*Kiss me, I'm Scottish* T-shirts. Margo could see all that from the corner of her eye. Yet her *focus* seemed to have narrowed to the tiny Scotswoman with her wizened face and sharp blue eyes.

"Did Patience send you after me?" Margo could imagine her employer being friendly with such a woman.

They probably belonged to the same pagan circle.

Though . . .

Margo knew most of Patience's friends. And this woman wasn't the sort to be easily forgotten. She reminded Margo of the witch in "Hansel and Gretel." Except this crone seemed a good one. Almost like the wisewomen in some Scottish medieval romance novels.

"Patience?" The old woman cackled, enhancing the comparison. "Nae, dear, that one didn't ask me to fetch you. But"—she stepped closer—"I know that she and your two other friends are saving a place for you at the Scottish luncheon buffet."

Margo blinked, not sure what to think of the woman having such intimate knowledge of her private life.

"You are Margo Menlove, eh?" The crone tipped her somewhat bristly chin.

Margo just looked at her.

White-haired, rosy-cheeked, and flamboyantly styled in a sweeping skirt of deep black velvet and an emerald jacket of the same material, she'd completed her outfit with an expertly draped blue-green tartan sash. A large ruby-studded Celtic brooch winked at her shoulder, where it held the sash in place. Tiny high-topped black boots with red plaid laces peeped from beneath her skirt, adding a touch of modern pizzazz to her Old World look.

Anywhere outside the Scottish Festival, she'd appear odd.

But lots of people did wear period dress to the event. Most didn't strike the same authenticity as this woman, but they did try.

It was part of the fun.

Still . . .

"How do you know my name?" Margo didn't like the chills prickling her nape.

The woman's smile turned mischievous. "Och!" She waved a knotty-knuckled hand. "I heard your friends blethering. They were worried that you hadn't yet joined them.

"I was about to come this way, so . . ." The crone didn't finish. She did glance across the grass, past the other souvenir and food stalls to the row of clan tents curving along the far side of the duck pond.

Thick mist was beginning to roll down from the low hills to drift across the water. Shimmering curtains of soft gray stillness glided toward the Cabbage Rose Gift Emporium and Tea Room and the sprawling auditorium just beyond. The mist reminded Margo so much of Scotland that her heart squeezed.

"Thon scene could be the Highlands." The old woman set a hand to her breast and took a deep breath. "No peat, but there's fine damp air and a wee touch o' leaf mold and moss. Such scents do delight the soul.

"Take away the hurly-burly and your boxy buildings and cars, and a body could almost be there. Maybe even on my own Isle o' Doon." She started to smile again, but

just then the two young girls—Margo's twits—pushed
through the crowd at the auditorium door, elbowing
inside.

"They'll no' be winning," the crone said again, sounding as if she knew. "Suchlike would lose heart fast in my
world. They're in love with the Highlands they see in
fill-ums." She spoke the word *film* as if it was strange on
her tongue. "They dinnae have the backbone to stand
beside a true Heilander."

"A true Highlander?" Margo was intrigued.

"Aye, just." The woman grasped Margo's arm with
surprisingly firm fingers. "Such men as walk my hills
need women of strength and courage. Women who appreciate honor and understand the need of blood feuds.
Bold-hearted lasses who can dress wounds and even
take up a sword if need be."

The crone's grip tightened. "Women worthy of a lord
of battle . . ."

Margo's ears began to buzz, a strange ringing that
increased as the old woman's voice faded. A wave of
dizziness washed over her and she leaned back against
the edge of a display table, vaguely aware of Donald
Junior showing a *sgian dubh* to a stocky, brown-haired
man wearing a sweatshirt decorated with a red Scottish
lion. Donald was holding up the little black dagger—
commonly worn as a sock knife—and repeatedly saying, "No, it's pronounced *skean do* . . ." as he turned the
horn-handled dagger this way and that, showing off the
knife's Celtic-knot-design mounting.

Neither man seemed aware of Margo and the strange
little Scotswoman.

Margo was very conscious of the crone.

"That's an odd thing to say. *Women worthy of a lord
of battle.*" Margo leaned harder against the table. Somehow, the woman's piercing gaze made her feel as if the

world were spinning around her. It was unnerving, and
worsened her slight sense of dizziness. Just as disturbing,
the crone was now shaking Margo's arm.

"Margo." Marta's concerned voice reached her, shattering the weirdness. "You're as green as grass." Her
friend let go of Margo's wrist and slid her arm protectively
around Margo's waist. "I told you it wasn't a good idea
to hang out here all morning, without eating. You should
have joined us at the scone booth for breakfast. Now—"

"I'm fine." Margo shook herself free, glancing around.

The little Scotswoman was gone.

The drawing box had also disappeared. One of Donald Junior's younger brothers must've carried the box to
the Cabbage Rose auditorium.

The box's removal meant the drawing was imminent.

Margo's heart began to thump. She turned back to
Marta. "Did you see a little old lady just now? A Scotswoman all tricked out in traditional costume?"

"You're kidding, right?" Marta glanced around at the
jeans-clad throng.

"No." Margo followed her friend's gaze. "She said she
was from the Isle of Doon."

Marta lifted a brow. "I don't think there is an Isle of
Doon in Scotland?"

"There isn't." Margo was sure. "Only a Loch Doon in
Ayrshire."

"Then she was pulling your leg."

"Maybe." Margo was still looking around.

Many women, including elderly ones, had turned
out in their own versions of Scottish dress. But in most
cases, their imagination was limited to a tartan sash or
a thistle-bearing T-shirt. A few wannabe vamps paraded
about in mini-kilts and thigh-high boots. Only the very
young girls—usually aged eight or so—who were Scottish dancers wore traditional Highland costume.

No one had on small black boots with red plaid laces. Not even the most eccentric of the granny set.

Purple hair seemed to be the hit with the geriatrics. Though there was an older woman who looked like an aged hippie walking about with heather sprigs woven into her thick, gray braids. She also boasted a blue and white saltire tattoo on her somewhat swollen ankle.

No escapees from the Brothers Grimm.

Margo frowned and rubbed the back of her neck.

She slid a glance at Donald Junior. But she knew without interrupting his *sgian dubh* sales pitch that if she asked him about the odd little woman, he'd say he hadn't seen her.

Because—Margo felt ill—there hadn't *been* a witchy-like crone.

She'd surely imagined her.

Her nerves were shredded.

That was all.

But the old woman had seemed so real.

"O-o-oh, look!" The pinch Marta suddenly gave her arm *was* real. "That has to be the Scottish author. Over there"—she pointed toward the row of clan tents—"heading towards the auditorium."

"Good Lord." Margo's eyes rounded. "I think you're right."

Wee Hughie MacSporran—if the tall, heavyset man in a kilt was indeed the Highland author-cum-historian-cum-touring-company-owner—had a patrician air about him that bordered on pompous.

He strutted like a peacock. A group of squealing, fawning women hurried in his wake, many clutching books they surely wanted him to sign. But he marched on without acknowledging them, his chin held high and his shoulders set in prideful determination. He really did look like a kilted teddy bear. But his arrogance ruined the cuteness of his apple red cheeks and bright blue eyes.

Margo's heart sank.

She hadn't expected a Magnus MacBride look-alike. But *Highland Storyweaver* had conjured very different images in her mind.

A swellhead wasn't one of them.

"He looks like he expects people to applaud just because he walks by." Margo glanced at Marta, then back at the Scottish author.

His thinning red hair and paunch dimmed the splendor of his tweed Argyll jacket and white, open-necked ghillie shirt. But the shirt's old-fashioned Jacobite styling did what it was meant to do. He looked as if he'd just walked off Culloden Battlefield. And his fur-covered, three-tasseled sporran appeared equally authentic. His kilt—Margo recognized it as a MacDonald plaid—swung smartly about his knees, his brisk strides showing the confidence of a man well accustomed to wearing Highland national dress.

"Maybe he's not as inflated as he looks." Ever the optimist, Marta grabbed Margo's arm and began pulling her across the grass, away from A Dash o' Plaid and toward the Cabbage Rose.

"He's probably very nice." Marta took another jab at playing diplomat.

Margo tried not to roll her eyes.

Wee Hughie looked so vain, she suspected he'd burst like a gas-filled balloon if someone pricked him with a pin. But she kept the sentiment to herself.

Pipes and drums were already sounding from inside the auditorium. The rousing tones electrified the air, stirring anticipation. And the crowd of people who'd been thronging the entrance was gone, everyone having entered the building and—Margo felt her heart flutter—no doubt hoping to hear their name announced as the grand-prize winner of the seven-day trip to Scotland.

"Come on, we need to hurry." Marta was almost running now. "They'll be getting ready for the drawing. Especially"—she flashed Margo a smile—"when Wee Hughie arrives."

That was true.

And suddenly Margo didn't care if Wee Hughie Mac-Sporran, Highland Storyweaver, used a golden trumpet to blast his glory before calling out the winning name.

As long as the name was hers, she'd be happy.

But nerves seized her when she and Marta nipped inside the auditorium and Darcy Sullivan, the Cabbage Rose's owner and sponsor of the annual Scottish Festival, greeted them with a brilliant smile.

"Margo! I hear you have excellent chances of winning the raffle." She winked at Marta. "A little birdie told me you bought three hundred and fifty tickets."

She leaned close, her green eyes sparkling. "I'm rooting for you."

"Thanks." Margo could hardly breathe.

She *was* shaking.

Now that the big day had arrived—so many of her hopes and dreams hanging on a single draw—her chest felt as tight as if someone had clamped an iron vise around her ribs, and her heart was pounding like a drum. Her legs felt like rubber and if anyone else spoke to her, she was sure she'd only manage to babble incoherent nonsense.

All the tables were filled and a crush of people crowded the aisles and lined the walls at the building's outer edges. The noise was deafening. A great din of excited voices rose and fell. On the stage, a pipes and drums band played a lively tune near the podium where Donald McVittie Sr. was just preparing to introduce

Wee Hughie MacSporran. At least that was what Margo thought Donald was doing.

It was hard to tell when the only thing she really saw was the big tartan-wrapped box sitting on a table near Donald and the Highlander.

A spotlight shone on the box, drawing attention to its importance.

Margo forced herself to look away. She was afraid she'd jinx her chances if she stared too long at the box that held her heart's desire.

Seeking calm, she glanced at the wall behind the Scottish luncheon buffet. Darcy Sullivan's Cabbage Rose Gift Emporium and Tea Room was actually Irish, and a local artist—who'd since married an Irishman and moved to Ireland—had painted huge, wall-filling murals of the Emerald Isle in the tea room and in the auditorium.

The images created a quaint and whimsical collage that reminded Margo of the Highlands—even though she knew that the winding country roads and gleaming whitewashed cottages were meant to be Irish. Scottish cottages also had thick walls and thatched roofs. And the portrayals of fiddlers entertaining foot-stomping crowds in smoke-hazed pubs could easily be set somewhere in Scotland. Likewise the windswept cliffs, gold-sanded strands, and endless stretches of blue, sparkling seas, could be ripped from Margo's own dreams. The artist—Margo couldn't recall the woman's name—had surely loved Ireland with the same passion Margo felt for Scotland.

Only the artist—lucky soul—hadn't just won a trip to the land she loved so much.

She'd found romance with a local and moved there.

Margo frowned, not liking the stab of jealousy that pierced her as she stared at the woman's paintings. She should be happy for the artist.

Trying to distract herself, she took a deep breath—
and another—as Marta led her to a front table where
Patience and Ardelle were looking their way, waving
hellos.

The two older women had dressed alike, each wearing a flowing ankle-length skirt, white long-sleeved shirt,
and blue-and-green plaid vest. A large hand-painted
poster announcing that *Margo is going to Scotland!* was
propped on the table, balanced against a bottle of cham-
pagne and four fluted cut-crystal glasses.

"You are going to win." Ardelle reached out to
squeeze her hand.

Patience leaned close as Margo took a chair. "I spoke
a good-fortune spell this morning."

Marta smiled. "See? What can possibly go wrong?"

A drumroll and flourish of pipes implied only thrilling
excitement, sweeping everyone from the bustling auditorium straight to the rolling vastness of empty heather
moors and wild, wind-whipped seas. Lights dimmed as
the stirring tones faded and Donald McVittie took his
place beside the tartan-wrapped drawing box.

The room fell silent.

"My friends, welcome!" Donald spread his arms,
beaming. "The moment we've all been awaiting is here.
But first"—he glanced at Wee Hughie—"I'll let Scotland's premier author and historian whet your appetite
for the Highlands with a wee taste of what Heritage
Tours has planned for you."

Wee Hughie straightened his shoulders, and joined
Donald beneath the beam of a spotlight. "Good afternoon." He bowed slightly, looking pleased by the clap-
ping that sounded from the crowd. "I'm delighted that
my U.S. book-tour schedule allowed me to join you today. It does my heart good to see so many Americans
enthusiastic about my homeland. You've heard of kilts,

clans, and tartans, Highland mist and castles. Scotland is all that and more.

"At Heritage Tours, we show you the Scotland of your dreams, ensuring you'll experience the holiday of a lifetime." He paused, taking a glossy brochure from beside the drawing box. "Today's grand-prize winner will start his or her adventure the moment they step from the plane.

"A luxury coach, fully climate-controlled and with large viewing windows, will whisk you into the heart of Glasgow city with its grand cathedral, followed by a visit to Stirling Castle and Bannockburn, Scone Palace, and on to the bonnie shores of Loch Lomond for lunch. Afternoon will take us to the wilds of Rannoch Moor, the mist-drenched hills of Glencoe"—Wee Hughie's soft Highland burr deepened, filling the auditorium as he read from the tour itinerary—"Fort William for tea and shopping, plus a look at the West Highland Museum there, and then more shopping at Spean Bridge and Fort Augustus. A Nessie-sighting walk along Loch Ness and a stop at Urquhart Castle before we drive on to Inverness, where you'll—"

A flurry of oohs and aahs rose from the listeners. The sound of faint rustling as people shifted in their seats, leaning forward to catch Wee Hughie's every word.

Margo stared at him, horrified.

Her dream of standing on a lonely heather-clad hill, mist swirling around her as she soaked up peat-scented air and atmosphere, shattered around her like glittering shards of broken glass.

"Is he reading the program for a single day?" Marta glanced at Margo, wide-eyed.

"I think so." Actually, Margo was sure.

She'd found a tour itinerary on the table and she was following along as he called out the stops. And every one of the seven days looked as busy and hectic as the first. If she won the trip, she'd be lucky to stand in one place long enough to snap a picture.

There wouldn't be time for anything else.

Marta snatched the brochure from Margo's fingers. "Gads!" She glanced up at once, her eyes even rounder than before. "You'll need a month off work to recuperate from a pace like this."

"Maybe I won't win." Suddenly Margo knew she would.

Such a tour fit her luck, after all.

Who else would win a trip to Scotland that would be such a whirlwind that she wouldn't actually get to see the land of her dreams?

Dina Greed would die laughing.

A metallic screech from the microphone, followed by a tap-tapping noise and a man clearing his throat, signaled that the big moment had come. Donald McVittie had lifted the tartan drawing box and was shaking it vigorously.

Wee Hughie MacSporran held out his hands and dramatically wriggled his fingers.

"In the name of my great-great-grandfather, Scotland's most famous hero king, Robert the Bruce"—he paused for effect, glancing regally at the audience— "I'm honored to declare that the grand-prize winner of my next Heritage Tour of Scotland is . . ."

He thrust his hand into the box.

Marta, Patience, and Ardelle leapt from their seats, each woman placing her hands on Margo's shoulders. Margo closed her eyes, her heart beating wildly despite her having seen the light speed of the itinerary.

It was still Scotland.

Margo's throat thickened and her eyes burned, her vision turning blurry. Blood roared in her ears, making it difficult to hear. But Wee Hughie was a big man and his voice was deep, carrying. He was also peering down at the small red ticket in his hand.

He looked up then, scanning the crowd. "My ancestry makes it a duty to act as Scotland's ambassador." His voice swelled on the words, pride shining on his red-cheeked face. "Therefore I'm delighted to welcome"—he paused—"Margo Menlove to my next Heritage Tour!"

"Margo!" Her friends pulled her to her feet, hugging her, as everyone in the audience cheered and clapped, calling good wishes.

Then—somehow—she had made her way through the throng and was walking up the steps to the stage and the podium, where Wee Hughie MacSporran, Donald McVittie, and Darcy Sullivan stood waiting to greet her.

Wee Hughie was smiling and holding an oversized air ticket, his pompous airs gone for the moment. He looked genuinely pleased to meet her. Dimples even creased his cheeks, making him appear almost boyish. Margo relaxed, suddenly hopeful that she'd misjudged him.

The tour would be wonderful.

And she was going to enjoy every minute.

Chapter 7

There was a saying about needing to be careful of wishes, lest they come true.

Three weeks, one Atlantic crossing, and too many days of Wee Hughie MacSporran later, Margo shifted in the aisle seat of her Heritage Tours luxury coach—named *Sword of Somerled* after one of Wee Hughie's illustrious forebears—and deeply regretted having never paid much heed to the adage. Working with Patience and at Ye Olde Pagan Times, she should know that anything you put into the cosmos can circle back and bite you.

Just now, she felt more than bitten.

Chomped struck her as appropriate.

The iron jaws of fate were having a field day with her, grinding down hard. Feeling the pain, she tried to stifle her irritability and failed.

At the front of the coach, Wee Hughie preened. Beside him, their driver expertly maneuvered them along a winding coastal road. A small and genial Glaswegian, he seemed immune to the Highlander's airs. He simply kept his eyes straight ahead, smiling the while.

Wee Hughie looked philosophical.

"Even today"—Wee Hughie sent an appreciative

glance at the vista of cliffs and sea beyond the coach windows—"Highlanders reflect the fierceness of their land. Study our faces and you'll see the same bold, unrelenting spirit. Listen to our voices and you'll hear the soft rain and birdsong, or the howl of a black autumn gale. We thrill to cold, gray seas and hills soaked with chill mist and the silence of winter darkness. The wildness and desolation that doesn't dampen our spirit, but makes our hearts soar."

Margo followed his gaze, for once agreeing with him.

She could almost smell the salt air. If it weren't for the coach's thick window glass, she knew she'd taste brine in the racing wind. It would lace the darker, richer scent of damp, peaty earth and pine. If she craned her neck, she just could see the surf boiling over the glistening black rocks that lined the shore.

But the man she imagined limned against such magnificence didn't bear any resemblance to MacSporran.

She saw Magnus beside the sea.

Her mind's eye put him there in all his war glory. His raven hair blew in the wind, and his gold and silver arm rings shone brightly, rivaling the glint of his sword and the sheen of his mail.

His dark gaze brooded on the sea and he held one hand against his sword hilt.

He was a hard-looking warrior.

And the most beautiful, wildly exciting man that Margo could imagine.

Her pulse quickened and she started to smile, her annoyance beginning to fade. But then Wee Hughie cleared his throat, shattering her dreams.

"Highland men are counted as the bravest and most daring in Britain's military forces." He put back his shoulders, standing tall. "This should not surprise us. Their valor was hewn of granite and cold, northern winds. Their courage ripped from the high, rocky crags and wild, steep-sided glens they called their home.

"My ancestors were the proud kings of this land and they—" He stopped abruptly, assuming a humble mien as he raised a hand to still the smattering of oohs and aahs that rippled through the coach at the mention of his blood connections to Scottish royalty.

"My forebears," Wee Hughie resumed, "played strong roles in forming the Scotland we know today. Their lives are the strongest and most golden threads in the fascinating tapestry that is Scottish history. I'm honored to share a few of their tales with you."

He looked down the coach, nodding regally to every passenger.

Margo forced a smile when his gaze lit on her.

"Pssst." The woman across the aisle, Tanya Long, reached to tap Margo's arm. Young, Southern, and bubbly, she bounced in her seat each time they shot past a castle ruin or a particularly scenic stretch of scenery.

Just now, Tanya lowered her voice and slid a meaningful look in Wee Hughie's direction. "Do you think he looks like Robert the Bruce?"

"I hope not." Margo blurted the words before she could stop herself. "Robert Bruce would've been mailed and helmeted, a long sword at his side, and his warrior's body as powerful and well honed as his weapons. If Wee Hughie is directly descended from the Bruce, I think it's a safe bet that the centuries have diluted the blood."

Tanya blinked. Her book—*Even You Can Speak Gaelic*—slid off her lap. She bent to snatch it off the floor, and then flashed another admiring glance at their kilted guide. "I think he's cute."

"I think he loves hearing himself talk."

"He told me people from the South have an easy time learning Gaelic." Tanya clutched the newly purchased book to her breast. "He says"—her Southern accent purred—"it's because so many of us have Scottish roots."

"There was a table with copies of that book at the petrol station in Fort William. I suspect"—Margo was sure of it—"Wee Hughie gets a kickback for every copy one of us buys when he stops there for gas."

"You're really cynical." Tanya slipped the Gaelic book into her backpack.

"I don't like being hoodwinked." *I also can't stand braggarts.* Margo kept the last sentiment to herself.

Leaning back in her seat, she debated if she dared using earplugs until Wee Hughie finished his latest oral discourse. He'd just left his kingly forebears and was beginning to expound on the knights, warlords, and chieftains in his ancestral gene pool.

Margo didn't think she could bear it.

She shouldn't have forgotten that the old gods were known to be capricious. After all, she was being chauffeured right through the ancient stomping grounds of those pagan deities. It would amuse the likes of Loki to take her heart's desire and turn its sweetness into something rancid just as she took the first, long-awaited bite.

Hoping Loki was busy making merry in Valhalla, she tried to stretch her legs.

Unfortunately, there wasn't room.

The Sword of Somerled boasted airplane-style comfort seats that allowed each coach passenger to push a button and recline his seat back.

And the man in front of Margo enjoyed taking advantage of that option.

Margo glared at the top of his dandruff-dusted head.

Heat was beginning to creep up the back of her neck, so she took several deep, calming breaths. Then she counted silently to ten.

Otherwise she might explode.

Who would've believed that the trip of a lifetime would turn out to be a nightmare?

Theoretically, she'd stepped into her own wonderland.

Not that her idea of tartan paradise ever included being shepherded about by a self-aggrandizing, kilt-clad teddy bear who wore a huge name badge that announced he was the Highland Storyweaver.

But that was where she was, so she adjusted her Aging Gracefully paisley shawl against the chilly blast of the coach's canned, climate-controlled air and determined to make the most of her time in Scotland.

Despite Wee Hughie MacSporran.

Outside the Sword of Somerled's much-vaunted touring windows, ranges of spectacularly steep and craggy hills delighted with tumbling waterfalls, skirts of autumn red bracken, and just the right amount of swirling mist to shout "This is the Highlands," without spoiling the view of the rugged, soaring peaks. There were glimpses of the sea, jagged cliffs, and inaccessible curves of pristine, golden sand.

Hauntingly beautiful islands looked close enough to touch. And the whole land- and seascape shone in more shades of blue than Margo would've guessed existed. Every hue was represented from the palest turquoise and mauve along the coast to the deep inky blue water rimming the horizon. Once in a while, the glistening black edges of a crofter's peat bank winked in a gentle roll of moorland, evidence that some lucky souls actually lived and worked here.

Several times she'd spotted the odd lonesome cottage, thick-walled, whitewashed, and so inviting in its setting of romantic seclusion. Dark slate seemed to have replaced the roof thatch, but laundry often fluttered in the wind, lending an old-fashioned touch. A time or two, she'd seen a dog sleeping on the door stoop. Sheep milled in rock-studded, heather-rich fields. And there were even the occasional Highland coos, the famed long-haired cows on so many Scottish postcards. If it was late in the day, soft yellow light could be glimpsed from behind the croft houses' small windows. And always, thin blue smoke curled from the chimneys.

Margo was sure the blue smoke was peat.

Sadly, they hadn't come close enough to any of those homes for her to actually get a whiff of the precious, typical Highland scent.

But she was grateful to have at least *seen* peat smoke.

Regrettably, such reminders of the quaintness inside the crofts also gave her a jolt at the harsh reality of having to board a return plane to Newark.

The hustle and bustle waiting for her there seemed as alien now as the dark side of the moon. Or maybe even Pluto or some as-yet-undiscovered planet. The noise and chaos of the real world also struck her—by comparison—to be as unpleasant as sticking needles in her eye.

Still . . .

There were moments when she wished she'd never left the States in the first place. A notion so unlike her, and so unsettling, she wondered a lightning bolt didn't zing down to strike her.

Just days ago, she would've laughed if anyone suggested she could go to Scotland and be miserable.

Yet she was.

Only it wasn't Scotland that disappointed her.

It was Heritage Tours.

Her head was spinning after five days of racing through castles, popping in and out of National Trust historic sites, each time staying long enough only to grab postcards at the visitor centers. She'd lost count of how often they'd jumped on and off the Sword of

Somerled at roadside beauty spots, quickly snapping photos before being herded to the next tourist-trap cafeteria-style tea and pit stop. Horrible, phony shops with tinny bagpipe music and the obligatory whisky liqueur and Scottish toffee samples. They'd roared past the good places at light speed, not even stopping. Like the neat-looking, thatch-roofed Folk Museum in Glencoe. Margo sighed, remembering. She'd have killed for an afternoon there.

Even a half hour would've been manna from heaven.

It was in such places that Scotland's past could really come to life. Havens where the surrounding rocks and moors held their breath, hoping to be appreciated by those who preferred walking through a sea of bog and heather to the maze of concrete, steel, and glass known as modern urbanization.

Margo bit her lip, not wanting to be ungrateful.

In truth, she'd seen more of Scotland than most Highland-loving Americans could cram into a single lifetime of plaid-filled longing.

Unfortunately, she'd only caught two-minute glimpses of each place of interest.

Her seven-day tour of the Highlands consisted of nanosecond intervals.

Nothing went right.

She'd even missed most of the free "wee drams" and tablet tastings—*tablet* was the Scottish word for toffee—because the comfort-and-shop places were always so crowded.

She'd learned to grin and bear the window-seat hoggers on the Sword of Somerled. The chance of an unobstructed, panoramic view of the Highlands brought out the worst in people. There was no such thing as sharing such prized vistas.

It was every man for himself.

And Wee Hughie's halfhearted efforts at persuading his charges to play musical seats failed abysmally.

Margo frowned, recalling his first such attempt.

He'd offered tartan-edged handouts of his lineage to anyone who voluntarily sat on the aisle during the scenic drive through the Great Glen.

No one had taken the bait.

So Margo hadn't managed to nab a window since the huge touring bus rumbled away from Glasgow Airport bright and early on the first day.

She'd landed a good seat then only because jet lag had slowed down most of the tour-goers. She'd been high on I-just-landed-in-Scotland adrenaline and developed the speed of a world-class sprinter.

No one stood a chance against her that morning. By evening, her fellow travelers had recovered from the rigors of long-haul flying.

Since then, she'd been on the aisle.

The only good thing about her fellow travelers' mad dash back to the bus—and their cherished place-by-a-window—was that their scramble allowed her to snap one or two peopleless pictures of the landscape.

In addition to hogging window seats, the Heritage Tour clients also seemed to have a penchant for barging in front of a camera lens.

"You've hardly bought any souvenirs, dear." The woman sitting next to Margo peered at Margo's carryall. Wedged beneath the seat in front of Margo, the satchel barely had breathing space amid her seat partner's ever-growing mound of shopping bags, cardboard boxes, and super-duper expandable cabin baggage.

The woman, heavyset and of indeterminable age—Margo believed her name was Pearl Wallace—leaned close, fingering a heather-gems pendant she'd bought at Spean Bridge Mill.

Margo had enjoyed their stop at the surprisingly cozy tourist mecca on the A-82, Scotland's best-loved scenic route through the heart of the Highlands. But she'd spent the time walking about absorbing atmosphere. She'd followed a path along the edge of a wood and then she'd stood on the little bridge, enjoying the cold air and watching mist hang over the river.

She hadn't bought anything.

Pearl eyed her critically. "Such a heather pendant would look good on you. Or"—she angled her head—"one of those lovely purple sweatshirts with the sequined thistles. They were even on sale.

"Tanya Long"—she glanced at the younger woman—"bought two of them."

Tanya was wearing hers now.

Looking proud, she smoothed a hand over her curly, honey brown hair. "I don't think you'll see a top like this again." She sat up straighter, displaying the sweatshirt. "You should've grabbed one when you had the chance."

"I rarely buy souvenirs." Margo took a sip of the bottled water she had picked up at Spean Bridge. Called Highland Spring and graced with a really pretty label, the bottle would make a nice planter for a tiny bit of ivy once she returned to the Fieldstone House.

And each time she'd see the bottle, she'd be transported back to Spean Bridge. Once again, she'd hear the rush of the river and feel the chill Highland mist damping her face, delighting her.

Such memories were her souvenirs.

But she doubted many people would understand.

Margo rested her foot against her carryall before a dark mood could descend upon her. She nudged the satchel with her toe, pleased when her best efforts wouldn't budge the bag. Heavy, iron-hard resistance met each push as her greatest treasures—rocks she'd picked up along the tour—proved their substance.

She didn't need factory-made heather jewelry or purple-glitter thistle sweatshirts.

And her stones hadn't cost her a dime.

Yet they were worth more to her than all the gold in the world. And they'd comfort her when she ached for the Highlands after the trip.

She'd always heard that the worst thing about visiting Scotland was the pain of having to leave.

Now she was dreading that moment.

But if she could get her Scottish rocks back home without giving some poor airline employee a hernia, she'd have a tiny bit of the Highlands with her always.

Constance Bean, a seventyish woman sitting across the aisle, lowered her glasses and gave Margo a look as if she'd read her thoughts.

"Can you believe we only have a few more days?" She shook her head wistfully. "But isn't it exciting that Wee Hughie arranged a Highland Night for us at the hotel in Gairloch this evening?"

She reached over to grip Margo's arm. "I've been waiting all my life to attend a genuine *ceilidh*." Her eyes shone with telltale brightness. "I've even practiced how to say it right: KAY-lee."

Sitting back, she dabbed at her cheek with a lavender hankie. "Who would've thought I'd actually get to experience one?"

Margo forced a smile. "It'll be grand."

She was lying out her ears.

And Constance's innocent enthusiasm only supported her sentiments about the cosmos. She also burned to prick MacSporran with a pin.

She wouldn't mind releasing some of his hot air.

His version of a ceilidh wouldn't be anything like a real one.

It should be a gathering of Highland friends and neighbors on a long and dark winter night to enjoy the warmth of a peat fire and entertain one another with stories, jokes, and song. An evening spent eating home-baked cakes, scones, and oatcakes. Drinking rivers of tea or ale, and then dancing to lively fiddle tunes until the small hours.

Such get-togethers used to take place in cozy croft-house kitchens.

Nowadays—Margo knew—some good ceilidhs were still held in the community centers of small Highland towns or in the pubs of outlying villages.

The Highland Nights sponsored by coach tourist-package hotels couldn't even be called a distant cousin of a real ceilidh.

And as soon as they reached Gairloch and had checked into the Old Harbour Inn, a rustic-looking, comfortable-sounding inn, Margo intended to pull a disappearing act. Any other time, she would've loved to spend an evening in the hotel's supposedly fabulous pub. It was said to be cozy, dark, and atmospheric. She'd even heard rumors of ghosts.

But the Old Harbour Inn was also just across the road from Gairloch's picturesque harbor.

Exploring the little seaside town on her own, and at dusk, seemed so much more appealing than enduring Wee Hughie's artificial version of a Highland Night.

Especially as she knew he planned to do a few readings from his books.

It was Gairloch and its harbor for her.

There was also—her heart thumped—a renowned crofting and fishing museum in the town. According to the map, she could walk there from the inn. She might not get inside the museum—it would surely be after closing hours before she arrived there—but something told her she needed to walk around the museum grounds.

It was a feeling strong enough to prod her to extreme measures.

"Excuse me." She lifted a hand to draw Wee Hughie's attention. "I have a question."

The Highland Storyweaver stopped in the middle of his spiel about the beautiful wooded loch they were just passing. He looked at Margo, lifting a brow inquiringly. "About Loch Maree?" He gestured at the sparkling blue water. "I was about to share some of the more romantic legends about the loch. The tales are many. Even Queen Victoria was impressed by the loch's splendor. She's known to have called it 'grand, wild, savage, but most beautiful.' So"—he nodded as if to silence her—"if you'll be patient—"

"I wasn't going to ask about the loch." Margo lifted her chin, not backing down.

"Then Slioch?" Wee Hughie gestured grandly at the huge sandstone mountain on the far side of the loch. "It's quite a bastion and has many good yarns of its own. I know them all and will gladly—"

"I have a question about a Highland hero." Margo rushed the words, feeling her face redden.

Wee Hughie beamed. "Ahhh . . ." He hooked his thumbs in his kilt belt, swelling his chest. "Which one of my ancestors are you curious about? Robert Bruce, Alexander Stewart, the infamous Wolf of Badenoch, scorned for burning Elgin Cathedral? Or maybe Somerled or Angus Og? The last two heroes"—he spoke indulgently, as if she'd never heard of the great Mac-Donald Lords of the Isles—"might not be as commonly known in America, but I can—"

"I know who they were." Margo felt heat spreading in her chest.

Wee Hughie looked bemused. "The wicked earls of Orkney?"

"I'd like to know about the Viking Slayer." Margo held his gaze. "Magnus MacBride."

"He's not one of my ancestors."

"But you've heard of him."

"Everyone has." Wee Hughie lifted a bottle of Highland Spring water from its holder by his seat and took a long sip. "Magnus MacBride is a legend. The man was a myth, fictionalized hundreds of years ago by Highland bards who were no doubt paid good silver to make their masters sound as if they were the notorious Viking Slayer.

"In truth"—he set down the water bottle—"Magnus MacBride never existed."

"There are many who say there's a kernel of fact in every tale." Margo was stubborn.

"No' in the stories about the Viking Slayer." Wee Hughie narrowed his eyes. "I'm surprised you've heard of him. Most people outside the Highlands never have. He's pretty obscure."

"I saw a drawing of him in a book. The background"— Margo hesitated, summoning courage—"looked like some of the places we've passed today. I saw similarities when we drove along Loch Torridon.

"That's what I wanted to know." Margo spoke quickly. "If this area belonged to the territory he protected with his sword?"

Wee Hughie just looked at her.

"I have a feeling"—Margo didn't care if he guessed it was a paranormal, woo-woo kind of sensation—"that he held influence in these parts."

"Held sway, you mean?" Wee Hughie frowned. "It's

said he chased the Norsemen from this entire coast, aye." He made the words sound sour, as if he didn't like being forced to speak of any heroes except his own noble forebears. "Legend has him having rampaged against Vikings from Cape Wrath at mainland Scotland's northwestern tip clear down to Applecross, which lies south of Loch Torridon."

"So I guessed right." Margo felt her heart start to race.

Wee Hughie looked annoyed. "You were right"—he drew himself up to his full, impressive height of at least six feet four—"in that Magnus MacBride is legended to have scourged any Viking wishing to raid these coasts. But that doesn't mean he lived."

"Maybe not." Margo couldn't disagree more. "But he sure left a reputation, didn't he?"

Wee Hughie harrumphed and—perhaps inspired by her mention of Vikings—launched into a dramatic spiel about an ill-starred love affair between a Norse prince and a local maid who lived on an island in the middle of Loch Maree. It was a sad tale of blood and heartbreak and Margo tried not to listen as Wee Hughie droned on, regaling the travelers with the young lovers' tragic ending.

Instead, she kept her gaze pinned on the loch's shining blue waters and made plans to slip away from the Old Harbour Inn in Gairloch that evening.

She meant to look for signs of Magnus MacBride, Viking Slayer.

She wasn't sure she'd find anything monumental.

But the prickles at her nape told her the Gairloch Heritage Museum was a good place to start searching.

Chapter 8

Later that evening, Margo slipped out of Gairloch's Old Harbour Inn. She crossed the little humpbacked bridge outside the hotel and then nipped across the road to the harbor. She walked briskly, making her escape. Heritage Tours expected their travelers to participate in the evening entertainments. Not attending was a breach of package-tourist etiquette.

Margo didn't care.

She did feel a twinge of regret.

The Old Harbour Inn was swoon-worthy. She'd fallen in love the instant she'd stepped inside the centuries-old hotel. A onetime coaching inn and so atmospheric that it seemed scandalous for the dimly lit interior to be crammed with tourists in modern-day clothes.

The public rooms were long, dark, and low, with black ceiling rafters and natural stone walls. The wooden floor was spotlessly clean, but creaked delightfully. A huge fireplace stood at the end of the bar and—Margo's pulse quickened—an authentic peat fire glowed in the grate, filling the air with earthy-rich sweetness. The pub also smelled faintly of fish-and-chips and ale and, best of all, the heady elixir of age.

The inn wore history well.

It was by far the best place they'd stopped on the tour.

Margo wouldn't have minded hanging around for a while and maybe meeting an eligible local. The servers were young, kilted, and good-looking. If she was lucky, one of them might have a nice older brother or cousin who'd just happen to breeze in tonight.

Someone alive, real, and attainable, who'd sweep her off her feet with a dimpled smile and a genuine, knock-her-socks-off Highland burr.

She could go for falling in love and staying in Scotland. She even knew a few women who'd had such good fortune. Such things did happen.

But she knew her luck.

And the MacHaggis Ceilidh Group had already claimed the inn's best corner—the one near the bar where the peat fire simmered in the hearth—and were already preparing for their performance of traditional music and dance. Posters cluttered the walls, announcing Wee Hughie as MC and praising the MacSkye Fiddle and Accordion Club, who'd join the MacHaggis folk singers and dancers to provide an unforgettable night of Highland hospitality and entertainment. Wee Hughie's readings and a book signing would start the evening's fun.

It was time for her to go.

She'd rather have sat alone in a dark corner of the pub, soaking in the atmosphere on a quiet evening, sipping a pint of real ale, and watching out for local cuties.

As things were . . .

She kept walking along the waterfront and enjoyed watching the colorful fishing boats coming in on the tide. Low whitewashed cottages lined the road, and the air smelled of salt, pine, tar, and peat smoke.

She thrilled to breathe in great, greedy gulps of what she considered the *essence of the Highlands*. She was sure anyone who could capture such a scent and market it to people like her would make a mint.

It was heaven on earth.

The gloaming, just as magical as she'd heard. It slid around her, a silken veil that turned Loch Gairloch into a mirror of smooth, molten bronze. Soft mist rolled down the hills, casting the seaside town in mysterious, dark blue shadows. And beyond the harbor—or so she'd been told by the people at the inn—a well-marked path would lead her to the crofting and fishing museum.

She still felt drawn there.

So she quickened her pace. But she hadn't gone far when she heard a tread behind her and swung around to find Wee Hughie almost upon her. He was walking fast, his kilt swinging about his knees.

"Margo." He caught up to her, slightly out of breath. "Pearl saw you leave the inn." He glanced down the quay to where the inn stood, well lit, against the dark curve of the hills. "Our entertainment starts soon. Did you forget the time?"

"Actually . . ." Margo didn't want to be rude. "I thought I'd walk for a bit."

"It is a fine night." Wee Hughie was looking at her strangely. "Though I'd feel bad to see you miss our ceilidh. We receive lots of e-mails from Americans who've been on tour with us and want to thank us for our Highland Night events."

I'm not every American, Margo almost blurted.

Instead, she looked out across the sea-loch, catching the flash of breakers out on the open sea. Huge Atlantic rollers, long and white-crested, they crashed ceaselessly against the rocky cliffs, regardless of the century.

Margo blinked, swallowing the sudden thickness in her throat.

"I wanted to walk along the harbor because the Hebrides are out there." She glanced at Wee Hughie, not expecting him to understand. No one would without intimate knowledge of her family history.

"My sister has strong ties to Barra." She refused to speak of Mindy in the past tense, even though she hadn't seen her in forever.

She knew Mindy was well and happy with her fourteenth-century MacNeil chieftain husband, Bran of Barra. They made their home on the Hebridean isle he called his own and that Margo wished had been on the tour.

If she'd had any doubts that her sister had time-traveled to happiness, an aged magnificently kilted Scotsman named Silvanus had appeared to her at Ye Olde Pagan Times and assured her that it was true.

Silvanus was a ghost.

And he'd proved that, too.

It wasn't easy to deny such a thing when the ghost in question vanished right before your eyes.

But Margo knew most people were too closed-minded to believe in ghosts and time travel.

She did believe.

Sometimes she envied her sister that she'd been the one lucky enough to experience such a wonder. She wasn't jealous that Mindy's late fiancé had left Mindy a genuine Scottish castle that had been transported stone by stone to Pennsylvania. Hunter MacNeil had been a first-class jerk and—in Margo's view—he'd owed Mindy that much and more. But after inheriting such a legacy, Mindy hadn't been able to keep or even sell the estate. She'd been forced into returning the castle to its original setting on Barra.

The rest was history.

And Mindy was on Barra still, living the high life as wife of a braw medieval chieftain who—Margo was sure—loved her sister fiercely.

Margo stepped closer to the edge of the quay, her gaze on the moored fishing boats. The wind was stronger and colder now, bringing the sharp tang of sea and shell-fish. Barra surely smelled much the same. The thought made her throat thicken even more. Her eyes began to sting and she dashed a hand across her cheek, pretending to tuck her hair behind an ear. Her personal life was no one's business.

But always, she missed Mindy.

So much.

That was why she rarely spoke of her. She didn't even keep pictures of Mindy around her apartment at the Fieldstone House. Such memories were too painful, since she knew they'd never see each other again. But it helped to walk along this Scottish coast and know her sister was out there somewhere. Just in a different place and time.

Margo felt close to her here.

"I knew your name was familiar." Wee Hughie smiled. "You must be Mindy Menlove's sister. I should've noted the resemblance. I met Mindy when she was on Barra, overseeing the restoration of MacNeil Tower."

Margo blinked. "Ahhh . . ."

No one had mentioned Mindy's name to her in over a year. Her friends in New Hope knew better. Now this kilted Highlander spoke of her as if he'd just seen Mindy yesterday.

"You met her?" It was all she could say.

"I did." Wee Hughie glanced at his wristwatch. "And I wish I didn't have to get to the ceilidh." He sounded regretful. "Your sister and I had lunch at a Barra pub called the Islesman's Pride. I'd like to tell you of that meeting."

"You took her out?" Margo couldn't believe it.

"Nae." Wee Hughie actually colored. "It was business."

"Oh." Margo was relieved.

"She was interested in the legend of the Heart-breaker, the fabled sword of Clan MacNeil. The sword has a fascinating history and, supposedly, a magical crystal pommel possessed of many powers."

"Mindy never believed in such things." Margo's heart squeezed, remembering. Mindy had always rolled her eyes over anything paranormal.

"Perhaps not, but"—Wee Hughie's voice took on an authoritative note—"Highland magic does exist. It's been known to turn the staunchest skeptic into a believer."

"I believe in such magic."

"It is real." Wee Hughie stood straighter. "The Mac-Neils' Heartbreaker is a classic example. There are some who'll tell you that the sword was powerful enough to shift time. And"—he eyed her speculatively—"to make a MacNeil chieftain aware of the woman destined to be his eternal mate. The crystal would then give off a brilliant blue light to alert the MacNeil that the woman of his heart was near and needed his championing."

"Mindy needed a champion." Margo's vision started to blur again. "She'd been through some difficult times before her trip to Barra."

Wee Hughie looked again toward the inn. "She's well now?"

"Oh, yes." Margo smiled, her heart filling. "She's married and very happy."

Wee Hughie lifted a brow. "In Pennsylvania?"

"Oh! Is that a seal between those boats?" Margo pointed at the water, tried to distract him. "I'm sure it was."

The loch's gleaming surface was just as empty as it'd been a moment before. But she wasn't about to tell the Highland Storyweaver where Mindy had settled.

"Did you know"—Wee Hughie stared out across the dark water, seeming to look far beyond the sea-loch— "that on your sister's last day on Barra, there were reports of an odd blue glow coming from within the little medieval chapel at MacNeil Tower?"

"No." Margo adjusted her paisley shawl, fussing with its loose knot.

"There are good, salt-of-the-earth men who swear they saw that blue light." Wee Hughie glanced at her, and then back to the horizon. "They worried that your sister was never seen to leave the wee isle where the castle stands.

"You do know MacNeil Tower is on a tiny island in Barra's bay?" His voice betrayed him. Wee Hughie knew where Mindy was and, it would seem, how she'd landed there. "There were questions."

"My sister is fine." Margo spoke brightly.

"I'm sure she is." Wee Hughie still didn't look at her. "The MacNeils are a good clan. They're a proud and noble race who take care of their own."

"I thought all Highland clans did that."

"They did." Wee Hughie turned to her. "They still do, much as clan spirit is possible today. But in olden times, days before the great Barra MacNeils, there were warriors who might not have been able to keep their loved ones safe no matter how hard they tried.

"Life was dangerous then." His eyes narrowed and his smile was gone. "Those were killing times, full of treachery and bloodshed. Magnus MacBride lived in those days. If"—he paused, watching her closely—"he even existed.

"The Viking Age was one of the reddest chapters in Scottish history." He reached to grasp her arm, squeezing lightly. "I liked your sister. I feel a debt to warn you to be careful walking about on your own. Here in Gairloch, and the farther north we go, the closer you'll come to the true heart of the Highlands. Deep, ancient places where the past does live on."

"I love the past." Margo did.

She'd embrace the chance to step into history. She wasn't afraid.

"Dinnae love it too much, lass." Wee Hughie's burr deepened. "There's a big difference between a MacNeil stronghold on Barra and finding yourself bound and freezing in the bilgewater of a Viking warlord's dragon ship."

Margo forced a smile. "I can see why they call you a storyweaver."

"I tell true tales." He winked and a dimple flashed in his cheek. "Now"—he rubbed his hands briskly, once again the tour guide—"are you for going back to the Old Harbour Inn with me? The ceilidh will begin shortly."

"I want to see the crofting and fishing museum." Margo was eager to be on her way. "I know it's just up the village road."

"They closed at five."

"I still want to go look around."

"So be it." Wee Hughie didn't argue with her.

But his words held a note of finality that sent a rush of shivers across Margo's nerves. Before she could say something light and breezy to chase her flare of alarm, he turned and strode down the quay toward the Old Harbour Inn.

Margo crossed the street and started along the road-side path to the museum. She'd taken only a few steps before something made her look back at Gairloch's sleepy little harbor.

Her heart stopped when she did.

Something wasn't right.

The quay looked the same as a moment before. And

so did the fishing boats, the whole bobbing fleet of them. There were still a few cars parked near the dockside fish-packing warehouses and one or two evening strollers on the harbor walk. But she couldn't shake the sensation that the atmosphere had somehow shifted, grown darker.

Her spine tingled, and she could feel the fine hairs rising on her nape. Nothing appeared out of the ordinary, but she couldn't shake the unease rippling along her nerves.

It was the sense of being watched.

Observed, and not in a good way.

Margo frowned. She also kept walking, trying to look purposeful and confident.

Unfortunately, the shadows cast by one of the quayside warehouses kept drawing her eye. A patch of deeper blackness there seemed to shift and swell on the wind, almost as if something was trying to form. She blinked, but the weirdness didn't go away.

Worse, the pulsing darkness had edges.

She was reminded of the shadowy mass she'd seen near the bookshelves at Ye Olde Pagan Times. This oddity had the same feel. And the seams appeared to glitter like Fourth of July sparklers.

Only the sparkles were inky, not bright.

Then someone—a crusty old fisherman—stepped from the warehouse, a wedge of yellow light flooding out into the evening with him.

The patch of blackness vanished.

Margo took a deep, relieved breath and reached to smooth the chills from the back of her neck. It'd been an optical illusion, nothing else. She gave herself a shake, letting the tension slide from her shoulders.

She also felt a bit silly.

The night couldn't have been more peaceful.

Threads of peat smoke—the earthy-rich scent made her heart tumble in her chest—rose from the chimneys of the stone houses along the road. Light from streetlamps shimmered on the water. And surf broke on the rocks. She also caught faint snatches of the ceilidh tunes. Jigs and reels from Wee Hughie's Highland Night, which would now be in full swing back at the Old Harbour Inn.

Margo kept walking.

A sign promised that the museum was just ahead.

The wind had freshened and carried the damp chill of coming rain. And it was getting late. The hillsides were already black with evening darkness. But the moon shone through the clouds, silvering the cobbled court-yard of the crofting and fishing museum.

Buffeted by the wind, Margo drew her jacket tighter and looked around.

A charming place, the huddle of low, whitewashed and rough-stoned buildings held just the right touch of yesteryear. Moonlight spilled across the slate roofs and fell brightly on the diamond-shaped windows of the museum's pièce de résistance, a mock lighthouse near the entrance.

As she'd been warned, the place was closed.

Or so she thought until a shadow moved behind the main building's lit windows just as she'd been about to walk around the replica lighthouse.

Margo froze.

Someone was inside the building.

And whoever it was had been watching her. Not just watching, but observing her carefully, and with stealth. The chill bumps on her arms told her that much. Her nape prickled again, indicating the same.

The air filled with menace.

She could feel it swirling around her, souring the cold night wind.

Wee Hughie's words of caution flashed across her mind as she stared at the museum. A curious rustling came from behind her, almost like the crackling of brittle, aged paper. Margo's heart began to beat rapidly. The strange feeling she'd had at the harbor returned with a vengeance. She took a deep, steadying breath, and willed calm.

It didn't come.

Something evil was near.

She started to turn, meaning to make a run for it, but just then she saw a small, old-lady face at the window, peering out at her.

"Oh, man . . ." Margo clapped a hand to her breast. She felt such a wash of relief, she laughed out loud.

The old woman smiled and waved.

Clearly a museum volunteer, she must've been working late to close out the gift shop. Or maybe she was just tidying up after a busy day. Either way, Margo felt ridiculous for letting nerves get to her.

The tiny woman cracked the museum door, beckoning Margo near. "We be closed since five"—she opened the door a bit wider, letting cheery light spill out onto the path—"but you can have a wee peek if you're quick."

"I was just leaving." Margo didn't want to get the woman in trouble.

She'd guessed right. The lady could be only a staff volunteer. A bit stooped, she had a whir of frizzled white hair and bright blue eyes. She was clearly pushing eighty, if not more. But she looked sprightly in her ankle-length tartan skirt and matching vest. And her white blouse was crisply ironed. She also had the contented air of someone who really loved her work.

"I only wanted to see the lighthouse." Margo seized the first excuse that popped into her mind, and then started to turn away.

But somehow, her feet carried her forward and she was crossing the threshold, into the museum's display-case-crammed entry.

"Och, a few minutes' nosey willnae hurt anyone." The old woman—her volunteer name badge read DEV DOONIE—twinkled at Margo. "We have a wealth of Highland history within these walls. And there's no one who knows these hills better than me."

Looking proud, she smoothed her tartan skirt. "Truth is, I'm older than the hills, as you can see." Her bright blue eyes crinkled at her joke. "If there be something you wanted to know, just ask."

"Well . . ." Margo hesitated. "Do you anything about Magnus MacBride?"

"*The Viking Slayer?*" Dev Doonie beamed. "I know of him, aye."

"So he was real?" Margo's pulse quickened. "I'd heard he was just a myth."

"Mythic would be more apt." The old woman's eyes lit with pride. "And, aye, he's real. No one hereabouts would tell you otherwise." She spoke as if she knew him. "Folk remember how he protected these parts with his sword, a huge gleaming brand called Vengeance."

Margo blinked. "He was liked around here?"

Dev Doonie hooted. "Lass, to the folk up and down this coast, he was a god."

Margo wasn't surprised.

The old woman took on the air of a conspirator. "Those days were bloodthirsty and folk lived in fear. When Vikings raided these shores, Magnus MacBride filled his warship, *Sea-Raven*, with his best fighting men, mounds of weaponry, and then came beating down from his stronghold, Badcall Castle."

She leaned close, her eyes glittering. "He brought other ships with him, a small fleet. They left stout warriors in each village along the coast. They were fierce, good-hearted men who taught sword-craft to the local lads so they'd know how to protect their homes and families if they were attacked again.

"The Viking Slayer also made sure the villagers had enough men and fuel to light balefires on the hilltops." Admiration filled her voice. "He wanted beacons lit if the Northmen were spotted off the shore."

"He did all that?" Margo had known he was that kind of hero. She'd felt it when the book *Myths and Legends of the Viking Age* sprang from the shelf and she'd picked it up, opened to the illustration of Magnus standing in the surf, raising his sword.

She'd known then he'd been larger than life.

Dev Doonie confirmed it. "Och, aye, he did all that. And he did more than see that the villagers had balefires. He sent swift help each time such flames reddened the sky." She nodded sagely. "That's the kind o' man he is."

"Is?" Margo blinked.

"Heroes ne'er die, do they?" Dev Doonie rubbed her hands, smiling again. "It's a pity"—her gaze went to the still-open door—"dark comes so quickly this time of year. There's a little strand not far from here where you'd have a fine view of the bay. A stroll there would put you close to the scene of some of the Viking Slayer's greatest battles.

"But . . ." She hesitated, tapping her chin. "It's a bit of a wild and remote place—"

"I love wild and remote." Margo didn't hesitate.

Wild places were her dream.

Remote was her middle name. Solitary and isolated became her.

Dev Doonie angled her head, considering. "Thon strand would be treacherous this time of night, the rocks slippery. But the moon is high now—you'd see well enough. . . ."

Margo glanced at her feet. "I have sturdy shoes."

'Tis a sturdy heart you'll be needing.

Margo started. She wasn't sure if Dev Doonie had spoken, or if she'd imagined the words.

The old woman had already moved to the door. She'd picked up a duster, hinting tactfully that it was time for Margo to leave.

She looked at Margo and winked. "Just follow the coast road about a quarter mile and you'll see a footpath down to the strand."

"I will. And"—Margo impulsively hugged her—"thank you so much for telling me about Magnus Mac-Bride."

"Och!" Dev Doonie wriggled free, her eyes dancing. "My like doesn't need thanks."

"But—"

"No buts, lassie." Dev Doonie wagged a finger. "Just you hie yourself to thon strand and do what you must.

"And remember"—she patted Margo's shoulder as she stepped out the door—"a true Heilander needs a woman of strength and courage."

"What?" Margo turned, but Dev Doonie had already closed the door and flicked off the lights inside the museum.

Margo stood in the darkness, frowning. She was sure she'd heard the woman's last words before.

She just couldn't recall where.

So she set off down the moon-washed path, taking the opposite direction along Loch Gairloch from the Old Harbour Inn. Dev Doonie's parting comment kept circling in her mind, keeping pace with her as she climbed the road, walking past a huddle of stone houses on the crest of a hill above the harbor.

"A true Heilander needs a woman of strength and courage."

Who said *Heilander* these days?

Even Wee Hughie MacSporran used *Highlander*.

There had to be something significant about those words.

She could feel them scratching at the edges of her memory. Much like a dog will scrabble at a door when he wants to go out. Or tap at your knee with his paw if you're eating and he wants table scraps.

If only she could remember . . .

Still puzzling, she paused at the top of the rise to gaze again at the sea. Rich, velvety darkness now cloaked the little harbor town and its quay. But she could see the hills, black outlines against the deeper night. Lights glittered along the docks and shone in the windows of the Old Harbour Inn, off in the distance. Yet she felt as if she were alone in another world, surrounded by nothingness and with no real trace of the twenty-first century anywhere for miles.

It was the all-enveloping silence that transported her. No city noises intruded on the stillness. Wind and the surge of the sea ruled here.

And the sweetness of such quiet almost broke her heart.

"Damn." Margo fisted her hands and blinked against the stinging heat at the backs of her eyes.

Scotland made her fragile.

She closed her eyes for a moment and listened to the heaving seas, the rush of the wind. Her throat burned and she swallowed hard. Her heart ached and she wondered if anything could stir a soul more deeply than a Scottish night wrapping around you like a caress.

She wanted to stay here so much.

"Damn." She cursed again, blinking furiously.

Then she sat on a roadside boulder to shake a pebble from her shoe. But the instant she leaned down to untie her boot's laces, she jumped back up again, so many chills streaking through her that she felt as if she'd thrust her fingers into an electrical socket.

"Oh, my God!" She stared at her feet, not seeing her own clunky walking boots, but remembering the tiny high-topped black boots worn by the white-haired, rosy-cheeked Scotswoman from Donald McVittie's A Dash o' Plaid booth the day of the Scottish Festival.

Dev Doonie at the crofting and fishing museum wore the very same boots.

And she tied them with red plaid laces.

Margo sank back onto the stone, almost dizzy. The world was spinning around her and her blood rushed in her ears, loud and ringing.

Dev Doonie *was* the little old lady at A Dash o' Plaid.

The woman had even claimed to have come from a nonexistent Hebridean isle called Doon. She'd been the one who'd made the Heilander comment.

Twice now.

There could be no mistake.

Margo should've recognized her at once. But she'd been sporting a typical museum-volunteer outfit and even an official-looking name badge.

People believed what they expected to see.

Margo knew that well.

The phenomenon probably also explained why a whirling, dark luminance was beginning to form across the road from her. It was the same weirdness she'd seen on the waterfront, and this time, she had no doubt as to the shape's malignancy. The smell of rotten eggs thickened the air, the stench burning her eyes and making her gag.

Rolling blackness blotted the road, cutting off her escape as the night came alive, seeming to breathe clouds of tiny jet-colored spangles.

Margo leapt to her feet and started to run.

The only place she could go was down the footpath to the strand.

Chapter 9

Margo ran like a gazelle.

The foul-reeking luminance at her back put wings on her heels as she flew down the rough-hewn steps carved into the steep headland. Her rotten luck definitely enjoyed the sticking power of gum on the sole of a shoe, because whatever horror had tried to materialize on the road swirled everywhere now. She could feel it swelling on the wind, pressing against her until she could hardly breathe, and even clawing at her back as if terrible, talon-tipped fingers were reaching for her.

Panic flooded her.

Adrenaline kept her legs pumping.

She'd always loved the paranormal, even priding herself on her acceptance of things like ghosts, time slips, Wiccan beliefs, and magic.

She'd felt sorry for people so narrow-minded they couldn't believe in the unseen and unproven.

Now . . .

She was ready to rescind her opinion.

If this was the supernatural, she wanted nothing to do with it.

This wasn't amusing.

Margo . . .

A hollow-sounding female voice called her name, the cry echoing along the headland.

"Oh, no!" Margo's heart slammed against her ribs, terror gripping her.

She ran faster, one hand pressed to her breast.

Halfway down the cliff, the path curved and seemed to end in a tumble of broken rock, thick with nettles. Margo sailed over the rubble in one leaping bound and tore down the remaining steps at light speed.

Relief was hers when she reached the strand. The air was cold and fresh here. Moonlight gleamed on the water and the tide was coming in, breakers foaming white up and down the coast as far as she could see. No miasmic clouds hovered anywhere and the only sound was the sea. She didn't see a single stir of movement that wasn't natural.

"Thank God." She braced her hands on her thighs and leaned forward, struggling to catch her breath. Night wind rushed past her, cooling her brow and bringing the clean tang of the sea.

For the moment, she was safe.

And she wasn't going anywhere until she was sure that the thing up on the road was gone.

Just now . . .

She straightened, pulled a still-shaky hand down over her chin. The strand *was* beautiful and any other time, she'd have swooned to be here. Incredible rocks were spread up and down the beach. Great masses of the loveliest stones she'd seen anywhere in Scotland. Most were the size of a man's fist, though some looked as large as a cantaloupe. They were all round or oval-shaped and perfectly smooth, each one well polished by the surf.

Every hue imaginable seemed represented. Many of the stones were speckled, some banded, and all of them sparkled or gleamed. They were so remarkable that each one struck her as more appealing than the last.

She wanted them all.

Unfortunately, her carryall was already so crammed with Scottish rocks that the seams were splitting. Her suitcase was no better. She'd used every available inch of space, even stuffing smaller stones inside her extra pair of shoes. Some of her toiletries and makeup had been sacrificed so a few stones could be wedged into her cosmetics case.

Who needed eye cream or a change of lipstick when you could hold a little bit of Scotland in your hand?

Not her, anyway.

Precious memories clung to each rock and she couldn't bear to leave any behind.

Still . . .

Margo tapped her chin, glancing at the temptation all around her.

Surely she could find room for just one more? A really special stone she couldn't resist and that jumped out at her, begging to be taken back to Pennsylvania.

A stone that was so *hers*, she'd carry it home in her hand if need be.

Glad for a distraction—and hoping to convince herself she'd only imagined the nightmare on the road—she clasped her hands behind her back and began walking the strand. A few times she held her breath and closed her eyes, certain that her stone would leap out at her when she looked again, scanning the lovely selection.

It was impossible to choose just one.

Until her gaze fell on the dazzling quartz band circling the large, round stone a few feet ahead of her. Similar to the other banded stones on the strand, this one somehow stood out from the rest. Just looking down at the stone made her skin prickle with awareness.

This was the one.

She could almost feel its power, the stone's heartbeat matching its rhythm to hers. A sensation that strengthened the longer she looked down at the stone, drawn by its spell.

She shivered, stepping closer to the stone. Dark gray in color and smooth as polished glass, it bore an inch-wide band of snowy white circling its middle. Pure quartz, she was sure, though the band sparkled with the brilliance of diamonds.

She tried to walk away, testing the vibrations, but her feet wouldn't move. Her fingers itched, burning to close around the stone.

When she started to reach for it, the band around the stone's center started to move, coming to life.

"Gah!" Margo leapt back, her eyes widening as strange symbols appeared and disappeared on the stone's broad ring of white quartz.

The characters shifted and glowed, blazing like the sun one moment, then gone the next.

She saw why when the moon slipped briefly behind a cloud, darkening the strand. There weren't any glowing symbols forming on the quartz band.

She'd been fooled by a trick of moonlight.

But she still wanted the stone, magical or not.

So she bent again to retrieve it, curling her fingers around its cold weight.

The stone turned white-hot in her hand.

"Agh!" Margo jumped. Her fingers tightened around the stone, unable to let go.

Oddly, the fiery heat didn't burn her. But a loud humming noise filled her ears and a series of shocks surged into her hand. The tingling jolts streaked up her arm, and raced across her shoulders and down her back, sizzling through her entire body.

It was like sticking wet fingers into an electrical socket.

Except that it didn't hurt.

It was just weird.

And when the strangeness ended, she heard a faint jangling behind her. The light crunch of footsteps on stone and—she was sure—the soft rustling of a woman's skirts. She also caught a distinct whiff of some kind of exotic, musky perfume. Almost like she imagined a Byzantine tomb might smell: dark and mysterious, with a hint of cold ash and lots of stale incense. The scent curled around her, intense and cloying.

Chills sped down her spine, icy and unpleasant.

Anxiety rose in her throat, almost choking her as the weird jangling came nearer and the rich, ancient-smelling perfume grew stronger.

The evil from the roadside was on the strand.

Margo . . .

Her name rode the wind again, the voice calling her, sounding pleased to spread such terror.

Whoever—*or whatever*—the entity was, she definitely knew Margo's name. There could be no mistaking this time. This was for real.

The presence was coming for her.

Heart thumping, Margo turned to face the long stretch of moonlit strand behind her. Her blood iced when she saw what was there.

It was a solid black mass.

A humming, inky cloud of malice that hovered about a foot above the ground, and—her stomach clenched—it was the same shadow she'd seen near the bookshelves the afternoon at Ye Olde Pagan Times.

The day she'd "met" Magnus MacBride.

Margo clapped the stone to her breast, staring. She was sure she wasn't mistaken. The presence brought the same dreaded energy. Worse, something pulsed inside the cloud. Iridescent specks spun at its heart, forming a vortex.

It was the small shapely form of a woman.

"Dear God." Margo felt horror sweep her. The manifesting female looked frighteningly like Dina Greed.

Margo's greatest rival in all things Scottish.

Except that was impossible.

Margo knew that her diminutive archfiend was already back in New Hope. And she couldn't have died and moved on to another plane, thus having the power to appear now for the sole purpose of frightening Margo to bits. If anything dire had happened to Dina, Marta or Patience would've called with the news. Maybe even Ardelle Goodnight of Aging Gracefully.

They had looked out for Margo, always.

But she was alone now.

Wishing her friends were near, she closed her eyes and breathed deeply, hoping the apparition would be gone when she looked again. It wasn't, and at second glance she could see now that the creature wasn't really Dina, however strong the resemblance. But the entity and her creepy black shadow were drifting closer to where she stood.

Her heart beat much too fast, making her blood chill. Shock pounded through her, blotting everything except the nightmare before her.

She couldn't run.

Her gaze was somehow fastened on the whirling vortex. And her legs felt like cement. She was sure that someone invisible had nailed her feet to the ground. No matter how much she wanted to bolt, she wasn't going anywhere. It was impossible.

She'd clearly been put under a binding spell, powerful witchery that would thwart any chance of escape.

Margo knew such spells existed.

Patience had once cast one on a purse snatcher outside Ye Olde Pagan Times. Her magic had held him in the shop's vicinity until the police arrived.

Margo swallowed hard, fear closing her throat.

"Who are you?" Margo's voice was a croak.

The specter smiled. "Look again, more closely." She spoke in the soft lilting tones of a Highland woman. But her voice was full of malicious pride.

And each word oozed venom, however pleasingly musical her Scottish accent.

She was of petite stature and voluptuous, with large breasts and a welter of dark curling hair that shone like a raven's wing. She had bold, flashing eyes. They were the color of rich, brown black peat. There the similarities to Margo's rival ended. This woman didn't favor Dina's tartan-tart mini-kilt getups, with thigh-high black leather boots and clinging, low-cut tops. The woman in the vortex wore a swirling black cloak that looked tissue thin and was luminous, giving off tiny speckles of light.

Bands of silver and jet hung from her neck, wrists, and ankles. The delicate jewelry chimed together with her every move.

Her strong, stale perfume was almost overpowering. It soaked the air, reminding Margo more than ever of a musty ancient tomb or chapel. Cold damp walls steeped with old smells like frankincense, myrrh, and maybe some gone-bad sandalwood.

"This isn't happening." Margo spoke with more bravura than she felt. If she rejected the woman's power, she might have a chance. "You're not here and I'm not seeing you. You're a figment—"

The woman laughed. "You're the will-o'-wisp."

Shaking her head, Margo held out her arm, as if she could ward off the woman and her shifting black cloud.

"Look here...." She took a step backward, then another. Every inch was like wading through thigh-high sand. "I don't know who, or what, you are—"

"I am many things, many faces." The woman's tone chilled her. Her gaze was like a blast of burning ice. "And you are the face I'm using to torture Magnus MacBride."

"Magnus?" Margo's heartbeat kicked into overdrive.

The woman's eyes lit with amusement. "I see his name is known to you. As I knew it would be, for I've spent long hours at my craft, searching for the perfect vessel to break him."

"I don't know any Magnus." Sweat trickled between Margo's breasts on the lie.

"Ahhh, but that's the sweetness of my revenge." The vortex-woman laughed. It was a cold, brittle sound.

The black cloud drifted closer, the woman's eyes revealing she was amused by Margo's passion for Magnus.

"I have worked dark spells, showing you to him. He burns for you, yet"—the entity's tone was pure evil—"he knows he can never possess you. Soon, desire will drive him to madness. His carelessness will bring his end."

Margo gulped.

The woman lifted a hand, examining her talonlike fingernails.

"I know something of magic. I can block your spell." Margo's heart hammered and her palms were slick with terror. She had no idea how to ward off such evil. She also wished her voice had rung stronger. The malice in the entity's eyes scared her more than anything she'd ever seen in her life.

She put back her shoulders, trying to look brave. "A friend of mine is a powerful sorceress." Margo knew Patience wouldn't mind the exaggeration. "She'll hunt you down, turning all her skills on—"

"No one's powers can touch mine." The vortex-woman smiled, the tilt of her lips chilling the air.

Margo tried to back away again, but her legs felt leaden.

The entity's eyes glowed, showing she knew. Wind whipped around her—strong, icy currents illuminated by a dazzle of whirling blue-black sparkles—as she lifted a hand to her lips, whispering ancient words against her fingertips before pointing to an empty space between Margo and the tide line.

"See him now, while he yet breathes." She swept her arm in a circle, making the air crackle like rustling paper. A tiny burning light appeared within the space she drew, a speck of brightness no larger than the shine of a candle. Then the flame burst into a sheet of fire, vanishing as quickly in a swirl of smoke.

When the haze cleared, Magnus stood on the strand.

He was dressed for battle, with his arm rings glinting brightly and his sword at his side. Wind tore at his plaid and he stood with his legs slightly spread and his hands on his hips, his broad mail-clad shoulders just brushing the ring of eerie sparkles encircling him.

His long, silky black hair spilled down his back in a glossy skein, the shining strands lifted by the unholy wind that had conjured him.

He didn't see them, his fierce gaze fixed on something distant.

He *was* magnificent.

And so real-seeming that Margo's knees weakened. She started to cry out, but no sound came. Her tongue felt weighted, her throat too tight to form words. When she tried to step forward, her feet still wouldn't move. Even breathing was difficult.

She did tighten her grip on her stone, trying to ground herself with its cold solidity.

She kept her gaze on Magnus, both horrified and enthralled.

"You'll never have him." The entity taunted her, triumphant. "My magic will trap you in an in-between place where you'll exist and yet not exist. Not in your world or mine. You're as cursed as the Viking Slayer."

She pointed her finger at him then and he disappeared, vanishing with an awful popping noise.

The terrible wind that had been circling him rushed at Margo, whipping around her with blasts of frigid air.

"No-o-o!" Margo's denial ripped free, the effort making her throat burn like fire.

Her cry only caused the entity to drift nearer, her luminous cloak floating about her like a shining black cloud. To Margo's amazement, the creature plucked several tiny sparkles off the gossamer material. Murmuring again, she thrust out her hand and the teeny lights danced across her palm, bursting into a blazing ball of light the size of a man's fist.

"Behold the Viking Slayer's destiny." She held up the fiery ball with her fingers, clearly protected from its flames. "As this fire is dashed"—she threw the ball into the surf, where it landed with a hiss, quickly vanishing beneath the waves—"so will he always yearn for you, only to find himself plunged into cold darkness, his passion thwarted. His desire shall remain unfulfilled, its fire snuffed out as swiftly as my ball of flame.

"You will come with me now." She started twirling, spinning faster as she spoke. "Innocent and naked as you came into your world, so shall you enter mine. Your arrival will blind Magnus, laming him with shock and making his steel as useless as sand spilling through his fingers. You'll see him cut down and he'll stare at you as he dies, his blood flowing red onto this strand.

"So mote it be."

Her eyes flashed silver then, her final words echoing down the strand.

And then she was gone.

The terrible black cloud went with her. And her cloying, Byzantine-tomb scent.

Margo stared at the spot where she'd been, then dropped to her knees, her legs too shaky to hold her.

It was then she noticed she was naked.

"Oh, God!" Her eyes rounded as disbelief sluiced her. She began to shake, uncontrollable tremors rolling through her body. Her stomach heaved, clenching as if she was about to be ill.

She still held her rock, gripping so tightly her knuckles shone white.

Everything else was gone.

Even the night's darkness, for it was now morning. A cold, blustery morning on the same pebbled shore where she'd just stood. Nowhere did she see a trace of the vortex-woman. And despite the entity's threat, Magnus MacBride wasn't anywhere, either.

She was alone.

Nothing stirred except a shimmering veil that stretched across the strand. It reached as high as the low, scudding clouds and shone like spun glass.

Margo guessed it was a time curtain.

But she could still see the stone steps carved into the cliffside. She even saw the wooden handrail that followed the path a few turns down from the road. But then the rail and the steps faded from view, first losing color and substance. It looked briefly like a black-and-white negative before they were simply gone.

The cliff remained.

As did her terror, for in the moment the steps and the handrail vanished, the strange symbols on her stone's white quartz band returned. They blazed red, pulsing brightly around the stone. Not a trick of light, the fiery, sticklike characters were recognizable as runes.

Norse runes.

More specifically, they were ancient Elder Futhark runes. Margo knew because Patience sold sets of them at Ye Olde Pagan Times.

Now they were almost on fire on her stone.

And the instant she realized what they were, the world disappeared.

"Agggh!" Margo clutched the stone as the earth tilted and bucked beneath her feet. She fell, spinning and tumbling as if she were caught in a cyclone.

Everything flashed black-and-white, one blinding burst after another, like a bad lightning storm. Loud *popping* noises hurt her ears, worse than an airplane piercing the sound barrier. She reeled, trying to see, but there was only darkness shot through with spears of brilliant light.

Then everything slammed to a jarring, teeth-rattling halt.

Margo tried to scream, but her chest was tight, burning like fire, the air knocked from her lungs.

She still held the stone.

She was on the same strand as before.

But now the vortex-woman's curse claimed her.

A terrible battle raged around her. Huge, wild-eyed men with swinging, waist-length hair and bushy, braided beards ran everywhere. In a killing frenzy, they shouted and cursed, oblivious to the blood streaming on their mailed shirts and spilling down the bright blades of their slashing swords and arcing axes.

None of them seemed aware of her.

They were too intent on their mad slaughter, too busy plunging swords into one another and lopping off arms with giant axes. No one bothered to glance at an unclothed, trembling woman clutching a stone to her breast. Her mouth opened in a silent scream.

"O-o-oh, God . . ." Margo closed her eyes, praying the strand would be empty when she looked again.

But it wasn't.

If anything, it was worse, the details rushing at her.

The pebbled shoreline was garishly crimson. And— her stomach rolled—bodies of dead warriors lay everywhere, their limbs at unnatural angles, or missing. Other men had lost their heads or suffered ghastly, gaping wounds, the cuts splitting them wide. One poor soul had been pinned to the ground by a spear. A flooding tide raced in, the long foaming rollers spreading the bloodshed so that the whole of Loch Gairloch swirled in an ocean of deadly, surging scarlet.

Everywhere men yelled insults and roared in rage, the shrill cries of the wounded and the moans of the dying made more terrifying by the clashing of swords, the knocking of shields, and—Margo felt sick—the awful sound of spear blades and axes sinking into flesh.

The sea landscape was more terrible.

Men stood thigh-deep in the surf, hacking, stabbing, and slashing at one another. Margo wasn't sure, but it seemed as if those men fought even more viciously than the ones racing about the beach. Many of the surf fighters grinned as they thrashed in the waves, swinging their swords and axes in ferocious, killing blows. When one fell, three more flung themselves into the fray, raising their swords and shouting with glee as they leapt off the scores of square-sailed, many-oared, Norse warships beating back and forth just off the shore.

"Oh, no, oh, no, oh, no . . ." Margo stared at the warriors, her eyes wide.

Her blood drained as she watched them, so grateful they didn't seem to see her.

If this was to be Magnus's death scene—as the entity had sworn—she was even more thankful that she still didn't see him.

Perhaps the woman had plunged her into the wrong battle?

Maybe she hadn't been sent anywhere.

If she was lucky, she'd wake in her bed at the Old Harbour Inn and this would be a bad dream.

But her stone was scalding her fingers and the fighting looked real.

Margo shook her head, disbelief sweeping her. "This can't be happening. Vikings—"

The world shook on the word *Vikings*, the powerful jolt snatching her cry and shaking the air with strangely silent explosions that reminded her of a powerful earthquake without the rumbling.

There wasn't any noise at all.

Total silence surrounded her, a quiet so heavy she could feel it weighing on her like a thick, lead blanket. Her hands were empty because, in her terror, she'd even dropped her special stone.

She was afraid to open her eyes.

She feared she'd been swept to a place far worse than Viking Scotland.

A cold, silent place that might mean she was dead.

Then she heard a shout and a splash. *"Sea witch!"*

She cracked her lids, peeking around her. She was just in time to see Magnus vault over the side of one of the warships and run through the surf, coming straight at her. And he was wearing a thunderous scowl.

Some might even say murderous.

"Dinnae move, you!" He was on the sand now, sprinting along the tide line, swiftly closing the distance between them.

She was still naked.

It was a circumstance that hadn't really bothered her until this moment because no one had been aware of her before. Now Magnus and everyone else could see her. And although Magnus's dark eyes burned with anger, his men were staring at her as if she wasn't just unclothed, but also two-headed, horned, and sporting a long forked tail.

She saw why at once.

Although Magnus and his warriors still bore signs of hard fighting, their long hair tangled and their mail and weapons smeared with blood, there were few remaining traces of the battle.

Sure, some of his men sat on the strand clutching wounds and moaning. And the warships under his command still rocked in the red-tinged water. The surf was just as crimson, bearing testimony to the slaughter.

But the Norse dragon ships had vanished.

The Vikings were gone.

And it was clear that Magnus and his men held Margo responsible.

They thought she was a witch.

Maybe even something worse.

And—Margo gulped as Magnus pounded up to her, his fury alive—she didn't know how to convince them otherwise.

The evidence against her was damning.

Chapter 10

"O-o-oh, no!" Margo stared at Magnus as he pounded across the strand toward her, his drawn sword glinting lethally. Hot fury burned in his eyes. And his scowl was fiercer than any she'd ever seen. She clapped her hands to strategic places and backed away, shaking her head as her sweetest dream turned into a nightmare.

"You don't want to use that." Her gaze didn't leave his sword.

The blade glistened red, fresh blood staining its length and dripping from the tip.

"I don't like violence." She prayed she'd waken any minute.

Her stomach lurched.

Magnus was almost upon her. He didn't look very sympathetic. If he noticed she was naked, or afraid, there was no indication. He appeared ready to toss her over his shoulder and carry her to the nearest bonfire.

"What devilry is this?" he roared, sweeping his blood-ied sword in a huge arc that took in the sullied, Viking-less strand and his white-faced, gog-eyed men.

"Speak." He pointed the blade at her. "Now, before I lose patience."

"I . . ." Margo could only stare at him.

He glared at her, his dark eyes flashing. "If you're powerful enough to banish Vikings into thin air, you'll have the strength to answer me."

Margo blinked. His voice was just as rich and deep as she'd imagined, and by some miracle she could understand him. But while the husky tones rumbled through her and could've been seductively intoxicating, his words were full of anger and distrust.

She took a backward step, shaking her head.

"I wait." He held her gaze, his brows low and fierce.

"I don't know what happened." Margo's chest was so tight she could hardly find breath for words. She'd obviously chosen the wrong ones because his expression turned blacker.

He tossed a glance at his men, now gathered nearby, gawking. "I see no one else capable of such witchery."

"It wasn't my doing." She wasn't going anywhere near the *w* word.

Besides, he looked more like the devil than her.

Cold sea wind whipped his long black hair. And he was so tall, much larger and more harsh-looking than she'd pictured him. His plaid was wet, torn, and smeared with blood. Even the bright silver and gold rings on his well-muscled arms bore speckles of red. He was clearly a man who struck terror in the hearts of his enemies, but whose power and magnetism left women breathless.

Unfortunately, at the moment, he was more terrifying than sexy.

"It couldn't have been anyone else." He kept his sword aimed at her belly.

Margo swallowed.

He prodded her with the blade. "Speak."

"I just did." That was the best she could manage.

Any moment she was going to break out in a cold

sweat. Her churning stomach and odd light-headedness warned that she might even be sick.

She did take another backward step, scanning the strand for the vortex-woman. As had happened with Patience, her spell had obviously gone wrong. She hadn't sent Margo hurtling back in time to witness Magnus's demise. She'd whisked her here for the terror of living her own death at his hands. She'd probably even planted the banded stone on the strand, needing its help to work her dark magic.

But the entity was nowhere in sight.

And Margo couldn't distinguish the stone from the gazillion other banded stones scattered everywhere.

She tried to tamp down the panic rising inside her. She failed abysmally. Although she didn't see the vortex-woman or her stone, she did see Magnus and his long-bladed sword. She could even smell the weapon's cold steel, the metallic reek of blood staining its length. This wasn't a dream or a vision, spun by Patience's faulty book-peering spell.

This was real.

The hard knot throbbing between her shoulder blades told her as much. She'd always wakened at the point her nightmares became too frightening to bear. Now she was horribly aware that she wasn't going anywhere. Nor would relief come with the ringing of an alarm clock.

Alarm clocks hadn't yet been invented.

Any other time she would have smiled at the irony. She'd always wanted to time travel. Now she *had*, yet her bad luck had gone with her.

She'd dreamed of Magnus pulling her into his arms and kissing her.

Not threatening her with his sword.

The unfairness of it gave her the anger to glare at him. She lifted her chin, felt the heat staining her cheeks.

"If you were the hero I thought you were, you wouldn't let me stand here shivering and naked."

Something sparked in his eyes then and he lowered his sword, ramming the blade into its scabbard.

"Who are you?" He reached her in a stride. "How did you make the Vikings disappear?"

"I didn't."

"You lie." He grabbed her wrist, gripping hard. "Your face is known to me, sea witch." He lowered his voice, speaking only for her. "I'd hear why."

"If I knew, I'd tell you." Margo kept her chin raised, hoping she looked braver than she felt. His rich burr was heavy, liquid seduction. Even in his anger, each word poured over her, making it hard to think. "My name"—she tossed back her hair, trying anyway—"is Margo Menlove and I came here as a tourist. I'm from New Hope, Pennsylvania, and—"

"*Too*-rist?" He narrowed his eyes. "I ne'er heard suchlike, nor anyplace called Pen*seal*—"

"*Tourist* is a traveler. And you wouldn't know of Pennsylvania because it doesn't exist yet." Margo held his gaze. "Not in your time."

He frowned. "No' in my time?"

Margo nodded. "That's right. Not in your century or for many hundreds of years yet to come."

"Say you?" Skepticism rolled off him.

"I do." Margo tossed her head.

He went very still. "My name, lass, is Magnus Mac-Bride. Men call me Viking Slayer. I'm no' fond of witches, either. Be glad I do not lop the head off your shoulders for speaking such foolery."

"It's the truth."

"The devil you say!" Scowling, he grasped her arms and turned her so that his big, powerfully muscled body shielded her from his men. "See here"—he leaned close, his fierceness making her heart hammer—"I willnae be made the fool. I already know Sigurd Sword Breaker or Donata Greer, the sorceress, conjured you to plague me.

"I have seen you naked as you are now." His voice went deeper, turning rough. A muscle leapt in his jaw, as if he was struggling to restrain himself. "You rode me in Orosius's kettle steam."

Margo blinked.

None of her fantasies about him had included kettles or anyone named Orosius. And she wasn't about to touch such a prickly theme. Not after the way he'd practically growled the admission.

If he had seen her naked in a dream, vision, or whatever, the experience hadn't been to his liking.

Just now, he was looking her up and down, a heated appraisal. "Aye, you are the same sea witch. My enemies are using you."

"I'm not a witch." Margo flushed, furious that her chill-perked nipples hardened even more beneath his scrutiny.

"And I don't know your enemies. Not Sigurd Sword Breaker. I never heard of a sorceress named Donata Greer." She could feel his disbelief beating between them. "They certainly didn't conjure me. Unless . . . Oh, God!"

"You do know them?" He tightened his grip on her, his gaze piercing.

"I might have seen Donata"—Margo took a deep breath, seeking courage—"if she's a small, raven-haired woman who favors black and lots of jangling silver and jet jewelry. Dark eyes filled with malice." The entity's image flashed across her mind, making her skin crawl. "Musky, exotic perfume that's heavy and cloying—"

"Donata, aye." He was watching her more closely than ever. "She is many leagues from here, locked behind cloistered walls. You couldn't have seen her."

"Well, I saw someone." Margo held her ground. "And she looked just as I described."

She wasn't ready to tell him the woman had arrived in a glowing black cloud.

She kept her chin lifted. And she knew her eyes were snapping.

She didn't like being called a liar.

"You have described Donata. You know her because she is your mistress." He loomed closer. Not so near that his bloodied plaid touched her, but close enough for her to feel the heat pouring off him. His breath brushed her cheek, the intimacy scalding. And beneath the salt tang of the sea that clung to his plaid hovered a trace of woodsmoke and man, the scent making her pulse skitter.

As if he knew, anger darkened his eyes and he took another step, crowding her.

Margo swallowed, her heart thundering. "I don't have a mistress."

He arched a brow, saying nothing.

His broad shoulders blotted much of the beach from her sight. His long black hair spilled free and wind lifted the gleaming strands, some of them teasing her face. His expression was harsh, cold, and dangerous. His towering proximity made her breath catch and left her dizzy. She had to tip back her head to meet his gaze.

Looking elsewhere wasn't an option.

He was so handsome in a fierce, rugged way. His potent male virility thickened the air, heady and overwhelming. Her body hummed in response, craving him against all reason. Fluid warmth began tingling low by her thighs, and her nipples thrust almost painfully, straining to make contact with his broad, hard-muscled chest.

He was the sweetest intoxication.

If only the circumstances weren't so surreal.

And terrifying.

She glanced at his sword hilt, grip-ready at his side. "So she was real. The woman I saw." Nerves rippled in her voice and she hoped he didn't notice. "When she vanished, I thought I'd imagined her. Everything she'd threatened. Then when I found myself here and—"

"She threatened you?" Suspicion flashed across his face again. "How could she when you banished her?"

"I didn't *banish* her."

"Then what did you do?" His tone said he wouldn't believe her no matter what she told him.

"She just disappeared." Margo puffed a hair off her forehead, annoyance beginning to chase her fear. "And she did that after she threw a fireball into the surf, cursing you the while."

Heat flooded her when she realized what she'd blurted.

But it was too late now.

"I had nothing to do with it." She narrowed her eyes at him, indignation shooting through her veins. "I can't even make my own luck improve. I sure as hell can't make vortex-women go poof in the night!"

"Vortex-women?" His brows snapped together.

"Yes." Margo didn't feel like explaining.

She didn't like how he was looking at her. And she wished desperately that she weren't naked. It didn't matter if he'd somehow dreamed her nude and astride him. In fact, that made it worse. So she squirmed, trying to free her arms from his grasp so she could clap her hands over her breasts.

She shouldn't be surprised that medieval men had different sensibilities.

Especially a hot-eyed, sword-packing warlord who defined the term *alpha male*.

But still . . .

Anger and adrenaline gave her the strength to loosen his grip. Again, she arranged her arms over strategic places, one hand above and the other below. Then she opened her eyes very wide, fixing him with a frosty stare.

If he had any honor, she might be able to shame him.

"Do you always let women stand around naked? Or"—she couldn't believe her daring—"is that how men of your day make themselves feel superior?"

He was on her in a beat, his hands locking so roughly around her arms that she was sure he'd snap her in two. "Dinnae speak again of 'my day.' No' here, with my men staring at us. Their ears are as sharp as their noses long. If they hear suchlike, they'll do more than cut off your head. They'll burn you here and now."

"And you won't?" A flicker of hope flared in Margo's breast.

"I—" He clamped his mouth, glowering at her.

He clearly did see her as a creature of the devil.

But something was shifting between them. A glimmer of doubt in his eyes, a lessening in the hard set of his jaw, it was an indefinable change that she prayed meant he was beginning to believe her.

"Well?" She lifted her chin, challenging him.

She had nothing to lose.

"Death by the elements is no different from biting it by a sword." She couldn't hold back a shiver. The sea wind *was* bitter cold. "Either way you'd be rid of me."

"Damnation!" He released her, clenching his fists at his sides. For a long moment he glared at her, his expression a frightening blend of fury, hunger, and frustration.

Margo hoped the hunger would win.

"Keep yourself covered." He snarled the command. Then he whirled to face his men, his legs spread and his hands on his hips. The stance was pure male aggression. Riled, roused, and full of rage.

Margo knew his next words would seal her fate.

Knowing her luck ...

She braced for the worst.

"Orosius!" Magnus kept his back to *Margo Menlove* and roared for the seer, knowing the big man—a formidable fighter, much to the surprise of those who didn't know him—would have retrieved his heavy bearskin cloak now that the fighting had ended, however odd the battle's close.

The seer appreciated his comforts.

Magnus still puzzled that Orosius had come along, as he'd sworn off warring years ago. But he had joined them, astonishing everyone.

And he'd fought with a ferocity that rivaled some of Magnus's younger men.

Magnus was secretly proud of him.

But just now ...

"Orosius! Where are you? I'll have your cloak, man!" He ignored the stares of his men and glanced up and down the strand, searching for the black-bearded seer.

The lout seemed to have vanished with the Vikings.

Magnus scowled. Such a fate would serve the old goat right.

His absence sent fury coursing through Magnus's veins because it was so damned hard not to look at the sea siren's nakedness.

She'd also scalded him with shame.

He'd have torn off his plaid and flung it around her— even if she was a devil-spawned temptress conjured by Donata—if he hadn't wanted to avoid sullying her with the blood drenching his plaid.

She thought him without honor.

And that stain bit deep.

Furious, he kept searching for the seer. "I need your

cloak, Orosius!" He raised his voice, shouting with all his lung power. "If you dinnae come quickly, I'll find you and rip the damty rag off your back."

He'd also cut the eyes from his men if they didn't stop gawking at Margo.

"Take your stares from her, you lechers!" he snarled at them, yanking Vengeance halfway out of her scabbard until the bastards turned their backs and fixed their gazes on the horizon.

When two of them glanced over their shoulders, surely spelled by the round fullness of her breasts and the tempting curve of her hips, he knew there was only one way to protect her from his men's gawking.

"God's eyes!" Knowing he was damning himself in the by-doing, he yanked off his soiled plaid and threw it onto the strand.

Bare-chested, he stormed around and hauled Margo into his arms, lifting her easily and gathering her to him, effectively shielding her nakedness.

"Dinnae think to fight me, sea witch." He flashed a warning at her, aware his eyes were blazing. If she so much as wriggled a toe, his honor would shatter.

His infernal loins were already tighter than a bowstring.

And his manhood was a raging, granite-hard agony.

"Unhand me!" She ignored the danger and squirmed in his arms, trying to twist free. "I'm not a witch."

"I heard you the first time." Magnus glared down at her, trying hard not to glance below her collarbone.

Unfortunately, in trying to shield her from his men, he was holding her so tightly that her breasts were crushed against his chest. Her chill-hardened nipples pressed into him, a torture beyond bearing. Worst of all, the silken curls of her womanhood kept rubbing across his hip. And the hot, slick heat of her was making him crazy.

"I know you heard me." She wriggled again, her

damned female curls brushing perilously close to his groin. "You don't believe me, so I have no choice but to tell you again. I am not a witch. I think Donata disappeared on purpose. But I don't know what happened to the Vikings."

"And pigs fly." Magnus tightened his arms around her. "Now be still."

Afraid he'd embarrass himself if she moved again, he set his face in his worst scowl, hoping to deter her.

She only glared back him, so beautiful in her rage that raw need clawed at his chest.

In truth, she didn't need to wriggle to best him.

Her scent assailed him. Minding him of cold, clean air on a frosty winter night, but with a trace of rose, the fragrance swirled around him, tantalizing and more annoying than a bee beneath his collar.

Every muscle in his body tensed and hot blood roared through his veins, scalding him. Soon he wouldn't be able to breathe. He could feel the lust and anger churning inside him, seething and boiling.

For two pins, he'd lean down and nuzzle her neck just to drink in her beguiling scent.

"Orosius!" He yelled louder this time. "Where—"

"I'm here." The seer ambled over to them, the big Norse war ax he preferred in battle still in his hand. Its blade and haft were smeared with red, but the seer's prized bearskin cloak looked clean.

Leastways it was as unsullied as it would ever be.

Orosius carried the cloak over one arm, as if he knew why Magnus wanted it.

"I'll have that." Magnus yanked it from his friend's arm, and setting Margo from him, he swirled the cloak around her.

"Thank you." She snatched the bearskin tight against herself, her eyes still shooting blue fire at him.

"I'll find you suitable raiments later." *If you don't disappear into the mist.* Keeping the sentiment to himself, he glowered back at her, for the moment glad to have her out of his arms.

Now that she was covered, he could breathe again.

He dusted his hands, demonstrably.

Sadly, he burned to pull the mantle right back off her shoulders, once again freeing her smooth, silken skin, the sweet curve of her hip, and those full, round breasts to his hungering view.

She was a lavish feast he was so tempted to fall upon. Desire ripped through him, especially now, fresh from battle and with the rush of victory hot in his blood. He took a step toward her, halting only because he was so furious that he'd erred about her.

She *was* the sea siren from the kettle steam. And he'd been so sure she was innocent.

Now ...

She'd proved that her dark magic was potent. She might be trapped in Donata's thrall, but she was the more skilled.

Who but a powerful she-devil could make a score of Viking ships and their crews simply vanish?

It was unthinkable.

So frightening, he doubted he'd sleep well for weeks.

And he was the Viking Slayer.

Nothing had scared him since he was a suckling bairn at his mother's breast. And though he'd never admit it, he suspected he'd been fearless even then.

Yet this day, here at Loch Gairloch, and in the midst of some damned fine fighting, the sea vixen had shown her true colors, teaching him the new face of terror.

And still he burned for her.

Chapter 11

She'd spelled him.

Magnus was sure of it. Why else would her shivering have shaken him to the core, his heart turning over when he'd stepped near to glower at her and then caught the chattering of her teeth? What other reason outside a witchy one could make him pledge to find her clothes?

How could any female save Satan's own seductress hold such power over him that just looking at her made him ache to roll her beneath him and bed her?

She wasn't a witch, she claimed.

She was a *too*-rist.

Magnus hardened his expression as he watched her fuss with the bearskin, smoothing the cloak's heavy furred folds. *Penseal-where'er.* He shuddered, wondering if she'd made up the name to muddle his wits. But the word had sounded true on her tongue. A small part of him believed her. Her horror and anger were too real.

Even now, she glared at him.

"You call me a witch. Don't you think I would've have used my craft to conjure clothes if I were?" She jutted her chin, defiance in her tone. "Or maybe cast you into a three-toed, wart-backed toad!"

Magnus spluttered.

Beside him, Orosius hooted.

"Keep out of this, you loon." Magnus bent a look at the seer. He'd forgotten Orosius was still there, hovering close by, his good ear tilted toward them.

"She speaks true, what?" The seer's words proved he hadn't missed a word. "If she were a witch, she'd have made good both those threats, eh?"

"That's exactly what I meant." Margo seized her advantage.

"Humph." Magnus folded his arms. He determined to ignore both of them.

"Your friend only stated half of it." She was suddenly toe to toe with him, having moved with incredible stealth while he'd been fuming. "If I had any witchy powers, I'd zap myself out of here. I always thought I'd love to see medieval Scotland. And then when I—" Her voice cracked and she swallowed, her eyes glistening as she pressed a fist to her lips.

"You've upset the lass." Orosius turned a dark look on him.

"Bah!" Magnus cut the air with his hand. "I've done naught but find a mantle to cover her, you arse." Even so, heat shot up his neck and a muscle twitched in his jaw.

He *had* put the sheen of tears in her eyes.

He would not allow himself to feel bad for her.

But he *did*.

And the knowledge only made him the angrier.

So he went over to her and took her chin in his hand and tilted her face upward so she had to meet his eye. "I'll only ask this once, lass. Answer me true. Did you use dark powers to fire-blast the Vikings, knocking them and their dragon ships into infinity?"

"Something knocked *me* into the ether and"—her eyes flashed blue sparks at him—"much as I wanted to be here, I'm now sorry I came."

She broke away from him and set her hands on her hips, trying to look fierce.

"You're not a hero, Magnus MacBride." Her words gave his heart a jolt. "You're an ogre."

"Hah!" Orosius thumped his shoulder. "She knows you well, aye?"

Magnus ignored him.

Tears sparkled on the sea vixen's lashes and he could see the wild beat of her pulse at her throat. She was distraught, likely terrified.

And her horror echoed through him like a distant pain, minding him of another young blond woman who'd trusted him to protect her and then died cruelly when he'd failed to keep her safe.

This woman wasn't Liana.

Yet the longer he stood watching her heart beat in her throat and seeing how she struggled to keep her composure, the more he felt drawn to her.

Steeling himself, he fought against the urge to pull her into his arms again. She was stunningly beautiful and even more desirable than in the kettle vision. But it was her courage that most impressed him. He could feel his heart racing with admiration. And—the admission disturbed him—he had the uncomfortable feeling that she could see into his soul. That it was breaking her heart that he doubted her. Even so, he had to know the truth.

Much as he was glad to rid his coasts of Vikings, he preferred banishing them on his own and in the tried-and-true ways.

He did so with the wicked thrusts and slices of Vengeance's trusty blade. A fine Norse battle-ax, when the need arose. *Sea-Raven* and his other ships, and as many good and loyal fighting men as he could gather to his banner. That was how a warlord dealt with Vikings.

They didn't use dark magic.

Such was life in his world.

If Margo spoke true, what he needed to do now was help her return to wherever she belonged.

So he cupped her face again, this time brushing his thumb back and forth along her jaw, hoping to soothe her. "Tell me how you came to be here and I'll try to find a way to return you safely to your own realm. Then—"

"I'm from Pennsylvania, not a realm." She twisted away from his grasp, the movement causing the bearskin cloak to fall open for a moment, giving him a fine look at her golden female curls and sleek thighs.

He also caught a glimpse of her breasts, which, just then, jigged enticingly.

Lust speared him, his entire body tightening.

"Keep yourself covered." He scowled at her, his moment of chivalry gone. Too much temptation waited behind the mantle's furred edges and she'd already pushed him past his limits. "Or are you trying to tempt me?"

"I'd rather have you believe me." She looked at him levelly, without her earlier belligerence. She wore an expression he couldn't quite place. And her eyes shone so brightly that his heart hurt.

He *did* want her.

And he couldn't look away from her luminous blue eyes, the soft pleading he saw there. He broke the glance and shook back his hair, letting its unbound weight swing about his shoulders, reminding him that he was a warrior. A man not swayed by naked bouncing breasts, sleek, shapely thighs, or even beseeching looks from sparkling sapphire eyes.

"I don't know what happened to the Vikings." She stepped closer, placing a hand on his arm. Her touch spilled through him, reaching places he shouldn't allow her. "I can't explain how I came here, though I'll admit I've long been hoping for such a miracle.

"Just not like this." She glanced at the cliffs edging the strand and Magnus saw a shudder ripple through her. "This was not my dream."

Magnus nodded. "I'm sure it wasn't."

Although he wasn't sure of anything.

Following her gaze, he wondered what she saw that troubled her. He saw only a rocky headland, a few dunes covered with marram grass. A morning sky, thick with low, dark clouds. "Where is Pen*seal* . . ." He frowned, unable to pronounce the name. "Pen—"

"Pennsylvania." A thread of pride ran through her words. "It's a beautiful place, very special. New Hope—where I'm from—is especially nice. But it isn't Scotland and I've always dreamed of—"

She broke off, her eyes rounding as the color drained from her face. "Oh, my God!" She pressed both hands to her cheeks. "I think I know what happened to the Vikings. I might have done it, after all. I—"

"Dinnae say another word!" Magnus clamped a hand over her mouth and glared at Orosius, who'd edged so close his big booted feet were almost nudging Magnus's own. "You'll hear the tale after I have, you long-nosed rascal."

"Could be I already ken how she did it?" Orosius sounded smug.

Magnus didn't care.

Ignoring the lout, he started pulling Margo across the strand, away from the seer and the surf line where his men stood in sullen, suspicious circles. Honorably, they still had their backs to the strand. Some had already boarded *Sea-Raven* and the other longboats, and were clearly waiting for Magnus's command to pick up the oars and beat south to Redpoint, where they'd planned to slay more Vikings.

For now, his men would have to wait.

Margo—he realized he'd been calling her by her given name, not "sea witch" or "*too*-rist"—said she knew how she'd banished the Norsemen.

It was his duty as chieftain and warlord to hear what she'd done.

Unfortunately, his ears filled with the sound of Orosius's hurrying feet.

"Ho, Magnus, wait!" Orosius caught up with them near the bottom of the cliffs. "I ken what it was. She used a Highland Curs—"

"A Highland Cursing Stone," Margo finished for Orosius. She looked at him, deciding by his wild and rustic appearance that he was some kind of pagan hermit.

Or maybe he was a warrior monk.

Whatever he was, she liked him.

He reminded her of the bearded eccentric who carved the Elder Futhark rune sets that Patience sold at Ye Olde Pagan Times. Old enough to be her grandfather, Earl Wyndhall was the same kind of big, lumbering man as Orosius. And she suspected that, like Earl, Orosius enjoyed being cantankerous. She'd also bet that he shared Earl's soft heart, even if he'd never admit it.

So she smiled at him now. And the dark frown that settled on Magnus's face as she did so made her feel all the better.

She wouldn't swear it, but she almost believed he might be jealous.

"So you cursed the Northmen?" Magnus sounded displeased again.

"Not intentionally." She hadn't. "But I might've vanquished them when I found myself here and called out the word 'Viking' as I clutched a stone I'd picked up on the strand. It might have been a Highland Cursing Stone, a magical stone that will banish a foe if you call out their name while holding the stone."

"Aye, just!" Orosius nodded. "That be the way of it."

Magnus looked like he couldn't decide whether to roll his eyes or laugh.

He did frown. "I ne'er heard of such stones."

Orosius gave him a reproving look. "You would have done if you'd paid more heed to my tales beside the fire at Badcall, rather than sitting alone at your high table when everyone else left the dais to make merry in the lower hall.

"Highland Cursing Stones hail from the days when time itself was young." Orosius's voice swelled importantly. "They're relics of the Old Ones and inscribed with ancient runes. If danger is near, you need only to grasp the Cursing Stone and speak the name of the offender."

"Once the name is uttered," Margo put in, "the foe will disappear."

This time Magnus did snort. "If such wonder stones existed, everyone in the Highlands would be scouring the hills to find one."

"That's just it." Margo remembered the legends from Patience's books on Celtic magic.

She shifted beneath the bearskin, not wanting to seem ungrateful. But the cloak was terribly itchy.

"Such powers were often misused by those who sought to wield them to their own gain and not, as intended, as protection for the innocent." She looked at Magnus, pleased that she still had his attention. "As a result, it's believed the Old Ones took action, scattering the indestructible stones across the land. Only a few were said to exist and they were all hidden in remote places.

"Areas where there were many similar-looking stones." She took a breath, remembering how the stone's warmth and energy had flowed through her fingers and up her arm, filling her body with its power. "The ancients hoped that doing so would lessen the chances of the Cursing Stones ever again falling into the wrong hands.

"If they should"—a chill rippled down her spine at this part—"a further spell was cast over the stones so that the magical runic script inscribed around their edges will appear to most as an ordinary quartz band encircling the stone. Only those of—"

"Pure heart"—Orosius boomed the rest, flashing a meaningful glance at Magnus—"and in dire need can see the enchanted runes, and then only briefly."

"Aye, well." Magnus looked at Margo. "You're saying you picked up one of the Cursing Stones and then banished the Vikings by calling out their name?"

Margo shrugged. "I told you, I don't know. But I can guess. And so I think that's what happened."

She paused to tuck her hair behind an ear. His suspicion hung in the air between them, the guarded look in his eyes making her defensive. "I was holding a stone and it did have a band of white quartz around the middle. And"—she stood straighter—"I did see runes flash red along the quartz ring. That's all I remember before, well, what happened."

Magnus nodded. "I will think on the possibility."

It wasn't the response Margo had hoped for, but as it wasn't a full denial, her heart soared.

"She speaks true." Orosius sided with her. "I saw her find the stone. It's why—"

"Saw her where?" Magnus rounded on him. "Here at Loch Gairloch or in your kettle steam?"

"Here, you nosy brine drinker." Orosius tapped his head, glaring at Magnus. "I dreamed it. That's why I came along on *Sea-Raven.*"

He jammed his hands on his hips and thrust out his bearded chin. "Belike I knew you'd think the poor lassie was the devil's own helpmate or something worse. I wanted to be around if you had any fool ideas when you saw what I knew would happen here this morn."

"I see." Magnus did.

Orosius might make him grind his teeth, but he didn't lie.

"So you believe me now?" Margo touched his arm, the light graze of her fingertips sending warmth all through him. "Please say you do. If you don't"—she glanced at the sea, then back at him—"I don't think I can bear being here."

"I . . ." Magnus pulled back his arm and reached to rub his nape.

But the truth stood in Margo's eyes just as the tight, burning knot deep inside him had been trying to tell him the while.

She was what she said she was.

A *too*-rist, though he wasn't about to admit the term baffled him.

Traveler, he could accept. But no woman journeyed about full naked and unescorted.

"If you saw Donata, she will have spelled a vision-image of herself from behind St. Eithne's walls." It was the closest he'd go to admitting he accepted such an out-landish tale. "That means she possesses greater powers than we knew."

"She was evil." Margo shivered again, visibly.

"You know what we must do?" Orosius spat on the pebbly strand.

"I'll no' kill a woman, howe'er vile she is." Magnus was firm. "We'll order the good abbess at St. Eithne's to keep a constant guard on her, even while she sleeps. If she's e'er under someone's eye, she'll no' be able to spin her foul deeds and curses."

"Say you." The seer looked doubtful.

"I do." Magnus threw a glance at the *Sea-Raven*,

where some of his men now stood on the steering platform, watching him. "Margo"—he turned to her now, setting his hands on her shoulders—"my men and I have business at Redpoint, a wee fishing village south of Gairloch. You cannae stay here on your own. Are you for joining us on the *Sea-Raven*?"

She didn't hesitate. "I'll come, yes. Th-thank you."

The hitch in her voice split Magnus's heart. And the same sweet, heady warmth that had washed through him when she'd rested her fingers on his arm poured through him again now. The sensation was stronger than before, this time melting places that had long been crusted with ice.

"Aye, well." He spoke briskly, hoping she wouldn't notice.

Then, before he could change his mind, he gripped Orosius's arm. "Orosius." He put respect into his tone. "You have a fine way with words. We'll be leaving for Redpoint anon. It'd be a fine help if you'd gather our men and tell them something, anything that comes into your mind, to explain what happened this morn.

"And let them know"—he glanced at Margo—"that we'll have an additional passenger on board the *Sea-Raven*."

"I shall." Orosius grinned and turned on his heel, striding swiftly across the strand.

When he was out of earshot, Magnus slid his hands down from Margo's shoulders, gripping her lightly by the hips. "Donata *is* dangerous. If she saw what you did with the Cursing Stone, she'll use all her powers to find you, hoping to get the stone. And you as well, I vow."

"She wanted to use me to hurt you." Margo confirmed what he now knew to be true. "She said I would distract you and then you'd be—"

"Cut down?" Magnus was beginning to understand the sorceress's scheming.

He grinned, the knowledge empowering him. "You do distract me, sweet. But"—he reached to smooth his thumb lightly over her lips—"no one is going to cut me down.

"Nor is anyone going to hurt you." He looked deep into her eyes, willing her to trust him. "From this moment onward, I'm no' leaving your side."

"That's good." She closed her eyes and took a deep breath, looking relieved.

As he watched her, the warmth inside Magnus swelled and spread. His need to protect her was fierce as the hot flames of desire burning at his loins. Only his wish not to frighten her, and the staring eyes of his men, kept him from pulling her hard against him and kissing her hungrily.

He would soon.

But for now, he was pleased to escort her onto the *Sea-Raven*.

The more he thought about it, the more he liked the notion.

Chapter 12

Margo's second thoughts kicked in as she let Magnus lead her across the strand toward his warship, the *Sea-Raven*. Pausing at the tide line, she stood with one hand holding the bearskin cloak against her nakedness. She puffed her bangs off her forehead, wondering where in the world she'd find the courage to board a medieval ship.

She'd never been keen on boats.

And in addition to looking like a fire-breathing sea serpent, this one was crewed by hard-faced, fierce-bearded men who bristled with arms and surely whetted their sword tips every morning. They were all staring at her. And each one appeared eager to test his blade's sharpness on her. Without exaggeration, they looked hostile.

Some might even say murderous.

Only Orosius was friendly, flashing a broad grin at her before he threw back his plaid and strode into the sea. Head high, he splashed through the surf as if he loved every step, and then vaulted over the side of the waiting longship.

Margo swallowed.

She had to board the *Sea-Raven*.

It wasn't like she had an alternative.

Even if she scrambled back up the cliff, the coastal road would no longer be there. And the Old Harbour Inn wasn't even a blip in anyone's imagination. Empty hills and wilderness would greet her. Perhaps a few villagers who'd take one look at a naked, bearskin-cloaked woman and, thinking the worst, do what Magnus had implied could so easily happen: they'd burn her as a witch.

Hanging around here alone, waiting for the *real* witch to return, was equally unappealing.

The dice had been cast.

And, as so often, she didn't much care for the luck of the throw.

"Oh, dear." She could feel her eyes rounding as the *Sea-Raven* tossed in the surf. Men were raising the ship's square red-and-white striped sail. Others already sat at the rowing benches, ready to get going.

Margo would almost swear the ship looked impatient, straining and eager to shoot forward, cleaving the waves.

Her stomach tightened at the thought. Dread skittered along her nerve endings and her heart was beginning to beat much too fast. Even her palms were growing damp and her mouth had gone bone-dry.

This was so not like her fantasy of time travel.

This was, in two words, the pits.

"We'll no' journey far this day. A wee inlet, Badachro Bay, just off Loch Gairloch, is where we're headed." Magnus was looking down at her, his voice deep, calm, and reassuring.

He knew exactly why she'd stopped so close to the water's edge.

He'd sensed her fear and wanted to take it from her.

Margo shivered a little, his hero image beginning to return.

"My business is a bit south of Badachro, at a place

called Redpoint." He reached to draw the bearskin closer together and then used a huge Celtic pin he took from his own plaid to fasten the cloak more securely. "Some of my men must travel there overland to lay preparation. We'll spend this night in Badachro. We'll moor the *Sea-Raven* at Sgeir Ghlas—"

"Where?" Margo blinked. She was glad to be distracted from the sensation of his strong, warm fingers brushing against her skin as he eased the brooch pin through the thick skin of the cloak.

"*Sgeir Ghlas* means 'gray rock.'" He stood back, the pin now in place. "It's the smallest of several islands in the bay and is a secure sheltering place for *Sea-Raven*. My men will sleep aboard ship."

"And us?" The intimacy of those two words speared straight to Margo's center, the tingling anticipation almost making her forget her fear of the tossing longship.

He meant to pass the night with her somewhere, and alone.

She looked at him, waiting.

"We'll stay the night onshore in a wee cothouse." He looked down at her then, regarding her as if he expected her to argue. But—she couldn't help it—the thought filled her with giddy expectation.

"A cothouse is a small cottage, right?" Margo's pulse quickened as sensual awareness beat through her, making her almost light-headed.

She knew what a cothouse was.

Magnus was watching her closely, a slight smile playing across his lips. His dark eyes were branding her, setting her on fire. "Aye, it's little more than a reed-thatched hut." His deep voice stirred her, and she ached to touch him. "But there'll be a store of driftwood we can burn and I'll bring enough plaids to make you a comfortable pallet to sleep on."

Plaids to sleep on.

Margo nearly gasped with pleasure.

She bit her lip, almost afraid to breathe. She could feel hot, sensual want sizzling between them. It was like an unrestrained electrical current, charging the air as it leapt around them, fanning her desire.

"I'm sure it'll be fine." Was that her voice, so breathy and excited?

It was, but she didn't care.

This was her dream coming true. Her luck was changing, transformed with the mention of tartan. Magnus would be on that plaid with her, she knew. They'd be naked, hotly entwined, and kissing all through the night. She might even ask him about the kettle-steam episode.

Life was looking good.

Magnus glanced out to sea, then back at her. "There's also a woman at Badachro, Orla Finney, who will surely have an extra gown and whate'er other female goods you might need."

Margo's elation faded. "A woman?"

"Aye, she is a joy woman, if you ken the term?" His dark eyes twinkled, showing her a very appealing side of him.

If he weren't speaking of a medieval prostitute.

Margo frowned. "I know what *joy woman* means."

He grinned then, dimples flashing. "Orla is a friend, no more. She'd a good-hearted woman who serves the fishermen and others who visit these shores. As she doesn't bar her door to Northmen, she also provides me with much appreciated news of their whereabouts and doings."

"Oh." Margo felt a wave of relief wash through her.

Until the morning sun shone through a cloud and the sudden light reflected brightly off the mailed shirts and swords of the men crowding the *Sea-Raven*. They were stony-faced, regarding her with sullen, down-drawn brows.

"They will no' hurt you." Magnus stepped close, smoothed her hair back from her face. "They answer to me and know I'd slit them from their bellies to their gullets if they so much as look cross-eyed at you."

Margo didn't remind him that they were doing that now.

She didn't have the breath.

The ray of sunlight also fell across the dragon ship, picking out the fearsome details of the red-and-black-painted raven heads carved on the high stem and prow. The birds appeared to be screeching, their wide-opened beaks seeming eager to chomp into enemies.

Or her, she was sure.

"It isn't your men. . . ." Not so much, anyway. "It's just that"—she looked up at him, the concern shadowing his eyes touching her so deeply that it made her chest hurt—"I've never been much for boats."

There, she'd said it.

Magnus's expression cleared, a smile spreading across his face. "You will love the *Sea-Raven*, ne'er you fear. There are few greater joys than feeling life surge into a fine ship as she dances across the waves, spume gilding her sides and the wind in your face. The glory of it can make a man feel like a god."

"I'm a woman."

"Aye, you are." Magnus's voice warmed, his gaze sliding over her from her windblown hair to her bare feet, now lapped by icy cold surf. "And"—he took her face in his hands, looking deep into her eyes—"you mind me that there are much greater pleasures than standing at the steering oar and feeling my ship's heartbeat thrum beneath my feet."

"O-o-oh . . ." Margo's breath caught, his words slipping through her like honeyed seduction, making her own heart beat hard and slow.

For a moment, her fantasy image of him flashed across her mind. As in her dreams, she saw him as a tall, powerfully built Highlander with his long raven hair tied at his nape and a plaid slung boldly over one shoulder. Gleaming mail winked from beneath his plaid and he wore a huge, wicked-looking sword strapped low at his hip. Gold and silver rings glittered on his powerful arms, and his handsome face was hard, almost as if carved of stone.

Now she saw him for real.

Vivid and alive, in full 3-D color in his own time and place. His rich Scottish burr seduced her senses and the heated look in his dark eyes tempted everything female inside her.

The wonder of such a miracle was almost too much to bear.

He wore his hair loose now, the sleek, blue-black mane spilling nearly to his waist. Sunlight fell across the glossy strands, emphasizing their silky sheen, and before she could stop herself, she reached to run her fingers lightly down the flowing raven tresses.

"Have a care, lass." He seized her wrist, locking his fingers firmly around her arm as he moved her hand away from his hair. "My men are watching and they may think you're laying a spell on me."

Margo could hardly breathe. "And if I was?"

"You already have." The smoldering heat in his eyes proved it. "As I think you know?"

Margo felt herself blush all over. "I know"—she moistened her lips—"nothing."

She did know.

At least, she guessed. *Hoped.*

Something had shifted since he began believing her,

and that altering perception unleashed a powerful connection between them. Margo had never felt so drawn to a man, nor so desperate to be crushed in his powerful embrace. Need heated the air around them, sizzling like living desire, and making her ache to be held tight against him. She craved the feel of his big, strong hands sweeping over her bared skin, questing and exploring, even as she ran her own fingers along the tight, muscle-hewn lines of his warrior's body.

She craved him with a longing she wouldn't have dreamed possible.

The hunger in his eyes said he wanted her as badly.

But she needed to hear the words. She couldn't guess how much time she might have in his world, so she wanted to see the burn of desire darkening his eyes, hear his liquid-seduction voice deepen and turn rough like skeins of smooth, raw silk rolling all over her.

"Now you are speaking untruths." His tone was low and gruff now. "You know fine what you do to me." He held her gaze, circling his thumb over the sensitive skin of her wrist before he released her. "This night, if you will let me, I'll prove it to you."

Margo nearly swooned.

A swirl of emotions rose inside her, elation, giddy excitement, and a tiny sliver of fear. If he meant what she thought and they made love, and she then lost him, she'd never get over the pain.

For now, her blood rushed and tingles danced across her nerves. The very idea of actually sleeping with him—and on a plaid!—had her knees knocking and her heart hammering like a drum. Then one of the men on his ship shouted and waved at him. He turned away from her toward the *Sea-Raven*—once again all medieval warlord.

"Come, lass, we must be off." He took her hand, leading her into the surf. "Orosius will have ordered the men to stretch an extra sailcloth over the stern. You'll be sheltered there, with plenty of plaids and furs to keep you warm. I'll be close by, on the steering platform."

Margo froze, the icy water foaming about her knees. "I'm not worried about keeping warm." All thoughts of lovemaking had fled her mind. "It's the possibility of drowning that scares me."

"Bah! *Sea-Raven* surrenders no one to the briny depths." Magnus reached for her, scooping her into his arms and holding her tight against him as he plunged into the surf. He strode through the tossing waves, heading away from the shore and right up to his beast-headed dragon ship.

"No ill will come to you, I promise." He leaned down to kiss the top of her head.

"There's always a first time." The wind caught her words, snatching them away before he could hear.

"Aye, there is." He flashed a grin at her, proving that he had heard. "And I'll make this one so good you'll beg me to sail on *Sea-Raven*, knowing the bliss that awaits you at the journey's end."

His vow sent delicious shivers racing through her, making her feel hot and tingly even as cold, choppy water swirled around them, drenching them to the waist.

But then the *Sea-Raven*'s high-prowed sides loomed before them and Magnus was holding her above his head, shouting for someone named Ewan to help her board. A strapping young lad with a broad, freckled face appeared at once, leaning down and plucking her over the ship's side as if she weighed no more than a sack of goose down.

"My lady." He grinned and set her gently on her feet near an empty rowing bench. "Ewan, at your service," he offered, helping her onto the oar bank. Leaning close to her ear, he lowered his voice. "Thon buffoons aren't as grim as they look. They'll come around. Ne'er you worry."

Then he was gone, hurrying away to join Orosius near the big steering oar.

And now that he'd left and she had a clear view down the center aisle of the ship, she immediately saw why he'd given her a warning.

The men lining the oar banks were turning their gazes aside, avoiding her eyes. One shuddered and several others made signs against evil. A small, wiry man who looked hard and strong despite his size, even appeared to be muttering a silent prayer.

Margo blinked.

I don't bite, she started to say, until the genuine fear on their faces made her hold her tongue. In their world, she knew, they had good cause to think she was a witch. Even so, such a reception wasn't a very propitious beginning.

But before their rejection could sting too badly, Magnus swung over the rail, landing lightly beside her. "Come, you'll have more comfort at the stern." Taking her hand, he pulled her to her feet, sliding his arm around her waist to steady her as he led her down the narrow aisle to the makeshift shelter he'd arranged for her.

When she was settled, he reached to adjust the bearskin cloak about her shoulders. That done, he threw open a kist and withdrew a fresh plaid, slinging it expertly across his own shoulders. Then he shut the chest and straightened, bracing his hands on his hips as he peered down at her.

It was a look that made her breath catch in her throat. Could he be any more handsome with his plaid highlighting his broad shoulders and the wind molding his kilt to his powerful thighs? Was there anything sexier than watching his long raven hair streaming in the blowing sea air?

Margo didn't think so.

Unless it was pure male hunger blazing in his eyes as he kept his dark gaze locked with hers.

"Dinnae make me regret believing you." He leaned close, bracing one hand on the side of the stern platform, caging her, as his gaze slid into her, intimate and deep. "I ne'er give my trust lightly."

"You can trust me." Margo hoped fervently he could. As the least techy, scientific person in the world—she so *wasn't* a physicist—she couldn't be sure she might not evaporate any minute, disappearing in front of his eyes as Donata had vanished before her.

It was a possibility she didn't want to consider.

She especially didn't care to think about it when just breathing in the same air was making her weak-kneed with wanting him.

"Raise!" A male voice Margo recognized as Ewan's roared the sudden command, and even before she could blink, twenty-four oars shot upward, sparkling water flying from the poised wooden blades.

"Dear God!" She jumped, terror sweeping her. "What are they doing?"

"Naught they shouldn't be. We're leaving." Leaning in again, he reached one hand around her neck, forcing her to look at him and not the rowers. "You've no reason to be afraid, *mo ghaoil*." The Gaelic sounded rich and beautiful on his tongue, making her forget her fear.

He'd used the Gaelic term for "my dear."

Margo knew the word from her failed attempt to learn the language.

But before she could consider the implications of Magnus calling her his dear, Ewan shouted again. "Lower and strike!"

The oar blades whipped downward, biting into the sea as the *Sea-Raven* surged forward in a burst of spray and cheers from the men. They were flying, shooting across the waves at incredible speed. Cold, white water shrieked along the hull and seabirds screamed above them as the oars flashed, bringing the *Sea-Raven* to life.

"Holy moly!" Margo was going to die.

"Hush, you." Magnus's warm breath touched her cheek. His fingers slipped from her nape into her hair, twining there, caressing. Delicious chills rippled down her spine and all through her, soothing and tantalizing her.

"O-o-oh . . ." His touch was magic.

"Shhh, I said." He was massaging the back of her head now, letting her hair spill over his hand.

And then he kissed her, soft and sweet. A slow, barely there brushing of his lips back and forth over hers, and so scintillatingly intimate that she forgot all about the men on the rowing benches and what they were doing with the oars.

She didn't even care that she was on a boat.

A medieval warship to boot.

Magnus was kissing her and nothing else mattered.

Nothing at all.

Something that would've mattered to her if she'd known was the icy chill pouring off a petite, raven-haired woman who sat on a stool in a tiny, dank cell many heather miles from Loch Gairloch and the *Sea-Raven*. St. Eithne's by name, the nunnery could easily have been called hell. Good, holy women did live quietly there, praying, stitching, and offering viands to any beggars who called at their gates. But the nuns of St. Eithne took their piety seriously, shunning all comforts and graces for themselves and any females unfortunate enough to find themselves in the sisters' care.

Donata Greer was one such unwilling guest.

And if another timid, uncooperative servant brought her a wooden bowl of gruel instead of the cold, sliced capon breast and roasted meats she demanded, she'd rake the miserable creature's face with her poison-tipped nails, ensuring she wouldn't be bothered again.

She'd sooner eat dust off the floor and drink raindrops from the window ledge than suffer the unpleasantness of slime-coated oats and soured ale.

The good sisters of St. Eithne's clearly weren't aware of her importance. She should have been afforded some status as the sister of the late Godred Greer, the mightiest chieftain to walk the land until Magnus MacBride had slain him. She was also the lover of Bjorn Bone-Grinder, a powerful Viking raider, whose amassed riches and growing number of followers would soon make him a formidable warlord, feared the length and breadth of Scotland's west coast and far beyond.

Above all, she was a highly skilled witch.

A sorceress who planned to take her dark magic to never-before-reached heights.

If she could extract herself from St. Eithne's infernal clutches.

Seething, Donata rose and kicked the rusty brazier that held an ashy lump of peat no larger than a newt's eyeball. She'd do better to strip herself naked and burn her clothes, maybe even her fine silver and jet jewelry.

Bone-Grinder would shower treasures on her when she escaped this miserable pit.

But she didn't want to annoy the good sisters overmuch.

Shocking them with her unclothed beauty might inspire them to whip her loveliness from her. Such punishments weren't unknown and she'd seen the birch switches in a corner of the abbess's quarters.

She also didn't want them to deny her the gruel, much as she detested the pap.

She needed her strength.

Finding the perfect woman to crush Magnus Mac-Bride had cost her much. She'd spent weeks bent over her runes, casting and studying them, always seeking. Until—at last—the very curtain of time had rolled back for her, revealing the female she'd sought so diligently.

Transporting herself into Margo Menlove's world to fetch her had nearly broken her, draining all her energy and leaving her almost powerless.

But she was resilient.

She'd recovered swiftly.

And even if her plans hadn't gone quite as she'd hoped, bringing the end of Magnus MacBride, she now had a much higher goal.

It was an ambition that would wipe Magnus and his soon-to-be lover off the face of the earth.

She'd be done with them, and anyone else who dared to cross her.

She and Bone-Grinder could even rule the world.

If her energies hadn't dwindled, preventing her from accompanying Margo into Magnus's presence, she would have snatched the Cursing Stone then and there. But she'd *seen* the stone, and its power.

That was enough.

She would find a way to escape.

Then . . .

Donata pressed her hands against the small of her back and stretched, preening like a cat.

Unfortunately, the horrid clanging from St. Eithne's bell tower signaled that the dinner hour was nigh. Soon, light footsteps would patter up to her locked cell and then the small hatch in the door would slide open, a thin, pale face appearing to announce the arrival of her nightly gruel.

As always, Donata would assume a humble mien and accept the slop they gave her.

And when she'd suffered its taste, she'd return to her stool and her spellings. She'd work long into the small hours, plying her darkest magic. As the good sisters of St. Eithne's slept, she'd spin her plans.

Soon, she'd be triumphant.

It was only a matter of time.

Chapter 13

Magnus's men knew that he had kissed her.

Margo was sure of it.

No one said anything. Nor did any of them openly show disrespect. Even so, as she braced herself against the edge of the *Sea-Raven*'s steering platform, trying to keep her balance, she could feel their displeasure rippling the air. With one or two exceptions, they were horrified that their leader had succumbed to the wiles of a woman they believed to be a witch.

Just now the *Sea-Raven* rowed steadily through Loch Gairloch. But when they'd first surged away from shore and Magnus led her down the ship's narrow center aisle to the bow platform so she could better watch the *Sea-Raven*'s high-beaked prow slicing through the waves, more than one oarsman had pointedly leaned away from her as they'd passed.

The slights were infinitesimal.

Magnus hadn't noticed.

Margo, whose heart had ever only beat for Scotland, wished the men didn't find it so difficult to accept her. They didn't need to *like* her, though that would be nice. A good start would've been for them to recognize that she wasn't going to pull a tall black hat from behind her back and call out the flying monkeys.

Even if she wouldn't mind the wicked little creatures buzzing overhead, keeping the *Sea-Raven* afloat.

Suspecting even flying monkeys would have trouble finding her here, not to mention a dragon ship with a crew of fierce-eyed, big-bearded men in mail, she drew a deep breath of the cold, salt air as they beat past Gairloch's waterfront.

Had she really been there in her own time, just a short while ago?

It seemed impossible.

Inconceivable that Wee Hughie and everyone on the Heritage Tour could still be at the Old Harbour Inn, enjoying the Highland Night ceilidh. Even now, as the *Sea-Raven* sped her right by them. So close, but worlds and centuries apart, an impassable chasm yawning between.

Yet she'd made it. . . .

She glanced at Magnus, standing at the steering oar with Ewan and an older, kindly man introduced to her as Calum, Ewan's grandfather.

"Do you need aught?" As Magnus met her gaze, the innocent contact shivered through her, making her face heat because she was sure he knew he just needed to look at her and she melted.

"A sip o' *uisge beatha*?" He patted the leather-covered flask attached to his sword belt. "Fine Highland spirits to keep you warm?"

"No, thank you." Margo almost choked.

If she were any warmer, she'd combust.

And if she imbibed anything as supposedly potent as early whisky, she'd surely get seasick.

What she needed—beyond the obvious, namely Magnus—was to be on solid ground again. She could see how some people might find speeding across the waves in a medieval warship exhilarating.

But she doubted she'd ever become a fan.

It was too darn scary.

The look of concern in Magnus's eyes said he knew she was still terrified. True dread jellied her bones, and for that reason, she preferred thinking about his kiss. How she wished he'd deepened it, delectable as the kiss had been. Reliving the moment, and all the delicious sensations it'd stirred, kept her mind off the cold, empty water separated from her feet by only a few planks of medieval wood.

Margo shuddered, unable to help herself.

"We'll be at Badachro soon." His gaze was intense. The implications of his words—that a small, firelit cottage and a pallet of plaids awaited them—made her even hotter than before.

She was sure her face must be glowing.

"Why no' enjoy the view the while?" He nodded toward the harbor, already beginning to fall behind them. "Gairloch is a busy settlement."

Margo bit her tongue, wondering what he'd think of New York.

But Calum was leaning close to him now, speaking in his ear. So she did as he suggested, and turned to watch the little township glide past.

Chills swept her as she did.

The dark blue hills hugging the harbor were still there, same as when she'd walked along the quay. Modern inconveniences—oh, how she loved the term—no longer dotted the shore. Instead, a straggle of squat, thatched-roof huts followed the same path as the coast road. And several large driftwood fires burned where she'd seen the crusty old fisherman step from a dockside warehouse. Rough-hewn, red-faced men worked the fires, using the smoke to dry fish. The docks were where she remembered, but now they were rickety wooden piers crowded with tubby medieval fishing and trading boats. One or two sleek medieval galleys, similar to Magnus's *Sea-Raven*, were moored close by.

It was like a movie set.

Only real-life.

This was the dream of a lifetime for her, made even more perfect by the rolling mist beginning to slide down the cliffs and drift across the loch's glassy black surface.

Margo's heart began to pound.

She'd never tire of Highland mist. It swirled and glistened, a shimmering gossamer veil, softening the day. This was a still world full of natural sound and iridescence, showing her the origin of every sentimental myth about the Highlands. She glanced at Magnus, her gaze skimming over the hard line of his jaw and cheekbones, and, because she'd been thinking of his kiss, his incredibly sensuous mouth.

She admired his long, black hair streaming in the wind, his broad shoulders limned against the steep blue hills. His arm rings flashed bright, rivaling the gleaming white crests of each swell creaming past the *Sea-Raven*. Her awareness of Magnus beside her was so strong that her pulse raced. He truly belonged here, in this beautiful, timeless place.

Watching him with such grandeur all around them helped her to ignore the long lines of dangerous-looking breakers rolling in from the open sea.

Until an outraged bellow shattered the peace.

"Hand o'er my shirt or you'll go to sleep this night as a woman!"

Margo started, whirling around to see the short, wiry man she'd noticed earlier brandishing a dirk at the belly of a larger man. Nimbly, the smaller man hopped about in front of his foe, his stature giving him an advantage in the aisle's narrow space.

The big man held a tattered rag aloft, waving it out of the little man's reach. " 'Tis mad you are, Dugan, keeping a shirt after the Greer witch cursed it. I'll have my wife sew you a new one. She—"

"I dinnae want another!" Dugan jumped, trying to grab the bit of dirty cloth. "Thon's my good-luck shirt, you flat-footed loon!"

"Magnus! Please, do something." Margo flashed a glance at him. But he only winked and cut the air with a hand, the gesture telling her the two men fought often and perhaps gladly.

Still . . .

Margo didn't like it. Roughhousing was one thing. Men going at each other with knives was something else altogether and she didn't want to see blood spill.

She'd seen enough bloodshed at the little strand in Gairloch.

"Two ales with Orla and you can have your smelly shirt." The big man kept the prize in the air.

Dugan, who obviously possessed an extra shirt, for he wasn't bare-chested, roared and made another fast-wristed flourish with his dirk. This time, he sliced the big man's plaid, though he didn't draw blood.

"You can buy your own ale from Orla." He was still dancing about, his blade flashing. "I'll have my shirt. And it's no' cursed, it isn't. The smears are mud Donata threw at us when we took her to St. Eithne's. They're no' witchy-curse stains, you fool."

"Then why can't the laundresses get rid of them, eh? They're the devil's hoofprints, they are." The big man balled the shirt in his fist, making to pitch it into the water.

"Nae! Dinnae do it!" True panic filled Dugan's eyes.

Dropping his dagger, he flew at the other man just as he drew back his arm.

"Wait!" Margo sprinted down the aisle, grabbing the big man's arm before she could think through her actions. Surprise worked in her favor and she easily plucked the shirt from his grasp.

"Saints o' mercy!" The giant leapt backward, stumbling over an oar bench in his haste to get away from her.

Dugan accepted the shirt when she handed it to him, his flushed face showing a strange mix of fear and appreciation. "It do be my best shirt, see?" He smoothed the soiled cloth over his arm. "I dinnae care that it has mud stains. It brings me good luck."

"Everyone needs that." Margo smiled at him, pleased when the fear eased from his face. "I could use some good luck, too, see? But"—she decided to take a chance—"I do know something that might get the stains out of your shirt."

Dugan's eyes rounded. "The laundresses have tried to clean it twice now. And"—he shook his head—"my own wife has washed it three times."

"Then tell her to try again, this time when the moon is waning." Margo suspected the shirt had been washed at full or waxing moon, the worst possible time to get rid of stains. "If she does, using very little soap and lots of clean, fresh water, I'm sure the smears will disappear."

If they didn't, she might be toast.

But as a Luna Harmonist, she did know how to take advantage of the moon's helpful rhythms and cycle. Waning moon was the best time for housework and laundry.

It was worth a try.

"Waning moon, eh?" Dugan cocked his head, eyeing her.

At the steering oar, Magnus looked amused.

Margo stood straighter. "That's right. Your wife can come to me if she has any questions."

"I'll tell her, I will." The little man actually bowed. Then he scuttled off down the aisle, making for his place on the rowing benches. He turned back to her before he sat down. "I thank you, Lady Margo."

"My pleasure." Margo struggled to speak past the thickness in her throat.

Who would've thought a little man named Dugan would make her cry?

Or help her break the ice with Magnus's crew?

"That was well-done."

Magnus spoke from just behind her, close by her ear. Her heart leapt. She could feel his warmth flowing into her as he placed his hands on her shoulders and turned her to face him.

"I didnae ken you were no' just bonnie but also a champion for the needy." His voice went a shade deeper, the words meant for her alone.

"Dugan didn't strike me as needy." Margo looked up at him, wondering if he'd guess how needy she was. "He could've done some serious damage with his dagger if he'd wanted."

"He wouldn't have because he and Brodie are good friends." He kept his hands on her shoulders and the connection sent spools of pleasure through her. "Brodie would've still hurled the shirt into the sea. He's superstitious and thinks Donata cursed the shirt."

Margo shivered, almost as if a cloud had passed over the sun.

"Did she really throw mud at Dugan?" She could believe it.

"Donata fights like a hellcat when riled." Magnus circled his thumbs lightly across her neck, intensifying physical sensations that already felt unbearably sensual. "Mud, sticks, rocks, anything she could get her hands on, I'm told. I wasn't there when my men took her to St. Eithne's, a nunnery where she's now kept under guard in a cell."

"Yet she appeared to me." Margo frowned, his touch making it difficult to think. "I saw her likeness."

"You did." He stepped back, ran a hand through his hair. "No' Donata out of her cell at St. Eithne's, but her wickedness cast in a spell-conjured guise."

Margo shuddered. "That makes her the more dangerous because she can't be contained."

"So we could say, aye."

His face cleared then, and a smile twitched at the corner of his lips. "This day is full of wonders."

Margo blinked. "What?"

"Here's you, standing midship in the aisle and no' reaching for a handhold." He rubbed his chin, observing her. "Truth is, you're no' even swaying."

"Oh!" Margo lurched crazily, grabbing for him before she fell. "I can't—"

"You were doing fine until I told you." He took her arm, leading her past the men at the rowing benches and into the soft darkness cast by the sailcloth shelter at the *Sea-Raven*'s stern platform.

He released her only long enough to undo the ties at the edge of the makeshift tent. The heavy flap dropped into place, separating them from the long center aisle and the men on the rowing benches.

"That is better." His voice roughened as he checked the flap, apparently making certain it fell properly. "We'll be in open water soon. You'll be protected here."

When he turned back to her, his eyes darkened and he started across the small space between them. A sliver of light slanted through a corner of the shelter, glinting off the bright steel of his long sword. The sight made her heart race, reminding her who he was and *when* they were.

She bit her lip, inhaling deeply.

He came closer, his gaze never leaving hers. "Margo."

The way he said her name, Mar-*go*, the last two letters rising on a lilt after he rolled the *r*, almost undid her. Her heart tumbled in her chest. An aching hunger began somewhere deep inside her. Fierce and insistent, it wound so tight she feared she'd break.

He was still looking at her, but she couldn't speak.

Then he was right in front of her, so near that she wasn't sure if the loud roar in her ears was her own blood racing, or his.

"You are a wonder. And I . . ." He trailed off, shaking his head.

Margo scanned his face, expectant, hoping.

"I dinnae ken what to make of you." His tone roughened even more. "I do want you."

Once again, he set his hands on her shoulders and stood peering down at her. The shelter's closed flap muted the creak and splash of the ship's oars, and even the grunts of the straining rowers. But the intimacy cast by the dim, tightly confined space was fiercely loud. Vivid awareness pulsed between them, thickening the air. Anticipation, excitement, all kinds of heady emotions, swelled and eddied around them, making words unnecessary.

Margo could tell he felt the same potent energy.

She could hardly breathe.

"Tell me, lass. . . ." He lifted a section of her hair, letting the strands glide across his fingers. "If Dugan's woman washes his shirt by the dark moon, will Donata's mud smears truly disappear?"

"They should." Margo tried not to sigh as his knuckles skimmed her cheek. "The wax and wane of the moon affects every aspect of our lives. All of nature bends to her rhythms and cycles. Those who observe and"—he was tunneling his fingers through her hair now, luscious sensations blurring everything but his caress—"study the moon can do much to help others if they so choose."

"Are you a wisewoman?" His tone held amusement.

Margo was glad he hadn't said witch.

"No." She met his gaze, almost intoxicated by his touch. "I am a woman who has always been fascinated by the moon and made the effort to learn what I could. In my"—she started to say *other life*, but bit back the words because the whole situation still felt so unreal—"hometown, New Hope, I worked as a Luna Harmonist, advising those who came to me."

"So you *are* a spaewife." A smile lightly tugged on his mouth.

"No, I'm not." Margo shook her head. If she were a wisewoman, she'd work a spell that would keep her from getting zapped back into her seat on the Sword of Somerled tour bus. "I'm simply a—"

"You are a beautiful woman who smells of cold winter snow and roses." He closed his eyes briefly and inhaled, as if savoring her scent. When he looked at her again, he touched her face, tracing the back of his hand along the curving line of her cheek.

He rested the whole of his hand against the side of her face. "You are fond of the moon."

"I am." She took a breath as sensual heat built between them. Prickling tingles ignited along her skin, sweet rivers of molten warmth flowing all down her body, rousing and soothing her.

She looked at him, seeing the hard pulse beat at his jaw. He wanted her as much as she desired him. And it wasn't just intense physical attraction. It was more. It was something incredibly powerful from deep within their innermost selves. Maybe from the farthest reaches of their souls, corny as that sounded.

Margo liked corny.

She was an old-fashioned kind of girl.

Her mother used to say that she had been born old. It had been her left-brained, nonfanciful, full-of-logic, parent's way of expressing what Margo preferred to think of as being born out of place and time.

Now she was where she should have been all along. The man she knew she could love through this life and many more was caressing her face and had just said she smelled like clean, cold air and summer roses.

And all she could worry about was accepting a sliver of happiness only to have her luck rear up and snatch it right back from her.

Such things happened in life.

She could almost feel old Murphy—of Murphy's Law—slinking around her and Magnus, watching and waiting, rubbing his hands in anticipation.

Pushing her old nemesis from her mind, she returned to a more dangerous one. "Do you think we should return to Gairloch later and look for the Cursing Stone? I doubt we'd find it. Not now, but—"

"I ordered one of my ships to stay there so the crew could scour the strand." He lifted a brow, watching her. "Did you no' see they didn't leave with us?"

"No." She hadn't seen anything except great sheets of sea spray flying along the *Sea-Raven*'s hull and the two screaming red and black raven heads mounted on the prows. She hadn't wanted to even glance at the other ships, each one equally fearsome.

"Aye, well." He ran one finger down the side of her neck and back up again, as if learning the texture of her. "They're there now, searching. If they find the stone, they'll take it to the edge of the sea and sink it. Such powerful magic has no place here.

"There are too many black-hearted, greed-filled men and dark souls like Donata who'd use such a stone for evil." He frowned, looking fierce again. "Orosius instructed my men, telling them what to seek. Though he warned they'd only turn up similar-looking stones."

"He's right." Margo recalled everything she'd read about the stones. "Highland Cursing Stones only reveal themselves when they wish, or so the legends claim. Their powers are boundless. If they feel threatened in any way and wish to hide, they're said to be able to conjure countless twin stones in less than an eye blink.

"Some folklorists even believe Cursing Stones can vanish and reappear elsewhere, many miles from their original location. Though . . ."

Margo paused when he cupped her face again, the heat of his palm branding her. She wanted to lean into his hand, beg him not to break the contact. She was so aware of his nearness—so close their breath mingled—that the intimate sharing began to make her sex clench, even now.

"Though?" He lifted a brow, waiting.

"Ah . . ." Margo shifted, urgent need rising inside her. She half wondered if he'd worked some kind of desire spell on her.

She cleared her throat. "As powerful as Donata's magic is, perhaps she can route its energy? I'll never know if it was her curse or the stone that brought me here. If she possessed the stone, she'll want it back. If the stone wasn't hers and she saw what happened, she'll be after it, hoping to harness the magic."

Magnus frowned. "Stronger guards will be set on her at St. Eithne's. She'll ne'er have an unobserved moment to weave her dark craft."

Margo wasn't so sure.

She remembered how the vortex-image's eyes had turned silver. The fireball she'd snatched out of thin air and thrown into the sea. Margo felt a chill sweep down her spine, the *hiss* of the fireball hitting the water ringing again in her ears. Donata practiced the blackest of magic and her skills could be unparalleled.

"She frightens me." She hadn't meant to admit it.

"You have naught to fear." He took her face in his hands, looking deep into her eyes. "Donata needs to be afraid, no' you. If she so much as breathes an ill wish your way, I'll have her taken to a worse place than St. Eithne's. There are grimmer keepers than the good sisters of thon nunnery.

"She cannae touch you here." He stroked her cheek, holding her gaze. "You are safe here."

"Your men—" Margo broke off, her face flaming.

She bit her tongue, not wanting to cause trouble on his ship.

"No one will hurt you." He slid his hands to her waist, his strong fingers gripping her through the thick pelt of the bearskin. "They know better," he vowed, holding her firmly as the *Sea-Raven* plunged into a trough and then shot up the other side. "I spare no man who does harm to a woman. No one."

He spoke fiercely, the hardness in his eyes proving his words.

Margo nodded. She started to take a deep, calming breath when the *Sea-Raven* pitched again, hurtling down another steep trough, the timbers screaming as sea spray doused the sides of the sailcloth.

"Agggh!" Margo threw her arms around his neck, clinging.

"It's nothing, lass. A few ripples, no more." He made light of the huge seas. But he kept one arm locked around her, a solid band of iron. He braced his other hand on the side of the steering platform, trapping her in the shelter of his powerful arms.

They were so close now, his breath against her face, his lips almost touching hers. "Oh, dear . . ." Margo twisted her fingers in his hair as sensations rushed through her. "I think . . ." She couldn't finish.

"Margo. *Valkyrie.*" He inhaled sharply, tensing as his expression changed, his eyes darkening with a look she could describe only as raw, savage need.

Then he growled deep in his throat and pulled her roughly against him. His mouth crashed down on hers, hard and fast, and he kissed her deeply. Nothing like the soft, sensual kiss he'd first given her—this was a bold, devouring kiss, and so heady that everything around her dimmed. Nothing existed except his plundering mouth on hers, the wild tangle of their tongues, and the feel of his strong, muscle-packed body pressed against her.

"O-o-oh . . ." She melted into him, tasting his passion and the heat of his desire, in every hot swirl of his tongue. He pulled her tighter against him, deepening the kiss, so his mouth almost crushed hers. Their breath mingled and it was glorious, the intimacy sending fiery need racing through her veins. She sighed in pleasure, encouraging him, wanting more. He smelled of the sea, plaid, and woodsmoke. An intoxicating blend so rich, earthy, and masculine that she felt almost dizzy. She drank him in greedily. She also felt the hard swell of his arousal nudging her belly. Even through her cloak, his need for her was strong, insistent. And such tangible proof of his desire filled her with feminine triumph.

She wanted him so badly.

She tingled everywhere, thrilling waves of excitement rolling over and through her body, the force of her desire throbbing at her core. A low, purely female cry escaped her as she clung to him. Heart hammering, she returned his tongue-tangling kisses, lost in the tantalizing haze of their abandon. He kept kissing her, his mouth more demanding now, hot and ravenous as he claimed her.

Until the waters around them settled and the *Sea-Raven* stopped pitching wildly. The calmer course worked like an upturned bucket of ice water as he stiffened and broke the kiss, setting her away from him.

"Sorry, lass. I shouldn't have done that. No' just now, at sea." He stepped back, shoved both hands through his hair. "I need to keep you safe out here, no' allow my need for you to distract me.

"These waters are killing grounds." His face turned fierce again and he glanced at the closed sailcloth flap. "No place for females, nowhere along this coast."

Margo hardly heard him. She pressed a hand to her breast, needing to calm herself. Arousal still swirled inside her neediest places, urgent and demanding. She took a deep, shaky breath, her gaze locked on his, her heart thundering against her ribs.

No one had ever kissed her so fiercely.

She'd heard of hard, bruising kisses. Now she knew the glory of them. And she craved more, her body responding even now to the residual pleasure washing through her.

He looked at her, sensual heat still pouring off him. Like her, he'd clearly not wished to abandon their pleasure. Even so, his brows were down-drawn with concern. "I'll no' let aught happen to you."

"I'm not afraid." She wasn't. She knew he'd keep her safe, always.

"You needn't be, I've told you." He smoothed back her hair, his touch giving her another rush of delicious tingles. "But the dangers exist. I cannae allow myself to forget them."

He stepped closer again, his powerful, ring-banded arms reaching for her. He gripped her shoulders, staring down at her as his heady male scent rose between them. Her legs weakened, need sweeping her anew. In the closed space, his scent was high, the earthy blend as intoxicatingly Highland as peat fire and heather.

Margo swallowed, aching for him so badly.

Breathing him in was heaven, but it was still not nearly enough.

His eyes were heating again. The blaze of hunger she saw there made her want nothing more than to feel his powerful male body against her again. More than that, she wanted to lie with him. She burned to have him deep inside her, possessing and completing her.

She'd never needed a man so desperately.

His fierce hold on her shoulders said he felt the same about her.

"Magnus . . ." She lifted her hand to trace the hard line of his jaw, her fingers then lighting softly across his mouth, lingering there. He flicked his tongue over her fingertips, nipping her skin. The contact shivered clear to her toes, sweeping her so close to an orgasm.

Then he frowned and seized her wrist, lowering her arm. "I cannae do this now, lass."

"Please." Margo was prepared to beg. Any moment now she was going to shatter, breaking into a gazillion tiny pieces.

He released her wrist, glancing again at the shelter flap.

"I need to be with my men, at the steering oar." He didn't move, his gaze burning her. "My crew will . . . *Damnation!*" He pulled her roughly against him, grasping the back of her head as he slanted his mouth over hers in another breath-stealing, knee-weakening kiss. His arm locked around her, holding her so tight she could feel the pounding of his heart.

Then he tore his mouth from hers, all medieval war-lord again. "This night, at Badachro, we'll finish this." His promise made her pulse quicken. His gaze swept over her possessively, as if he knew exactly what was hidden beneath her cloak.

"I'll leave you for now, sweet." He pressed his hand to her cheek, and then stepped away. "This sailcloth isn't just for your privacy. Northmen ply these waters and I'm no' of a mind to fight them with you on board. They'd come like bees to a hive if they spotted your bright head amongst my ugly, bushy-bearded crewmen.

"I'll no' see your life risked." He gripped his sword hilt, the same huge medieval blade he'd raised to the skies in the book illustration. "It's no' that much farther to the inlet we're seeking. Stay in here until I come for you."

"I will." Margo nodded, fear beginning to claw at her again.

A sea battle with Vikings wasn't something she wanted to experience.

"I know you'll look out for me." She did, but his warning put a knot in her chest. "There haven't been any Vikings about, have there? Not since we were at ..." She let her voice trail off, not wanting to mention the Cursing Stone and the brutal scene at the strand.

He'd been about to throw open the shelter flap, but instead his hand fisted, the heavy cloth bunching beneath his fingers. "The Northmen are aye about, lass. Their pagan hordes are in these waters now, even though we haven't seen them. They hide in the mist and behind rocky islets along the shore, flashing out from nowhere to surprise their chosen prey.

"They're devils who'd do more than hurt you if you fell into their hands. Things so vile that"—a dark shadow crossed his face—"you might be tempted to escape the horror any way you could.

"I'll no' let that happen." His gaze was burning now, and a muscle twitched at his left eye. "No woman should suffer their depredations."

"I'm not afraid." That wasn't true, but it didn't matter.

He hadn't heard her.

He was looking into a past she couldn't see. And when his jaw clenched and he gripped his sword hilt tighter, so hard that his knuckles shone white, she suddenly knew what fueled his rage.

A woman.

The revelation sent waves of jealousy crashing through her, needle-sharp and dazzling green. The thought of him kissing another woman as he'd just kissed her made her feel sick inside. Imagining him making love to someone else—she knew he'd be incredible in bed—was beyond bearing. Knowing he'd *loved* someone felt like a knife to her heart.

And she knew she was a terrible person for feeling that way.

But she couldn't help it.

She wanted him for her own.

"The Vikings killed your wife, didn't they?" Margo knew she was going to hell because the words *your wife* tasted so sour on her tongue.

The title held power because his eyes widened and he jerked as if someone his own size and strength had punched him in the gut.

She'd give anything to be the woman who'd meant so much to him.

"I dinnae have a wife." His voice was terse, cold as if it came from a distant, frozen place. Somewhere he didn't like remembering. "My betrothed took her own life before raiding Vikings could rape her." The shadow returned to his face and stayed there this time, etching darkness across his proud, chiseled features. "She thrust a dagger into her belly, preferring death to being whored by the Northmen who burned her village."

"Dear God." Margo stared at him.

"It was Orosius who learned the truth of her death." He looked at her, his beautiful peat brown eyes dulled with torment. "Her spirit came to him, wanting to let me know. As a rune master, he's more accessible to those in the otherworld, or so he explained to me.

"I was glad to know what happened. But"—he pulled a hand down over his chin—"it changed naught. Liana was still dead."

The green wave of jealousy that had swept her on imagining him married congealed into a cold lump of shame.

"I'm sorry—" She started forward, reaching for him, but he turned and ducked through the shelter flap before she'd taken two steps.

His pain remained in the little space, thick, acrid, and terrible. The horror of his loss surrounded her; she could feel it seep into her bones. Outrage also flared through her, constricting her chest and taking her breath. She knew now how much he'd lost and what drove him. And why he'd become a Viking slayer.

He truly *was* a hero.

And just now, she wanted only to hold him.

Tonight, if she was still in his world, she'd try and make him forget all he had lost.

Chapter 14

"Badachro's quiet."

At the *Sea-Raven*'s bow, Magnus glanced at the young warrior standing beside him. He agreed with Ewan's assessment. Badachro Bay did look empty. But no sign of Vikings didn't mean they weren't about, hidden somewhere. It was a truth Magnus knew well, so he kept his gaze sharp as the *Sea-Raven* beat deeper into the woody, steep-sided inlet.

"Peaceful or no', we'll still have two men keep watch from Sgeir Ghlas this night." Magnus glanced at Ewan. "You, I'm thinking, and Dugan."

Ewan grinned. "Last time we moored here, you kept vigil on thon gray rock." He gaze flicked to the barren islet and then to the sailcloth stretched across the other end of the ship. "Can it be you'll make your bed in *Sea-Raven*'s stern this e'en?

"I would"—he looked back to Magnus, winking—"if the lass fancied me."

"Watch your tongue if you wish to keep it." Magnus thumped the lad's shoulder to take the sting from his words. "Now get you back to the steering oar before your grandfather runs us into a rock. He isn't the steersman he once was. But"—he gripped Ewan's arm as the young man started away—"dinnae be telling Calum I said so."

"I willnae." Ewan grinned again, and was gone.

Magnus caught a flutter at the sailcloth flap and saw Margo ease aside the heavy cloth just enough to peek out at the high, tree-covered hills they were gliding past. The highest peaks were lost in heavy mist and her eyes shone as she looked there, as if the rolling blue haze delighted her. When the flap gaped a bit more and he saw that she'd pressed a hand to her breast, he knew he'd guessed right.

She *was* thrilled by the mist.

His chest tightened, watching her. It'd been many years since he'd looked at a simple thing like sea haar and seen a wonder. Surely not since he was a wee lad and his mother told him tales that Highland mist was the realm of faeries and that the luminosity of such mist was truly the glow of their raiments and the sparkling of their wands.

He'd listened, round-eyed. And he'd believed every word.

Until the harsh realities of life in these beautiful but harsh hills had taught him differently.

The pull in his chest became an ache, a longing for something he'd lost and he didn't know how to retrieve. And it worsened when Margo sensed him watching her, and instead of nipping back into the shadows and closing the flap, she locked eyes with him.

Her face softened as she looked at him, her huge blue eyes seeing into his soul, he was sure. But just when he was about to shift on his feet like a fuzzy-bearded youth, she let the shelter flap drop.

He waited for her to peek out again—he could feel her wish to do so, as if they were somehow connected and he knew her mind—but the sailcloth didn't stir.

The moment had passed.

And he needed to keep his gaze on the water and land before him, watching for any sign of Vikings. His days of searching for faeries flying about in the mist were gone and no more. So he turned back to the bow and took a deep breath of the cold air blowing in from the north.

He welcomed the relief that sluiced through him.

Ewan had been right.

Badachro *was* still.

The scatter of reed-thatched huts dotting the shore sent up thin blue curls of peat smoke, the sight assuring Magnus that the fisherfolk who dwelt here hadn't been troubled. Six fat cattle grazed behind the hovels, near to the wood's edge. Magnus's own beasts, each one a prize animal, they'd been brought here a short while ago to be used as bait at Redpoint.

Magnus rubbed the back of his neck, hoping all would go as planned.

Willing it so, he glanced away along the shore again, searching for any small indication of treachery.

He saw none.

There were no docks here. But several fishing boats bobbed in the bay and others had been drawn onto the shore, resting beyond the tide line. A small dog scratched and sniffed around a pile of drying seaweed. And a few skinny chickens pecked near the door of one of the fishing huts.

Nothing else moved.

Dim light shone from Orla's cottage, which could mean she had a visitor. Magnus frowned as he eyed her home. Whitewashed and recently thatched with thick, fresh heather, the cottage was a more sturdy structure than the rest and set apart at the far end of the settlement. The red door was closed and he hadn't been mistaken: soft yellow candle glow did glimmer in the two deep-set windows. Magnus knew she entertained at all hours. And he wouldn't relish interrupting her trade. His gut also clenched to imagine what the joy woman would make of Margo.

Above all, he hoped Margo wouldn't misunderstand his friendship with the other woman.

Orla was as attractive as she was perceptive.

She was also an invaluable helpmate.

Magnus hoped she wouldn't let him down now.

He'd soon know, for Ewan was expertly guiding *Sea-Raven* toward the sloping strand, preparing to glide the ship onto the shingle.

Needing to be sure all was well, Magnus cast one more look across the quiet waters.

But he hadn't missed anything.

No Norse warships lurked in the bay, hiding their heathen presence behind the handful of islets guarding the inlet. Had his enemies been here, he'd have sent them to the sea bottom before they could blink. But he shuddered at having Margo on board during any such encounter. It was bad enough that she'd be at Redpoint.

Frowning, he touched Vengeance's hilt, knowing the red-sanded cove would be a scene of slaughter.

A necessary warning to his foes—especially after what happened at Gairloch—his plans for Redpoint couldn't be avoided.

He would ensure that Margo remained well away from the blood spilling.

For now, he strode down the ship's center aisle, swiftly covering the paces to the sailcloth shelter and the woman who was as responsible for the knot in his chest as for the hot, throbbing ache in his loins.

"Margo." He drew aside the flap before his good sense warned him to leave her where she was. "You can come out now. No more need to peek, lass. There is no danger here."

"No Vikings?" She stood in shadow, but enough light fell through the flap opening for him to see the unasked question in her eyes.

"No dangers at all." He ducked through the opening and went to her. He took her face in both his hands. "I wouldn't take you ashore if I thought harm would come to you."

"So . . ." She hesitated, her blue eyes luminous in the shelter's dimness. "Nothing will happen that might cause me pain?"

"Nae. You have my word." He held her gaze, knowing she hadn't meant marauding Northmen.

She'd meant him.

She'd wanted assurance that the sizzling need that scorched the air every time they so much as looked at each other wouldn't burn her.

He was already on fire, as he was sure she knew.

But he also saw the worry shimmering at the backs of her eyes. She might not admit such concerns, and she might love Scotland—any fool could see that she did—but he knew it must be hard to find herself in a strange world filled with dangers she'd never before encountered.

She needed reassurance.

He smoothed her hair behind an ear, and then leaned down to drop a kiss on her brow.

"So long as you are with me, you have my protection." He wouldn't lie and promise anything more. Not knowing she could be ripped from him any moment, plunged back into the distant place she claimed was her home. "I'll no' leave your side."

"Thank you. But I don't want to be a bother on your ship." She stepped closer, her cold-winter-air and rose scent coming with her, teasing and taunting him. "I'll try to get my sea legs," she added, the determined tilt of her chin making his heart hurt.

"You will." He took her hand, linking his fingers with hers as he led her out of the shelter and into the ship's narrow aisle. "Now come. My men will set us ashore, leaving us at Badachro. Then"—he nodded across the water to the spit of gray rock that was Sgeir Ghlas— "they'll take the *Sea-Raven* over to moor by thon islet for the night."

She followed his gaze, looking calmer than he'd expected. "Where is the 'wee cothouse with its driftwood fire and pallet of plaids'?" Keeping a hand on the edge of the stern platform, she turned away from Gray Rock to scan the shore, studying the turf-walled fisher huts before her attention settled on Orla's cottage.

"That one looks substantial." Her eyes narrowed.

"Thon is Orla's cottage." Magnus tried to keep his tone neutral. "There, beyond the treeline"—he pointed to the opposite end of the bay—"is the wee cothouse I meant. You can't see it because it's in the wood. No one has lived there for years. Folk use it for shelter only."

"I don't see anything." She leaned forward, trying for a better view, and Magnus saw that her lips were swollen from his kisses.

The soft ripeness made her look vulnerable and incredibly desirable. As if she knew, she straightened and lifted a hand to touch her mouth.

"Oh, dear . . ." She traced a fingertip across the curve of her lips. Tapping her lower lip's fullness, she tested for tenderness.

Her eyes widened, her finger exploring her lip. "I must look awful. . . ."

"Nae." Magnus could hardly speak. His gaze was frozen on her questing finger, the glimpse he caught of her tongue when she parted her lips just a bit. "You look . . . You are—" He clamped his own mouth tight, aware he was spluttering.

Worse, his men were gawking.

He glared at them until they looked elsewhere.

Then he turned back to Margo and immediately wished he hadn't. The sight of her damping the tip of her finger with her tongue froze him. And as his brows flew down in another scowl, she felt again along her lower lip.

Magnus nearly roared.

Something inside him clenched and it was all he could do not to grab her to him and plunder her sweet mouth again. And this time, he'd kiss her for hours and hours, tasting and ravishing her ceaselessly, sating himself on her, until the morrow's sun rose and set once more. Then he'd begin all over again.

She was maddening him.

And something told him she was doing it on purpose.

"Hold her, Magnus!" Ewan called the warning just as the *Sea-Raven*'s bow started to glide toward the shore's sloping strand.

"Oh, God!" Margo paled and grabbed Magnus, clinging tight.

"All is well." He whipped an arm around her, pulling her hard against him. "We'll settle in a moment."

"Back oars!" Calum's deep voice boomed beside his grandson as the rowers quickly reversed their pulls. All around them water seethed and foamed as the long oars churned the surf, the rowers expertly keeping the ship from grinding onto the shingle.

Then the *Sea-Raven* came to a halt, riding the choppy waters about ten feet from shore. Knowing there was only one way to get Margo off the ship, Magnus swept her up in his arms, carrying her to the bow.

"Dugan, come along!" He threw a glance at the little

man as he marched down the ship's aisle. Dugan had more strength than some men three times as large. And, unlike a few of the other warriors on board, he wouldn't be tempted to let Margo fall into the water when he handed her over the side and into Magnus's waiting arms.

Proving it, Dugan sprang to his feet, grinning. "Are you taking me ashore?" He caught up with them, eager. "I'll guard the lady—"

"Wait!" Margo squirmed, eyeing the rough surf. "I'm not ready to go anywhere. I liked the sailcloth—"

"You've been itching to see land." Magnus held her firm. "Now you're almost there. Stop wriggling."

"But—"

Ignoring her, Magnus turned again to Dugan. "There are others to guard her. You're to keep watch with Ewan on Sgeir Ghlas. Just hand the lass o'er to me." Quickly, he placed her in Dugan's arms and then swung over the side before Margo would have time to protest or become frightened.

Or so he hoped.

But when he reached up to take her as Dugan lowered her over the side, he saw that she'd squeezed shut her eyes.

Her face was ghostly white.

Magnus understood. The water was waist-deep and freezing, the current strong and making it difficult for even him to keep his feet.

"Have a care!" he roared at Dugan, not liking the fool's cheeky grin.

But the little man handled her gently, easing her into Magnus's arms as carefully as if he held something truly precious.

As well he did.

The truth of it made Magnus lift her even higher

against his chest so that she was almost riding his shoulder as he stood, watching Ewan back the *Sea-Raven* away from the strand and into the deep waters of the bay.

"Come for us at sunrise!" He nodded sharply as Ewan responded with a flourish, letting the oars dip and flash in a quick farewell before the *Sea-Raven* whipped around in a plume of spray and sped away toward the Gray Rock and the other islets.

Now he was alone on the strand with Margo.

Or they would be as soon as he marched out of the icy water.

She'd gone still as stone.

"You can open your eyes, lass." Magnus turned to splash through the surf, making for the shore. "We're on solid ground again."

"I don't call this solid." Margo wasn't cracking an eyelash.

Not yet.

"I willnae let you fall, Mar-*go*." Magnus nuzzled her neck, nipping her ear as he shifted her higher against his shoulder. "You needn't look if you'd rather wait. We're almost ashore."

Margo wanted to believe him.

His neck nuzzle and ear nibble made her skin tingle, providing a welcome distraction.

But she still wasn't ready to look.

Keeping her eyes shut left her in a world that was cold, wet, and dark. Seeing it would be scarier. She'd never believed in peering beneath rocks. Ugly things always lurked there, waiting to pounce. This was one of those times she was leaving the rocks alone. She didn't need to look to know the world had turned nasty. Icy waves were crashing into them and she'd felt Magnus's foot slip once. Worse, the *crack* and splashing of the dragon ship's oars filled the air, the noise so terrifyingly close that she expected one of the long, flashing oars to bop them any minute, knocking them under the waves, where they'd drown.

If doom was coming, she didn't want to see its arrival. She wasn't that brave.

But then the waves stopped hurtling into them, and the smell of peat smoke and pine was suddenly high on the wind, seasoning the cold, salt air. She also caught a trace of cooking smells—a rich, savory stew?—as they reached solid ground and Magnus carried her out of the surf and up the sloping shoreline.

"There, see you?" He set her down, but kept his hands at her waist, holding her. "We're here. Soon you'll be warm and have new, dry clothes." His gaze flicked to the red-doored cottage at the far end of the little bay. "Orla is about your size and will have everything you'll need."

"Won't she wonder who I am?" Margo was torn between her desire to see the last of Orosius's heavy, now-wet bearskin cloak and hesitation at meeting the medieval joy woman.

A woman who was obviously on very good terms with Magnus.

"Orla is a friend, no more." Magnus cupped her face, his dark gaze earnest as he repeated what he'd already told her.

"Many women are friendly until they sense competition." The argument slipped out before she could bite her tongue.

Magnus smoothed his hands down over her shoulders and then along her sides, sliding his arms around her. He pulled her close. "You dinnae have any competition." His voice was low and gruff, his gaze intense. "You ne'er have, if you'd know the truth of it."

Margo's heart dipped. "I know you were . . . You must've—"

"You dinnae hear well, aye?" He placed his palm against her cheek, pressing gently. His warmth soothed her. "I said no one."

"I—" Margo broke off when the fisherfolk began stepping out of their huts, gathering in a ragtag huddle to stare down the strand at her and Magnus.

They didn't look hostile. And none of them made an attempt to approach, instead staying in a tight circle where they were, near their turf-walled hovels. The small dog she'd noticed earlier ran back and forth, barking. But he looked more excited than ferocious. And his tail was wagging.

Still . . .

Margo swallowed, remembering how easily Magnus's men had taken her for a witch.

"They're only curious. They've been expecting me. But they'll be surprised to see you." He turned their way then, lifting a hand in greeting as he called to them. "You'll have three of the cattle returned to you soon." His promise earned smiles. "The beasts will be your own then, after Redpoint."

The smiles turned into grins.

A little boy, thin-shouldered and wearing a tattered plaid, danced a jig.

Magnus smiled as he watched the sprite, a dimple flashing once in his cheek.

"I'll send a few more from Badcall, and a fine pair o' pigs," Magnus shouted, and Margo was surprised when the villagers didn't throw themselves on the ground, bowing to him.

They'd looked that happy.

She glanced at Magnus, puzzled.

"What was all that about?" She hadn't understood

anything he'd said. She had seen that the villagers idolized him.

"I'll explain later, at the cothouse." He wasn't looking at her. He'd set his hands on his hips while he watched the villagers trickle back inside their huts.

They seemed to have forgotten she was there.

Magnus hadn't.

He turned back to her, and his eyes were fierce again, reminding her so much of how he'd looked in the book illustration. As in the drawing, his long hair streamed in the wind, and as if he'd read her thoughts, he'd set his hand on his sword hilt, his strong fingers lightly circling the hilt. His arm rings shone brightly and his wet plaid clung to him, molded to the broad, hard-muscled expanse of his chest. He stood with his legs apart, the warrior stance making her breath catch.

He was her dream turned reality.

Being near him, breathing the same air, listening to his beautiful, deep voice, and seeing his passion, all lit a simmering desire inside her. She was almost light-headed with wanting him.

And she wanted more than his lovemaking. She wanted him to care about her with the same burning fervor she'd seen in him when he'd stopped to call out to the fisherfolk.

She knew now he'd never love her. No woman could compete with a ghost, especially not a martyred one.

But she so hoped he would care for her.

"Thon folk have suffered much." He was still watching the villagers, looking on as a few stragglers disappeared into their humble dwellings. "I've sworn an oath to do all I can to keep them safe and spare them grief."

His words speared Margo's heart.

She shivered in the wind—it was freshening, the sky darkening with heavy clouds—but a deep, molten heat spread inside her, growing warmer when he took her hand, meshing their fingers.

"Come, now." He led her along the curving strand, skirting the tide line and taking her up near the edge of the trees toward the tidy, whitewashed cottage with its red painted door.

Margo hurried beside him, one hand gripping the bearskin mantle to keep it from gaping wide. The cold stones shifted under her bare feet, making it difficult to walk. And several times she stumbled, slipping on the shingle. But Magnus caught her each time, steadying her and giving her a moment to regain her balance.

It was after one such pause that a glint of silver in the wood caught her eye.

"Magnus." She froze, scanning the thick edge of pines. "I saw something in the trees. I think"—her blood chilled at the possibility—"it was the flash of mail."

"It was." To her surprise he grinned.

She blinked. "You saw it, too?"

"Nae." He started forward again, seemingly unconcerned. "But I know there are men in the wood. They are my own warriors. They're crewmen from one of my other ships, the *Wave-Dancer*."

He stopped briefly, glancing at the dark pines before they moved on. "Calum had orders to send them here. They'll circle the cothouse as we sleep this night, standing guard to alert me should an enemy approach."

"Oh." Margo was both relieved and—she couldn't believe this—disappointed, because she was so sure he'd meant to make love to her at the little cottage.

She still felt reasonably sure.

And that only tied her belly in a worse knot.

Privacy might not be a big issue in medieval times, but she wasn't keen on getting naked and intimate with a circle of hard-faced, sword- and ax-packing men-in-steel anywhere within hearing range.

The very idea sent a wash of heat up her neck.

Magnus smiled and gripped her fingers tighter. "You'll no' ken they're there. They've been told to keep at a good distance."

Margo's face burned even hotter on his words. It was almost as bad that he obviously knew she expected him to ravish her. Mortified, she took a deep, calming breath.

It didn't help.

And when they started forward again, she promptly stubbed her toe against a rock. "Ow-w-w!" She faltered as she grabbed her throbbing foot. "I didn't see—"

"Hush, you." He scooped her into his arms, holding her close to his chest as they reached the end of the bay and approached the joy woman's home. "I should've carried you the whole way."

"I didn't mind walking." She hadn't. But being in his arms was better.

Even so, she wanted to be standing on her own two feet when she met Orla.

"You can let me down now." She was watching the cottage, dreading their arrival. "My toe doesn't hurt that bad and—" Her jaw slipped, her protest snagging in her throat as the red door swung open and Orla stepped out onto the cottage's tiny stone stoop.

"Dear God in heaven." Margo stared at the other woman, her heart racing as Magnus lowered her to the ground, oblivious.

Margo was anything but.

She was shocked to the core.

She could only stare, disbelief sweeping her as Orla smiled a greeting, gesturing them inside.

Orla had a face Margo recognized.

She could've been Marta Lopez's twin.

Chapter 15

"Magnus, it is too long since you darkened my door."
Orla waited until Magnus and Margo were inside, then
grasped Magnus's arm and lifted on her toes to kiss his
cheek.

Margo watched, stunned. Amazement and surprise
gathered tightly in her chest, shivers rippling up and
down her back. Her breath locked in her throat, making
her glad the other woman addressed Magnus first, giving
her time to recover before she was forced to respond.

"I've been hoping you'd come soon." Orla led them
inside the candlelit cottage, her warm brown eyes as-
sessing Margo, her smile full of welcome.

And it was Marta's smile.

Marta's rich chocolate eyes looking at her.

They were beautiful eyes, fringed with thick black
lashes, and so familiar. They also brimmed with a secret
knowledge as if Orla understood exactly why Margo
was staring at her, still unable to speak.

And the reason wasn't only that Orla resembled
Marta so strongly.

Her home could've been a medieval version of Ye
Olde Pagan Times.

Charmingly feminine, and with the same candle-wax, aromatic essential-oil scent, the cottage was low-ceilinged and heavily beamed. All manner of dried herbs, flowers, and leaves hung in clusters from the thick black rafters, and the stone-flagged floor looked painfully well swept. Odd bits of driftwood, wooden bowls of pinecones, and innumerable pebbles and stones crowded the thick window ledges and the shelves arranged artfully across two walls. A large plaid curtain hung across one corner, discreetly hiding Orla's sleeping quarters, a niche where, according to Magnus, she likely plied her trade when such men came to call.

Marta would've loved the cottage.

Patience and Ardelle would've swooned. And Margo's chest tightened as she imagined how the three women's eyes would've lit with wonder if they'd been here with her. They would've walked about, examining everything, and exclaiming their delight, deeming the cottage perfect.

It made Margo felt right at home.

Magnus looked out of place. His head almost brushed the heavy black ceiling rafters and he had to duck to avoid the hanging clusters of flowers and whatnot. Towering above her and Orla, he sent a look at the tray of fresh-baked oatcakes and cheese set upon the room's lone table. Along with the earthen jug of ale and three cups placed invitingly beside it. A brace of candles burned nearby, their golden glow lending to the cottage's homey atmosphere.

Magnus cleared his throat, plainly uncomfortable. "Three ale cups, Orla?" He looked at his friend, one brow raised questioningly.

"*Magnus.*" Margo blushed, his meaning obvious.

Orla's eyes only lit with amusement and she laughed. "I still leave such *delights* to my less discerning friends in the trade," she announced, not looking at all embarrassed. "The truth is . . ."

She lifted her chin and met his gaze, her dark hair gleaming in the firelight. "Something told me you'd bring a friend here this day."

"Humph." Magnus frowned. "Dinnae start with such-like. I hear enough second-sight and rune-casting foolery from Orosius. I dinnae need you—"

"I have a woman's good sense, no more. That is all." She smiled at Margo. "Though I'll own that living so close to nature"—she gestured to the treasures displayed all around the cottage—"allows one to observe and discover truths some folk never notice.

"I also trust in my dreams." She tucked her hair behind an ear, her gaze still on Margo. "All women do. It's why we're wiser than men."

"Say you?" Magnus didn't look impressed.

"I do." Orla turned her smile on him, and then took Margo's hand and ushered her to a low bench against the back wall, urging her to sit. Her no-nonsense, take-charge personality reminded Margo so much of her friend that a terrible hotness swelled in her throat. She had to blink rapidly to keep from embarrassing herself.

Orla was shaking her head, tutting over her as she took a length of soft linen from a basket near the bench. Stepping close, she used the cloth to dab sea spray from Margo's hair and off her face.

"I can see you've suffered an ordeal, *mo ghaoil*." She chose the same Gaelic term of affection as Magnus. And she glanced at him now, a frown marring her brow. "What have you done to her, h'mmm?"

"Naught, as you surely know." He stood near the cottage's central hearth, warming his hands before the strangest fire Margo had ever seen. The flames shone blue, purple, and gold as they hissed and spat, dancing almost sinuously atop a small heap of elegantly twisted silver-hued wood. "Margo is from a distant land to the south," he improvised, avoiding Margo's eyes. "She's the sole survivor of a foundered ship. We found her just north of Gairloch and took her on board the *Sea-Raven*."

"Did you, now?" Orla's arched brow said she didn't believe a word.

But she held her tongue, setting aside the drying cloth and dusting her hands. "Then you have come seeking raiments for her, h'mmm?"

She flicked a glance at Margo, winking as if they shared in a conspiracy Magnus knew nothing about. "As it is . . ." She tapped her chin, looking about the one-room cottage as if searching for something.

Margo watched her, more drawn to the laughing-eyed joy woman by the moment. She had what Patience called *heart*.

Just now, she gave Margo another quick wink, proving it.

"It could be," Orla began again, "that I set aside some goods that would serve Margo. Two gowns and a linen chemise, a fine wool cloak, and a butter-soft pair of good leather *cuarain*"—she paused, and Margo was so glad she knew *cuarain* was Gaelic for slippers—"plus a few bits of frippery.

"I needed to clear space for my pebbles and suchlike. I have so little room. . . ." Orla shrugged expansively, a smile playing across her lips. "You are very welcome to the goods, if you wish?" She looked at Margo, waiting. "I do believe everything will fit."

"I'm grateful to you." Margo didn't hesitate.

She couldn't keep walking around naked and in a heavy furred cloak, her feet bare-soled.

She was also sure that Orla's hand-me-downs would be the right size for her. She and Marta had often exchanged clothes on weekends and special occasions. Doing so allowed each woman to wear something different without the expense of purchasing a new outfit.

"I've put everything in a leather satchel. Though . . ." Orla started tapping her chin again. "I can't recall where. . . ."

"Come, Orla." Magnus circled a hand around her wrist, lowering her arm. "How did you know I'd bring Margo here?"

Orla beamed. "The men from *Wave-Dancer* passed this way a while ago. I offered them refreshment and"— she shrugged again, her tone affectionate—"men do speak when they're enjoying a good cup of ale and what-have-you."

"They told you about Margo?" Magnus sounded surprised.

"They mentioned the cothouse in the wood and that they were to stand watch there." Orla went to the table and poured three cups of ale, offering Magnus and Margo each a cup before taking one for herself. "As I know you would never order a full ship's crew to guard your sleep, it was clear you wanted protection for something much more precious.

"And"—she took a sip of ale, smiling at him over the cup's rim—"what is dearer to a man than his woman?"

"Margo isn't—" Magnus clamped his mouth tight.

Orla lifted a brow. "You see, women *are* wise."

"Long-nosed, some might say." Magnus remained stubborn.

"Mayhap, I'll not deny." Orla set down her cup, her expression turning earnest. "I did hear something disturbing from a visiting friend not too long ago." She slid a glance at Margo, and then looked back to Magnus. "It was troubling news."

"You can speak plainly." Magnus folded his arms.

"I don't want to frighten someone unaccustomed to

life here." Again she flicked a look at Margo, her eyes seeming to say so much more than her words. As if she knew Margo was genuinely out of place.

"I have seen Viking battles." Margo wished she hadn't seen such a horror.

She shuddered before she could stop herself.

Orla crossed the room quickly, placing a comforting arm around Margo's shoulders. "They are not easily forgotten, h'mmm?" She gave Margo a squeeze, and then went to fetch the ale jug, topping Margo's cup. "We're all revisited by such terrors in our dreams, aren't we?

"But"—she returned the jug to the table—"my news is disturbing in a different manner. Good folk have been disappearing from the countryside." She looked at Magnus. "Whole families vanished from their farms without a trace. There have been three discoveries so far, all in the hinterland west of Gairloch.

"No one knows what's happening." She looked between Margo and Magnus. "There's never been a sign of struggle and not even a speck of blood. As I heard, they're simply gone from their homes. Folk up that way are worried."

Margo glanced at Magnus. She wasn't surprised to see him wearing his fierce warrior look again. His eyes blazed and he'd reached to rub the back of his neck.

"I don't care for the sound of that." He frowned, looking at Orla. "Get word to me if you hear anything else. And if you see"—he hesitated—"a small dark-haired woman in a black cloak and who covers her wrists and ankles with jangling silver—"

"The sorceress, Donata Greer?" Orla's face hardened. "I never could abide that woman. She is at St. Eithne's last I heard. Her captivity has caused a stir among the Northmen. None seemed overly bothered when you slew her brother, Godred. But there's a simmering anger that Donata is locked away at the nunnery.

"But why do you ask?" Orla's glance flicked again to Margo. "Is it because she cursed you?"

"Pah!" Magnus cut the air with his hand. "Her mutterings couldn't curdle milk."

Margo knew he was speaking for her benefit.

Donata Greer could probably alter the earth's axis if she wished.

Nothing she did would surprise Margo.

But the mention of her name tinged the atmosphere. The light also dimmed in Orla's eyes and she now looked worried. Magnus reminded her of a caged tiger, furious to be confined and ready to rip flesh the instant he could bend the bars and break free.

His face was harsh and dark, his eyes glinting dangerously. "We'll have the clothes, then, and leave you, Orla." He glanced around the room, his expression turning fiercer when he didn't see the desired leather satchel. "There is much to do and—"

"Oh, I know." Orla's expression softened as she took a polished pebble from the window ledge, rolling the little stone in her palm.

Magnus's brows lowered. "I'll no' be hearing your tales, Orla. No' that kind. Pebbles are no' runesticks, howe'er often you claim to see things in them."

"I do." Orla smiled. "Though not *in* them, but by reading their cast."

A chill rippled down Margo's spine. Marta read tarot.

In that moment, she felt so close to her friend that emotion gripped her like an iron vise around her chest. Her breath snagged again. Especially when Orla glanced at her, her expression turning almost wistful as she carefully returned the pebble to the window ledge.

Margo stood, aware that Magnus's patience was thinning.

He'd folded his arms, his gaze level on the joy woman. "Whate'er you think you know, Orla, I'm warning you to keep it to yourself. I'll no' be hearing strange tales up and down this coast. If I do, my next visit willnae be a friendly one."

Orla didn't look concerned. "You should know me better." She glanced at Margo. "Your lady does."

"I told you, she's no' my lady."

Orla laughed.

Then she took his arm and hastened him across the room. "Wait outside while I help Margo dress." She'd no sooner spoken the words than she'd maneuvered him across the threshold, closing the door firmly behind him.

She turned to Margo. "He can be a great fearsome brute, but he has a good heart beneath his scowls and bluster. And"—she bent to whip a plaid off a bulging leather satchel near the door—"he has been too long without a woman. Many long years, it is. Or so I believe."

Margo felt her face heating. "He wasn't lying. I'm not 'his lady.'"

Although how she wished she was.

Margo took a breath, remembering his passion when he'd spoken of the woman he had loved. "He told me about Liana. She was—"

"Liana was an innocent child." Orla's voice held respect, but wasn't particularly warm. "A good lass, to be sure, and beautiful. But . . ."

Orla set the satchel on a bench and opened it. "I do not believe she'd have made Magnus happy, had her life"—she hesitated, clearly not wishing to detail the young woman's tragic death—"been different. She desired babies and a family, but a man needs more.

"If they didn't"—she bent over the satchel, her dark hair falling across her face, hiding her expression—"there'd be no need for women like me."

Margo bit her lip, not sure how to respond. She liked Orla and didn't want to offend her.

"Liana was chaste?" Margo chose the safest reply.

She was surely going to land in hell because it mattered to her, but she hoped the young woman *had* been virginal.

That would mean . . .

Margo's heart began to pound, the hot desire flaring in her letting her know for sure she was hell-bound.

"Aye, Liana was pure." Orla's words confirmed Margo's suspicion. "She died a maid. Magnus never touched her, nor any woman since, though many have tried to catch his eye. He lives only for vengeance.

"There are many of us"—Orla's tone became agitated, proving how much she cared for her friend—"who feel he's been alone too long. He needs a wife to not just sit proudly beside him at the high table and bear his sons, but who will bed him well of a night." She spoke frankly, her words making Margo blush. "Someone to heat his blood, make him burn, and remind him that being a man is more than carrying a sword and killing Vikings."

Margo didn't know what to say. "I think vengeance is important to him."

"Pah!" Orla snorted. "To be sure it is, and rightly. But he needs to remember that there are other important things in life. Things that remain when vengeance is served and sword blades rust and dull, and when a man's powerful shoulders begin to thin and slump. True love burns eternally, my lady. No power on earth can dim it. And"—there was a catch in the joy woman's voice—"I believe that is why you're here."

Orla had been pulling garments from the satchel, but now she straightened, eyeing Margo up and down. "You are a desirable woman and he hungers for you. A woman of strength and courage," she added, the familiar words sending a rush of chills across Margo's nerves.

A woman of strength and courage.

They were the exact words Dev Doonie had used at the Bucks County Scottish Festival and again at the Gairloch Heritage Museum.

Margo swallowed, half-certain the floor had dipped beneath her feet.

Orla's gaze flicked to her pebbles on the window ledge and then back to Margo. "True friendship never fades, either, my lady. Those who love us deeply do so always, no matter where we are."

Margo blinked.

The other woman's words were strange. And so apt that Margo's heart squeezed so hard, her chest hurt. Her eyes were stinging again, the cozy cottage beginning to blur and swim.

She hoped she would see Orla again.

If by some miracle she stayed here, she'd ask Magnus to bring her on visits to Badachro. She'd insist, even if the journey would mean suffering the ordeal of traveling on the *Sea-Raven*.

She started to glance aside, not wanting Orla to see her emotion. But the other woman was already fussing briskly over her, smoothing Margo's hair and deftly undoing the large Celtic pin holding the bearskin cloak at Margo's neck.

The strange moment was gone, spinning away as Orla swept the mantle off Margo's shoulders, leaving her naked before the strange blue-flamed fire.

Then, from nowhere—or so it seemed—the joy woman produced a small bucket of steaming, rose-scented water and a soapy linen cloth. Humming softly, she busied herself bathing Margo's shivering body.

It wasn't until a short while later, dressed as a medieval Scottish woman, and with Magnus leading her deep into the thick, piney wood, that Margo recalled something that sent chills coursing through her again.

The tune Orla had hummed as she'd helped Margo bathe and dress was a melody Marta had favored, often humming the lyrical notes beneath her breath when she studied her tarot.

The memory made Margo's blood thrum.

And it gave her as much comfort as if Marta, Patience, and Ardelle were walking beside her on the woody path. But then thoughts of a very different nature seized her when the trees suddenly thinned and a tiny turf-walled hut loomed right ahead of them.

The cothouse in the wood.

They were there.

The time had come.

Chapter 16

"Wait, lass." Magnus stopped a few yards from the cothouse, thrusting out an arm to bar Margo's way. "Those are stinging nettles round the door." He nodded toward the little hut and Margo saw the thick, green underbrush crowding the narrow path.

She also caught the silver gleam of the sea, flashing in the distance, just visible between the trees. She puffed her bangs off her forehead and looked around. Dense pines made the wood dark and the air was cold and sharp, and smelling of salt and resin. They'd been steadily climbing and the cothouse was higher up the hill than she'd realized. It looked cold, empty, and forgotten.

The nettles at the door were waist-high.

Magnus grinned, eyeing them.

"Stay where you are, sweet, and you'll no' feel a single sting." Striding forward, he whipped out his sword and scythed it across the underbrush, cutting the nettles to harmless stubble.

Sheathing his blade, he strolled back to her and lifted her in his arms, kissing her forehead. "There are many ways a man can use his sword, see you?" He looked down at her and his eyes darkened with the heat she remembered from the sailcloth shelter on board the

Sea-Raven. "More ways than there are stars in the night sky."

Margo knew he was no longer speaking of the huge medieval long sword sheathed at his hip.

His *real meaning* made pure female need flame inside her.

Shivery with anticipation, she breathed deeply of the cold, piney air as he worked the cothouse's door latch. Damp had swollen the wood and he had to give a hard push to make the door creak open. Musty air rushed out to greet them, icy-cold and smelling of old leaves and rich, loamy earth.

"You'll be safe here, lass." He paused in the dark opening, his eyes narrowing as he looked down at her. "No Vikings, nor the Greer sorceress, will come anywhere near this hill tonight. But"—he pulled her close, more tightly against him—"I cannae protect you from my own good self. If you're of a different mind, say so now, and I'll have the guardsmen in thon trees return you to the *Sea-Raven.* They'll no' lay a hand on you, I promise."

"And you?" Margo's heart was thundering. "What about your hands?"

"My hands . . ." He drew a ragged breath. "The truth is I want my hands running all o'er your smooth, bared skin."

"I want that, too." Margo couldn't believe she'd just said that.

But two words circled in her mind, pushing her to be bold.

Strong and *courageous.*

"Margo." He leaned down and kissed her, hard and swift. "You'll no' regret this." He broke the kiss, breathing the words against her cheek.

"I know. . . ." She nipped his lower lip, flicking her tongue against his.

Strong and courageous, strong and courageous . . .

Those were her fighting words.

And she knew that if she caved, showing doubt or hesitancy, Magnus's eyes would shutter and his shields would rise—his honor and sense of duty would keep him from "taking advantage" of a woman who might not be completely keen.

She was more than keen.

And she desired Magnus badly enough to jump over her shadow to make him hers.

As if he guessed, he crushed her to him then, practically squeezing the air from her lungs. "Margo . . ." Holding her securely, he ducked beneath the door's low lintel and set her on her feet on the hard-packed earthen floor. "You will bring me to my knees, lass. It has been too long. . . ."

He pulled her to him again, taking her face between his hands and kissing her deeply. Slow and languorous kisses, full of tongue and soft, hot breath. Each kiss tantalized and melted her, curling her toes as their eyes adjusted to the cothouse's gloom.

When he pulled back, stepping away from her, Margo gasped. "Someone must've been here." She turned in a circle, surveying the tiny one-roomed space, impossibly tight and earthy-smelling. The floor had been swept clean and the walls and ceiling were free of cobwebs. The promised plaid pallet looked fresh and newly plumped. And someone had placed a cloth-covered basket of viands and an ale jug on the floor near the door.

Most telling of all was the mound of elegantly twisted, silver-hued driftwood waiting to be lit on the room's central grate.

"Orla did this." Margo's heart warmed.

Magnus shrugged. "She may have done. I'd ordered

my men to ready the place, but they wouldn't have taken such care."

Margo adjusted the soft wool of the shawl Orla had given her. "She is a good woman."

"You are a beautiful woman." Magnus's voice was deep, smooth, and rich as cream-laced whisky. He touched the side of her face, tracing a finger down the curve of her cheek, and then along the line of her jaw. "I have ne'er desired a woman so fiercely. Have you spelled me, Mar-*go*?"

"No." She could hardly breathe. "But if some kind of magic brought us together, and that seems the only way we *could* have met, then I am not sorry."

She wasn't.

Just standing so close to him was a sensory overload. Being alone with him here, in a teeny cottage on a Highland mountain, where the Scottish wind sighed in the trees and the surf shushed against the distant shore—*a Highland shore*—felt as romantic as if he were already making love to her. . . .

It was almost more than her heart could bear.

"I thought you were a Valkyrie." His voice softened as he looked down at her. "Or mayhap a sea witch . . ." One corner of his mouth lifted as he slipped a hand into her hair, letting the strands spill through his fingers. "A temptress sent to lure me with her spume-kissed glistening nakedness, making me so hard I could no' breathe."

"I was covered with sea spray this morning." Margo leaned into him, slipping her arms around his waist. She needed his closeness.

"Spume-kissed, aye." His breath was soft and warm against her face, and the intimacy excited her. "But"— his dark gaze flicked her length—"you weren't naked as I saw you the first time."

Margo shivered. The thought of him already having seen her naked almost pushed her to a climax.

"I also saw you riding astride me in Orosius's kettle steam." He slid his hand down her back, splaying his fingers across her hips and pulling her closer. So near that she could feel his heat through the rough wool of his plaid. She also felt his arousal, long, hard, and thick. The manliest part of him proved his desire with an impressive kilt-bulge.

"You were naked then, too, Margo-lass." The kilt-bulge nudged her belly. "And now . . ." He bent his head to kiss her, thrusting his tongue between her parted lips, sharing breath as he slowly twirled and tangled his tongue with hers. He slid his hand lower as they kissed, gripping the round curve of her bottom, kneading her flesh.

"Now, Margo"—he broke the kiss and stepped back, his dark eyes burning—"I would see you naked again. I want to hold you. Kiss you everywhere and make you mine—"

"Will you undress, too?" Margo blurted her wish, acting strong and courageous before excitement made her stutter and spoil everything. She did not want him to worry she was frightened or unwilling.

"Highlanders love to be naked, sweet." His hand was already at the big Celtic brooch holding his plaid at his shoulder. "We are earthy, lusty men."

Margo melted on the word *earthy*.

No one but a Highland Scot could make such a simple word so toe-curlingly sexy.

The word rolled through her, echoing in his rich, butter-rum burr.

"Oh, dear . . ." Her eyes rounded as he unclasped the pin, pulling off his plaid and tossing it onto the tartan pallet at his feet.

"Och, aye." He smiled, a slow, wicked smile that warmed her most private places as he pushed back his long black hair. The gleaming strands spilled across his shoulders, falling nearly to his waist. Margo's mouth went dry as she wondered how it would feel to have all that silky raven hair swing back and forth across her breasts when he made love to her.

Half-naked, he took her breath away. His shoulders were broad and just as powerful as she'd expected, while his hard-muscled chest delighted with a dusting of glistening black hair that arrowed downward, disappearing beneath his kilt belt. And—Margo's pulse leapt—a scatter of silvery scars proved he was indeed a lord of battles.

She swallowed, aching to see more of him.

The part she really wanted to see pressed more insistently against his kilt now, looking even longer and harder than before.

Following her gaze, Magnus reached to unlatch his sword belt, then lowered the great brand carefully to the floor. When he straightened, he made short work of his kilt, reaching for her and pulling her roughly to him the instant he was completely unclothed.

She leaned into him as he loosened her shawl and slipped it from her shoulders, tossing it onto the pallet with his plaid.

"I have wanted you all these nights, Margo." He was undoing her bodice laces, his eyes locked with hers as his hands worked the fastenings. His fingers brushed her bared skin, each tantalizing touch sending ripples of pleasure straight to her center.

But when her newly donned medieval gown gaped wide at the front, her breasts spilling free, modern-day sensibilities reared their ugly head as she threw an uncomfortable glance at the rough-planked door.

"There's not a lock on that door." Strong and courageous shouted protest at the hesitation, but Margo-of-the-Bad-Luck could just see the medieval equivalent of a troop of Boy Scouts parading by and peeking inside the shelter.

And if such an embarrassment was going to happen, it would most likely be just when she'd be in the throes of a rip-roaring climax.

Magnus was frowning, his dark gaze on the rain-warped door. "My men are out there, in the wood. They'll no' let anyone pass."

"They might overlook a small herd boy and his pals." Margo stood her ground, using her best substitute for a medieval Cub Scout. "What if—"

"You are with me, lass." His arm whipped around her, a hard band of iron, dragging her to him. "No one would dare come anywhere near this cothouse while we are here. The very wind will skirt this hill tonight, and even the leaves shall skitter in the opposite direction.

"This night is ours." His voice was fierce, his dark eyes glinting. "Whate'er comes, we shall have these hours."

Something in his tone told Margo that he, too, feared their pleasure might be fleeting.

She bit her lip, wishing she hadn't worried about the door.

But it was hard to shrug off a lifetime spent worrying about things like privacy and locked doors. A circle of mailed and armed warriors standing vigil in a wood all night as their leader made love to her was totally out of her experience.

Now . . .

His words, though romantic, only reminded her of the dangers swirling all around them.

Her *gown* was swirling around her head.

Margo blinked, her thoughts about medieval Cub

Scouts and dangers spinning away as Magnus lifted the gown's voluminous skirts. With a skill that hinted he'd once done this often, he pulled the gown up over her head and off, then sent the whole blue linen bundle sailing onto the pile of his own discarded clothes.

"Sweet holy heather..." He stepped back, the appreciation in his eyes making her heart race. "You are lovelier than I'd thought. Just stand there and dinnae move. I want to look at you."

At ease with his own nakedness, he bent to retrieve something from a small leather pouch attached to his sword belt. Seeing flint, steel, and a char cloth, Margo realized his purpose. It made tingles sweep across her most vulnerable places as he knelt before the little pile of driftwood and set to building a fire.

He wanted light to see her.

And that notion did very wicked things to her.

She'd never stood naked this long in front of any man. Most of her past boyfriends had been of the old one-two-we're-done, beneath-the-bedsheets, and all-lights-out variety.

Magnus wanted to look at her.

And his wish to do so electrified her. There was something blissfully decadent and oh-so-arousing about knowing that he wished her to stand here, unmoving and so wrenchingly vulnerable, simply for him to gaze upon.

He glanced at her now, his eyes dark with barely restrained desire as he carefully lit the driftwood. He straightened as blue, purple, and gold flames sprang to life, licking hungrily at the slender twists of silver-bleached wood. It was a beautiful sight.

But the look on Magnus's face was heart-stopping. His eyes blazed brighter than the fire, and his raven black hair shone almost as bright, the loose strands spilling around his shoulders as he folded his arms and gazed upon her.

His manhood stood, too. Thick and large, it rode his belly, his eagerness for her making her tingle even more.

She wanted him so badly.

"My *too*-rist." His voice was low and rough. "I could look at you for all my days and ne'er tire of your beauty."

"O-o-oh . . ." Margo hoped he hadn't heard her sigh. But she hadn't been able to help it. His words excited her; the fierce look on his face unleashed a dark, echoing need deep inside her.

The fire was larger now, the colorful flames leaping as the driftwood hissed and popped. They threw dancing shadows on the walls. In the shifting of light and dark, mysterious shadows whirled, lending a sensual, almost otherworldly feel to the atmosphere.

Margo started forward, wanting to go to Magnus, but he held out a hand, staying her.

"Nae, lass, no' yet." He spread his legs and crossed his arms, the stance giving her a good look at the large, heavy male sac between his legs. Even as it was drawn tight in arousal, its size made her blood thicken with aching female need. "I haven't yet looked my fill of you."

His words sent a rush of liquid heat to the aching place so low by her thighs.

Even her breasts were heavy and aching, her nipples taut and thrusting, begging for his touch.

She couldn't recall having ever been so excited.

"Open your legs, Mar-*go*." He gestured, encouraging her, as she did as he bade. "More. Spread your legs wider. I would see all of you."

"Oh, God!" She began to tremble.

"That is better, lass." His gaze skimmed over her, and then settled at the tops of her thighs, burning her. And it felt so good, so thrilling as he looked at her with such heat in his beautiful dark eyes.

He went to her then, placing one hand on her breast, his thumb gently circling her nipple, while he slid his other hand between her legs, gripping her firmly.

Margo's knees almost buckled. She rocked her hips, needing the contact. When he tightened his fingers on her, lightly squeezing, her climax did begin to crest. Sweet strings of hot pleasure wound through her, each tingling twist and curl making her crave release.

"I didnae want this." He lowered his head, trailing kisses across the top swells of her breasts, his thumb continuing to rub back and forth across her sensitized nipple. "I'd vowed to care for no woman again." His voice was deep, roughened by desire as he looked up to hold her gaze, locking eyes with her as he swirled his tongue around her nipple. He stroked and caressed the slick softness between her legs. His touch was the headiest torment.

"By whate'er powers brought you here"—he found her most sensitive spot, rubbed tiny circles there—"I cannae turn away from you. I have ne'er wanted a woman so fiercely. I'll no' be letting you go, Margo.

"No' e'er." He dropped to one knee before her, leaning in and using his chin to nudge her legs farther apart. "You are so fine, my *too*-rist. And here"—he looked up at her, his tongue now flicking across the sensitive spot where he'd just been circling a finger—"you smell of cold winter mornings, roses, and a wee touch of musk."

He moved to nuzzle her belly, closing his eyes and breathing deeply as he pressed his cheek against her feminine curls. "You are headier than mead, Margo." He looked up at her again, once more caressing her with his hand, circling her special spot with maddeningly delicious circles, slow and deliberate. "I could devour you whole. . . ."

"Then do." Margo opened her legs wider, feeling very strong and courageous by giving him better access. "It feels so good. . . ." She thrust her fingers into his hair, grabbing handfuls of the thick, silky strands as he did just as he'd promised, licking her with long, measured strokes as if he'd never tasted anything more delicious.

"I am ravenous for you." He flicked his tongue over her clit, then again and again. Glancing up at her, he slid the tip of one finger along up her center, light as a butterfly touch, and then back down again. He stroked her gently, up and down the very heart of her, as he teased her with his tongue.

Margo twined her fingers in his hair, twisting the thick strands around her wrist, holding tight, needing something to balance her.

He turned his head and nuzzled her inner thigh, nipping the tender flesh there before he returned to her center, his tongue probing and explorative. Delicious.

"O-o-oh, don't stop. . . ." Margo couldn't stand it. Any moment she was going to shatter.

Waves of erotic sensation whirled inside her, spreading from her core, then circling back again as exquisite pleasure danced between her legs. She rocked her hips and squirmed, his swirling tongue bringing her closer and closer to the edge.

Need burned in her.

"Magnus . . ." She reached for his hands, threading their fingers, as she dropped to her knees. She knelt face-to-face with him on the cold, hard-packed floor. "Please, I can't wait much longer. Kiss me. . . ."

She grabbed his face, kissing his cheeks, his forehead, and his throat, before locking her fingers behind his head and pulling him close, moaning as she kissed his mouth with a fierceness she couldn't control.

"Sweet lass." He kissed her with equal hunger, plundering her lips with deep, openmouthed kisses, his tongue thrusting greedily. "The plaid . . ." He broke away long enough to throw a meaningful glance at the pallet only an arm's length away. But instead of moving onto it, he brought his hands up between them and cupped her breasts, plumping, weighing, and squeezing them. He rolled her nipples between his thumb and fingers until she cried out and seized his wrists, pulling his hands from her breasts.

"I will shatter. Please, wait." She was trembling, on the verge now.

And still they kissed, their mouths locked tightly together, their breath mingling, as their tongues swirled and glided. Then—Margo didn't know how it'd happened—they were rolling on the earthen floor, their arms and legs entwined, their bodies pressed so close that their heat scorched the cold, damp earth.

The ancient smell of a thousand summers rose around them, warm and beguiling, blending with the faint tang of lost seas as the driftwood burned, and the sharper musk of their own desire.

Intense pleasure stormed through Margo in thick, unstoppable waves of concentrated ecstasy so powerful she couldn't bear to tear her lips from Magnus's even to gasp a breath.

"Lass, I must have you." He drew her onto the pallet, settling her on her back, running his hands over her breasts and her belly. Still kissing her, he let his hands glide deeper, smoothing down the tops of her thighs and back up the insides, cupping her sex and squeezing in rhythm with their stroking tongues.

Margo was floating.

She'd known he'd be a grand lover.

But this . . .

Need pulsed deep inside her, a surging tide so demanding she stilled, opening her legs wide and reaching for him, closing her hand around his iron-hard length, so large, hot, and silky smooth beneath her fingers. She stroked and caressed, rubbing him in the same deliberate way she ached to feel him sliding in and out of her.

As if he knew, he rolled on top of her, positioning himself between her thighs. He reached between them, bringing himself where he needed to be. Then, inch by inch, he eased into her, until he was deep inside, filling her completely. He pulled back and reentered several times, letting her adjust to him.

"Margo." He pushed up on his elbows, holding her gaze, seeking her center with a finger, and rubbing her there as he began moving slowly in and out of her. "You feel so good, lass, sweeter than all my dreams."

"O-o-oh . . ." Margo arched back against the plaid, wrapping her legs around him. She ran her hands up and down his back, tunneling her fingers through his wonderful hair, her sex clenching around him as he began thrusting harder, faster, and deeper.

The incredible pleasure crashed over her, its force stunning her as wave after wave of her release flooded her, taking her breath and hurtling her onto a dizzying sea of shattering peaks.

And still she clung to him, everything female in her thrilling to hear him shout her name in his own release, then glorying in the same triumph when he collapsed atop her, his body still jerking inside her, spilling hot seed.

It was, in a word, epic.

And Margo was sure she'd never move again, for her limbs felt weaker than wet noodles.

But some barely coherent part of her feared that such a mind-blowing orgasm would attract her usual bad luck as surely as if she'd marched down the street with a target on her back.

It wouldn't surprise her to wake up and discover she'd been napping aboard her Newark-bound flight, her vacation over and everything a dream.

It seemed a possibility, considering how good she felt just now.

So she lay very still, almost afraid to breathe.

She *was* afraid to crack her eyes.

"Mo ghaoil. My dear." Magnus rolled onto his back and pulled her against him, proving that he, at least, still had the strength to move. He settled her against his chest and shoulder.

The Gaelic endearment speared her heart. Longing filled her chest, along with fierce, soul-splitting joy. Whatever happened now, she'd have this night to remember.

No one could erase their bliss.

As if he wished to strengthen it, Magnus slid his hand up her side and over her breasts, lightly flicking her nipples with the tips of his fingers.

Margo purred, arousal beginning to stir again.

"M'mmm ..." She snuggled close, after-pleasure still heavy inside her. Magnus's fingers circling her nipples made the blood simmer and pulse anew between her legs. It was a luxurious feeling, totally decadent.

And thank goodness, so real.

That reality was underscored by Magnus's arm wrapped possessively around her. And the hiss and popping sounds of the driftwood fire that filled the little cothouse.

She hadn't gone anywhere.

And no medieval Cub Scouts had arrived to dash cold water on her pleasure.

Life might be getting good for a change.

"Margo." Magnus's tone told her that wasn't so. "There was another reason I brought you up here."

She stiffened, all her senses snapping to high alert.

"I wished to speak with you alone, away from the ears of my men." He was skimming his fingers across her breasts in a series of slow, tantalizing circles.

It was a delicious, deliberate exploration, the caresses both soothing and incredibly sensual. But Margo didn't like the tension humming between them. Dark emotions poured out of him, staining the air.

She slipped out of his arms. "Then tell me."

He caught her wrist, frowning. "I will. But stay here with me." He pulled her back down beside him. "I told you I'd explain Redpoint. That is what you must know. Your life might depend on it."

Oh, great.

She'd managed her first voyage on a medieval dragon ship and now she had to survive Redpoint.

The mere place-name sounded ominous, after she'd seen Magnus and his men run around Gairloch with blood dripping from the tips of their swords.

"So what happens at Redpoint?" She wished she didn't have to know.

She did reach for her discarded chemise, pulling it over her head before giving Magnus her full attention.

Somehow she wasn't up to hearing bad news while naked.

Magnus took one of her hands, meshing their fingers. "I've planned an ambush at Redpoint." He didn't mince words. "Six of my best cattle beasts will graze along the shore, attracting a few Viking ships that will rush in, expecting an easy provision raid.

"When they do"—he brought her hand to his lips, kissing her fingertips—"my men and I will attack from the cliff tops, firing their ships and fighting their warriors on the strand. Afterwards, the ease of their slaughter will act as a warning to others of their ilk to keep clear of this coastline."

"And if they beat you?" Margo looked at him.

For a moment, she thought he was going to smile and tell her no Viking could defeat him.

A slight tug *did* appear at one corner of his mouth.

But then his face cleared and he frowned. "That is why we're having this talk. Should aught go wrong, Calum will look after you. He won't be joining the fight, so he'll get you away—"

"I'm going to be there?" Margo felt her stomach clench in knots.

"You must be at Redpoint." He turned over her hand, kissing her palm. "I willnae leave you on your own here. No' even on *Sea-Raven*, guarded. You'll no' be too near the battle, but above the fighting, on the cliffs. You needn't watch. Just promise me you'll stay with Calum if need be. He'd see you back to Orla's, where you can stay until he can escort you to my home, Badcall Castle.

"If that happens, my aunts, Agnes and Portia, will welcome you. They can be difficult." He slipped his arms around her, drawing her back against his chest. "Aunt Portia fancies she knows herbs and healing and often mixes bad cures and potions for folk, sometimes causing more havoc than good. And Aunt Agnes can be forceful. She's a bold woman, and likes to bluster. But they mean well."

Not at all happy, Margo bit her lip. "If I'm going to see Badcall, I'd rather go there with you."

She remembered what Orla said about Magnus needing to learn there was more to life than vengeance.

"Why don't we go to Badcall directly?" The idea seemed brilliant. "Surely you killed enough Vikings at Gairloch. And what happened with me . . ." She paused, still puzzling at the power of the Cursing Stone. "That wiped out a lot of Vikings."

It had.

But he seemed to have forgotten because he was shaking his head.

"There you have it." He pulled her closer into the shelter of his body, keeping his arms clasped around her. "If Gairloch hadn't happened, I'd leave the six cattle here at Badachro and sail with you for Badcall at first light. But too many Northmen and their ships vanished that day and they will be missed."

"Oh." Margo was beginning to understand. "You want victory at Redpoint so that word of the battle will spread. The Norse will then believe you annihilated the Vikings at Gairloch in a similar fight?"

"You are a clever lass." He kissed the top of her head. "Redpoint has been planned for a while. We brought the cattle down weeks ago. Even my dog, Frodi, is here. He is old and came in a litter with the cattle. I wanted him along because no other dog is better trained for such affrays. And Frodi loves a good adventure. After the fight, he'll be treated by a journey home on the *Sea-Raven*."

"The cattle, too?" Margo hoped they wouldn't be on the ship.

She loved dogs. But the *Sea-Raven* was horror enough without six bellowing cattle on board.

"The cattle stay here, dinnae you worry." Magnus had surely guessed her alarm. "Three of the beasts will be brought back to Badachro. The other three will be my gift to the fisherfolk at Redpoint for letting me site my ambush in their cove.

"I'd only hoped to give the Vikings a warning. Now"—he took a breath—"they must be made to believe I sent the ships at Gairloch to the bottom of the sea. I'll no' have them swarming these coasts, looking for stranded war bands or searching for the Cursing Stone."

"The Cursing Stone?" Margo's stomach clenched. She didn't want the stone turning up again, zapping her back into the twenty-first century. "I thought we agreed it'd vanished on its own?"

"We did. And I am sure that it has." His answer confused her. "Orosius believes so."

"But?" Margo hated buts.

"Donata might yet be after the stone." His voice hardened. "She is known to consort with Vikings. If she enlists their aid, hell would be unleashed on us. I'd sooner act first and put out word that I burned a great fleet of Viking warships at Gairloch, leaving no' an ash in memory."

Margo considered. "What if the Vikings don't believe you?"

"They know my reputation." Pride rang in Magnus's voice. "They will no' doubt the story."

Margo wasn't so sure.

She also knew he was leaving something out.

Her.

If Donata rallied Vikings to help her search for the Cursing Stone, she'd also tell tall tales about a "mysterious blond woman" who'd possessed the wonder stone. Margo wouldn't be safe anywhere.

Magnus was trying to protect her.

And to do so, he was going to plunge right into another Viking battle.

The thought chilled Margo to the core.

Chapter 17

Two mornings later, Magnus stood closer to the Red-point cliff edge than most men would dare. Even his war-riors held their distance. Unfortunately, a rustle of skirts warned that Margo had difficulties staying where he'd left her. He'd placed her out of sight, behind a thicket of broom and whin bushes, well away from the precipice.

Now . . .

He shoved back his hair, listening intently. Then his heart began to pound when, along with the telltale rus-tling, he caught a trace of clean snowy air and roses on the morning wind.

There could be no mistake.

His men were even swiveling their heads, exchang-ing glances and under-the-breath mutters. Their eyes, for the moment, weren't on the oh-so-important horizon and whatever enemies might appear there.

They were gawking at Margo.

Furious, Magnus turned.

She was nearly upon him. "I can't see from behind those bushes." She made that sound as if it was a prob-lem. "Perhaps I can—"

"You'll stay where I put you." Swift, fierce heat raced through Magnus's veins. He could feel his brows sweeping low in a fearsome scowl. "That spot was chosen so you wouldn't see anything. And so that no one will see you.

"Just now"—he took a step toward her—"every ship between here and the horizon will spot your bright head. Your hair blazes like the sun."

"My cloak has a hood." She was already reaching for it.

Magnus stopped her with a quick grip to her wrist. "The thicket, lass. Go back there now, stay with the villagers waiting there, and dinnae show yourself again until I come for you."

"But—"

"I'll no' have you distracting my men." Magnus's head was beginning to pound.

Several of his warriors were already edging near, bending their ears. Their appearance proved his words.

What red-blooded man wouldn't have his head turned when she paraded past? High color slashed her cheeks, her eyes flashed blue sparks, and the wind tossed her shining, sun-bright hair about her beautiful face. Most damning of all, her lips were fetchingly kiss-swollen.

Magnus eyed those lips, remembering how heatedly they'd kissed through the night.

Would that he was plundering her mouth now.

Instead, it annoyed him to see that Orla's woolen cloak fell in a much more appealing manner than Orosius's heavy bearskin mantle. Margo's new clothes drew attention to the full curve of her breasts and the ripeness of her hips. Charms made all the more evident because the wind molded the cloak's folds to her feminine shapeliness.

His men couldn't help but stare at her.

Even so, he glared at them.

"Just be careful." Her mouth set in a disapproving line. "I remember what I saw at Gair—"

"You'll be seeing none the like here"—he took her arm, urging her away from the cliff edge and back toward the thicket—"if you stay behind thon bushes."

When she stood in place, her blue eyes starting to spark again, he cupped her face in his hands and kissed her hard. It was a rough, bruising, no-quarter-given kiss that he hoped would keep her too stunned to argue with him.

"Now go." He set her from him, sharply aware of his men's stares.

"There's been enough of this vengeance stuff," she said—or so Magnus thought—before she turned and strode away, her back straight and her shoulders rigid.

Magnus scowled after her.

He waited until she disappeared around the thicket, and then he went back to the cliff edge. His men still lingered a good distance behind him. He stepped closer to the edge than before. He was too steady on his feet to slip. And his anger appreciated the challenge.

He also didn't worry about being seen, for the deep shadows of a large, broken-stoned outcrop hid him well. And even if it didn't, he and his men had prepared the strand below with care. No Norse raider intent on easy plunder would waste glances on the soaring bluffs that hemmed the little cove where such ripe pickings beckoned.

It was a fail-proof plan.

Peering down at the beach now, he flexed his fingers, and then rolled his shoulders, waiting.

Cook smoke curled lazily from the clustered hovels of the fishing village, and drying nets hung from stunted, wind-bent trees at the far end of the curving strand. Magnus said a silent prayer of thanks that the Redpoint fishers' huts were bunched at the south edge of the cove. Their boats lined the sand directly beneath Magnus and his men. That was a shame, but boats could be replaced and he'd do so gladly. No one stirred at this early-morning hour, but somewhere a dog barked, the sound making him smile.

The bark meant that Calum and Frodi were in place on the strand, out of sight behind the thatched cottages, but doing their job. Which was to keep the six fat cattle—some of Magnus's best—from getting bored and wandering away from the cove and up onto the more tempting grazing grounds beyond the dunes.

The beasts wouldn't be seen there.

And Magnus wanted them noticed.

Just as he hoped that the pile of sand-filled barrels near the cottages would be mistaken for a generous supply of plump, brine-soaked herring.

Viking warriors had ravenous appetites and the need for food was as great as their constant hunger for gold, women, and easy-to-capture slaves. Knowing how they treated the poor souls who fell into their hands made his gut clench and—for what seemed like the thousandth time since climbing onto the ridge—he narrowed his eyes to scan the horizon.

He was eager for a good bloodletting.

But the waves still stretched bleak and dark, a rolling sheet of beaten gray.

Thunder rumbled in the distance and a mist dampened the air, but he welcomed the day's wetness. Later, after the killing, a good rain would wash the Norsemen's blood from the cove's dark red sand.

"The sea is quiet." Ewan lifted his head from where he lay in the grass. "Nothing's moving except the tide and"—he tore his gaze from the water long enough to glance at Magnus—"maybe those thick clouds gathering in the west."

"They'll come." Magnus slapped his sword hilt; there was no doubt in his mind.

He could smell the Vikings' taint in the air as surely as he could still taste Margo's rich, womanly sweetness on the back of his tongue.

His sword, Vengeance, also knew the Northmen were coming.

Magnus could almost feel the blade's readiness to sup blood. There was no denying the sword's thin-as-air quiver when she smelled battle.

It was a joy to feed her.

But just now, he had others needing nourishment. Food to fill bellies and ale to take the edge off the terror of souls who lived from catching herring and eels and not by how fiercely they could wield steel.

He also hoped that the need to calm and soothe frightened villagers would keep Margo occupied, her mind off the horrors that would unfold on the still-peaceful stretch of lovely red sand.

Turning his face into the wind, he cast another glance at the empty sea, and then looked again at Ewan. "Do the villagers have enough to eat?"

"More than we had this morn." Ewan grinned. "They're all back there." He nodded to the thick line of broom and whin bushes. "They're feasting on bread, herring, cheese, and enough ale to have them sleeping through till the morrow. Your lady, too, if she knows what's good for her."

A muscle jerked in Magnus's jaw, but he didn't correct Ewan for calling Margo his lady.

Leastways, he wished a true union with her would be possible. It was one reason he'd been so disappointed when his crew had failed to turn up the Cursing Stone after searching the strand in Gairloch.

He didn't just want to toss the enchanted stone into the sea to keep such powers from landing in the hands of dangerous, evil men.

He also feared the stone's existence might always present a threat to Margo.

Something might snatch her from his arms as swiftly as the stone's magic had helped her appear.

He frowned, liking none of it.

For now, he nodded at Ewan. "The villagers are still guarded?"

"Och, aye." Ewan sounded amused. "My grandfather told the guards he'd cut off their balls in their sleep if they left their posts."

"Calum would." Magnus stifled a laugh. Sound carried on water. "And"—the humor left his voice—"if a single villager is harmed, I'll slice off the rest o' the guardsmen's bits and make each man eat his own danglers.

"If aught befalls Margo, they'll lose more than their danglers." Magnus set his hand on Vengeance's hilt. "I'll have their heads."

"They know that, lord."

"Then pray they stay with Margo and the fisherfolk when it comes to a fight." Magnus shot another glance at the thicket. The glint of spear heads and mail could just be seen through the broom's yellow blooms if one knew where to look. "I'll no' be having them rushing down to the strand if the battle joy takes them."

"They won't, lord." Ewan's gaze was on the sea again, watching.

A curlew called then, the haunting cry coming from farther along the cliff.

Magnus's pulse quickened. "Vikings have been spotted."

He shot a look at Ewan. The lad's hand already hovered near his sword hilt, his fingers twitching. A broad smile was spreading across the younger man's red-bearded face. Magnus nodded, pleased. Then he glanced at the other warriors, each man behind a rock or hidden by grass. Every one bristled with arms, ready to kill.

The sea still stretched empty.

But the prickling at Magnus's nape told him they were no longer alone.

And they weren't.

Suddenly Magnus could see the enemy. Dark shapes beneath the blackening sky, three dragon ships slid out of the mist, their long oars rising and falling, sending up plumes of bright silver spray. Each ship boasted fearsome beast heads on stern and stem, and the oarsmen beat faster on every smooth, sweeping stroke. The ships rode the flooding tide, coming fast, and were filled with howling, fierce-faced warriors, their helmets and mail glinting in the dim morning light, their swords and battle-axes already drawn.

"Hold, men." Magnus spoke only loud enough for his warriors to hear. He threw a glance over his shoulder at the thicket, relief sluicing him when he didn't see Margo peeking out through the underbrush.

Turning back to his men, he jerked a nod. "We wait until the ships run ashore and Frodi chases the cattle from the strand."

Releasing his grip on Vengeance's hilt, he flattened his hands against the large, deliberately loosened boulders before him. He splayed his fingers and took a deep breath, willing victory.

From below came the loud hiss of sheared water, the splashing of oar blades, and the wild shouts of the Norse marauders.

Fury, hot and seething, scalded Magnus's blood. But he stayed where he was, unmoving. He kept still as stone, out of sight behind the sheltering outcrop. It was a reprieve of heartbeats, for very soon hell would open and the quiet little strand would become a killing place.

He peered around the outcrop and down to the cove, and for one terrible moment, he imagined Liana running across a similar beach, her innocent eyes wide with terror as she tried to flee the wild-eyed, huge-bearded men chasing her. To his horror, he couldn't recall her face clearly.

He saw Margo instead. His mind's eye conjured her lithe, naked, and terrified, as she raced along the surf, chased by Viking hordes and—his gut twisted—Donata, who rode the wind on a birch switch.

Magnus shuddered, banishing the image.

Then nothing else mattered because in that instant the first of the three dragon ships roared onto the shore, its keel crunching into the strand in a wild spray of foam and flying pebbles. The other two boats came as quickly, grinding to the same screeching halt even as mailed, screaming Norsemen leapt down from the prows, swords, axes, and spears in their hands.

Magnus felt a surge of elation.

This was the moment he'd been awaiting.

He flashed a look at Ewan, jerked a swift nod.

The younger man grinned. Then he set a hand to his lips and made the sharp drumming notes of a great spotted woodpecker. The sound rippled the air, echoing across the hills like drifting smoke rings. It was all the encouragement Magnus's warriors needed. On the strand, the Vikings didn't notice the birdcall as they splashed through the surf, shouting taunts and swinging axes.

But the world around them split wide as Frodi shot onto the strand, barking wildly as he herded the six cattle into the safety of the dunes. Frodi flew across the strand, excitement letting him forget his old bones as he ran faster than he had in years.

Laughing, the Vikings chased after Frodi and the cattle beasts, oblivious of impending doom. Coming death swept near as Magnus and his men sprang to action, heaving as one to send a barrage of boulders hurtling over the cliff to crash onto the marauders. Other men burst from inside the fisher huts, shooting fire arrows into the beached longboats as they ran out onto the sand.

The arrows streaked into the ships with unerring accuracy, some slamming into hulls, others piercing sails or thudding into the rowing benches. Flames caught swiftly, crackling to life and licking across the planking, blackening the masts and rearing beast heads. The fire grew quickly, sweeping the timbers and leaping high to turn the sky red and fill the cove with clouds of whirling, choking smoke and ash.

A vile stench filled the air and burned his eyes, but the moans of dying Norsemen—and the rage of those Vikings yet living—was a sweet song in Magnus's ears as he hastened down the cliff path, Vengeance drawn and ready, his men on his heels.

Chaos met them.

Many of the Vikings lay sprawled on the strand, their big mail-clad bodies mangled by the rocks. Most had whipped around and run back to their burning ships, where they dashed about, yelling and scooping up sand and water with their shields, trying to douse the flames. But a few whirled to attack Magnus and his men as they thundered down the cliff track and raced into the confusion.

"I want blood!" Magnus swung Vengeance, the great sword's blade clashing against steel, then slicing through the wooden haft of an ax.

The ax wielder roared, casting aside the useless weapon and reaching to whip out his sword. Before he could, Vengeance whistled through the air, taking off the Norseman's wrist in a lightning-fast strike. Howling, the man staggered, then dropped to his knees, clutching the bloodied stump to his chest. Magnus stabbed deep with Vengeance's tip, ending the Viking's misery with a swift jab to the throat, the force of his thrust almost severing the man's head.

"MacBride!" A huge Norseman snarled his name, proving they knew whose coast they'd dared ravage. Agile for such a giant, the man danced around Magnus, his war ax swinging, already dripping red. "You'll not fell me! Come try"—the man's eyes flashed challenge—"and the gulls will feast on your eyes before the blood dries on my blade."

Magnus grinned coldly and reached to yank the leather band from his hair. "Hold tight to your ax, Northman, if you wish to dine in Odin's hall this e'en!" Still smiling, he tossed his head, letting the loose strands swing about his shoulders. "Word is, there's an empty chair there, waiting for you."

"You're cursed, MacBride." The Viking kept dancing, tossing his ax from hand to hand, a gap-toothed grin splitting his bushy blond beard. "Donata's cast her spell on you, speaking death and misery to you and yours."

"I dinnae believe in spells," Magnus lied, eager to redden his steel on the man's blood.

He wanted this Norseman's soul.

There were fine rings of thick silver on the man's large, mail-sleeved arms.

"I keep a chest o' those." Magnus flicked his wrist, using Vengeance's tip to point at the Viking's arm rings. "I take them off dead men and tonight I'll be tossing yours in with the others.

"Except"—he implied delight—"the two or three I'll wear in my feast hall this e'en."

The Viking lunged, bellowing his rage. Magnus side-stepped him with ease, scything Vengeance to counter the man's vicious blow. But the sword's blade glanced off the heavy mail of the Viking's sleeve, the failed strike only serving to enrage the man more. He whirled on Magnus, hacking wildly, his bloodied ax blade cutting air when Magnus spun, then swept Vengeance in a great, whistling arc. And this time, his blade sliced into the vulnerable gap beneath the Norseman's raised arm, the powerful cut cleaving deep, splintering bone and sending a fountain of red to brighten the length of Magnus's sword and splash across his chest.

"Vengeance!" Magnus yelled his battle cry as he yanked free his blade. The huge Norseman toppled, falling face-first onto the sand.

Magnus wheeled away, eager to slay his next challenger.

"I'll give you vengeance."

The taunt came from another tall, mail-coated Norseman. Blond as the slain axman's, this Viking's wheat-colored hair spilled free to his waist, and the battered faceplate of his helmet shone red in the firelight. Ten or more gold rings glittered on each arm, proclaiming his status. As did his jeweled belt buckle and the gem-studded clasps adorning the thick plaits of his proudly braided beard.

"You're the dead man, Viking." Magnus wasn't impressed.

The Norseman didn't care. "If the fates so will it." He shrugged, unconcerned. "I think it's you who'll miss the morrow's sunrise."

"Shall we see?" Magnus was keen.

"Tell Odin that it was Harald Skull-Splitter who sent you into his company." The Viking grinned, whipping his sword in a flashing figure-of-eight flourish. "I keep him well amused."

"Then he will be pleased to meet you at last." Magnus twirled Vengeance in an equally bold display. "Perhaps"—he flicked his gaze to the three burning ships, guessing that this man was the warlord who owned them—"he'll like you so much that he'll replace your fired boats in Valhalla."

"I'll build new boats from the riches I'll be taking from your lands, Viking Slayer." He spoke Magnus's byname as a slur. "After I dine on your liver and then whore your women in your bed."

Harald Skull-Splitter's men stopped fighting long enough to jeer. Magnus's warriors snarled, their outraged protests heating air already scorching hot from the flames of the Norsemen's burning dragon boats.

Together, their own fighting momentarily forgotten, Magnus's men and the Viking warriors formed a circle, ringing Magnus and Harald Skull-Splitter. Each man edged near, drawn by the lure of a fierce and deadly combat of arms, a battle that promised a spectacle of blood sure to please the most jaded warrior.

"A boon for you, Skull-Splitter, in honor of your bravery . . . and in small recompense for the loss of three fine ships." Magnus glanced at the ring of men, searching the Norsemen's faces. "Which man lives to carry my message to Sigurd Sword Breaker? You decide. Now, while you still have breath to utter a name."

Harald Skull-Splitter spat on the sand. "There'll be no need."

"I insist." Magnus moved with eye-blurring speed, the tip of Vengeance jabbing beneath the Viking warlord's chin before the man could blink. "Choose a survivor."

Harald Skull-Splitter set his mouth in a tight hard line, his face showing no emotion. But his gaze did flash to a young well-armored warrior. Blond, good-looking, and the least burly of the Northmen, he still had the freshness of youth about him. And, surprisingly, an air of innocence that shone bright in his startling blue eyes.

"You." Magnus jerked his head at the youth. "Who are you?"

"I am Arnor Song-Bringer." The young warrior stepped forward.

"A good name—as your leader has lost his tongue." Magnus kept his sword tip at Skull-Splitter's chin. "You have broken his quiet."

Several of Magnus's warriors sniggered.

The other Vikings remained silent, anger rolling off them.

"The name is because my birth ended my mother's silence." The youth's voice was clear, proud. "She lost my father and my brothers before I was born and vowed in her sorrow to never speak again. When I came, she sang to me, forgetting the oath in her gladness."

Magnus frowned, feeling oddly chastised.

Skull-Splitter took advantage, knocking Vengeance away from his jaw. "Arnor is Sigurd Sword Breaker's nephew."

Magnus eyed the youth sharply. His blood chilled and he was sure that Vengeance's blade vibrated, demanding to bite deep into the youth's flesh.

Whipping Vengeance back up to point at Skull-Splitter's belly, Magnus snarled. His rage seethed and he tasted hot bile as his world took on the shimmering red haze that always came with killing.

He shot another fierce glance at the youth.

Arnor glared at him, defiant.

"Who he is, or"—Magnus turned back to Skull-Splitter, his scowl deepening—"how he received his name, doesn't matter. Only that he will be left alive to carry my warning to Sword Breaker and every other Viking warlord who dares to eye this coast."

"You've just spoken your last words." Harald Skull-Splitter attacked then, leaping forward in savage anger, his sword a flash of silver that struck Vengeance so hard Magnus reeled, almost losing his footing.

He recovered swiftly and roared a challenge as he lunged forward. He swung Vengeance with a fury, the vicious arc catching Skull-Splitter in the side. Vengeance's blade screamed across the tight steel rings of the Norseman's mail coat, bruising but drawing no blood.

Skull-Splitter laughed and slashed down furiously with his own blade, trying to slice through Magnus's arm. Magnus blocked the blow with Vengeance's broad side, thrusting the Viking backward with such force he should have crashed to his knees. Instead, he spun around, his own blade swinging in another death-bringing stroke. Except Magnus wasn't yet ready to die. He was eager to kill, so he whirled, slashing Vengeance in an even mightier arc. This time the blade sliced through the Norseman's mailed sleeve, cutting straight into muscle and bone. Blood sprayed onto the sand and Skull-Splitter's sword dropped from his limp fingers.

Magnus grinned, not surprised when his foe growled and used his left hand to pluck his huge Norse war ax from its jeweled belt ring.

"I've taken worse scratches from the women I bed," Skull-Splitter sneered, ignoring his bloodied arm and raising his bright ax blade.

"You've had your last whore. Save"—Magnus eyed the long-handled ax, unconcerned—"any toothless hags Odin might share with you."

Magnus lunged then, aiming deadly, but Skull-Splitter leapt aside and the sword glanced harmlessly across the Norseman's massive steel-clad shoulder. Eyes blazing, the Viking charged, lifting his good arm to rain ax blows and hacks at Magnus's head and arms.

"Donata's curse is on you, MacBride." Skull-Splitter hissed the words as he brought his ax slashing down, missing Magnus's shoulder by a hairbreadth. He hacked again, wildly. "You're wasting breath trying to kill me because you're already a dead man."

"Nae, that's you." Magnus narrowed his eyes, refusing to acknowledge the chill that swept him on the Viking's words. Furious, he flicked Vengeance with blinding speed, taking two fingers from his foe's ax hand.

Skull-Splitter howled, his remaining fingers still gripping his ax. "You'll not fell me," he jeered, coming at Magnus again.

"I'm slaying you now." Magnus sidestepped the blow with ease. "Hold on to your ax if you wish to dine with Odin this e'en."

"Cur!" Skull-Splitter tried to rally.

But the sand beneath his feet was growing slick with his spilled blood and the force in his left arm wasn't as powerful as the might of his useless sword arm. He kept fighting, snarling fiercely as Magnus continued to spin and lunge, avoiding the Viking's ax swings and dealing his own vicious strikes with Vengeance.

Roaring now, the Viking slammed down his ax in a fierce swipe that could've cleaved an ox in two equal halves. But Magnus was prepared and on Skull-Splitter's downswing, he rammed Vengeance forward in a terrible two-handed thrust, piercing mail and leather jerkin to sink the sword's blade deep in the Norseman's gut.

Magnus's men cheered and raised their own reddened blades, renewing the fight with the other Vikings even before Magnus could yank Vengeance from Skull-Splitter's belly. The Nordic warlord twitched on the sand, his bloodied fingers groping for his ax hilt.

He didn't moan, but his eyes met Magnus's, pleading for that mercy.

Northmen dreaded nothing more than dying without a weapon in their hand. If they did, the way to Valhalla and the glories of Odin's feasting hall was barred to them. Instead they fell straight to Niflheim, the Norse hell where such ill-fated men shivered in endless cold and dark while Nidhogg, the Corpse-Tearer, a huge scaly-backed dragon, gnawed on their bones as they wailed and writhed in eternal agony.

Magnus relished the thought.

Skull-Splitter's eyes were beginning to glaze, the plea in them fading.

The man had fought hard. He'd been fierce, braver than many men Magnus knew.

He deserved to die well.

His eyelids fluttered, drifting shut.

"God's curse!" Magnus ignored the fighting around him and bent, snatching up the Viking warlord's ax and thrusting the weapon into the man's hand. He dropped to one knee beside the bastard, curling his trembling fingers around the hilt and holding them there until Skull-Splitter gave a last gurgling sigh, shuddered, and fell still.

The Norseman's soul had fled.

And—Magnus stood—Skull-Splitter would already be taking his place at Odin's table. No doubt reaching for a brimming horn of ale and grinning broadly at the plump, half-naked beauties eager to wriggle onto his lap. Life for Harald Skull-Splitter just became paradise.

Magnus was still cursed.

The Vikings' taunts filled his mind again, clear as the clashing of swords and axes, the grunts, shouts, and curses of the men fighting across the red-streaming sand. A chill tore through him and he dragged his sleeve over his brow, wiping away blood and sweat.

He could almost feel darkness swirling around him, drawing nearer and searching for him.

He looked for Arnor Song-Bringer.

Then—at last—the killing slowed and the insults, screams, and yells lessened, the battle drawing to an end. Only Magnus's warriors stood on the sullied, smoke-hazed strand. But one Viking yet lived, just as he'd ordered. Calum and another older warrior held the youth at the tide line, Frodi sitting guard before them.

"Ewan!" Magnus glanced at his friend, and then nodded toward the end of the cove where a small two-man skiff was beached near a pile of drying seaweed. "Ready that boat for Arnor Song-Bringer."

"With pleasure." Ewan sheathed his bloodred sword and sprinted along the strand, quickly dragging the little boat to the water's edge.

Magnus then narrowed his eyes at Sigurd Sword Breaker's nephew. "Calum and his cousin are about to put you in thon skiff." Magnus remained where he was, arms folded. The insult would be greater if his men, not him, put the messenger in the boat and shoved him off. "You'll go naked and stripped of weapons. Nor will you have oars. Your own gods and the sea will determine where to take you. If they're kind, you'll reach your northern shores, or a Viking ship, before you die of cold or thirst.

"If you make it to your uncle"—Magnus did come forward now, for Calum and the other warrior had tossed the bare-bottomed Norseman into the skiff and were already shoving the boat into the waves—"tell Sword Breaker what happens to raiders who dare set foot on my shores. If he and his ilk wish to land at the bottom of the sea, their ships' ashes soiling the strand as at Gairloch, they can come.

"Tell him"—Magnus raised his own foot, kicking the skiff deeper into the surf—"Magnus MacBride, Viking Slayer, is waiting. And that I'm eager to feed every last one of you to Corpse-Tearer. I showed mercy to

Harald Skull-Splitter. I have none for your uncle or his
followers."

"My uncle doesn't need your mercy." Arnor Song-
Bringer sat ramrod straight in the tiny boat, his chin
raised defiantly. "He shows quarter to no man and will
cut out my tongue for delivering your message."

"But you will." Magnus lifted his voice above the rising wind.

"I shall." The young warrior's blue gaze bit deep into
Magnus's own. "For I am as brave as you, MacBride, and
fear no man. Not even—"

The rest of his words were carried away by a gust
of whirling smoke from the burning dragon ships. And
when the soot-filled air cleared, the little skiff was much
farther out to sea, a black speck bobbing wildly in the
foaming, red-glinting waves.

Then Arnor Song-Bringer was gone.

He was vanished, off on his way to whatever end the
fate spinners planned for him.

Magnus felt a bump against his leg and looked down,
seeing Frodi leaning hard into him. "You did well, lad."
He rubbed the dog's ears, and then took a twist of dried
meat from a pouch on his belt, giving Frodi the treat he
loved best before sending him to gather the six cattle
from wherever they'd wandered beyond the dunes.

The cattle would make a fine gift to the fisherfolk
here and at Badachro.

As would the watch Magnus intended to place on the
cliffs above both bays. A deterrent should the Norsemen
ignore his warning.

He just wished he knew what to do about the warning
bells in his head. They rang loudly now. And even this
day's good work couldn't dispel them. Worst of all, he
couldn't shake the ghastly suspicion that his ill ease had
more to do with Margo than with him.

Donata might've cursed him. But he shook off her threats as a seabird repels water.

It was Margo who was vulnerable.

Donata would be after Margo's soul, trying to use her to crush him. Especially if she guessed how deeply Magnus was coming to care for Margo.

Women were aye more cruel to their own kind.

And that knowledge sent him sprinting across the strand, away from his men, racing for the cliff track and the thicket of whin and broom bushes waiting above.

He tore up the path, his legs pumping, only one thought on his mind.

Margo.

Chapter 18

Two weeks later, Margo stood on a high crag above Badcall Castle, staring out at the rolling sea. A brisk northern wind blew past her, tossing her hair and tearing at her clothes. She didn't mind the afternoon's rawness. Far from it. She turned her face to the gusts, enjoying a rush of pure, undiluted pleasure. She lived for such weather, always had. Her woolen cloak kept her warm, anyway, though she appreciated the additional comfort of the light linen shawl draped across her shoulders.

Given to her by Magnus's aunt Agnes, who had claimed she stitched the shawl's age-faded thistle border when she was just a lass, the offering did more than keep the cold off Margo's neck.

The gift made her feel welcome.

Accepted, and at home at Badcall.

At least, as far as that was possible.

As she touched the shawl's soft linen folds, hoping she'd never have to leave here, she deeply wished the cloth held the same powerful magic as the Highland Cursing Stone.

But the shawl was just that, a length of linen, however old and precious.

So Margo pushed away any overly sentimental thoughts that would lead her down roads she didn't want to travel, and simply watched the long Atlantic rollers crashing onto the jagged, black rocks. It was an awe-inspiring sight, and the booming of the waves echoed down the coast.

It was also a vista she allowed herself to enjoy every afternoon, just before the gloaming began to close in, making it too treacherous to be on the bluff.

Public footpaths and guardrails hadn't yet been invented, after all.

Not that she'd have it any other way.

Or any other place.

She could breathe here. She'd never felt more vital, so alive, almost intoxicated. The landscape's beauty drenched her senses. Everywhere she looked, there was wonder and heart-wrenching splendor. Clouds raced across the sky, their hurrying shadows painting the moorland and hills. Seabirds wheeled above her and wind sighed through the pines.

She couldn't imagine a place more perfect.

So she closed her eyes and breathed deep, seeking connection with her surroundings.

A waft of heather rewarded her. Then a hint of cold, clean air, kissed with the tang of the sea. Her heart began to pound, slow and hard. A wonderful sense of contentedness spread through her.

Until a cough from somewhere to her left reminded her that she wasn't alone.

As they did every day, Dugan and his brawny, oversized friend Brodie accompanied her, never letting her from their sight. They trailed her like faithful hounds, watching over her whenever she ventured anywhere outside Badcall's castle gates without Magnus at her side. Just now Magnus was overseeing the sword and ax practice of some of his younger warriors, so Dugan and Brodie were with her.

They were her medieval bodyguards, following Magnus's orders.

Margo knew Dugan performed the task gladly.

In recent days, Brodie was also warming to her.

She'd taught him some easy Luna weather lore. So when, last week, a large halo shone around the moon, two stars glimmering within, Brodie proudly warned several friends not to make a planned journey because a bad storm would descend before two days had passed.

Brodie claimed an "ache in his bones" told him so.

Margo didn't mind.

It was reward enough to see Brodie's eyes light when the predicted storm did break, just when he'd declared it would happen.

Men were awed by the accuracy of his "aching bones."

And Margo gained a new champion.

She looked for the two men now, the clean brightness of Dugan's lucky shirt making it easy to spot them against the dark edge of the pines. They kept a discreet distance, allowing her a degree of privacy. Both men sat on large rocks, their drawn swords resting across their knees.

Catching her glance, they stopped talking and looked her way. Each man nodded politely and lifted a hand in acknowledgment.

Margo did the same, enjoying the warm, wonderful sense of belonging that filled her as she turned back to the sea. Soon evening dark would draw in and she'd return to the hall. But for the moment, she needed to be outside.

This was the Scotland that had always called to her. And she was here at last.

Her beloved Highlands.

A wild and rugged landscape that so appealed to those who loved solitude and thrilled to cold brooding days full of mist, wind, and drizzle. People like her, who'd rather hear the nightly weather report announce dipping temperatures and rain than heat and fry-your-eyeballs sunshine.

She didn't do summer.

And if she was still here in another month or so, she'd excel at Scottish winters.

Too bad she wasn't very good at Highland magic.

The one time she'd had a brush with true Celtic legend and lore, she'd lost her wits and let the Cursing Stone slip from her fingers.

Everything had gone so horribly wrong that day.

Just remembering Donata with her glowing black cloak and silver-disk eyes damped her palms and made her stomach queasy.

Yet without that nightmare, she wouldn't have Magnus. She knew well that nothing worth having came easily. She had Magnus, and Donata was no more than a small annoyance in the great scheme of things.

Not that she really had him ...

They enjoyed a powerful physical attraction and he was beyond incredible in bed. But he meant so much more to her than the great sex and even his irresistible burr. She'd fallen desperately in love with him. And she wanted him to feel the same.

She needed his assurance so that if she was whisked back to her time, she could wrap herself in the comfort of knowing he'd loved her.

Not knowing how he truly felt was ripping at her.

Yet the closest he'd come to any verbal declaration was to call her *mo ghaoil*.

Margo frowned, ducking when two swooping gulls sped right past her head, almost clipping her ear. It was when she straightened, brushing at her hair, that she saw Magnus. He stood farther along the cliff, his position a good distance from her two protectors.

Margo's breath hitched, her heart thundering. As always when she caught her first glimpse of him, she came alive, her skin tingling with awareness. The most delicious warmth began flowing through her body. Sinuous, needy heat started pulsing deep between her thighs.

She swallowed, her gaze locked with his.

How long had he been there?

She flicked a glance to Dugan and Brodie, surprised they hadn't called a greeting to their lord, alerting her that he'd arrived. But seeing their master, they'd gone, circumspect as always. They'd left her alone to brave the desire simmering in Magnus's eyes.

As she didn't hide her feelings, she was sure they knew she welcomed every private moment that she and Magnus could spend together.

Anticipation beat inside her, hot and thrilling. He still hadn't left the trees, where he leaned against a tall Scots pine, the tree's red bark glowing softly in the fading light. He'd crossed his legs at the ankles and his arms were folded, his head slightly angled as he watched her.

But then his eyes darkened and he gave her a slow, knowing smile. His gaze not leaving hers, he pushed away from the tree and strolled toward her. Even at a distance, she could see how much taller and larger he was than most men. He was definitely more magnificent, with his plaid slung proudly over one shoulder and his arms bright with rings of silver and gold. His gaze was focused, his jaw set. The fierce determination on his face excited her because she guessed the reason behind his appearance.

He carried a plaid draped over one arm, his intent igniting a slow burn deep inside her.

"My *too*-rist." He stopped about halfway to her, wind whipping his plaid as he stood with his legs slightly spread and his hands on his hips, his gaze sweeping over her boldly.

He'd freed his long, silky black hair from its usual leather band and it streamed in the wind, a glossy skein of pure, unbound temptation.

He *was* magnificent.

But his use of the word *tourist* nibbled at the edges of Margo's bliss.

She didn't want to be an outsider.

She ached to belong.

To him, to the wild and spectacular land he loved so much and protected so fiercely, and—a hot pang stabbed her chest—even to the proud, superstitious people that were his blood kin and friends.

She wanted everything, most especially his love.

"Dinnae look troubled, *mo ghaoil*." He was striding forward again, his expression more fierce than ever. "It is a grand day and"—he reached her, sweeping her hard against him, holding her close—"I have loved watching you enjoy it just now." He kissed her, crushing her mouth beneath his in a deep, ravenous claiming so hotly possessive that a flood tide of heat and desire swept her.

"It has been long since I've seen anyone look out across the sea with wonder on their face." He cupped the back of her head, his fingers in her hair, gripping fast as if she'd disappear if he didn't. "Did you know your eyes light, turning starry, when you watch cloud shadows glide across the hills?"

He leaned in, kissing her again, slow and soft this time. "It warms me inside to see you that way, Margo-lass. You remind me of the beauty I'd forgotten. The truth that for those of us who love this place, there is nowhere else in the world. You bring that peace back to me."

"Oh!" Margo's heart nearly split. Her eyes were more than *starry* now.

She blinked, glancing aside just as a whole new battalion of the cloud shadows he'd mentioned turned the hills into a shifting kaleidoscope of blue, purple, and gold. Looking back at him, she took a deep breath, hoping her words wouldn't shock him because she so wanted him to understand her.

"I've always loved Scotland." She kept her hands around his neck, her fingers clutching his plaid. "Do you know ... ?" She sought the right words, and then just rushed on. "Whenever I come up here, I keep looking for some kind of enchanted portal that I can slip through and fix time, some trick or other that will let me stay here, guaranteed.

"Or I could rig a blockage that would seal the time rip after I popped safely back here, to you. Just anything"— her voice cracked—"to keep me with you."

"You dinnae need the like, *mo ghaoil*." His voice deepened. "You are here. I'll no' let anything take you away from me, no' now."

Her heart squeezed, but she couldn't keep her gaze from flitting about, searching the rocks and heather for some tiny hint of unusualness.

There was nothing.

"Come, lass." He nuzzled her neck, nipping her ear. "I know there is Highland magic, dark and light. Donata's mutterings couldn't have brought you here without the power of the Cursing Stone. Thon stone is gone now. Orosius swore it and he would know. That danger is passed and cannae touch you. But enchanted portals"—he straightened, shaking his head—"and rips in time?"

"I passed through one to get here." Margo shivered. Someday she'd tell him of Mindy and Bran of Barra, but she didn't want to make this more complicated than it already was. "Magical stone or not, there had to be an opening in the veil between your world and my own. Donata used it to find me, and the Cursing Stone added a new twist, one we'll never really understand."

He frowned then, doubt clouding his eyes even though—like her—neither one of them had a choice but to believe.

She *was* here, after all.

"Such things exist." Margo slid her hands deeper into his hair, twining her fingers in the cool, silky strands. "Time gates."

She really had hoped to find one hereabouts.

After all she'd been through, nothing surprised her anymore. So she'd wanted to try.

Unfortunately, no mysterious fairy rings had appeared in the grass, allowing her to nip inside just long enough to seal the opening and secure her place in Magnus's time.

But it wasn't that easy.

Such portals, though surely real, were next to impossible to locate. And they were even more difficult to use properly if she had encountered one.

Scottish romance writers used them all the time. With a sweep of their pen, or a flourish on a keyboard, they let their time-traveling heroes and heroines pop in and out of the past as if such portals were revolving doors.

Margo knew better.

And she wanted to live her romance, not write or read one.

"Margo . . ." Magnus stepped back and gripped her chin then, tilting her face so she had to look at him. "I have no wish to speak of time gates. I see only you before me and that you are soft, warm, and desirable." His words caressed her, warming her from within. "Your scent enchants me. It is like the clean, fresh air of a cold winter morning and heather, and—"

"Not cold air and roses?" Margo knew her rose scent was no more. It'd been a Lunarian Organic perfumed body spray, Sea of Clouds, travel size.

She also knew why she smelled of heather, but bit her lip.

Magnus's eyes heated and he pulled her close again, once more nuzzling her neck. "You bathed with my aunt Portia's soap, didn't you?"

Margo nodded, the look in his eyes making her breath catch. "I mentioned loving roses and she told me she makes a special rose-scented soap. She gave me a jar and—"

"You discovered it smelled of heather?" Magnus's tone held amusement.

"Actually, yes." Margo smiled, loving the easy banter. It was a new side to him along with the dimple that flashed in his cheek as he smiled down at her. She met his gaze, her pulse fluttering. "The 'rose'-scented oil she poured into the bathing tub also smelled of heather."

This time Magnus laughed. "Poor Aunt Portia. She makes all manner of soaps and essences, always announcing a new scent with such pride. Yet—"

"It's always heather."

"Aye, though none of us has the heart to tell her."

"I won't, either. Don't worry." Margo's heart warmed as she remembered the older woman's pleasure in presenting her with the "rose"-scented toiletries.

But when she felt her eyes starting to go starry again, she touched the plaid still slung over Magnus's arm and looked up at him.

"Why did you bring this?" She hoped her guess was right.

He grinned, wickedly now. "To do this," he said, shaking out the plaid and spreading it across a soft patch of low-growing heather.

Turning back to her, he bracketed her face, kissing her deeply. "I would love you as only a Highlander can, beneath the wind and surrounded by heather, taking you on my plaid again and again until the light fades."

"Oh, Magnus, I—" She couldn't finish. He stole her words with another kiss, this one harder and deeper than the last. The taste and scent of him flooded her senses, rousing and intoxicating her. His kisses were magic, the feel of his big muscle-bound body against hers beyond irresistible.

She wanted him desperately.

Before she could say so, he moved with lightning speed, rolling them to the ground so that she was sprawled on her back across the plaid. He straddled her, bracing his arms on either side of her and leaning forward so she was trapped by his powerful, kilt-clad body.

"I want you, Margo." His words made need well inside her, sharp and intense. "Here and now, the whole of me deep inside you." He reached to pull up her skirt, baring her legs as he slid his hand up the inside of her thigh, stroking her nakedness, finding her slick and damp with arousal. "I can think of nothing but you, lass.

"You are with me always." His hand gripped her hard, squeezing. "Haunting my dreams and filling my days. There are times I think you always have been with me, even before . . . when I loved Liana. A part of me will love her always. She was good and—"

"Please." Margo pressed her fingers to his lips. "Don't speak of her now."

He straightened his back, looking down at her. "But you should know that I—"

"I know this is good." Margo arched her back against

the plaid, lifting her hips to increase the exquisite pressure of his hand clamping her mound.

She had rather begged him to tell her that he loved her, but she wasn't feeling particularly strong and courageous. Hearing of his shining devotion to his long-lost betrothed would shatter the bliss rippling all around them.

It was a beautiful energy, and not purely from their own physical sensuality. There was something else, something that felt mystical. An elemental force that rose from the deep, peaty ground beneath his plaid, swirled out of the heather, and flowed strongly from the ageless, lichen-covered rocks. Perhaps the lifeblood of the land, it warmed the earth and thickened the air with its magic.

"Liana is no more, lass." The finality in Magnus's words made her heart jolt.

He didn't sound crushed or even angry. He sounded only matter-of-fact. And—Margo gulped—he was using his free hand to tug off his plaid. He tossed it aside, and then reached for his sword belt, his fingers expertly working the clasp as he leapt to his feet, stripping so fast she saw only a blur of flashing tartan.

Naked, he offered her his hand, pulling her to her feet in front of him. "I want you to ride me, Margo." His hands were at her neck, undoing the knot of her shawl, then the clasp of her woolen cloak. "Like you did when I saw you in the kettle steam, but now, and here on my plaid."

"O-o-oh . . ." Excitement made Margo light-headed until a rustling in the trees behind them burst her sensual bubble. She remembered that even though Dugan and Brodie had tactfully stepped back into the trees, they were still around. And they'd surely be watching.

She could feel her cheeks coloring as she glanced

at the wood. "Maybe this isn't such a good idea." She
scanned the dense fringe of pines, seeing nothing.

Still . . .

"Thon men will have their backs turned. Ne'er you
worry." He was pulling up her gown, already easing her
arms from the sleeves. "They will have slipped deep into
the gloom lest they wish to make me very angry, which
they willnae."

Margo wouldn't argue that.

Besides, it was too late.

He had her fully naked now. Their clothes were strewn
about the heather and he'd once again thrust his hand
between her legs, gripping her possessively. And just
as he slid one finger inside her, teasing and tantalizing
her, he lowered his head to lick her nipple. Margo cried
out at the inferno of desire that flamed in her veins. She
rocked against his hand and raised her breasts, offering
them to him as he suckled her. Whatever concerns of
modesty she'd had were now racing away on the cold
Highland wind.

It was too late to care.

She wanted Magnus more than decorum.

But she did hope he was right about Dugan and
Brodie.

Then she knew nothing except the liquid hot need
rolling through her in great, glittering waves of pleasure.
Incredible, sweeping desire crashed over her, nearly
cresting, when he lowered himself onto the plaid and
stretched out, opening his arms in invitation. She went
to him eagerly, her entire body hot and trembling as he
pulled her down on top of him and ran his hands up and
down her sides.

And as they kissed, Margo sensed the strange energy
almost crackling in the air around them, the passion-
warmed earth seeming to hum and breathe in tandem

with them, keeping pace in an ancient, soul-binding rhythm.

It flashed across Margo's mind that Scotland was claiming her, too.

Welcoming her, and sanctifying her love for this Highland man, initiating her in a long-forgotten pagan rite when people believed that making love so intimately close to the naked earth made them as one with the land.

She loved the notion.

But just now, she had to do something about the rivers of heated tingles racing back and forth across her neediest places, making her desperate, hungry inside.

Surely knowing how much she desired him, Magnus gripped himself, holding the long, hard length of him in place for her as she scrambled over his thighs. She planted one knee on either side of him, and—being very strong and courageous now—arched her back to better display the fullness of her breasts as she lowered herself onto him, slipping down slowly, savoring each and every hot, rigid inch of him.

"Margo . . ." Never had her name sounded more beautiful as in his deep, buttery-rich burr, turned so husky by his passion. "Precious lass, you will split me."

He'd been running his hands all over her, but now he spread his arms out to the sides, fisting his hands until his knuckles gleamed white. His jaw clenched and his entire body tightened, veins standing out in his neck as he closed his eyes, inhaling through his teeth, as she lifted herself up and down, riding him.

Margo threw back her head, pulling in great, greedy gulps of the chill air as molten pleasure heated her from within. Never had she felt this way, so fiercely connected to a man—and to the earth, wind, and sky all around them. It was a heady, empowering sensation.

And so wondrous, so stunningly incredible, she couldn't bear for it to end.

But her heart pounded furiously and her fast-approaching release roared through her blood, urgent, demanding, and relentless. Any moment, she would shatter, splintering into nothingness.

And she wanted that so badly.

"O-o-oh, God . . ." She lifted and dropped back down on him faster, bending her back. She'd braced herself with her arms and now her hands slid off the edge of the plaid, her fingers digging deep into the soft, peaty earth.

"Magnus, I . . ." The words became a gasp, a shuddery cry, as an intense rush of pleasure spiraled through her. She was suddenly aflame, soaring to the headiest heights. She was only vaguely aware of Magnus lifting his hips up beneath her, shouting her name as they shared their completion.

Panting and drained—but in a delicious, wonderful way—she would've collapsed limply on top of him, if he hadn't reached for her, easing her into his arms.

"How did I e'er live without you?" He rolled them onto their sides, careful to make sure his arm and shoulder supported her. "You needn't worry about being swept away from me, Margo-lass."

He stroked her hair, traced a finger along the curve of her breast, then gently circled her nipple. "I'd rip open the sky to find you. And I'll no' frighten you by saying what I'd do to anyone who'd even try to injure you. You're safe with me. Always."

"I know." Margo could hardly speak.

She did snuggle closer against him, the after ripples of her climax still rolling through her, beautifully languorous.

Somehow, she dosed, stirring only when Magnus lifted her shoulders to ease her gown back down over her head, dressing her with an ease she'd have to ask him about someday, when she didn't want to break the mood.

His hands were wonderfully skilled. Even his most innocent touches made desire spiral inside her, tempting her to arch her body against his. She wanted his mouth on hers again, needed his kisses so much she could scarcely breathe. He could so easily sweep her away on a rush of passion. And she was so blessed to be with him.

Already dressed, he stood looking down at her, a smile tugging at his lips. "You are now a true Highlander's woman, Margo-lass. No woman can make the claim"—his gaze flicked to the rumpled plaid—"until her man has had her in the heather."

"Some might say I had you." Margo looked up at him, pleased when his smile deepened, showing his dimple.

"And you may have me again, later this e'en if you wish." He placed a hand on his sword hilt, his expression turning serious. "For the now, I must return to Badcall and see if my lads are doing well with their sword and ax training. Will you come back with me?"

"I don't know." Margo started to rise, but her limbs still felt like wet noodles. Each breath was an exertion and her heartbeat was yet ragged. And now that they were both dressed again and the strange pulsing earth magic that had thickened the air had faded, she did have a slight niggle of propriety concern.

People could always tell when someone had just had a hot tumble in bed.

She was sure medieval Highlanders knew when a woman had just enjoyed a lusty roll in the heather.

A quick glance at the trees, where Dugan and Brodie had reappeared like clockwork, proved her theory. The two men looked painfully uncomfortable.

No way was she going to place everyone at Badcall Castle in such a position.

"I'll stay here a bit. Thank you." She leaned back on her arms, tipping her face into the wind. "It is a lovely afternoon and . . . you know, it's very special for me to be here. I'll come back before dark, and then I'll take another of Aunt Portia's 'rose' baths before supper."

"You're sure?" Magnus lifted a brow.

"I am." Margo smiled.

"As you wish, sweet." He bent to ruffle her hair and kiss her brow.

Then he turned and was striding away from her, heading for the thick line of trees and the darkness beyond. Margo's heart seized when he disappeared from view. She loved him more than life itself.

And he might not have said the words, but she was starting to suspect that he could love her, too.

Whatever happened, she knew she'd never forget this time with him.

Not that it would matter.

Because if she lost him, life as she knew it would no longer exist.

Her heart would be left in turmoil. And she knew she'd go through her days walking blind and unable to breathe. She'd be living proof that the old adage about time healing all ills was a total falsehood.

The passing years wouldn't soothe her.

They'd destroy her.

Chapter 19

Hours later, Magnus stood in his torchlit hall at Bad-call Castle, looking on as Gilbert, a kitchen laddie, piled driftwood onto the hearth fire. Magnus's two aunts, who were secretly known as the *Ship-Breast Sisters* because of their sturdy size and large, shelflike bosoms, were fussing at the lad. Agnes kept warning him to take care as he thrust the twisted, silvery wood in with the peats. Driftwood hissed and spat, and Agnes had set a basket of tatty, moth-eaten plaids, shirts, and table linens close by the fire.

She wanted to sort through the discarded goods and hoped the fire glow would aid her no-longer-so-sharp eyes as she searched for reworkable bits of cloth.

Aunt Agnes enjoyed giving new life to her *treasures*, as she called such rescued scraps.

Magnus folded his arms, hoping he wouldn't have to intervene.

His aunts were forceful women and arguing with them only made them cross. But in truth, he loved them dearly.

He was especially pleased by how well they'd taken to Margo. They'd accepted her quickly, cosseting her as if they'd loved her forever. There wasn't a day they didn't show her warmth. And more affection than he'd ever seen them give anyone. They clucked over her like two mother hens.

Magnus suspected they looked on her as the daughter neither of them ever had. For a number of unfortunate reasons, the sisters hadn't wedded, remaining lifelong maids, much to their unspoken sorrow.

At times, they could be daunting.

This was one of those instances. Gilbert was a wee mite and a timid lad.

He was terrified of the two women.

Sadly, he was also afraid of Magnus. He had only to glance at Gilbert and the boy nearly jumped out of his skin. Something Gilbert did because, according to Calum and others, Magnus so often walked about wearing a dark scowl.

Lately, he smiled much more often.

Now that Margo was with him.

He'd even surprised himself by laughing on occasion. It'd been a greater wonder to learn how good that felt, to laugh again. But Gilbert hadn't seen him in a while, certainly not in the weeks since returning from Redpoint with Margo on board the *Sea-Raven*. So Gilbert was avoiding looking in Magnus's direction, although Magnus was sure the boy knew he was there.

"Don't be putting it there, lad." Agnes *tsk*ed just as Gilbert stretched to drop a twist of driftwood onto the top of the peats.

"His name is Gilbert." Magnus spoke low from the shadows. "You'll scare him less if you call him rightly."

"You're one to tell a body how not to frighten a soul!" Agnes bent an annoyed look on Magnus as she bustled between the boy and the fireplace. Huffing as only annoyed older women can, she maneuvered her bulk so that Gilbert couldn't thrust a large piece of driftwood into the smoldering peat fire.

"Put the wood in the back, see?" She pointed, indicating where she meant. "That way we'll not have sparks shooting onto my creel of treasures."

Gilbert complied, quickly tossing the driftwood deep inside the hearth.

"Agggh! Not that way." Agnes waved her hands, wailing. "Don't be throwing the wood. You'll have ash raining all over us."

"And let's have the next piece here, eh?" Aunt Portia lent her opinion, her heavy heather scent wafting in the air as she extended her arm to direct the lad.

"Aye, Lady Portia." Gilbert bobbed his head and picked up another twist of driftwood, moving toward the fire to do as she bade.

But he didn't look happy.

And when Magnus saw Agnes swell her formidable breast and prepare to scold the boy anew, he strode forward to snatch her basket of discarded cloths off the floor.

"We need a good fire this night, Aunts." He braced the basket against his hip, looking at them levelly. "Even"—he winked at Gilbert—"if driftwood spits like the devil hisself.

"I like the blue flames." He wasn't about to tell his aunts why. That the seductive blue-purple fire with its haunting hint-of-the-sea scent swept him back to a tiny cothouse in Badachro where he'd first made love to Margo by the light of a driftwood fire.

Instead, he straightened his shoulders. "After we've dined and the hall is cleared for the night, I'll have extra candles taken to your quarters. You can sort the cloth remnants there, Aunt Agnes.

"By the light of a few fine candelabrums and no' here before the hall fire, where you had to know the driftwood hisses and spits." He set a hand on Gilbert's shoulder, his grip firm as his aunts fussed and spluttered before sailing away into the gloom of the great hall.

Once they were gone, he roughed the boy's hair.

"Dinnae tell anyone, Gilbert"—he leaned down, lowering his voice—"but there are some who call thon two women the Ship-Breast Sisters.

"Now finish your work. They'll no' be pestering you again." Magnus straightened, feeling both awkward and inordinately pleased when Gilbert looked up at him, his freckled face lit by a shy smile.

Standing taller, Gilbert returned to his task with vigor. Soon, the blue-purple flames would dance and leap and Magnus was glad for it. The additional warmth was welcome, as a fierce autumn storm had rolled in from the sea, chilling the air and sending rain hammering across the roof. Hard wind tore at the shutters and howled past the towers. And even through the stronghold's thick walls, the crash of waves could be heard as angry seas pounded the cliffs.

It was a night for quiet comforts.

Magnus was pleased to offer his men a warm, dry hall with plenty of ale, bread, and meat. They had one another's company, their swords within reach if needed, fine hounds sprawled on the floor rushes, and a halfway decent musician plucked harp strings in a darkened corner.

Nothing was amiss.

Except that he burned to sprint up the winding turret stair, burst into his bedchamber, and toss Margo over his shoulder, and then carry her back down to the high table so he could enjoy the simple pleasure of having her beside him.

After he'd stopped halfway down the stair to back her against the wall, toss up her skirts, and ravish her as they stood in the shadows.

He needed her that fiercely.

Even now, a few short hours after taking his ease with her on the bluff.

He also meant what he'd told her on the cliff. Watching her as she'd gazed out at the sea had touched him deeply. The look in her eyes had tugged on something deep inside him. Seeing how much she loved his home had taken his breath.

His heart had beat faster, his chest filling with pride.

Too many of his own people lived in dread, always casting their gazes over their shoulders, watching and waiting for the next raiders from the north to bring death and sorrow to their shores.

They'd forgotten the beauty.

They were no longer awed by wild mountains and foaming rivers, or empty, windy places where one's spirit took flight. They'd grown blind to the wonder of soft twilights when the light faded from the heather and silence walked gently, cloaking the cold, dark nights.

Such appreciation had also slipped from Magnus's mind.

But it'd all slammed back into him each time he caught such wonder on Margo's face.

She gave him a piece of himself that he had lost.

She made him remember the things he'd once loved so fiercely—all sadly forgotten through the years of warring and vengeance. There were times he felt as if he'd always known and needed her. She completed him.

He hadn't yet told her that he loved her, but he would.

It rode him hard that he'd once suspected she was a sea witch come to plague him. Guilt lanced him, though he knew he'd had little cause to think otherwise. Even so, he felt a need to undo his early doubts and do right by her. And that desire went deeper than the longing at his groin. Above all, he wanted to know her safe.

And he couldn't do that when she let his aunts bundle

her into steaming, scented baths that lulled her into such a relaxed state, she preferred sleeping away the evening to spending it with him at the high table.

It especially annoyed him that she'd do so on a night when he'd swear odd shadows were creeping through the hall like a plague.

Frowning, he turned and snatched his sword off the bench where he'd placed it earlier. Carefully, he buckled the blade's belt around his hips, glad to have Vengeance's familiar weight at his side.

"You feel it, too?" Calum joined him, his face harsh in the firelight.

Like Magnus, the older man had strapped on his sword.

"Feel what?" Magnus cocked a brow, not ready to voice the prickles at his nape.

He enjoyed a good day's fighting as much as the next man, perhaps even more. But on such a cold, wet night, he was more of a mood to seek his bed—and Margo's arms—than to swing Vengeance and spill Norse guts.

The Northmen had heeded his warning at Redpoint.

The coast had been quiet for weeks.

And the break was more welcome than he would've believed possible.

He glanced at Calum. "You're in a strange mood."

"I'm feeling my battle wounds this night." The older man rubbed an ancient scar on his neck. "But that's no' what I meant."

"Then tell me."

"There's blood in the air." Calum spoke what Magnus already knew.

Magnus forced a smile and patted Vengeance's hilt. "You smell the traces of my sword's last meal."

Calum snorted. "I hear Vengeance stirring in your scabbard, screaming her hunger."

"She isn't starving, as well you know." Magnus kept his hand on the sword.

Calum's chin jutted. "You weren't wearing her a moment ago."

Magnus flashed another glance at the torchlit stair tower, this time relieved not to see Margo coming down the steps, slipping into view.

He wouldn't want her to catch any war talk.

She'd made clear what she thought of "brute force and violence," as she called a good day's bloodletting. Magnus shoved a hand through his hair, hoping he'd be able to persuade her to think differently.

A man without a sword was like a tree without roots and branches.

Totally useless.

"For an old man, your eyes are sharp." Magnus didn't hide his annoyance.

"Glower all you wish." Calum wasn't daunted. "I knew you when your shoulders were no wider than the span of my hand." He stepped closer and poked a finger into Magnus's plaid-slung chest. "I could still fight off you and six o' your best men if you pressed me."

"That I know." Magnus allowed the older man his pride.

Years ago, Magnus had watched him cut down six Viking warriors. Big, fierce men who'd fought like howling demons. They'd died grandly, their blood flowing like rivers in spate. Calum—Magnus's father's most trusted battle companion—had walked off the field with little more than scratches.

He'd taught Magnus everything he knew about sword-craft.

Calum had also shared his vast knowledge of women, divulging secrets that Magnus had put to good use in the years before he'd met Liana and vowed to keep her innocent until he could make her his bride.

Now . . .

For the first time, his heart accepted that he could no longer call Liana's features to mind.

Instead, Margo's face flashed before his eyes. Beautiful, vibrant, and alive, she filled his soul and made his heart soar. As if they were still on the cliff, he could feel the cool silk of her hair beneath his fingers. How she'd thrown back her head as she rode him, her smooth, sleek thighs gripping his hips. His vitals stirred as he recalled the hot, tight glide of her womanhood, descending and lifting on him. The tempting views of her breasts, bouncing and flushed with desire. Then—his entire body tightened—he recalled letting his fingers delve through the bright golden curls topping her thighs. He knew exactly what waited for him beneath that gleaming triangle and he wanted her now, so fiercely he could hardly breathe.

He did glare at Calum.

His friend's war-battered face could wipe the lust from any man's mind.

Calum was rubbing his neck scar again, worrying the long-healed wound.

"Blood in the air, eh?" Respect made Magnus repeat the aging champion's concern.

Calum nodded. "The stench fills my lungs, aye."

Squaring his shoulders, the older man set a hand to his sword. "I could walk out into thon wee blow gusting past our walls and still smell the evil. It's so strong even the wind can't chase its taint."

Magnus agreed.

Ill ease rolled through him, thick and dark.

He glanced again at the stair tower, relieved to know

that Dugan and Brodie stood guard outside Margo's door as she bathed and rested.

They'd stand there all night, even without supper, if Magnus didn't relieve them, which he intended to do very soon.

He was weary of waiting for her.

But when Magnus followed Calum to a narrow slit window, he immediately wished he hadn't. The moon had slid out from the clouds, and the sea gleamed like a sheet of beaten silver, made eerie by swirls of blowing mist. It was easy to imagine the high beast-headed prow of a Viking warship gliding out of such fog, one ship after another.

"I could almost choke on bile." Calum's gaze went to the shifting mist. "Something vile is afoot. If I'm wrong, then I'm an archangel, glittery winged and haloed."

"You're the devil and all his minions rolled in one. The closest you come to angels is having them for breakfast. And"—Magnus punched Calum's arm, pleased by the spark his words put in the older man's eye—"I dinnae mean holy angels."

"I do like the ladies." Calum's lips twitched. But then he peered again through the window, looking toward the horizon. "Still . . ."

"There's no threat from the sea this night." Magnus knew that was true. "The danger lies elsewhere. I can feel it simmering and shaping, but I cannae say where—"

A loud *crack* shattered the hall's peace as the entry door flew open and slammed against the wall. "Holy heather, but it's a foul night." Orosius's booming voice announced his unexpected arrival.

"Magnus!" The seer stamped his feet and shook the water off his shoulders. "I've brought grim tidings." He whipped off his dripping bearskin cloak and threw it on a bench. "Where are you hiding?"

"I hide from no man." Magnus strode up to him.

"That may be." Orosius stood with his hands on his hips. "But I'm here to tell you there's a woman you should hide from."

Some of Magnus's men sniggered.

Others hooted, perhaps not seeing the earnestness in the seer's eyes.

"There's ne'er been a MacBride born who feared a woman." Scowling, Magnus stepped around his sooth-saying friend and shut the hall door against the wind. "I'll no' be the one to start such a fool tradition."

Orosius huffed. "Do you think I'd leave Windhill Cottage on such a night for foolery? I rarely leave my peat fire, as well you know."

Magnus did know.

There were few men who savored solitude more than Orosius. He didn't suffer others gladly. If he did seek company, he had good reason.

Worse, Orosius looked genuinely alarmed. His shaggy black hair and his huge beard appeared more tangled than usual, whipped by wind and spattered with raindrops. And he kept darting glances behind him to the hall's closed door.

"What are your tidings?" Magnus gestured for some-one to fetch the seer a cup of ale. "Were you peering into your kettle steam again?"

"I wasn't scrying o'er my cauldron, nae." Orosius let his voice boom. "I cast my runesticks is what I did. They showed me the sorceress Donata Greer." He shuddered visibly. "She's escaped."

"That cannae be true." Magnus stared at him. "How could she get away from St. Eithne's? The nunnery sits on an island in Loch Maree and"—he glanced at Ewan and some of the other warriors gathered near—"I sent a score of my best fighters to guard the isle. They wouldn't let her go."

"I saw her free." Orosius's jaw set stubbornly. "The runes dinnae lie. They fell clear and true, showing me all."

"What did you see?" Magnus felt a throbbing pain begin between his eyes. "Speak fast."

"Bjorn Bone-Grinder fetched her." Orosius spoke the name with scorn.

"Bone-Grinder?" Magnus's anger surged.

Bjorn Bone-Grinder was one of Sigurd Sword Breaker's most formidable shipmasters. A huge man with flaxen hair down to his waist, he enjoyed a reputation as a ferocious fighter. But his byname didn't come from the men he crushed in battle, though the assumption was close to the truth, for he ground the bones of men he felled. He then mixed the dust into the sand he used to polish his weapons and mail.

He boasted the bone added strength and magic to his ax swing.

Magnus had been trying to kill him for years.

But the bastard was slippery as an eel.

"Even if Bone-Grinder managed to near the isle"— Magnus's mind was whirring—"he couldn't have made it away alive. The men I sent to the nunnery are expert bowmen. They could've picked off Bone-Grinder and his men before they'd had a chance to run a ship onto the isle. Or they could've filled her timbers with fire arrows when she tried to beat away."

"Aye, they could've done." Orosius took a sip of ale. "But they didn't, eh?"

"What else did the runes show you?"

Orosius tugged at his beard. "Bone-Grinder was cunning. He—"

"That rat is e'er clever." A sick feeling was beginning to spread through Magnus's gut. The Viking shipmaster was more than crafty. He was twisted. "What did he do? I already know it was treachery."

"It was that." Orosius spat onto the rushes. "He brought hill folk with him. A whole second ship filled with feeble old men, cowering young women, and bairns. Somewhere he'd also captured a few monks and a nun."

Magnus suddenly understood the tight knot in his belly.

"The hill folk . . ." He didn't want to voice his suspicion. That the hill folk were the vanished farmers Orla mentioned.

"A monk was the first to die." Orosius fisted his hands on the words. "Bone-Grinder slit the man's belly in view of the nunnery walls. Then he demanded Donata's release, saying he'd kill the poor folk in the other boat, one after the other, if your men didn't row her out to him."

Magnus's blood chilled. "Your runesticks showed you all that?"

"They did, aye."

"I'm no' surprised Sword Breaker wanted Donata." Magnus ran a hand through his hair. "I should've realized he'd have seen her when he dealt with Godred. He's known as a lusty bastard and—"

"Bone-Grinder is the one who desires her." Orosius's shrewd gaze met Magnus's. "When the runesticks showed me the scene, I saw him claiming her as his woman. He might've acted with Sword Breaker's approval, but he went to St. Eithne's to force the return of his bride."

"So . . ." Magnus considered. "The unlamented Godred didn't just advise Sword Breaker where he'd find rich and easy plundering. He was also willing to whore his sister as bride to one of Sigurd's fiercest shipmasters. Some of the gold and silver we found in Godred's hall must've been payment for Donata."

"Could be . . ." Orosius rubbed the back of his neck.

"To be sure it was." Magnus snatched an ale cup off a

table and drained it. He needed to clean the taste from his mouth of a man who'd sell his sister so vilely. He couldn't stomach the ill treatment of any woman. Even if she was a wicked, coldhearted sorceress who'd spew a curse if someone just looked at her wrongly.

"If Godred yet lived"—Magnus slapped down the empty ale cup—"I'd kill the bastard again."

"You'd be wasting effort." Orosius lifted his voice above the men's angry murmurings. "Donata went to Bone-Grinder eagerly. My rune cast showed her as a bitch in heat, throwing herself into Bone-Grinder's arms as soon as your men handed her onto his ship.

"Like as not"—he sounded disgusted—"they were rutting in the ship's bilgewater even before Bone-Grinder's rowers took up their oars."

Magnus scowled, regretting his moment of sympathy for the sorceress.

"Did the runes show where Bone-Grinder went?" Magnus could feel Vengeance humming in his scabbard, scenting Norse blood.

"Aye." Orosius strode to the hearth fire and stretched his hands to the flames. "But the waters where I saw his ships could've been anywhere. There was too much mist to tell rightly. With St. Eithne's at Loch Maree, I'd wager I saw the coast along Torridon or Gairloch.

"Either way, you'll no' need to go looking for him." He turned to warm his backside. "The last thing I read in the runes was Bone-Grinder promising Donata he'd avenge her brother's death.

"The bastard will be coming after you." Orosius's voice was loud in the quiet hall. "He'll bring shiploads of friends and they'll want vengeance."

"And they'll meet her." Magnus patted his sword hilt. "She'll look forward to the feast."

"The day will be soon." Orosius sounded cheerful, as

if he relished the fight. "It'll be a great slaughter. And I dinnae need my runesticks to know." He grinned. "I feel it in my bones."

"So do I." And Magnus really did.

But before he could press his fingers to his throbbing temples, the hall door burst open again. The door crashed against the wall as six men from Magnus's night patrol burst in from the rain, one of them carrying a limp and drunk-looking Dugan, while two others lurched under Brodie's weight. The two guardsmen were hardly able to support the big man.

Brodie appeared as befuddled as Dugan.

"Found 'em up on the cliff, we did." One of the patrol guards threw a glance at Magnus. "Out cold, they were, flat on the ground."

Both men's heads lolled on their necks, their limbs hung loosely, and they babbled like witless fools.

Magnus stared at the spectacle, fury scalding him.

Fear lamed him.

He was aware of his jaw slipping and his eyes flying wide, but no words left his mouth. His throat had snapped tight, dread stealing his ability to speak, making it impossible to even breathe.

Dugan and Brodie weren't abovestairs, standing guard at Margo's door, after all.

They weren't watching her.

They were ale-taken and he was going to kill them.

Seeing red, he started to reach for his dirk—a quick neck slice was what the bastards needed—when his aunts appeared out of nowhere. The two women were making a fast line for the men. Portia had her healing basket clutched in one hand, and Magnus grabbed the basket now, slamming it down on a table.

"They'll no' have pampering." He glared at his aunts, putting himself between them and the creel of herbs and cures. "They're stone drunk and will have naught but my fist in their noses—"

"They look something other than ale-headed to us." Portia drew herself up to her full height. "And"—Agnes darted around them, snatching the basket before Magnus could stop her—"my potions aren't for them. We want to help Margo. If Dugan and Brodie have been set upon, she'll also be in need of tending. We—"

"What?" Magnus roared as the hall around him dimmed, then reared back—everything near him flashed black-and-white. "Margo isn't bathing?"

"How could she be?" Agnes kept the healing basket behind her, out of Magnus's reach. "No one made a bath for her. We went to look in on her a few times this evening, thinking to offer her one, but not a sound came from behind her door and so we left her alone."

"We thought she was sleeping." Portia was starting to look gray.

"Where is she?" Magnus's head was going to explode. He glanced round, his heart icing, blood thundering in his ears, absolutely deafening.

"She's gone." Portia sank onto a bench, her fingers pressed to her mouth.

"Dugan and Brodie didn't bring her back from the cliff with them." Agnes voiced Magnus's dread. "She must've gone missing," she repeated her sister's words. "Oh, dear, oh, dear . . ."

"Nae, she was taken." Dugan spoke with great effort, his words slurred. He'd been laid on a cleared long table and now he rolled his head to the side, trying to focus his glazed eyes on Magnus. "It was Donata. She—"

"Donata?" Magnus felt the floor open beneath him.

Dugan nodded. "She appeared out of nowhere just after you left. We shook our swords at her, thinking to scare her away, but"—he took a long, shaky breath—

"she smiled and pointed a finger at our feet, making flames shoot up out o' the ground.

"It was a wall of fire, but *cold* fire." He looked at Magnus, the horror in his eyes showing that he spoke true. "That fire whipped around us, trapping us where we stood as she chanted and raved, staring at us with glowing silver eyes until our legs buckled and we fell to our knees.

"I dinnae remember much after that, everything went dark." His eyes started to fill, glistening brightly. "If aught happens to Lady Margo . . ."

On another table, Brodie struggled to speak. "L-last thing we saw, Donata was sneaking up behind your lady. The Lady Margo was napping, where you'd left her on the cliff, and—" He couldn't finish, a rough, rattling cough seizing him.

"No-o-o!" Magnus threw back his head and howled. He clamped his hands against his temples, twisting his fingers in his hair. All the horror and darkness he'd ever known came rushing back to crush him now.

He'd promised to keep Margo safe, even vowing to rip the sky if she was taken from him.

Now . . .

What hollow promises he'd given her. Cold guilt and anguish pressed the life from him, filling him with bitter ash. His body was frozen, heavy and leaden as if he'd been cast to stone.

He looked around his hall, seeing no one and nothing.

He *heard* everyone. The low, rumbling voices of his men, his aunts' distress, and even Frodi's whine, but that was all. Everything else was dead for him.

His world had slammed to a shuddering halt and he couldn't bear the thought that Margo was gone. Even worse, she was in Donata's clutches. He was living Li-ana's tragedy all over again. And once more he hadn't been there to stop the horror. The woman he loved had been taken and he hadn't even known it until it was too late.

He had to find her.

This time he couldn't fail.

Chapter 20

Three days and much searching later, Magnus stood on the bow platform of *Sea-Raven*. He cast a scowl at Ewan, who skillfully manned the sleek warship's steering oar. The lad's face was grim-set, his eyes swollen and darkly shadowed, as were the eyes of all men on board. Magnus knew he looked worse than the lot of them. Even Frodi whined and hung his tail between his legs in Magnus's fearsome presence. But it wasn't often he spent full days and nights tearing through every clump of heather, knocking apart each tumble of stone on the moor, and wading through bog pools, dreading what he might find at their oozing black bottom.

Unfortunately, he'd ripped the sky in vain.

They hadn't found Margo.

She remained gone without a trace.

Now they were following Magnus's last, desperate hope. They were rowing the *Sea-Raven* south toward Gairloch, riding the huge gray swells of a flooding tide. The men were silent, each warrior sending his oar biting hard into the cold, wind-whipped water. Needle-sharp rain and a thick, blowing mist obscured the line of jagged black cliffs that marked the nearby coast.

Not that it mattered.

Magnus and his crew knew every inch of these waters.

There was also the stench of blood on the wind that drew them onward. And like good hounds, they needed only to follow that foul smell and they'd come to the fishing hamlet where Orosius swore they'd find trouble.

The taint in the air proved the seer right.

Magnus just hoped that Margo's lifeblood wasn't adding to the reek.

If he couldn't find her, if he failed to save her . . .

"Damnation!" He clenched his fists and clamped his jaw, cursing whatever cruel gods had tossed her into his arms only to rip her away again. He could feel her now, the urgent press of her lush curves against him, how she wrapped her arms around his neck, returning his kisses with singeing ardor.

The memories made his blood roar. Fury raced through his veins like liquid fire, flaming his need to find her.

And to tear apart the heathen devils who'd taken her.

Magnus drew a tight, furious breath. He squeezed shut his eyes for a moment, wishing he could open them and still be on the cliff with her. He should have swept her up in his arms and carried her back to Badcall with him. But he'd gone, leaving her vulnerable.

Now . . .

He shoved a hand through his hair. His heart was a cold stone in his chest, his soul hollowed and black. Margo's scent was still on him. It was faint, only a trace, but enough to madden him.

" 'Tis glad I am you're no' aiming such a look at me." Calum's deep voice boomed close by. "I'm no' of a mind to feed Vengeance with my blood."

Magnus turned to the older man. "Pray God that Vengeance will soon gorge herself on Viking blood. And that none of the bastards challenge us before we reach

Gairloch. My gut tells me that's where Margo is, trapped and helpless in the thick of the horror there."

Calum didn't argue.

And his silent agreement skewered Magnus's heart.

When a glimmer of sympathy flickered in Calum's eyes, Magnus turned swiftly away, returning his gaze to the sea. They hadn't yet seen any Norse ships, but that didn't mean they weren't there.

Magnus just hoped that if any Northmen spotted *Sea-Raven* and her escort ships shearing through the waves, they'd assume the long-keeled, high-prowed fighting ships were their own and not come to investigate. If they also caught the gleam of mail and helmets, Magnus was counting on such marauders simply raising their oars in greeting and then speeding on their way, accepting that *Sea-Raven* and his other ships were hastening south to do their own raiding.

There was a certain code of honor among such cravens.

Any other time, he'd have welcomed a chance encounter with a well-manned Norse longboat. Better yet, several of them. He'd developed a liking for fast and furious Viking slayings at sea. Smearing the waves with Nordic blood was gratifying. As was watching the howling bastards sink like stones to the seabed. A dressed-for-war Viking, weighted down with heavy mail and steel, vanished beneath the waves in an eye blink.

Just now his only wish was to find Margo.

He kept his gaze on the dark smudge of the coast, what little of it could be seen. If he squinted, he could just make out the faint glow of hearth fires above some of the cliffs. The smoke haze was reassuring because it meant those scattered fishing settlements were as yet unmolested.

If the villages were untouched, there'd be folk able to take in Margo if she escaped Donata's clutches.

It was a thin hope.

Magnus leaned into the wind, peering hard through the flying mist and rain. They were just entering Loch Gairloch, and dim lights shone far ahead where the large sea-loch ended and the fishing village's harbor awaited them. A few flimsy thatched-roof hovels already dotted the shore. Magnus studied each one carefully, but nothing stirred anywhere near them. Several piles of driftwood could just be made out through the fog, showing where men dried herring on the strand, but no one was there now. All seemed quiet as his ships rowed through the cold dark morning. Until they approached the first moored fishing boats and entered the gates of hell.

Blood smeared the water.

Torch-bearing villagers scurried along the shore, the flames casting a reddish glow on the stained water as they pulled bodies from the sea.

Orosius hadn't erred.

Nor had Magnus's own gut instinct failed him.

Bone-Grinder had killed more than one captive. The heap of limp bodies near one of the piers indicated that he'd slit the throats of every villager he'd captured.

Some had suffered worse than neck cuts.

And to Magnus, staring at the carnage, the cold, wet wind racing past him felt more like scorching blasts of sulfurous hellfire.

Suddenly he wished his instincts were wrong, prayed that Margo would be found somewhere else. Anywhere but trapped in the red-stained nightmare all around them. He'd rather spend endless days searching for her, as long as she was safe and spared such a heinous sight.

He gripped Vengeance's hilt, his rage surging. Bile hot in his throat, he scanned the harbor, looking for the Viking warships.

He saw only fishing craft.

So the heathen dastards had escaped. Sword Breaker's brutish shipmaster was nowhere to be seen. Nor was there any sign of his raven-haired whore. Bone-Grinder and Donata had fled the scene, leaving only a bright stain of red and swollen, broken bodies in their wake.

"Mar-go!" Magnus cupped his mouth and yelled her name as the *Sea-Raven* neared the shore. Again and again, he bellowed, many of his men taking up the cry.

But there was no sign of Margo anywhere.

Nothing stirred except the villagers who'd turned, freezing where they stood, to stare in horror at *Sea-Raven*. Others screamed and ran, sprinting for the dunes or behind the nearest cottages, the bravest reappearing with scythes and hoes in their hands.

"Row faster!" Magnus swung round to glare at the men on the oar banks. "Mother of God, pull! Pull hard! They're too beset to see clearly. Calum"—his gaze flashed to the older man—"wave Badcall's banner so they'll recognize us and remember we're friendly."

When they were close enough, he leapt down from the *Sea-Raven* and splashed to shore, running up to the nearest villagers and grabbing one of the men.

"A fair-haired maid, so tall"—he thrust out a hand, measuring Margo's height—"have you seen her? She's no' local and speaks with the accent of the south," he improvised, furious by the man's uncomprehending stare.

"She's with a small, dark-haired woman, dressed in black." He shook the man, flashed a desperate look at the other fisherfolk gathered near. "The fair-haired lass is my wife." He would make that true when he found her. "She's been taken, stolen away by—"

"Pssst . . . MacBride." The hissed cry came from the shadows near the docks.

Whipping around, Magnus saw nothing. But he knew he'd heard a man call his name furtively. Narrowing his eyes, he scanned the deserted fishing huts and flicked his gaze over a large pile of herring barrels.

Nothing stirred.

Except—he tossed back his hair, scowling—the terrified villagers, who'd used his distraction to run away.

Furious, Magnus turned back to the fishing huts, this time seeing a glint of mail in the darkness between the tumbledown cottages. He started forward, Vengeance already half-drawn.

"MacBride, I greet you." Arnor Song-Bringer stepped forward to the edge of the shadows, not leaving the dimness of the narrow alley between the cottages.

He was the young Viking from Redpoint—Sigurd Sword Breaker's nephew, and the warrior Magnus had sent forth, stripped and weaponless, in a tiny skin boat without oars.

Now he was dressed for war, glittering in mail and arm rings, a long sword at his side and a huge Viking war ax slung from his shoulder. But he held his shield upside down, extending it before him in the accepted sign of peace.

Magnus frowned, not taking his hand off his weapon. "Song-Bringer." He drew up in front of the younger man. "You lived, I see."

"Northmen are not so easily killed." Arnor Song-Bringer looked past him, his gaze darting up and down the now-empty harbor. "Nor are fair and brave young women, praise Odin." He turned back to Magnus, lowering his voice. "I was left here as a lookout and must be away, but first—"

"You know where Margo is?" Magnus grabbed the Viking's arms. "She lives?"

"She's in a fish-drying shed on the other side of the loch." He nodded across the water, and Magnus could just make out a tiny turf-walled hut, standing alone against a spill of fallen rock. "The witch-woman is with her. Soon, Bone-Grinder will come to fetch them. My uncle will be with him." The young Viking glanced at the water. "They mean to cross the sea to Ireland, where they'll sell your woman at the slave market."

"This is true?" Magnus reeled, a strange mixture of disbelief, hope, and horror crashing through him.

He flashed another glance at the tiny shed across the loch. "You are no' lying, setting a trap for me?"

"I might do that on the morrow." Arnor Song-Bringer didn't turn a hair. "But I speak true now. My uncle needed someone to stay behind and watch the seas, make certain no one approached the shed where Donata holds your lady. I asked to be that man. I was sure you'd come looking for such a prize."

He shifted, adjusted the upturned shield on his arm. "I owe you the debt of my life. That burden is now paid, and with my appreciation. I hope to wed soon"—for a moment he looked very young, no longer an enemy—"and I can do that because you spared my life at Redpoint.

"If we meet again . . ." The young Viking shrugged, his meaning clear.

"I am now in your debt, Song-Bringer." Magnus's throat was thick as he reached to grasp Arnor's arm with both his hands. "Live well."

Then he turned and ran back into the surf, plunging through the waves until he reached the *Sea-Raven* and one of his men reached down to help him on board.

"Margo is here! She lives, but Donata has her." He leaned forward, bracing his hands on his thighs, gulping air. "We must make haste. Bone-Grinder, Sword Breaker, and their warships are returning for the women. They'll be here anon."

"*Back oars!*" Calum shouted the order. "Back the oars," he yelled again. "Slew her round, now!"

And the crew did, Magnus's escort ships following suit, each craft back-rowing at speed so the sleek war-ships surged to life and sped around, shooting past the harbor's long, wooden piers and out across the red-stained waters toward the far side of the loch.

Margo was there.

And if the gods were kind, Magnus would have her on board the *Sea-Raven* and halfway to Badcall before the Vikings beat into Loch Gairloch.

"See there, my lover is returning."

Smiling benignly, Donata gripped Margo's arm and hustled her to the cracked door of the drying hut. "Bone-Grinder has brought his friends, just as he promised. Have a look. . . ." She shoved Margo forward, giving her no choice but to stare out at the terrifying sight before her. "Sword Breaker will take you on his ship and then you'll be rid of me."

Donata stepped close, lifted a lock of Margo's hair, and rubbed the strands between her fingers. "I tried to seduce him myself once, but he prefers fair women. He'll make the journey to the slave market in Dublin enjoyable for you. Many women say he's a good—"

"He's a devil." Margo whipped her head around and glared at the other woman. "I'll kill myself before I'd let him touch me." She snarled the words, not even sure where they'd come from.

Unfortunately, she wasn't feeling strong and coura-geous enough to fight the smaller woman.

Donata held a wicked dagger at Margo's side.

And she'd nicked her more than once. Margo's gown was already red-drenched at the middle, her hips and belly sticky with warm blood. Thank goodness, the cuts were only flesh wounds, nothing deep.

Still . . .

She didn't want to provoke her captor into doing anything worse.

And now . . .

She stared out at the loch, terror sluicing her. There were so many ships, a whole Norse fleet, and with more racing in from the horizon.

They filled the sea in every direction.

With their high, beast-headed prows and narrow lines, they looked as beautiful and proud as they were frightening. They *flew* across the waves, their flashing oars ripping the water and sending up great plumes of spray. And each ship was filled with mailed and helmeted men.

Men who loved to fight.

And they were coming to take her to a slave market.

On the journey south, Donata had gleefully told Margo that female slaves rarely lived more than a few days. Some survived a week or two, at most. The Viking shipmaster or warlord used them, then the crew and other men until there was nothing left of the woman.

Margo shuddered.

She gripped the edge of the hut's door, unable to take her gaze from the spectacle.

Until a sudden movement from the opposite side of the bay caught her eyes and a loud splashing rose above the chaos, making her turn toward several large and fierce Viking ships that flashed out from the harbor and straight into the bay. The dragon ships' long oars rose and fell like pistons, and white water hissed down their sides as they sped toward one of the other large warships.

Before Margo could blink, the lead ship sheared down the side of the other one, snapping her long oars like wooden matchsticks, laming the ship.

She tore her gaze from the frightening sight, and it was then that she saw the tall, raven-haired warrior at the prow of the attacking warship.

A ship with fierce black and red raven heads decorating the tall stem and stern posts.

The proud warrior lord was Magnus in all his battle glory.

"Magnus!" Margo's heart split. Relief rushed her and her knees almost buckled. "Oh, God, he's here! Magnus has come for me."

She was safe now, whatever came.

"He'll see me slice you to ribbons is all he'll do here." Donata shot an arm around Margo's waist, pulling her close as she jabbed Margo's belly with the tip of her dagger. "I'll keep you in sight here, at the door, until he's on the strand. Then I'll cut you good."

"He'll kill you." Margo was sure of it.

"He can try." Donata wriggled the fingers of her knife hand, and tongues of red fire shot from her fingertips, the flames hissing in the cold, damp air.

"Magnus MacBride can't touch my magic." She closed her fingers around the dagger hilt again and the flame tongues fizzled away.

"No, you're wrong." Margo tried to speak as strongly as she could. "Your magic can't harm him. He doesn't fear you, so you have no power over him." She hoped to God she was right.

"We shall see." Donata's tone made Margo's blood run cold.

Margo willed courage to flood her senses and bolster her. She also kept her gaze on Magnus, taking strength from him as *Sea-Raven* spun in a tight circle, churning the water, as she shot after another Viking warship, clearly meaning to slice more oar blades.

The beating of the oars made the water boil; men's shouts blended with the splintering of wood as the attacking ship's bow raced down the side of her enemy, snapping the oar shafts. Margo's heart filled her throat as she watched, unable to look away. Other ships she recognized as part of Magnus's fleet were clashing just as fiercely with the Viking ships. Everywhere warships spun and attacked, slamming into one another, grapnel chains flying as the ships crashed together, men leaping from one bow platform to the next, swords and axes bright in the air.

The fighting was loud, red, and terrible. And never had Magnus looked more powerful, bold, or gorgeous.

He towered above his crew, all huge men. Dressed for warring, he was mailed and helmeted. Even from shore, Margo could see that his eyes blazed with fury. His hair was unbound, spilling loose from beneath his headgear. A glistening raven skein, the long strands flew around his shoulders in the wind. He held Vengeance high in the air and the glinting blade shone red, as did the steel of his mail shirt and the rings on his arms. And like so many of the other men, he was cheering as they sent fire arrows arcing across the sky, many of the arrows finding their mark in Viking sails or on deck.

Within moments, the loch was ablaze. The warships' sails were burning quickly, the fires leaping from ship to ship. And still men fought, yelling and screaming, many jumping into the sea to avoid the flames, and then sinking as their heavy mail weighed them down.

It was chaos.

Beside her, Donata mumbled, speaking low incantations Margo didn't understand.

She didn't care.

Donata was underestimating the power of love, a much greater force than any sorceress's babble and threats.

When Magnus reached the shore, he'd rescue her.

Margo didn't doubt it.

She kept her gaze locked on Magnus and the *Sea-Raven*.

He didn't see her.

Nor—her heart stopped—did he see the huge, half-naked Norseman climbing stealthily up the far side of the *Sea-Raven*, a wicked-looking dagger clutched in his teeth, deadly purpose in his eye.

Magnus had his back to the assassin.

Any moment, the man's long, thin blade would sink into Magnus's flesh, killing him.

A quick stab beneath the ribs or a fast slashing cut across the throat, and all would be over.

Their future stolen before Margo had a chance to run and leap back into his arms.

"No-o-o!" The denial tore from her throat, welling up and ripping open something hard and tight inside her, letting so much strength and courage burst free that she was able to knock Donata's dagger from her side. She wrenched from the sorceress's grasp.

"Magnus, watch out!" Margo ran forward, charging through the pockets of men who were now fighting along the shore, skirting and leaping over the fallen, screaming at the top of her lungs.

She could hear Donata chasing after her, yelling and cursing.

But Margo raced on.

The man with the knife in his teeth was already on board the *Sea-Raven*.

Margo stopped at the edge of the surf, staring at the scene in horror. Magnus was so close, but in such peril. She could see the flash of his grin, the white of his teeth, and even hear his deep, victorious voice shouting at his men to gorge their blades on more Norse blood.

But it was his blood that was about to be spilled.

His killer was creeping forward now, the dagger no longer in his teeth but raised and ready to strike. Obviously a well-skilled warrior, he used the distraction on the *Sea-Raven* to blend into the shadows, slinking quietly along the other side of the ship from where Magnus and his men fought against the nearest Norse ship.

He was almost upon Magnus.

"Magnus, no-o-o!" Margo waved her arms and screamed. "Behind you!" She yelled with all her might, so loud that her throat ached, burning like fire.

"Nae, behind you!" Donata's cry filled the air as she grabbed Margo, jerking her around. "You die now," she hissed, her hand raised and already slashing downward, aimed at Margo's heart.

Margo froze for an instant, terror icing her, her eyes on the flashing blade.

Then adrenaline, fear, or maybe just the sheer will to live exploded inside her and she leapt aside, flailing her arms with all her might to ward off the dagger's descent.

Her face twisted with rage, Donata appeared unable to stop the blade's trajectory. She reeled, slipping on the shingle, as she tried to capture Margo again. But the blade sliced down with lightning speed and the viciousness of hate, plunging deep into a heart that knew only darkness.

Donata's eyes flew wide, locking on to Margo's in the horror of her last breath.

"Oh, God!" Margo clapped her hands to her face and backed away as the other woman toppled, crumpling to the rocky shore. Her sightless eyes stared heavenward, no longer flashing silver and inspiring terror, but blank and powerless. The sea was already claiming her, lapping at her black silk cloak, pulling at her long raven hair, and washing red-tinged spume onto her silver and jet bangles.

Donata was dead.

And Margo hadn't even touched her except to defend herself.

Still . . .

She felt as if she'd killed someone.

"It wasn't you, lass." A deep, beloved voice called behind her and she turned to see Magnus striding up out of the surf, a score of his men coming behind him. They all held swords in their hands—bloodred swords—but they were grinning so broadly to see her that she sobbed and ran the rest of the way to Magnus.

His gaze flicked to her waist as she neared him, his eyes widening. "God's mercy!" He pulled off his helmet and stared at the bloodstains, his face turning ashen. "You're hurt!"

His men formed a circle around them, their faces equally grim now.

"What did she do to you?" He reached her, the horror on his face breaking her heart. "I'll—"

"It's nothing, only flesh wounds." Margo shook her head, glancing down at the red stains on her gown's middle. "She nicked me, that's all. She was taunting me, trying to scare me back in the drying hut. It hardly hurts."

"You are sure?" His face was fierce. He kept glancing at her waist, a muscle jerking in his cheek. When he looked up again, he was ashen with horror.

"Oh, Magnus, don't look that way. I'm fine, truly."

"Praise God." He closed his eyes, the color returning to his face. "I thought—"

"And you are safe! I'm so glad!" She flung herself at him, her eyes blurring as he grabbed her, sweeping her up hard against him and kissing her roughly. "I thought you'd be dead." She pulled back to look at him, smoothing his hair.

He stroked her cheek, soothing her. "Sword Breaker tried hard to kill me, but your cry warned me. I spun around, ducking as he lunged. And then"—he grinned—"he learned the taste of my steel even before I'd straightened."

He sobered, his gaze fixed on her face. "I have waited long to take vengeance on that one. If you hadn't yelled—"

"Don't say it, please." Margo touched her fingers to his mouth, stopping the words before he could speak them. "If I hadn't been here, you wouldn't have been—"

"Aye, I would have been fighting him." He took her hand, turning it so he could kiss her palm, the sensitive skin of her wrist. "Could be he might no' have crept on board the *Sea-Raven* this day, but there would have been another day, a new battle. Many such fights, and for as long as I would have needed to end his reign of terror."

"And now?" Margo could hardly speak for the tightness in her chest.

"Now"—he took her face in his hands and kissed her—"you have done more than show me wonder and joy. You have brought me peace. Something tells me there willnae be much warring in these parts from this day onward. With Sword Breaker dead and many of his friends at the bottom of Loch Gairloch with him, I'm of a mind to enjoy my hearth fire more.

"And"—he kissed her again—"a certain cliff with a very fine view. If you will join me there?"

"Oh, Magnus . . . you know I will." Margo's heart squeezed. She knew her eyes were misting.

Behind him, she could see the Viking ships burning, a few lone vessels speeding away toward the horizon, defeated and fleeing. Some men still fought, but halfheartedly, the battle now winding down.

Magnus and his men had won.

She had won.

Yet she twisted round to stare at Donata's body, her black cloak drifting back and forth with the washing tide.

"You didn't kill her, sweet." Magnus cupped her chin,

turned her face away from the sorceress's body. "We all
saw it happen. She lost her footing, stabbing herself after you leapt aside and her aim went off balance. That's
what happened."

"Aye, that was way of it." Orosius grinned, stepping
out from the circle of men. "The force of the strike she
meant for you drove the blade deep. No' that it matters
now. She's gone, and I'm for home!"

A chorus of ayes agreed with him.

Magnus grinned and lifted a brow at Margo. "And
you, lass?" He glanced across the water to where the
fierce red-and-black-painted dragon ship rocked in
the surf. "Are you up for another sea voyage on the
Sea-Raven?"

Margo didn't hesitate. "Oh, yes."

Magnus grinned. "Then all is well."

Turning to Calum, he nodded briefly. "Gather the
men and get any stragglers back on board. And"—he
glanced at Margo, a look of hope in his eye—"tell any
who haven't yet noticed that we found my bride and she
is well. We'll have an additional passenger for the journey home. A lady who, I have reason to believe, will be
staying with us for a very long time.

"I hope for the rest of my days," he added, leaning
close to her ear, the words for her alone.

"I hope so, too." Margo could hardly speak.

"I thought so." Magnus winked, and then kissed her,
hard and swift. The embrace was so full of passion that
it warmed her immediately, even after all the horror she
had witnessed. Setting her from him, he looked at his
men, waving them away. "Go back to the ship. I'd have a
moment alone with my lady."

The men turned, dutifully striding away, back into the
tossing surf. Only Orosius hesitated, returning after taking a few steps.

"Just one thing ..." He leaned close, lowering his voice so only Magnus and Margo would hear. "You erred about Lady Margo staying with you for a long time."

His words put a fierce scowl on Magnus's face and filled Margo with terror.

But then the seer grinned and thumped Magnus's shoulder. "Truth is she'll be with you throughout this life and all the ones beyond."

He stepped back then, looking proudly sage. "That, too, I saw."

Then he turned and strode back across the sand, his war ax still dangling from his hand and his step much too jaunty for a man his age.

"Do you think he's right?" Margo hoped it desperately.

"Aye, he is." Magnus's tone was firm. "Orosius always speaks true."

"But what if—"

"You willnae be swept away from me, Margo." He tucked her hair behind her ear, his dark eyes locking on hers. "If you think I'm fierce against Vikings, you haven't seen how I'll fight if anyone tries to take you from me again. No Cursing Stone, if e'er such a wonder reappears. No fool time gates or whate'er you called the like. No force on earth will separate us, I promise you."

"You're sure?" Margo needed certainty.

"I'll carve it in stone if you wish." His voice was rough, his eyes darkening with an intensity that sent warmth spilling through her.

She held his gaze, her mind warning her that their love couldn't possibly work. Her heart said otherwise. He was so tall, strong, and handsome. A bold, invincible man who could make anything happen.

Yet it wasn't his powerful build or his fierceness that convinced her.

It was the slow smile beginning to curve his lips. The

way he was looking at her, his expression melting her. She took a shallow breath, her heart turning over.

"You don't need to carve it in stone." She couldn't believe her voice didn't crack. "I believe you."

His smile deepened, but he also raised a brow. "You'll no' be missing thon Pen-seal place? You know I must be asking. I'll no' have you turning unhappy and—"

"Unhappy with you?" She blinked once, twice. "And here, in the Highlands?" She couldn't hold back her own smile. "There's not a chance of that happening," she promised, knowing she'd never spoken truer words.

Then she raised her hands to frame his face as she lifted up on her toes to kiss him, soft and sweet, gently and so full of meaning.

She leaned into him, hoping she could speak past the thickness in her throat. "Orosius was right. I know we belong together. I think I've always known it, known you. And you're so right. I'm not going anywhere. Certainly not back to—"

"Och, but you are going somewhere." He lowered his head, kissing her again, deeply and more thorough. "Did you no' hear? You're returning with me to Badcall and—"

"I know." She pulled back to look at him. "But Badcall isn't what I meant. That's where I want to be, with you, and always. I meant I won't be going anyplace else.

"I'm here to stay." She twined her arms around his neck, tunneling her fingers in his hair. "I've never wanted anything more."

"Valkyrie . . ." He took her face in his hands and kissed her again, hard, fast, and bruising this time. When he broke away, his face held a look that made her heart swell with happiness. "You are all I have e'er wanted. My love for you fills me so completely I sometimes wonder I can draw breath."

"I think I've loved you forever." Margo spoke the

words against his cheek, leaning into him. "Almost as if . . ." She let the words tail off, aware of the slow simmer beginning to darken his eyes.

"Be warned, Margo-lass, tempting me as you are." He glanced down to where her breasts pressed against his chest. "I've a great need for you. And this night, when we reach Badcall, I'm going to slake it." His smile turned wicked. "Unless you'd rather I no'?"

"Oh, no!" She pulled back to look at him. Desire whipped through her, hot, spearing pleasure. "I'd never deny you anything. I just don't want to wake up and find I'm only dreaming."

"You're no' dreaming, sweet." He shook his head, the love she saw in his eyes melting her. "And I promise I'll ne'er let you go."

"Would you swear that on Vengeance?" She decided to be daring.

He patted his sword hilt and grinned. "You have my oath on Vengeance, *Sea-Raven*, Badcall"—he glanced over at the shaggy gray dog loping back and forth along the surf line, waiting for them—"Frodi, and anything else dear to me."

Margo blinked, knowing that was serious.

"Did you no' hear me? I love you, my *too*-rist." He pulled her to him again, holding her so tight she feared he'd break her ribs. From the *Sea-Raven*, men cheered. Some were even thrusting their swords in the air, though Orosius's war ax could be seen flashing in a bright circle above the other weapons.

Frodi barked, his tail wagging.

Magnus ignored them all.

"I do love you, Margo." He bracketed her face again, smoothed back her hair as he looked deep into her eyes. "I think I may have done even before we met. I know I'll keep on loving you when we are no more."

"Oh, Magnus . . ." Margo couldn't speak.

But she did do the unthinkable. Hot, burning tears began to leak from her eyes as he held her, spilling down her cheeks one by one and falling softly onto the rocky shore of a real live Scottish strand.

And she was in her favorite time period, wrapped in the arms of the man she loved and had wanted more than anything else on earth.

Life didn't get any better.

Her luck had turned good at last.

And it felt glorious.

Epilogue

Ardelle Goodnight ran the edge of her thumb along the glass counter of Margo's old Luna Harmony station and then let her fingertips drift over the blue and silver jars and bottles of the Lunarian Organic cosmetics still arranged in a lovely display.

Her fingers came away black with dust.

"This is just not right." A big woman, she put back her shoulders and drew an indignant breath, her large shelf-like bosom rising on the inhale. "We owe it to Margo to keep her place tidy. If she comes back and—"

"She won't be and we all know it." Marta tucked her dark hair behind an ear and slid a worried glance to where Patience was seeing a customer out the door. "Something happened in Scotland, like with her sister."

Marta leaned close to the older woman, her voice low. "The authorities over there would've found something if there'd been foul play. But there was nothing, not a trace. Just like with Mindy."

"Humph." Ardelle brushed at her jacket, a tweedy

suit recently arrived at her own shop, Aging Gracefully, where she delighted in giving new life to discarded— Ardelle preferred the term *deserving*—items of heir- loom clothing and other odd-bit assortments.

"Look. . . ." Marta glanced toward the shop's back room where she did her tarot readings, a cozy corner that also served as Ye Olde Pagan Times' kitchenette and housed Marta's ever-growing collection of pol- ished river pebbles and driftwood she collected from the shore. "I have a reading soon. Please don't say any- thing to Patience about dust today. It's the anniversary of Margo's drawing win, remember?

"She'd want us to celebrate and be happy tonight." Marta touched the older woman's arm, squeezing lightly. "Please, don't make a fuss here, or later at the Cabbage Rose."

Ardelle pursed her lips. "There's even dust on Mar- go's stool."

She swiped a finger over the stool's blue and silver seat, proving victory with an upraised smudged finger. "It's disgraceful."

"It's Patience's way of coping." Marta threw another look at the shop owner, pinching Ardelle's arm when she saw that Patience was heading their way. "She doesn't want anyone touching anything that was Margo's."

Ardelle sniffed. "I think her new *Heather Mist* pot- pourri blend was her tribute to Margo?"

"It is." Marta glanced to where the prettily packaged potpourri dominated a low, round table near the book- shelves. "She's even talking about mixing the scent into Heather Mist soaps and essential oils, all in honor of our Margo."

"Well . . ." Ardelle flicked a speck of lint off her sleeve. "I'm glad to hear she's doing something positive."

"I'd do a lot more if we could just be sure Margo is

okay." Patience sailed up to them, defensively maneuvering herself between her two friends and Margo's dust-covered Luna Harmony station.

"I would have thought she'd send us some kind of sign." Patience looked down at her fingernails, fidgeting to hide the brightness in her eyes. "We were all so close, always. Sometimes I still feel her near, you know? As if she's still here, or we're there, wherever she is."

"I know, dear." Ardelle slipped a tweedy arm around her friend's shoulders, patted her arm. "And I didn't mean to fuss about the dust a moment ago. I understand."

Ardelle sniffed again, nodding thanks when Marta handed her a tissue. "It's just that she was so intuitive. She must know we're worried about her and—"

"Pardon me." A small, white-haired woman stood before them, looking between Marta, Patience, and Ardelle as she balanced a large cardboard box of books against her hip.

All three women jumped.

The door chime hadn't announced the little old lady's arrival.

Patience stepped forward, all brisk business. "How can I help you?"

The old woman hesitated, her eyes twinkling as if she found Patience's words amusing.

But then she set down her box and straightened, brushing at her long black skirt. A pair of tiny black boots peeked from beneath her hem, revealing that she used jaunty red plaid shoelaces.

Marta, Patience, and Ardelle exchanged glances.

The little old woman was still beaming at them, her gaze settling on Patience. "I do believe you deal in used research books?" Her voice was accented, lilting and musical. "Fine tomes on topics of mystical origin and the like?"

"We do." Patience nodded, peering down at the box. "Those look valuable, though. I might not be able to pay you what they're worth."

"Och!" The woman waved a hand. "I'm not after money. I'm just doing a bit o' tidying up, is all. I've no more space for these."

"They do look old." Ardelle bent over the box, already examining a few volumes. "Here's one for you, Patience." She held up a slim book on charms and spells for the "covenless white witch."

"Let me see." Patience snapped the book from her friend's fingers, flipping through the pages.

Marta ignored them, glancing at her watch to see if her tarot client would soon be arriving. "I'll need to get in the back— Hey!" She blinked, glancing around. "Where did the old woman go?"

Patience and Ardelle looked up from the book box. "What?" They spoke in unison. "She was just here."

"Well, she isn't now." Marta rubbed at the chills on her arms.

As when the little woman had arrived, the door chime hadn't tinkled.

"She'll be back." Patience pushed to her feet, a hand on her hip. "No one would leave such valuable books behind, whether she wants money for them or not. Why, look at this one. . . ."

Bending down again, she picked up a leather-bound brownish volume, its title, *Myths and Legends of the Viking Age*, raised in red and gold lettering.

"Isn't this the book Margo bought just before she went to Scotland?" Patience held out the book to her friends. "I'm sure it is."

Marta and Ardelle leaned close, peering at the book.

"Let me see." Ardelle snatched the book from Patience's fingers.

Frowning, she began flipping through the pages. She stopped when she came to a two-page color illustration of a Viking warship off the coast of Scotland.

"Look at this." She set the book on Margo's old display counter, holding the pages open to the drawing. "This is just the kind of place Margo would love."

Patience and Marta joined her, framing her, as all three women leaned over the book to admire the oh-so-romantic landscape spread across the rich, creamy pages.

Beautiful as a master painting, the illustration showed a rocky shoreline with steep, jagged cliffs soaring up around a crescent-shaped cove. The sky above shone with the blue, purple, and gold luminosity of gloaming and the sea gleamed like beaten silver.

A haven of a place, the dreamlike background was made perfect by the man and woman embracing on the golden-sanded strand. They stood at the water's edge and the man's long dark hair was tossed by the wind. Clearly a Highland warrior, he was big and strapping, and wore a plaid slung boldly over one shoulder. A huge sword was strapped at his side, and he was holding the woman's face with both hands, leaning down and kissing her fiercely.

He looked deeply in love with her.

And the blue-gowned, fair-haired woman enjoying his kiss was his perfect match.

"Hey, look at her hair." Marta frowned, leaning close to peer at the illustration. "She's wearing her hair cut chin-length with bangs."

"That can't be." Ardelle nudged her aside, examining the page. "Medieval women didn't—agh!"

Ardelle jumped back, her eyes round. "It's Margo! She looked at me and smiled."

"She was smiling at me." Patience grabbed the book,

clutching it to her breast, a bosom just as large and formidable as Ardelle's. "It was our dear girl and she was
looking right at me, not you."

Marta bit her lip, not wanting to ruin their claims with
the truth.

She'd been the one Margo had smiled at, even winking as if they held some special secret.

"Can we try again?" Marta turned to Patience, opting
for diplomacy. "Maybe if we all look at the drawing at
the same time, we can tell for sure?"

Patience frowned, not yet ready to hand over the
tome.

Ardelle snatched it from her, slapping the book
onto the counter again. But this time when she flipped
through the pages, the beautiful drawing was gone.

It'd vanished from the volume as if it'd never been.

"I know she was in there." Patience started pacing
back and forth in front of the display case. "My eyes
aren't deceiving me.

"You both saw it, too." She looked from Marta to Ardelle, and then back at the book. "Or will you be denying it?"

Ardelle shook her head.

"We could've been mistaken." Marta avoided answering truthfully.

She didn't want to see Patience hurt.

"There are probably a lot of copies of that book." She
eyed it again. "This one can't be Margo's and we—"

"It is Margo's!" Ardelle's voice rang with triumph.
"See here." She was pointing to something on the inside
front cover. "She's written her name in the book. I recognize her handwriting. Look."

And so Patience and Marta joined her, peering down
at the opened book and reading Margo's inscription
aloud:

Margo Leeanne Menlove.

And as the three women bent over the book, puzzling over the significance—or not—of Margo's full name, a tiny white-haired woman lifted her ever-so-curious nose from the shop's window glass and gave a most satisfied sigh.

Things were good in the world this day.

She'd done well.

So she smoothed her skirt, lifted her chin, and set off down the sidewalk, the heels of her small black boots with their red plaid laces tapping jauntily.

Don't miss the next delightful
Scottish paranormal romance
from Allie Mackay!
Read on for a sneak peek.
Coming from Signet Eclipse
in January 2012.

Balmedie Beach, Northeast Scotland

She wasn't alone.

Kendra Chase—a hardworking American from Bucks
County, Pennsylvania, and a woman much in need of
some private downtime—knew the instant someone intruded on the solitude of the wild and rugged North Sea
strand she'd been walking along for the last two hours.

In that time, she hadn't seen a soul.

Now her skin tingled and the fine hairs on her nape
lifted. Awareness flooded her, her entire body responding to the changed nuance of the air. The atmosphere
was charging, turning crystalline as her senses sharpened.
Everything looked polished, colors intensifying before
her eyes. The deep red-gold of the sand glowed, as did
the steely gray of the sea, and even the crimson sky. The
brilliance was blinding, the chills slipping down her spine
warning that the changes weren't just a trick of the light.

Something other than the sinking Scottish sun was
responsible.

Kendra took a long, calming breath. So much for surrounding herself with white light to block unwanted intrusions from the Other Side, though . . .

No ghost was causing the back of her neck to prickle. As one of the top spirit negotiators employed by Ghostcatchers International, she always knew when she was in the presence of the disembodied.

This was different.

And although she'd been assured by the desk clerk at her hotel that Balmedie Beach, with its high marram-grown dunes and long, broad strand, was a safe place to walk, the teeming city of Aberdeen was close enough for some wacko to have also chosen this strand for an afternoon jaunt.

She doubted there were many ax murderers in Scotland, but every urban area had its thugs.

Yet she didn't actually feel menace.

Just something unusual.

And thanks to her work, she knew that the world was filled with things that were out of the ordinary.

Most people just weren't aware.

She was, every day of her life.

Just now she only wanted to be left alone. So she pulled her jacket tighter against the wind and kept walking. If she pretended not to notice whatever powerful something was altering the afternoon, she hoped she'd be granted the quiet time she really did deserve.

But with each forward step, the urge to turn around grew stronger.

She needed to see the source of her neck prickles.

Don't do it, Chase, her inner self protested, her natural defenses buzzing on high alert. But the more her heart raced, the slower she walked. Her palms were growing damp and she could hear the roar of her blood in her ears. There was no choice, really. She had to know who—or what—was on the strand with her, affecting her so strongly.

"Oh, man . . ." She puffed her bangs off her forehead and braced herself for anything.

Then she turned.

She saw the man at once. And everything about him made her breath catch. She blinked, surprise, astonishment, and also a thread of alarm, rising in her throat.

For a peace-shattering interloper, the man was magnificent.

No other word could describe him.

He stood on the high dunes a good way behind her, his gaze focused on the sea. Even now, he didn't glance in her direction. Yet his *presence* was powerful, claiming the strand as if by right.

Tall, imposing, and well built, he was kilted and wore a cloak that blew in the wind. Even at a distance, Kendra could tell that he had dark good looks. And—she swallowed—there was an air of ancient pride and power about him.

Limned as he was against the setting sun, he might have been cast of shadows. But there could be no doubt that he was solid and real.

He was a true flesh and blood man, no specter.

Yet. . . .

Kendra's pulse quickened, her attention riveted by his magnetism. She pressed a hand to her breast, her eyes wide as she stared at him. The same wind that tore at his cloak also tossed his hair. A dark, shoulder-length mane that gleamed in the lowering sun and that he wore unbound, giving him a wickedly sexy look. His stance was pure alpha male. Bold, fearless, and uncompromisingly masculine. He could've been an avenging angel or some kind of sentry.

Whoever he was, he seemed more interested in the sea than a work-weary, couldn't-stop-staring American female.

And that was probably just as well because even if she'd hoped to enjoy her one night in Aberdeen, she wasn't in Scotland as a tourist.

She was working and couldn't risk involvement.

Not that such a hunky Scotsman would give her the time of day if he *did* notice her.

She had on her oldest, most comfortable, but terribly worn walking shoes. However warm it kept her, her waxed jacket had also seen better days. And the wind had made a rat's nest of her hair, blowing the strands every which way until she was sure she looked frightful.

It was then that she noticed the man on the dune *was* looking at her.

His gaze appeared deep, knowing, and intense, meeting hers in a way that made her heart pound. The air between them seemed to crackle, his stare almost a physical touch. A fluttery warmth spread through the lowest part of her belly. Decidedly pleasurable, the sensation reminded her how long it'd been since she'd slept with a man.

Embarrassed, she hoped he couldn't tell.

She didn't do one-night stands.

But she felt the man's perusal in such an intimate way—his gaze slid over her, lingering in places that stirred a reaction. He made her *want*, his slow-roaming assessment sluicing her with desire.

She tried to glance aside, pretending she hadn't stopped walking to stare at him. But she couldn't look away. Her eyes were beginning to burn because she wasn't even blinking.

Retreat wasn't an option.

Her legs refused to stir. Some strange, invisible band sizzled between them, then wound around her like a lover's arms, shocking and sensuous. The sensation dried her mouth and weakened her knees, making it impossible for her to move as he looked her over, from her tangled hair to her scuffed shoes. His gaze returned to her breasts, hovering there as if he knew her bulky all-weather jacket hid a bosom she considered her best asset.

Kendra stood perfectly still, her heart knocking against her ribs.

He was scrutinizing her, she knew. Perhaps he was trying to seduce her with a stare. He had the looks and sex appeal to tempt any woman, if that was his plan. Before she could decide how to react, the wind picked up, the chill gusts buffeting her roughly and whipping her hair across her eyes.

"Agh." She swiped the strands from her face, blinking against the sting of windblown sand.

When the wind settled and her vision cleared, the man was gone.

The high dunes were empty.

And—somehow this didn't surprise her—the afternoon's odd clarity had also vanished.

Sure, the strand still stretched as endless as before, the red-gold sand almost garnet-colored where the surf rushed in. The sea looked as angry as ever, with violent white-crested waves. Their roar filled the air, loud and thunderous. And the western sky still blazed scarlet. But the sense of seeing through cut glass had faded.

"Good grief." Kendra shivered. Setting a hand to her brow, she scanned the long line of grass-covered dunes. Then she turned in a circle, eyeing the strand. The beach was just as deserted as it'd been since she'd started her walk. Nothing broke the emptiness except the scattered World War II bunkers half buried in the sand up ahead of her. Built, she'd heard, so men could watch for German U-boats. Now they were part of the strand's attraction.

A little bit of history, there for those interested.

The bunkers were also a reason she'd shielded herself before setting foot on the strand. White light and a firm

word declaring her wish for privacy usually kept spirits at
bay. If any long-dead soldiers felt a need to hover around
their old guard post, she didn't want to attract them.

She was off duty, after all.

And it was clear that the kiltie from the dune had
taken off as well.

He was nowhere to be seen.

He must've headed away from the strand, disappearing across the wide marshland behind the dunes. There'd
be a road out there somewhere, a place where he
could've parked a car. Or maybe he'd gone to a nearby
farmhouse where he just happened to live. Something
like that could have been the only explanation.

Sure of it, Kendra pushed him from her mind and made
for the bunkers. She'd eat her packed lunch there—late
but necessary sustenance—and then head back the way
she'd come. Until then, a brief rest would do her good.

But as she neared the first one, she saw that someone else had the same idea. A tall, pony-tailed man
leaned against the bunker's thick gray wall. Dressed in
faded jeans and a black leather jacket, he could've been
a tourist. But Kendra sensed that he was local. Arms
folded and ankles crossed, he also looked very comfortable, like he wasn't planning on going anywhere soon.

Kendra's heart sank.

She'd so wanted just one day of peace. Her only wish
had been a walk along an empty strand, soaking in the
tranquillity after weeks of hard, grueling work counsel-
ing ghosts at the sites of lost medieval villages in England.

Her energy was drained. The prospect of quietude
had beckoned like a beacon.

Now even a beach reputed to be among Britain's wildest and most undisturbed had proved crowded. The man
at the bunker had enough *presence* to fill a football field.

Kendra bit her lip, wondering if she could slip past

him unnoticed and walk on to the other bunkers farther down the strand. Before she could make her move, he pushed away from the wall and turned towards her. As he did, she felt the blood drain from her face.

He was the man from the dunes.

And he was coming right up to her, his strides long and easy, his dark gaze locked on hers.

"This is no place for a woman to walk alone." His voice held all the deep richness of Scotland, proving she'd tipped right that he was local. "Sandstorms have buried these bunkers within a few hours of blowing wind. The seas here are aye heavy, the surf rough and—"

"Who are you?" Kendra frowned, not missing that his dark good looks were even more stunning up close. It didn't matter that he now wore his hair pulled back with a leather tie. The blue-black strands still shone with the same gleam that caught her eye earlier. "Didn't I just see you on the dunes? Back there"—she glanced over her shoulder at the long line of dunes running the length of the strand—"no more than ten minutes ago?"

"I'm often on the dunes." A corner of his mouth lifted as he avoided her question. "And you're an American." His sexy Scottish burr deepened, as if he knew the rich, buttery tones would make her pulse leap. "A tourist come to visit bonny Scotland, what?"

"Yes." Kendra's chin came up. Hunky or not, he didn't need to know her business here.

No one did.

"Weren't you in a kilt just a while ago?" She kept her chin raised, making sure he saw that she wasn't afraid and wouldn't back down.

"A kilt?" His smile spread, a dimple flashing in his cheek. Then he held out his leather-clad arms, glanced down at his jeans. "I do have one, aye. But as you see, I'm no' wearing it now."

Kendra saw how he was dressed. She also noted that his jacket hugged his shoulders, emphasizing their width. How his shirt made no secret that his chest was rock-hard and muscled. Her gaze slipped lower—she couldn't help it—and then even the tops of her ears heated. Because, of course, his well-fitting jeans revealed that a certain very manly part of him was also superbly endowed.

She took a deep breath, hoping he hadn't seen that she'd noticed.

"You did have one on." If she didn't know better, she'd swear he was trying to spell her. Use his hot good looks to fuzz her mind. "A kilt, I mean."

"You're mistaken, lass." He lowered his arms, fixing her with the same intent gaze as he'd done from the dunes. "I've been here at the bunkers a while, listening to the wind and keeping my peace."

Kendra felt her brow knit. "I know I saw you."

He stepped closer, his smile gone. "You could've seen anyone. And that's why I'll tell you again, this is no fine place for a woman alone. Youths from the city come here this time of the evening." He flicked a glance at the bunker's narrow, eerily-black window slits. "They dare each other to crawl inside and stay there till the moon rises. Such lads drink their courage. They turn bold and reckless. If a bonnie lassie then happened along—"

"I'm not a lassie." Kendra wished he wasn't standing so close. His broad shoulders blocked out the strand and the bunker, narrowing her world to him. His scent was heady and addictive—it invaded her senses, filling her mind with images that weren't good for her.

There was something terribly intoxicating about the blend of leather, brisk, cold air, and man.

Any moment she was going to blush like a flame.

She could feel the heat gearing up to burst onto her cheeks. A problem that escalated each time her gaze lit on his hands. They were large, long fingered, and beautifully made. She couldn't help but wonder how they'd feel gliding over her naked skin.

She wasn't about to look at his mouth. One glance at his wickedly sensuous lips had been enough. It'd been so long since she'd been properly kissed.

This man would kiss like the devil, she knew.

And no man had ever affected her so passionately, so fast.

He towered over her, his big, powerful body mere inches from hers. She could feel his breath warm on her face, teasing and tempting her. His nearness made her tingle. And his rich Scottish accent was melting her, wiping out every ounce of her good sense.

She never mixed work and pleasure. Early tomorrow morning she'd embark on one of the most important assignments of her Ghostcatcher career. She'd require all her skill and sensitivity to settle the disgruntled spirits of a soon-to-be-refurbished fishing village.

Souls needed her.

And she needed her wits. A good night's sleep, spent alone and without complications.

"So you're no' a lassie, eh?" The Scotsman gave her a look that made her entire body heat.

"I'm an American." The excuse sounded ridiculous. "We don't have lassies."

"Then beautiful women." He touched her face, tucking a strand of hair behind her ear.

Kendra's pulse beat harder. Tiny shivers spilled through her, delicious and unsettling. "There are lots of gorgeous women in the States. Smart women who—"

"I meant you." He stepped back, his withdrawal chilling the air. "Those other women aren't here and dinnae matter. For whatever reason, you've found your way to

Balmedie. It'd be a shame if aught happened to you here, on your holiday."

"I can take care of myself." She could still feel the warmth of his touch. The side of her face tingled, recalling his caress. "I'm not afraid of youths and their pranks." She couldn't believe her voice was so calm. "As you said, I'm American. Our big cities have places I'd bet even you wouldn't go."

"Rowdy lads aren't the only dangers hereabouts." He glanced at the sea and then the dunes. Deep shadows were beginning to creep down their red-sanded slopes and the wind-tossed marram grass on their crests rustled almost ominously.

"There are ruins here and there." He turned back to her, holding her gaze. "Shells of ancient castles set about the marshlands beyond the dunes. Many locals believe some of those tumbled walls hold more than rubble and weeds. Ghosts are said to walk there and no' all of them are benign."

Kendra bit back a smile. "Ghosts don't scare me."

Ghosts were her business.

And she was especially good with the discontented ones. They were, after all, her specialty.

"Then perhaps you haven't yet met a Scottish ghost?" The man's voice was low and deep, perfectly earnest. "They can be daunting. You wouldn't want to happen across one on a night of cold mist and rain, certainly not here at Balmedie in such dark weather."

"It isn't raining." Kendra felt the first icy drop as soon as the words left her mouth.

"If you hurry, you'll make it back to wherever you're staying before the storm breaks." His glance went past her, back toward the Donmouth estuary where she'd entered the strand. "I'd offer to drive you, but my car is probably farther away than your hotel."

"I don't need a ride." She wasn't about to get in a car with him, even if he had one close.

He was dangerous.

And he was also right about the weather. Looking round to follow his gaze, Kendra saw the thick black clouds rolling in from the west. Dark scudding mist already blew along the tops of the dunes and the air was suddenly much colder. Even in the short space of her backward glance, rain began hissing down on the sand and water.

She'd be drenched in minutes.

And that was all the encouragement she needed to leave the beach. Ghosts didn't bother her at all. But the last thing she wanted was to catch a cold. So she pulled up her jacket hood and then turned around to bid the too-sexy-for-his-own-good Scotsman adieu.

Unfortunately, she couldn't.

He was gone.

And—Kendra's jaw slipped as she looked up and down the strand—he also hadn't left any footprints. Not even where they'd stood just moments before.

"I'll be damned." Her astonishment was great.

Generally, only spirits could move without a visible trace. Yet she knew he wasn't a ghost. He'd been real, solid, and definitely red-blooded.

So what was he?

Burning to know, Kendra clutched her jacket tighter and hurried down the strand. Scotland certainly was proving to be interesting.

ABOUT THE AUTHOR

Allie Mackay is the alter ego of Sue-Ellen Welfonder, a *USA Today* bestselling author who writes medieval romances. Her twenty-year career with the airlines allowed her to see the world, but it was always to Scotland that she returned. Now a full-time writer, she's quick to admit that she much prefers wielding a pen to pushing tea and coffee. She spent fifteen years living in Europe and used that time to explore as many castle ruins, medieval abbeys, and stone circles as possible. She makes annual visits to Scotland, insisting they are a necessity, as each trip gives her inspiration for new books.

Proud of her own Hebridean ancestry, she belongs to two clan societies and never misses a chance to attend Highland games. In addition to Scotland, her greatest passions are medieval history, the paranormal, and dogs. She never watches television, loves haggis, and writes at a 450-year-old desk that once stood in a Bavarian castle.

Readers can learn more about her and the world of her books at www.alliemackay.com.

S0152